The ⊠ FORMULA ⊠

BY STEVE SHAGAN

THE FORMULA
CITY OF ANGELS
SAVE THE TIGER

The
⊠ FORMULA ⊠

□ □ □ □ □ □ □ □ □ □ □ □ □ □
□ □ □ □ □ □ □ □ □ □ □ □ □ □

A NOVEL BY

STEVE SHAGAN

WILLIAM MORROW AND COMPANY, INC.
NEW YORK

FOR MICHAEL AND GRETCHEN WAYNE

The author wishes to express his gratitude to the staff of the United States Mission—Berlin Documentation Center.

And to Willy Egger for his patient and expert guidance through Germany.

Money not morality is the principal
commerce of civilized nations.

—THOMAS JEFFERSON

The ⊠ FORMULA ⊠

PROLOGUE:

BERLIN—APRIL 3, 1945

CHAPTER

THE STEEL HELMETS BOBBLED ON THEIR SMALL HEADS, AND SOME OF them were having trouble balancing their automatic rifles. Major General Helmut Kladen thought they looked like a group of children playing war games in their fathers' uniforms. The squad leader, a boy of perhaps fourteen, walked up to the front of the open OKW staff car and asked Kladen's chauffeur for his transit papers. The others gathered around the gray Mercedes and stood silently, staring at Kladen, who sat stiffly erect in the luxurious leather of the rear seat.

One of the taller children mustered the courage to ask if he could touch the Knight's Cross, with Oak Leaf clusters, that rested on a red silk foulard at Kladen's throat. General Kladen nodded, and the boy came forward. He fondled the medal with great reverence, then quickly stepped back and whispered something to his comrades, who nodded solemnly. The bridge shook suddenly from the concussion of the massed Soviet artillery at the Seelow salient. Kladen began to feel uncomfortable and snapped, *"Schnell! Schnell!"* at the boy who was examining their papers.

The squad leader smiled at Kladen and motioned his chauffeur to go on. The driver slipped the Mercedes into low gear, and it rolled slowly across the bridge. Kladen looked back at the child soldiers. A pall of gray smoke from the burning city of Berlin some fifteen kilometers away had settled over the bridge, lending a ghostlike quality to the small figures in their ill-fitting uniforms.

Kladen lit a long pink Russian cigarette and shook his head sadly; the thought of the children holding the bridge depressed him. They were waiting for Wenck's Twelfth Army, the army group that would save Berlin from the Mongolian hordes. But there was no Twelfth Army. It had long ago ceased to exist. The Twelfth Army was a myth on a document in the Führer bunker. The children on the bridge would be dead in a matter of days.

Kladen felt a sudden rage. He remembered Rommel's last words when asked why he had joined the plot against Hitler. Rommel had replied, "If one knows how to begin a war, one had better know how to end it." But Rommel was gone. All the great men were gone. But perhaps fate had chosen him, Major General Helmut Kladen, hero of the Reich, master Panzer tactician, survivor of the howling sands of Africa and the arctic blizzards of Russia. Perhaps he could prevent the total destruction of the German people.

The big OKW staff car picked up speed as it moved along Reichsstrasse 96, heading north toward the colossal funnel of smoke that rose up from the heart of the ruined city.

The gray cloud cover over the Berlin skyline glowed with an eerie, orange luminosity; leaping tongues of flame were like the brush strokes of an invisible artist gone mad, determined to change the color of the sky. The constant fires fueled a fierce wind that whipped a vast wall of reddish dust down the abandoned, rubble-strewn streets. The wind carried with it the stench of seared flesh, burning rubber, and escaping gas. It was the foul smell of a modern civilization ground into oblivion. Peering through the dust, Kladen could discern the black skeletal remains of what once were tall office buildings. They loomed above the rubble like puzzled survivors of another time.

The big car turned into Königstrasse, jumped the curb, and traveled along the sidewalk. The street was impassable; piles of rubble were flung across the wide boulevard. Kladen saw girls wearing Antiaircraft Battalion uniforms attempting to clear a vehicular path through the ruins. Old men wearing Home Guard uniforms directed open cars full of staff officers who were lost. The nightly bombing kept changing the shape of the city. A section that existed one day disappeared the next.

They turned left onto the Kurfürstendamm. The devastation of the once-elegant boulevard took Kladen's breath away. The tall maple trees were gone. The exclusive shops, cinemas, and cafés were reduced to mounds of crushed cement, shattered glass, and smoking wood. A trolley car rested upside down in the center of a restaurant. The bodies of its last passengers were suspended at odd angles from holes in its shattered frame. A pack of wild dogs snapped and leaped at the corpses, anxious to tear into the charred flesh. An elderly policeman, carrying a small Schmeisser submachine gun, emptied a full clip into the dogs. A long line of women waited in front of a store for a handout of milk and bread. Small children clutched at their mothers' skirts and looked fearfully up at the sky; even infants knew from what direction the destruction fell.

They passed the ruined church at the foot of the Kurfürstendamm and swung into Budapesterstrasse and entered the Tiergarten Park. The world-famous park was a horrifying landscape out of a Picasso nightmare. The grass was black. The trees had been burned down to charred stumps. The bodies of German soldiers hung on the arms of the tall gaslamps with signs draped across their swaying bodies that read, "I was a traitor to the German people." On a knoll near the zoo packs of dogs feasted on the rotting corpses of women and children who had been caught in the daylight air raids. They drove slowly past the zoo, where eight hundred SS men manned the huge flack tower. They had their 88-millimeter artillery pieces aimed at the northern approaches of the city, where one could see the flashes of Marshal Konev's massed artillery. Kladen could clearly hear the bellowing of elephants and the anguished roars of lions and tigers. The animals as well as the soldiers had been under fire for months.

They emerged from the Tiergarten and headed for Unter den Linden. Directly ahead, the Brandenburg Gate was still standing. Kladen looked up at the top of the arch; the marble chariot was still there, but three of its four bronze horses had toppled over. Off to the left the Reichstag was in ruins, the slogan on its blackened face, "FOR THE GERMAN PEOPLE," still visible; on the east wall, a huge portrait of Hitler hung at a crazy angle.

On Unter den Linden people had emerged from cellars and were picking through the rubble. They seemed to Kladen like so many insects searching for tiny morsels in a huge garbage dump. There was a sudden thunderous roar from the northern horizon as the big guns of the First Russian White Army opened up on the German defense line at Küstrin. The frames of the ruined buildings shook, and the people gazed up from their rubble hunting, their dazed eyes glancing fearfully northward. They had been warned. The hordes from the east would kill, rape, and plunder, and now they were at the gates. The evil genius with his withered hand and shaking head was alive under the dead city. He still broadcast the same message: "Come up from your shelters, mass, prepare, be ready to die for the honor of the Reich. The last great battle to save the civilized world from the Mongol hordes has fallen to the German nation." But it did not seem to Kladen that anyone was listening. Not anymore. The only question was how to save the nation; perhaps Reichsführer Himmler had found the key. Kladen's mission was designed by Himmler. God help him that he was right.

At the corner of Pariser Platz and Wilhelmstrasse a sudden gust of red dust stung Kladen's eyes. He blinked rapidly to clear them, then pulled the top of each eyelid over the eyeball in a swablike fashion. It was a trick he had learned years ago in Africa. As the fluid in his eyes cleared, he stared in disbelief at a building whose ornate facade was miraculously unscathed. It was the Adlon Hotel, preserved in all its nineteenth-century elegance.

The Adlon was more than a hotel; it was a legend. Before the war it had been the favorite hotel of kings and queens, heads of great industrial cartels, diplomats, presidents, artists, composers, the hierarchy of the Reich, infamous courtesans and their affluent lovers. To be known by the concierge of the Adlon was a sign of importance. Kladen smiled grimly as he thought of all the buildings in the city that had been smashed, of all the monuments to the glory of the Third Reich that had been reduced to ruins; it was a macabre irony that the Adlon should be untouched.

They parked at the entrance between two staff cars. The drivers of the other cars in their field gray uniforms snapped to attention and saluted smartly as Major General Kladen stepped out of his car. For a moment he stood silently, studying the front of the hotel. Its windows were covered with tar paper, and a wall of sandbags supported the entrance all the way up to the second-story balconies. But despite the sandbags and the blacked-out windows, the old hotel, like some *grande dame* out of the Belle Epoque, retained her dignity.

Kladen lit a cigarette, inhaled deeply, then followed his driver up the steps of the hotel.

The great lobby with its marble walls, adorned with fifteenth-century tapestries, was gloomily lit by low-wattage bulbs and burning candles set at odd places. A shower of crystal hung from a priceless antique chandelier suspended from the high, frescoed ceiling.

Kladen felt the strange sensation of having gone from daylight to an interior world where night was permanent. Kladen removed his black leather gloves, and his eyes grew accustomed to the gloom. He noticed the isolated clusters of men and women huddled in various parts of the lobby. They were shadowy figures, wearing a variety of dress. There were blue-uniformed Luftwaffe fighter pilots in from Tempelhof Airfield, speaking in hushed tones to young blond girls. Kladen presumed the girls were prostitutes arranged for the pilots by the Air Ministry. Several black-clad Gestapo men of Himmler's AMT 3 stood together, silently surveying the people in the lobby. There were businessmen sitting on divans having tea and perusing documents which passed from one to the other. A badly wounded Wehrmacht captain leaned on his crutches, staring vacantly at the businessmen. A soft cloud of blue smoke drifted up into the gaslamps. And from the balcony a radio played a sad ballad sung by a throaty vocalist. Kladen removed his greatcoat, folded it over his arm, and walked up to the desk.

The concierge was on the phone speaking to someone in what Kladen thought was Swedish. The balding concierge motioned to Kladen that he would be with him in a moment.

The concierge concluded his conversation, and smiled a harried smile at Kladen. "How can I be of service, General?"

"I am Major General Helmut Kladen. I am to meet SS Brigadier General Schellenberg."

At the mention of Schellenberg's name, the concierge seemed to tense; his voice grew hurried and officious. "Yes. Of course. We've been expecting you, General. Please follow the bellboy."

Kladen walked to the small French elevator. The boy waited for him to enter, then closed the gleaming grilled-brass door. They rode up in silence, the boy occasionally glancing furtively at Kladen's decorations. The elevator came to a graceful stop at the fourth floor.

Again the boy stood aside for Kladen. "To your right, General."

Halfway down the corridor the boy stopped and knocked on an oak-paneled door. A voice from inside asked, "Who is it?"

Kladen spoke, "Major General Kladen."

The door was opened by a thin, effete-looking man, with soft blue eyes and gleaming black hair, which was flat to his scalp and parted in the center. He wore the black uniform of a captain in the Gestapo AMT 3.

"Welcome to Berlin, Herr General." The man smiled.

Kladen gave the bellboy three marks and entered a wide, high-ceilinged room, with two oak doors leading off to a bedroom. Tall French windows overlooking Unter den Linden were blacked out, but despite the ugliness of the tar paper, the suite still retained an air of undisturbed elegance. There were three men in civilian dress seated on Louis XIV chairs, near the windows. They were smoking and drinking champagne. Kladen could see the neck of the champagne bottle sticking up out of a silver bucket on a table alongside the men.

"Some champagne, General?" the captain asked. "Dom Pérignon, 1937."

"No, thank you," Kladen replied, and dropped his greatcoat and gloves on a sofa, and waited for the captain to introduce him. But the effeminate man merely stared at Kladen, the small, ironic smile never leaving his face. Kladen nodded at the businessmen, then addressed the captain: "I was told this was a matter of the utmost urgency."

"Yes, of course, General. One moment."

The Gestapo captain minced across the room to the bedroom door and knocked twice. Softly. A harsh voice from within the room growled, "What is it?"

"General Kladen has arrived, sir."

The gruff voice replied, "Give Comrade Kladen some champagne, introduce him."

The captain walked quickly to the silver bucket, lifted the sweating green bottle, and filled a glass with the gold-colored wine. He came back to Kladen and handed him the glass. "This champagne is from the Reichsführer himself, a gift from Himmler."

Kladen took the glass, lifted it, and said, "To the German people."

The Gestapo captain's smile vanished. He walked to the front door of the suite and faced the room. Kladen sat on the sofa and sipped the champagne. The businessmen stared across the room at Kladen. The silence was punctuated by a burst of shrill feminine laughter from the bedroom.

Kladen stood up and turned to the Gestapo captain. "I believe General Schellenberg asked you to introduce me, Captain."

The captain smiled nervously. "Yes. Yes, forgive me, General." He rolled his hips as he walked to the center of the suite. "Permit me to introduce first Dr. Hans Luschen, director of Reich Energy Resources."

Across the room a smallish, elderly, gray-haired man stood up and bowed from the waist. "An honor, General." He sat down.

The captain said, "Karl Saur, director general of Reich Armaments."

The paunchy, florid-faced man sitting next to Luschen nodded at Kladen. He did not rise or speak.

The captain concluded, "And finally, the distinguished Dr. Abraham Esau, head of Reich Research."

Dr. Esau was a tall, handsome, well-built man in his late forties. He rose and smiled at Kladen. "A pleasure, General."

Kladen nodded. Esau sat down. The Gestapo captain went back to his position at the door. The men sat in the awkward silence of the large suite. Kladen could hear the antique clock above the fireplace ticking. The silence was suddenly disturbed by a loud rattling of the blacked-out windows, followed instantly by the ominous rumble of Soviet artillery. Kladen noticed the three men squirm uneasily at the sound of artillery. Kladen knew there was a great distinction in the civilian mind between aerial bombardment and enemy artillery. The bombs were dropped from moving aircraft whose presence over the city was only temporary. The artillery was evidence of the permanent proximity of the enemy. There was no hiding anymore. The Soviet armies were punching their way toward the very heart of the city.

Dr. Esau was the first to speak. "Have you come in from the front, General?"

"Yes. I was attached to the Fifty-sixth Panzer Corps," Kladen said. "With Field Marshal Busse's Ninth Army at the Seelow salient."

"But Seelow is only twenty-six kilometers from this very room," Esau exclaimed.

"Twenty-two kilometers," Kladen corrected the doctor. He took a certain soldier's satisfaction in their fright.

Luschen then asked, "Is Wenck's Twelfth Army on the way?"

"I have no information about Wenck."

It was as if a dam had broken. The beefy, florid-faced Saur then spoke. "They say General Felix Steiner's Eleventh Corps is conducting a pincer movement to encircle Konev's advance armor."

"I have no information about General Steiner," Kladen replied curtly.

The men fell silent once again. Once again the antique clock could be heard ticking. After a long moment the tall oak doors of the bedroom opened.

SS Brigadier General Walter Schellenberg, chief of Foreign Intelligence for Reichsführer Himmler, entered the room. He was a stocky, hawk-faced man with black-agate eyes peering out of a very white face. Schellenberg was dressed in a freshly pressed black uniform with the death's-head insignia on his shoulder patch. An Iron Cross medal, First Class, was pinned to the breast of his jacket; a small gold medallion above the Iron Cross indicated that he was a founding member of the elite SS unit.

Schellenberg studied the men for a moment, then walked carefully up to the window, pulled back a piece of the tar-paper cover, peered out for a moment, then turned to Kladen. "You've met everyone, General?"

"Yes."

Schellenberg nodded. "Good." He stared at Kladen, then gently said, "Sit down, please."

Kladen sat down on the sofa, facing the civilians across the room. The SS captain remained standing, his back to the door of the suite.

Schellenberg addressed Kladen. "For the record, General, I personally have been charged by Reichsführer Himmler to conduct this operation. As you know, the Reichsführer has assumed command of the Fif-teenth Corps, facing Konev's Mongolians. Our mission is not only secret; it is sacred. It represents the final opportunity to preserve the German nation from Asiatic enslavement."

Kladen cleared his throat. "I understand."

Schellenberg blew a cloud of smoke at Kladen. "I knew you would, General." He nodded at the Gestapo captain, who left his post at the door and quickly crossed the room to the table with the silver ice bucket. He poured a glass of champagne, handed it to Schellenberg, and went back to the door. Schellenberg sipped the champagne and walked up to Kladen.

"The Reich is defeated. We must therefore save as much of the Ger-man nation as possible."

"I am prepared to carry out the mission," Kladen replied.

Schellenberg paced for a moment, then placed himself in the center of the suite. "SS General Wolff is at the moment in Zurich conducting secret negotiations with the chief of American Intelligence, Allen Dulles. Wolff has made the proposition to turn over to the Americans our most critical military documents concerning research and develop-ment of secret weapons. We offer this information in return for amnesty for those of us who have served the Reich in certain areas that may be construed as war crimes. In addition, we are seeking American guaran-tees that they will enter Berlin before the city falls to the Soviets." Schellenberg sipped some more champagne and turned to Dr. Esau. "Please describe to the general the materials we will be surrendering."

Dr. Esau spoke in a cold, clipped monotone. "The principal docu-ments pertain to: the ME-262 jet fighter; the new eighty-eight-millimeter antiaircraft battery with electronic Zeiss sights; the V-one and V-two rockets; the design engineering of the jet wind tunnel; the remote control ground-to-air heat-seeking missile; the long-range rockets known as A-four and A-nine; the design for the uranium-powered submarine; and finally all our files on synthetics."

Schellenberg said, "Thank you, Doctor," and turned to Kladen. "Dr. Luschen and Herr Saur have prepared the files and manifests. You will take a convoy of six heavy-duty trucks tomorrow morning from opera-tional headquarters at Zossen. You will make your way south to the vil-lage of Bodensee on the Swiss frontier. Once there, you will wait for final word pending Wolff's negotiations. If they succeed, you will cross the frontier and surrender the convoy to Swiss frontier police. Under-stood?"

Kladen shrugged his massive shoulders. "The route south is unreliable. The entire Reich consists only of a ninety-five kilometer corridor. At certain points, particularly near Munich, the gap is less than thirty kilometers between the Americans and the Russians. In addition, the roads at daylight are in full view of British Mosquitoes."

"That is why you were chosen, General." Schellenberg smiled. "You are, after all, a famous Panzer veteran. You will have an SS motorcycle escort and papers to clear all federal police checkpoints. You will follow the motorcycles in an armored car. The trucks will form a caravan behind you. As to the British fighter planes, we are in luck. The weather forecast predicts fog and low clouds."

"What are my orders if we are intercepted?" Kladen asked.

"In that unfortunate case, you are on your own."

"Meaning what?"

"Meaning you will not reveal the nature of your mission. Unless, of course, you wish to condemn all of us to death. Anything else, General?"

"Yes. What is the code name of this operation?"

"Valkyrie."

"That was the code used by the conspirators who plotted against the Führer," Kladen replied in a surprised tone.

"I'm well aware that 'Valkyrie' was their code. I chose it for this operation because the irony appealed to me. We are utilizing a conspirator's code to save the German nation."

Kladen picked up his greatcoat and said, "I will require the latest battlefield positions and precise cartography; I am concerned about the corridor south."

Schellenberg's white skin reddened, but he forced a thin smile. "You will be in Zossen tonight. You will have access to all relevant data. You have all night to prepare your route." He moved closer to Kladen, and the thin smile widened. "I stress again that this assignment is voluntary. If you wish to refuse, you can rejoin your unit at the front, and this meeting will be forgotten. It is up to you, General."

Kladen's voice trembled with anger. "I am here because I have spent my life serving the German nation. I will continue to do so to the end." He gasped for air, fighting his rising fury. "My devotion to the German nation is not for anyone to question!"

Schellenberg put his hand on Kladen's shoulder. "Forgive me. I did not mean to question your loyalty, but only to point out the voluntary nature of this mission." He turned to the three civilians and with a sweeping gesture of his hand said, "All of you carry the last hope for the salvation of the German people." Schellenberg then faced Kladen. "Godspeed, General. Heil Hitler!"

Kladen returned the salute. Schellenberg strode quickly to the bedroom door and disappeared inside. The Gestapo captain opened the front door of the suite. Kladen waited for the three civilians to leave, then extended his right hand to the effeminate captain, who placed a limp hand inside Kladen's and smiled. "Bon voyage, Herr General."

Kladen squeezed the captain's hand and increased the pressure until tears began to form in the captain's eyes. Kladen continued to apply the pressure, trying to break a bone in the graceful hand. The captain finally gasped in pain, and Kladen released his hand. "Now you can apply for an Iron Cross, Captain. You can say you were wounded in the Adlon Hotel." Kladen went out and softly closed the door behind him.

Inside the velvet bedroom of the suite a teenaged blond girl lay naked on the large bed, reading a French movie magazine. She looked up at Schellenberg as he began to undress and in a childlike voice asked, "Do you know Maurice Chevalier, General?"

CHAPTER

THE SIX CANOPIED TRUCKS FOLLOWED THE ARMORED CAR AND ITS motorcycle escorts. They had left Zossen at daybreak and had been on the road for seven hours, stopping only once to wait for a bridging tank to clear a section of Reichsstrasse 96. A three-mile sector of the principal artery had been blocked by the wreckage of an armored column. The big gray tanks with their small black crosses had been caught by a flight of British Mosquitoes. The burned bodies of the tank crews still clung to the steel sides, and columns of black smoke rose up from the open turrets.

A Wehrmacht officer suggested an alternate route to Kladen, a cutoff that led to a country road. The detour permitted them to circle the blocked highway. The road meandered through rolling hills with cultivated fields on either side. The sinister rumble of American artillery continued without let-up. Kladen ordered the convoy to halt in a wooded section just off the road. The men took care of their bodily functions, then quickly tore into their ration cans of sausage, cheese, chocolate, and crackers. Kladen did not eat; he smoked and drank a liter of white wine. After the break they resumed their route. Kladen was grateful for the gray sky and low cloud cover and the thick, shifting patches of fog that clung to the dips and hollows of the country road. They were skirting Reichsstrasse 96, staying wide to the east.

As they passed through a small village, Kladen could see a distant column of smoke rising from Nuremberg. The Americans were moving fast. Kladen's field reports did not coincide with the column of smoke to the west. He decided to take an even wider sweep away from the American armored units. He signaled the column to stop, clambered down from his armored-car perch, and walked up to the corporal on the motorcycle. He showed the man the field map and pointed to a thin blue line. "This is a single-lane country road; we reach it at kilometer stone five. We will take that road for the next eighty kilometers." The corporal nodded and saluted. The convoy started forward once again.

Kladen stood up in the turret of the armored car, his coat collar turned up against the wind. He felt slightly heady from the wine, and his thoughts drifted back to the great years in Africa. He would be up in the turret, like now, only he was not leading trucks in those days. He would be in the lead tank at the fulcrum of a huge arrow formation, roaring across the desert in a phalanx of three hundred tanks, heading the charge, engines roaring, clogging the eardrums, battle flags flying, tons of grinding armor speeding toward the entrenched British positions: man, machine, and the elements, meshing into a moving steel fist. The will of the mind and spirit overcoming all fears. They were the Panzers. The men of the blitzkrieg. The elitists. But those days were gone, committed to the refuse pile of memory. Kladen thought that perhaps there was a bizarre but correct irony to this, his final command of two motorcycles and six trucks.

They came to a slope where a federal police barricade had been thrown across the road. The officer in charge checked their transit pass and waved them on. As Kladen passed, the officer shouted up to him, "American patrols have been reported; take care, General!" Kladen nodded and saluted the man. He smiled at the words "take care." How could he take care?

They were making forty kilometers an hour on the rutted dirt road. The topography of the land had changed. They had been climbing steadily, traveling through a pine forest. The road began to twist and curve sharply. They were forced to slow to a crawl, but Kladen didn't mind. The sky was beginning to darken, and for the first time he believed they had a chance.

Kladen reached into the huge inside pocket of his greatcoat and took out a flask of French cognac. He unscrewed the cap and took a long pull of the strong brandy. His stomach warmed almost instantly, adding to his euphoric feeling. He tucked the flask away and clung to the sides of the turret.

They were coming slowly around a blind curve when Kladen saw the big olive-colored Sherman tank lumber out of the woods. He stared in stunned fascination as the tank's 90-millimeter cannon slowly revolved on its turret and homed in on the oncoming German vehicles. Kladen kicked the shoulder of his driver, who braked the armored car. He then turned back and motioned the following trucks to halt. The motorcycles up ahead slowed as three more Shermans rumbled out of the woods, taking blocking positions on the road. Kladen raised his arms above his head. A moment later a company of American infantrymen streamed out of both sides of the forest. The machine guns on the tanks chattered suddenly, and Kladen's motorcycle escorts fell off their cycles. The cycles ran driverless for a brief moment before exploding into bright orange fireballs.

The cannon of all four tanks were now trained on Kladen's convoy. Kladen kept his hands above his head and clambered down from the turret. He reached the ground, turned back, and motioned his truck drivers to do the same.

A big rawboned American captain walked slowly up to Kladen. His shoulder patch bore a white letter *A* on a blue field rimmed in red. Kladen was familiar with the patch; it belonged to General Patton's Third Army. The captain had a .45 automatic in his right hand. He was flanked by a staff sergeant and a corporal, both cradling Browning automatic rifles. The infantry platoon had fanned out, circling the trucks and their German drivers. The American captain had a black growth of stubble on his cheeks and chewed a wad of tobacco. He faced Kladen and spit a long stream of tobacco juice into the earth close to Kladen's gleaming boots.

"You *sprechen* English?" the captain drawled.

Kladen spoke with deliberate precision. "I am SS Major General Helmut Kladen; number four-three-six-zero-five."

"Captain Jesse Renfro," the American answered, "Company B, Sixth Battalion, Fourteenth Regiment, Third Division." He spit another stream of the brown viscous fluid. "Third U.S. Army."

Kladen tried a smile. "May I lower my hands, Captain?"

"You don't move your goddamn hands till I say so." Renfro then turned to the corporal. "Get those truck drivers' names, ranks, and serial numbers. Blindfold them and start them back to Weiden." The corporal nodded but didn't move. "What the hell are you waitin' for, Corporal?" Renfro growled.

The corporal's helmet bobbled. "I just never seen a kraut general before. Look at all those fucking medals!"

The big sergeant to the right of Renfro grunted, "Yeah, fucking SS. Maybe he was in on that Malmédy shit. Murdered all them guys in the Hundred and First."

Kladen remained silent. Then Renfro ordered, "Get going, Corporal!"

The corporal saluted and went up the road toward the trucks. Captain Renfro studied Kladen for a moment. "What's in those trucks?" he asked.

"I have no knowledge of the cargo. My orders were to transport them."

"Where to?"

"South. To a village named Bodensee."

Renfro turned to the sergeant. "Take a look at what's in those trucks."

"Yes, sir!" The big sergeant lumbered off.

A group of infantrymen herded the German truck drivers past Renfro and Kladen.

"What are all those decorations for?" Renfro asked.

"They represent my campaigns in Africa and Russia."

"In what?"

"SS Panzer commander," Kladen replied. "Do you suppose I might have a cigarette?"

Renfro said, "Let me tell you, General, this company's had Germans. I was a lieutenant two days ago. I'm a captain today because we lost six line officers in the last two weeks. You keep your goddamn mouth shut." The big sergeant came trotting back up to Renfro. "Captain!"

"Yeah?"

"You better have a look!" The sergeant caught his breath and continued: "Full of steel cabinets, top to bottom every goddamn one of them!"

"Stay with the general, and watch his hands," Renfro snapped. Renfro walked up to the lead truck. Two infantrymen helped him up onto the truck's interior. It was as the sergeant described, row upon row of gray steel cabinets. All locked. All unidentified.

Renfro took the big .45 automatic from his holster, cocked it, stepped to the side, and fired into the top drawer of a nearby file. The lock blew off. Renfro holstered the automatic and pulled the drawer open. There were ten orange folders, bulging with documents. Renfro took the first folder out, opened it, and looked at the top sheet. It was headed "KUMMERSDORF EXPERIMENTELLE ANLAGE—BRANDENBURG" and addressed to a Walter Dornberger. Renfro could make out the words "Ballistics" and "Rocket Designations A-1–A-4." He replaced the orange file in the drawer and slammed it shut. He jumped back down onto the dirt road and turned to a platoon leader. "Get six guys who can handle these trucks. Put two men inside each truck with orders to guard those files." The platoon leader saluted, went over to his squad, and started to call out names. Renfro put a new plug of chewing tobacco in his cheek and walked back up to Kladen. The big sergeant had Kladen covered with his BAR, and the general still had his arms raised above his head.

Renfro spit the juice of the new plug, then looked at Kladen. "You have a manifest for this convoy?"

Kladen started to reach into the inside pocket of his greatcoat. But as his hand moved, the sergeant shoved the muzzle of the BAR into Kladen's belly. Kladen winced in momentary pain and got his hand back up over his head.

"You don't move your hands until I tell you to," Renfro snapped.

"I was about to give you my orders. I have no manifest."

Renfro growled, "Fuck your orders! I asked you for a manifest. What's in them cabinets?"

Night was coming on. Kladen felt a chill and a wave of resignation. It was over. He was obviously dealing with an American officer of a lower station. He had spoken with them before. Years ago. At Kasserine Pass in Africa when they had routed the American 34th division and taken thousands of prisoners. Kladen's fluency in English had required him to assist the Abwehr intelligence officers, and he knew that with Americans there was nothing one could do in the face of ignorance and lack of breeding.

Renfro spoke to the sergeant. "Get them tank lights on." Renfro turned to Kladen. "I'm gonna ask you one more time. What's in those files?"

Kladen sighed. "The trucks are carrying secret military files."

The lights of the tanks had come on, and the big sergeant was back. Renfro smiled. He knew now that for the first time in his life, Jesse Renfro had made a score.

"Sergeant!"

"Yes, sir!"

"Listen carefully. Call Battalion S-Two and Regiment S-Five. Tell them we got a six-truck convoy loaded with secret documents. We got an SS major general covered with decorations."

"Yes, sir." The sergeant started off.

"Sergeant!" Renfro's voice stopped the sergeant. "Better tell them to notify First Army Headquarters, get a staff major from G-Two, and alert Command Intelligence at SHAEF in Reims."

The sergeant saluted and trotted off. Kladen and Renfro stood in the shadowy light thrown by the beams of the tank's headlamps.

"Now, General, you can reach into your coat pocket and hand me those orders."

Kladen lowered his hands. He wished there had been time to wire the convoy with explosives. His right hand went inside the huge inside pocket of the coat. His eyes never left Renfro's face. Kladen's right hand came out of the greatcoat with a spherical antipersonnel grenade. His left hand pulled a lever. The safety valve flew off. Kladen clenched the live grenade in his right hand and leaped forward to embrace Renfro, holding the surprised captain in a powerful vise.

There was a sudden yellow flash accompanied by an earsplitting explosion. In a matter of seconds Captain Jesse Renfro and Major General Helmut Kladen were reduced to a thick syrupy mixture of blood and intestinal fluids that slowly formed a dark puddle on the dry German earth.

CHAPTER

3 ⊠

A LIGHT SPRING RAIN FELL AS THE YOUNG LIEUTENANT ATTACHED TO
Staff G-2 walked up the narrow Rue le Sarge. He enjoyed his assignment in Reims. The town with its narrow streets and parks reminded
him of the Impressionist paintings of Pissarro. He smiled at a group of
blue-and-white-uniformed schoolgirls who followed two nuns wearing
their black habits and huge white-winged hats. The girls giggled as they
passed the handsome American lieutenant.

At the corner the lieutenant turned into a narrow street just behind
the railroad station. He walked slowly toward a plain, modern two-story
building. The lieutenant thought there was something romantic about
the rain. He approached the building and smiled at the sign plaque
above the entrance: "COLLÈGE MODERNE ET TECHNIQUE."
The former boys' technical school was now Supreme Headquarters for
the Allied Expeditionary Force. The lieutenant knew something important was behind this summons. Only General Eisenhower and his immediate general staff worked here. The balance of the twelve hundred
officers and twelve hundred enlisted men attached to G-2 was scattered
in a wide variety of buildings throughout Reims.

The lieutenant presented his ID to the MP at the desk. "Colonel
Hassler is expecting me." The MP nodded, picked up the receiver,
dialed four digits. The MP gave the lieutenant's name, received the
proper response, and hung up. He handed the lieutenant's ID back to
him.

"Last door on your right, Lieutenant."

The lieutenant went down the hallway and stopped at a doorway
marked "COMBINED INTELLIGENCE OBJECTIVES SERVICE."
Two MPs checked the lieutenant's ID and pass, then waved him inside.

The large former classroom had been converted into a maze of glass-partitioned offices. Cardboard signs were attached to each cubicle identifying their sections and operational officers. There was a cacophony of telephone rings and typewriters and the omnipresent clouds of cigarette smoke wafting up over the twenty or so personnel occupying the room. The lieutenant walked up to an enclosed cubicle marked "CIOS FIELD OPS. COLONEL HERBERT HASSLER."

The colonel was a thin, esthetic-looking man, wearing a wrinkled shirt, black tie and rimless glasses with thick lenses. His desk was dotted with neat piles of multicolored folders all stamped "Secret." The lieutenant presented himself, and the colonel removed his glasses, rubbed his eyes, and said, "Good morning, Lieutenant."

"Good morning, sir."

"I assume you are aware of the convoy we intercepted several weeks ago."

"Yes, I am, Colonel. It was a remarkable catch. I've been translating some of the documents for members of the civilian scientists. The ALSO group."

"Well"—the colonel sighed—"then you know that certain material has been classified 'black,' meaning critical, and other documents have been classified 'gray,' not vital."

"Yes, sir."

The colonel lit a Camel. "There is one entire truck loaded with formulas to do with synthetics. They are coded with a variety of German names." The colonel inhaled deeply and blew a cloud of smoke up at the lieutenant. "These code names run the gamut from the Greek gods to chapters in the Bible. Like Genesis. Our experts have little or no interest in these files. But our British allies do."

"Why is that, sir?"

The colonel abruptly ground out the Camel. "Ask them, Lieutenant. Your orders are to transport these documents and files to Hamburg. You will have an armed escort. The route is defined, and all checkpoints have been notified." The colonel handed the lieutenant a sealed manila envelope. "When you arrive at British headquarters in Hamburg, you report to a Major Anthony Carlin. You will remain in Hamburg on attached duty to the British. You will assist them in translation and coding of the documents."

"When do I leave?"

"This afternoon at thirteen hundred hours. You will personally check the manifest, have it countersigned, and seal the truck."

"Yes, sir."

"Anything else, Lieutenant?"

"A question, Colonel."

"What is it?"

"Have we determined the true purpose of that German convoy?"

"No," the colonel replied. "But we have identified its commanding officer. A heavily decorated Panzer general."

"Why would a Panzer combat general be charged with transporting secret documents?"

The colonel's voice hardened. "This is not an area of your concern, is it, Lieutenant?"

"No, sir."

"When you arrive, phone me," the colonel replied curtly, then added, "Dismissed."

The lieutenant saluted smartly and left.

The light rain had turned into a heavy cold downpour. The truck was parked at the intersection of Rue Ste.-Geneviève and Avenue d'Épernay. Four jeeps, their canvas tops raised against the rain, were parked in front of the truck. Two black MPs wearing ponchos and helmets were standing at the rear of the truck. The steel doors of the truck were open, and the young lieutenant emerged from the truck's interior, carrying a thick manifest. He was accompanied by a staff sergeant. The lieutenant nodded at the MPs, who swung the steel doors shut. The lieutenant addressed the staff sergeant: "I make it all in order."

The sergeant nodded, and a stream of water fell out of the saucerlike curve of his helmet.

The lieutenant signed the manifest, passed the pen to the sergeant, who countersigned. The lieutenant took a large lock out of his poncho and carefully hooked the ear of the lock through the truck's door handle and snapped it shut.

And in that moment, in the rain of Reims, in the late spring of 1945, the twenty-six-year-old lieutenant had no way of knowing he was sealing a formula whose value would be without parallel in human history.

BOOK I

LOS ANGELES-
MARCH
1978

CHAPTER

4 ☒

THOMAS NEELEY PULLED THE HEAVY DRAPES OPEN, THEN TUGGED THE black handle of the floor-to-ceiling glass door. The door slid smoothly open across its steel runners. Neeley blinked in the bright morning light and stepped out onto the large circular terrace. Columns of white steam drifted up from the aquamarine surface of the heated pool.

Beyond the pool and circling the terrace was an iron railing whose vertical struts were hidden by thick clinging ivy. Neeley drew his terry-cloth robe tighter against the morning chill. The sky was bright, but the sun was still fighting some low clouds. He walked slowly to the railing and looked out over the sprawling panorama of the city. The view was south, across Hollywood and Crenshaw, past Culver City, all the way to the Pacific.

Neeley's fieldstone split-level house sat on the highest ridge of the brown hills that overlooked Sunset Boulevard. It was part of a glossy, overpriced development. Neeley knew he was taking a chance when he bought it some five years ago; it was lofty living for a man in his profession. But then, he'd taken a lot more dangerous risks than the purchase of a house.

The view from the terrace always gave him a feeling of well-being, especially at night when the city turned into a dazzling carpet of multicolored lights.

Even now, in the first light of day, there was power and beauty in the vista. But it was an illusion. Neeley knew what life was really like down in those palm-lined streets and pink stucco ghettos, and the sudden violence that erupted on the graceful, serpentine freeways.

At sixty, Thomas Francis Neeley had seen it all. He had joined the Los Angeles Police Department on May 22, 1946. He moved up through the ranks quickly: from precinct patrolman to sergeant in Vice, to lieutenant first grade Homicide, and finally to the rank of inspector in Operations and Intelligence. After years of distinguished service he left the Los Angeles Police Department to assume the post of chief of the Beverly Hills force. Tom Neeley knew the system from its core out. He understood the process of justice. He knew the scales were always tipped in the direction of power and that being right never guaranteed anyone a just verdict. And along the rising curve of his career he had met them all: the professional and amateur killers, con men, dealers, junkies, pimps, and pistoleros. However, the criminals who fascinated Neeley were the white-collar money magicians. Those gifted wizards who could plot a money swindle with the infinite genius of an Einstein. He had pursued and dealt with them all. And more important, he had understood them. He had never sent a man to prison who didn't belong there. He had never taken a dime to alter his position on a case. He had never succumbed to power. But that was a long time ago.

His eyes narrowed as the sun broke through the hazy clouds; he felt its sudden warmth through the robe. It would be a hot, sultry day for March. A good day to sit at the pool and conduct a little business. He undid the knot on the robe, and it fell open. He patted his flat stomach and thought: Not bad for a man his age. The tennis helped keep it flat, but it was really his current work that kept him slim. Treachery was a marvelous appetite suppressant. He could no longer remember the precise moment when he had crossed the line into criminal activity. He suspected there was no real turning point; it was a combination of events, of time, of fear, and the incredible daily contrast of his own status with the profound wealth and power of those he protected in that small magical triangle of real estate known as Beverly Hills.

It had all hit him when he divorced Kay. He was fifty-five and turning into the homestretch, looking forward to a small pension and being alone. He could handle being alone, but not alone and broke. It was a time in life when a man is most vulnerable to dangerous persuasions. It was that time when a man realizes just how mortal he is. When he sits at the funerals of his colleagues listening to the priest and transposes the words of the eulogy from the corpse to himself. Neeley found himself possessed by a growing need to possess. And even more, a need to be needed, to be sought after. Well, he sure as hell had achieved that.

He walked over to a chaise lounge, he took off his robe, and slipped naked into the steaming water. He swam methodically, in a steady crawl, for sixteen laps.

He clambered out, caught his breath, picked up a body towel, and dried himself with short, brisk strokes. He glanced at a white pad on a small glass-topped wrought-iron table. There were three names on the pad, but it was too early to call those names. Neeley stretched out on the lounge, faced the sun, and closed his eyes, letting the sun soak into his body. But its warmth could not dispel the tongue of fear that licked at the back of his brain.

It was the German thing. It scared him. It had from the beginning. The score of the century. Hell, the score of all the centuries. And once he had been close, very close. But how could he have known? Hell, even the experts hadn't known. But why did he tell Clements? The old cop in Neeley knew that Clements couldn't be trusted, but then no one man could bring the German thing off alone. Besides, maybe his fears were groundless. Arthur Clements was a legitimate, well-connected businessman. A board member of half a dozen major corporations, including Tidal Oil, and Clements had put him in touch with the old man, Adam Steiffel. It was only natural he would go to Clements with the German thing. Still, there was something about Clements that went against Neeley's grain. But it was too late for second guessing.

Neeley thought about today's party at Leo's, but the German thing wouldn't let go. Christ, even if he found it, even if he succeeded, what could it do for him. Money? He had enough of that. The cocaine was steadily fattening the Swiss account, well over two hundred thousand tax-free, nonaccountable dollars. The cocaine had been all right. Why in God's name had he started the German business? It was dangerous but irresistible. But suppose Clements stirred up Adam Steiffel? The awesome power of the old man chilled Neeley right through the warm rays of the morning sun.

The high whine of a small car straining up the hillside dispelled Neeley's fear. He knew who was in that car. It was the girl. She was always on time. He felt a small knot of warmth ball up in his belly as he thought about her. She never said much. She didn't have to. She delivered eighty-seven percent pure cocaine. Some girl.

Neeley rose, put his robe back on, took a brown Sherman cigarette out, lit it, and walked to the railing. The gray Datsun looked like a small bug as it fought its way up the final steep curve to Neeley's house.

The girl fascinated him. He never came on with her. But he had thought about it. Often. It wasn't her beauty. The girl had something more profound and very rare. She was totally feline. And the effect was hypnotic. The way her fingers touched things. The way her lips closed carefully around each word. The way her long dark hair fell casually across her shoulders, as if it just happened that way. She wore no makeup, but there was a presence of a heavy perfume that took your breath away. Ivory bracelets jangled at her wrists, and expensive French jeans painted all her curves. And her smile was like the memory of an old love affair.

Neeley watched the car disappear below into his driveway and walked quickly back into the living room, closing the sliding glass door behind him and pulling the drapes. He turned a small rheostat on the wall, bringing the lights in the living room down. He went over to the mirror above the fireplace and fluffed up his hair so it rose and waved.

The girl pulled into the breezeway garage alongside the parked Mercedes and cut the engine. She opened her large bag, took out the voodoo doll with the hollowed inside that held half a kilo of almost pure cocaine. She checked her face in the rearview mirror and ran her tongue slowly over the curve of her lower lip. She took one final look, then opened the door and slid out of the driver's seat.

The doorbell chimes sounded. Neeley went to the door, looked through the peephole and saw her face . . . some girl.

CHAPTER

THE DOHENY-PALMS WAS A TALL, TERRACED APARTMENT BUILDING built into the steep curve of a street called Doheny that slopes from Wilshire Boulevard up toward Sunset Boulevard. Its tenants comprised a mélange of aging character actors, mediocre agents, call girls, whose prices were falling, and a sprinkling of senior citizens living on small pensions or the largess of their successful offspring. The common denominator for all was a permanent feeling of transiency. They were the refugees of broken marriages, lost relationships, and faded dreams.

Barney Caine stood on the sunlit terrace of his twelfth-floor apartment, sipping the last of his third cup of coffee. He shifted his shoulders slightly so that the snub-nosed .38 Smith and Wesson did not bulge from its holstered position under his left arm. He placed the cup down, took a lungful of smoggy air, and stared over at the pretty girl on the chaise lounge.

Kathy Barnes's lips moved slightly as she read the calendar section of the Los Angeles Sunday *Times*. She wore a red bikini that had trouble hiding her pink nipples and dark pubic hair. She was a tall girl with very blond hair that didn't seem to fit her black eyes. Barney thought her natural dark-colored hair would have been a better match. But Kathy was a stewardess who still believed the myth: Blondes were soothing at thirty-five thousand feet. Besides, she felt her blond ponytail coalesced with the slogan of the airline she worked for. Her figure was not spectacular; but it still curved in all the right places, and when she was on the ground, Kathy worked hard to maintain her firm lines. She played tennis, jogged, danced, and made love as often and as strenuously as possible with a wide variety of lovers: male and female.

They had met three months ago, on a flight from Chicago to L.A. Barney had been in Chicago to testify against a Mafia soldier who for a while had operated out of Los Angeles. Barney's testimony was required to fill in some details on the mobster's background. It was an easy trip, and everything had been first-class. It was, in fact, in the first-class section of his return flight that Barney had met Kathy. She was the smiling stewardess, the blonde in the red uniform, the bird with the golden tail.

After they landed at L.A. International, Barney waited for her to check out. He drove to La Dolce Vita restaurant in Beverly Hills. Kathy had a voracious appetite, and Barney enjoyed watching her eat. She reminded him of an actress he had once dated. The actress had eaten everything in sight, including the breadsticks from the adjacent table. Kathy ate with the same zest. She explained between forkfuls of linguine and clams that the airline food was not only inedible but dangerous. "Christ," she said, smiling through a mouthful of bread dipped in garlic sauce, "the preservatives in that stuff are strong enough to kill a horse." After the linguine she had veal piccata. Barney had zuppa di clams, and they went through two bottles of cold Orvieta. After dinner they sipped Sambucca, and Kathy unleashed a stream of anecdotes about the bizarre activity of passengers she had served in her ten years of flying. The stories were spiced with vivid descriptions of her sexual encounters. Barney found her frankness fascinating. He had never met a girl who so advertised her wide-ranging sexual experiences. They left the restaurant and drove to his apartment. She didn't quite live up to her billing, but it wasn't due to any lack of effort. It was only at the first light of day that she surrendered to sleep.

They had been sharing their weekends ever since—that is, when he was not on call and when she was not flying. Barney knew their relationship was thinning out. They really had nothing to say to each other; but the sex was good, and she was never a pain in the ass. Still, he found himself searching for new faces. Barney needed someone. He had needed someone ever since his marriage fell apart.

Barney lit a slim-line cigarillo, walked over to Kathy, and sat down at the foot of the lounge. She dropped the paper onto her lap and looked into his soft brown eyes.

"A new De Niro picture opened Friday," she said.

"De Niro's a hell of an actor," Barney replied.

"Want to go?" she asked. "It's at the Avco."

"If I get through with Timmy in time."

"Funny"—she smiled—"you're the third Sunday father I've been involved with." Kathy brushed a fly from the side of her face. "Being alone on Sunday is lousy. But I understand." She paused. "That's pretty good, that I understand, don't you think so?"

"Yeah, that's pretty commendable," Barney said. "The same way I understand when you have to fly on a Sunday." He got to his feet, turned his back to her, and looked out over the city. It was a splendid view from the terrace. The mean streets didn't look mean at all from this height.

Kathy swung her pretty legs over the side of the lounge, and walked slowly up to him. She curved her body into his; her arms went around his neck. She was almost as tall as Barney. She stared at the half-moon scar on his right cheek and the bump on the ridge of his straight nose. She brushed her lips lightly against his and murmured, "Do you have to go now? I mean right now. . . ."

"Right now." He kissed her softly.

The white phone on the round breakfast table rang suddenly and sharply. He walked over to the table and picked up the receiver. It was Charlie McKeever at Central. Barney could see the florid-faced, over-weight Irish mug scowling in his swivel chair in front of the communication console. McKeever's mood would get darker as the day wore on, and the bottle of Jim Beam in his desk would get lighter.

"Get outta bed, and get your ass over to Nolan at Tactical," McKeever growled.

"Tactical?" Barney asked. "Why Tactical?"

"How the hell would I know?"

"Whose orders?"

"Commissioner's orders," McKeever replied.

Kathy turned the FM radio on, and something soft and melodic by Carly Simon came on. She watched the muscles in Barney's face tense as McKeever let Barney stew for a moment.

"Why me, Mac?" Barney asked.

"Don't know." McKeever belched and chuckled. "Maybe because you're so goddamn smart. Ask the commissioner. I'm just a dumb cop. Working Sundays. Looking at piss-colored walls and waitin' for a pension. Now get your ass in gear, sweetheart." McKeever hung up.

Barney did not replace the receiver but depressed the button on the cradle closing the connection.

Kathy looked at him. "No Timmy. Right?"

"Right." Barney nodded. He took his finger off the button, got a dial tone, and dialed. He hoped Alice wouldn't answer. It would be the familiar assault: "How can you do this to your son? He was so excited he didn't sleep all night." And on and on, shoving the guilt deeper and deeper. But Alice knew the argument would lead to an old conclusion. The profession came first. It always had. It had destroyed their marriage.

Alice had enjoyed Barney's years in the CIA. She found something glamorous about that part of Barney's career. Under the guise of the State Department diplomatic service they had gone to Madrid, to Rio, to Mexico City, to San Salvador, and finally Santiago, Chile. And while Barney never mentioned the nature of his work, there had been a certain excitement, a touch of top-drawer, all-expenses-paid living. Alice never for a moment thought there was any danger in Barney's work. CIA was merely an exotic handle for the Diplomatic Corps. But when Barney resigned and decided to join the Los Angeles Police Department, it all changed. The glamour was gone. The work was mundane, and Alice found it almost embarrassing when her friends asked her what Barney did to reply, "He's with the police." The marriage soured, and they were divorced. Alice married a renowned neurosurgeon and lived in a sprawling Spanish mansion in a heavily wooded area of Bel-Air.

Barney was lucky. Timmy answered the phone. He explained the problem carefully without ever talking down to the eleven-year-old. He promised to call Timmy the moment he was free, and maybe they could see an early movie in Westwood and then have supper at McDonald's. Timmy took it like an adult and said, "Okay, Daddy, but be careful."

Kathy walked Barney to the door. Barney said he'd phone, but if she could make other plans, not to hesitate. She nodded, kissed his cheek, and closed the door gently behind him. She walked back out to the terrace, went to the phone, and dialed the number of an interesting man she had met on a flight from New York to Los Angeles on Friday.

CHAPTER

6

TACTICAL HEADQUARTERS WAS LOCATED IN A GLASS BUILDING ON Berendo and Wilshire. Its entrance was flanked by two tall but tired cactus plants. In the center of the glassed-in lobby there was a fountain with a marble figure of the goddess Diana. The goddess had a puzzled expression on her marble face as if she were wondering why a continual column of greenish water poured out of her open mouth.

John Nolan was chief of Tactical, and his office would have suited any high corporate executive. Three walls were oak-paneled; the fourth wall was glass and looked out over the city. Nolan was seated behind his desk, reading a long telex and chewing nervously on a dead cigar.

Nolan was a stocky, florid-faced man with sagging folds of skin, laying row upon row, starting just under his baggy eyes and proceeding down to his chin. He was fifty-three, but his fallen face and overweight, lumpy body tended to add ten years to his age. Nolan had been born in South Boston, and although he had spent most of his life in California, in moments of stress, the Boston accent could still be heard; "car" would become "cah," and "bar" would become "bah." Nolan wasn't very inventive, but he was a reliable bureaucrat who knew the political ropes and always adhered to the unwritten law "The department above all else."

Tactical was an independent police unit whose principal function was to coordinate evidence and information on special cases between the thirty-two detective bureaus scattered across the sprawling city.

Nolan had assumed control of Tactical fifteen years ago. He had survived six different commissioners. Nolan spoke softly but carried a big portfolio of skeletons; he knew where the scandals were buried. He was a true man of his times. Nolan was a survivor.

At the huge glass wall, Sergeant Louis Yosuta stared silently out at the city. Sergeant Yosuta was Nisei. Japanese-American, and no one was more genuinely Californian than Louis. He had been born on the grounds of Santa Anita racetrack in 1943, when Santa Anita served as a detention camp for native-California Japanese, most of whom had sons who had volunteered for combat and fought with valor and distinction against the Germans in Italy. Louis's brother, James, was killed when the 442nd Nisei led the 34th Division in the suicidal crossing of the Rapido River. Louis had been a top student and received a full scholarship to UCLA. He had served with the 1st Cavalry Intelligence Division Vietnam from 1962 to 1965. He joined the L.A. police in the fall of 1966 and compiled a record of distinction.

Nolan selected Louis for Tactical out of a potential two hundred candidates. And Nolan had not been wrong. Louis possessed a quiet intelligence and unwavering sense of duty. Nolan had assigned Louis to some highly political, volatile cases, and the slim, handsome Japanese had performed beyond Nolan's expectations. Louis was Nolan's main man.

Nolan placed the telex on his desk and glanced over at Louis. "For Chrissake, Louis, sit down."

Louis turned to Nolan. "You bring me in on a Sunday. Urgent. And you haven't said a word for fifteen minutes."

"When Caine gets here, I'll only have to say it once. Now, sit down."

Louis moved quietly across the thick dark carpet and sat down in a chair facing Nolan's desk. "I fail to understand," Louis said, "why we have to reach out into Internal Security and Intelligence when we have our own guys: Kupper, Stillman, Greene, Fitzsimons, and all the rest. Why this guy Caine from ISI?"

Nolan sighed. "I was so instructed by his eminence the commissioner. Okay, Louis?"

"Who is Caine?" Louis asked.

Nolan slid the telex across the desk to Louis. It was a printout from the IBM computer at Central.

CAINE, BARNEY
BORN: 11/8/42: AT—USAF Base Hospital, Langley Field, Virginia.
FATHER: HARRY LAWSON CAINE: Deceased: 1/13/43—8th AF
    Cologne, Germany. Full colonel. Killed in action. 36 missions.
    Distinguished Flying Cross. Purple Heart.
MOTHER: JANET FLORENCE: Deceased: 5/23/62: Cancer.
EDUCATION: Hawthorne Military Academy, Los Angeles, Calif.;
    Chicago University, Chicago, Ill.

DEGREES: Master's: Philosophy—Criminology.
LANGUAGE: Fluency—Spanish.
CAREER DATA: Recruited CIA: 3/30/65. Assigned: S.A. Bureau:
 Mexico City, Madrid, Rio de Janeiro, San Salvador, Santiago.
RESIGNED: 9/5/70: CAUSE NOT STATED. *SEE FED Com-
 ment, pg. 23.
LOS ANGELES POLICE: 3/4/71.
SPONSOR: Inspector Thomas Neeley.
ASSIGNMENTS: 4/6/71—VICE.
 7/2/72 through 8/25/74—HOMICIDE.
 8/26/74 through 9/12/76—METRO SQUAD.
 9/14/76 to present—INTERNAL SECURITY INTELLI-
 GENCE.
COMMENDATIONS: NARCO SQUAD (2) operations beyond the
 call of duty.
 HOMICIDE (1) superior performance.
MARITAL STATUS: DIVORCED: ALICE SPENCER 5/15/73.
DEPENDENTS: Son: Timothy William Caine: Born: 10/18/68.
COMMENTS (ISI): Capable. Resourceful. Operates at times outside
 procedural code. Respected by fellow officers. No close friends
 on force. No liaison recent with sponsor T. NEELEY. Main-
 tains liaison with certain former CIA colleagues. ISI-PR: Above
 average. Politics: Registered as Independent.

INFO REQUEST 11:26 A.M. 3/15/78
POLICE COMMISSIONER: MO: PERSONAL
CODE FILE: AR6743-LAPD: DUO

Louis slid the telex back across the desk. "I'm impressed," Louis
said.

Nolan picked it up and placed it in his top drawer. "I'm delighted
you're impressed, Louis. I'm certain the commissioner is delighted,
too."

The buzzer sounded, and Nolan pushed a small white pearl button on
the side of his desk, releasing the lock to his office door.

Barney came into the office. Nolan did not stand up but managed a
vague smile. "Hello, Caine."

Barney nodded. Nolan waved his right hand in Louis's direction.
"This is Sergeant Louis Yosuta."

Louis stood up, and Barney walked over to him and they shook
hands.

"Sit down, Caine. Sit down," Nolan said genially.

Barney sat down in a deep leather chair and turned to Louis. "I knew your former partner, Charlie Robbins." Barney paused, "He was a good man."

"Yes. He was," Louis replied.

Nolan got up from behind the huge desk, clutched his stomach, and belched loudly. "Goddamn ulcer!" He popped a Gelusil from the open bottle on his desk and looked at Barney. "Care for a cigar?"

"No, thanks."

Nolan bit off a piece of the end and spit a shred of leaf on the carpet. He lit the cigar with an onyx Dunhill lighter and rotated the end of the cigar through the bluish flame. He blew a great cloud of smoke up toward the ceiling pinspots and sat down heavily in his swivel chair. He used the cigar as a pointer as he spoke to Barney. "You've been selected personally by the commissioner. He spoke to Chief Adamson at ISI requesting you be temporarily assigned to Tactical. Adamson agreed."

"Naturally," Louis said.

Nolan ignored Louis and continued. "The commissioner then phoned me. I'll be frank with you, Barney. I told the commissioner we had competent men within the Tactical Division, but the commissioner insisted. He said you might have a personal stake in this case. And due to your service in ISI you are well aware of the need in special cases to protect the department's good name. And this is a special situation. That's why it's Tactical. That's why you're here. You're assigned to me. But you run this case. Louis is your partner. You report directly to me." Nolan leaned back. "Is that clear?"

Barney took out a cigarillo and used Nolan's onyx lighter.

Nolan pressed, "I asked if all that was clear, Lieutenant?"

Barney nodded. "The chain of command is clear. But what case am I running?"

Nolan leaned forward. "A little over an hour ago Captain Thomas Neeley was found shot to death. I believe Tom Neeley was your sponsor."

Barney exchanged a quick glance with Louis, then asked, "Where was Neeley found?"

"In bed. In his house. Up in the hills."

"The coroner's man there?"

Nolan nodded. "They woke Torres up for this one."

"Who found him?" Barney asked.

"Leo Mirell's chauffeur." Nolan moved a slip of paper across the desk to Barney.

"Who's Leo Mirell?" Barney asked.

Nolan sighed. "Leo Mirell runs the most powerful theatrical agency in town. Now hold the questions. Patrolmen Cauthen and Meyer are on the scene. Everything's frozen. The patrolmen haven't touched a thing. There's the address." Nolan got to his feet. "They're waiting for you."

Louis and Barney stood up. "Anything else we should know?" Barney asked.

"Yes." Nolan nodded. "We've all heard the rumors about Neeley dealing cocaine. We also know the rumors of Neeley handling some bag-money jobs. We know he lived way over his pension. We know he ran with a dangerous crowd. You knew Neeley. He served with distinction for a lot of years before he took over the Beverly Hills thing. Tom Neeley is a famous police name in this town. We got a hell of a lot of heat on the department right now." Nolan came around the edge of the desk and walked up to Barney. "We have forty-three police killings of unarmed suspects under investigation right now," Nolan went on wearily. "We've got that son of a bitch on Channel Seven up our ass and that goddamn *New West* magazine calling us a Gestapo."

"I know all about it," Barney said. "I'm conducting the Internal investigation on the last police killing."

"The guy that came out of the bakery naked?" Louis asked.

"Right," Barney said. "The officers claim the victim had a concealed weapon."

"Where?" Nolan asked. "Up his ass?"

"The officer who killed him says he had a weapon in a paper bag. Turned out to be a banana."

"Well," Nolan said, "that kind of shit has placed us all on the griddle. Now we have a top cop retired, and dealing in Christ knows what, found shot to death. I don't know who burned Neeley. I just hope to God it wasn't connected with any of his former police activities. You're on this case to insure the department against any public outrage. We keep this one inside."

"Has the press been notified?" Barney asked.

"No. Not even Neeley's former wife."

"Good. I'd like to handle that myself."

"It's your case, Barney."

Louis asked, "What if we find out Neeley was involved with former squeals?"

"It's simple, boys. Whatever you find comes to me. Now you better get over there."

Louis opened the door for Barney and followed him out. Nolan went back to his desk and dialed the commissioner's home number.

The afternoon sun cast a hazy, yellow light. The smog was heavy, and Barney's eyes smarted as he drove the restored ten-year-old yellow GTO Pontiac convertible through the heavy Sunday traffic. The eight-track cartridge played a series of numbers by the Bee Gees from the score of a current popular movie. They were traveling west on Wilshire, passing the last Art Deco buildings of the thirties.

"Nice car," Louis said. "I guess you hold something long enough and it comes back."

"Yeah. It's become a collector's item," Barney said. "I'm not a car nut. I just have trouble letting go of old things."

They crossed Robertson and turned north into Doheny. They were passing the Doheny-Palms, and Barney thought of Kathy. He wondered if she'd hold still for the day. He didn't think so.

"How do you know Neeley?" Louis asked.

"Neeley was a friend of my father's. They met in the Air Force in '42 or '43. Neeley flunked out of pilot school. He transferred into some other branch of the Army. After the war Neeley stayed in touch with my mother until she died."

Louis looked out the window and said, "Neeley was a good cop for a long time."

"Yes. He was," Barney agreed.

They crossed Sunset, going north toward the hills.

They passed a huge mansion recently purchased by a twenty-year-old Saudi sheikh. The sheikh had erected marble statues of Greek cherubs atop the long, high wall surrounding the mansion. The statues had one unique innovation: They all had pubic hair.

Louis asked, "How you gonna handle this, Barney?"

"We just go by the book."

"Nolan's book?"

"I think we have to play it the way it comes down . . . and protect the department if we can."

There was a pause, then Louis asked, "You were CIA, right?"

Barney knew it would come. Every cop he had ever worked with would pop that question sooner or later. "That's right. I was with the Agency," Barney replied.

"How come you quit?"

Barney sighed. "A good agent delivers blind obedience. I couldn't do that anymore."

They stopped at a light, alongside a henna-haired youth in an open 450 SL Mercedes. The boy had his tapes playing at a deafening decibel. He wore a Mickey Mouse shirt and had a ring through his left ear. As the light changed, he winked at Louis, gunned the car, and roared off.

Barney turned left into the Canyon Estates and started the long climb toward the top of the ridge. They were passing the honey-combed hills where the half-million-dollar homes nestled into the ridges on either side of the road. The same houses had sold for less than two hundred thousand only five years ago.

Barney glanced at Louis. "You think Neeley was dealing in coke?"

"That's what's around," Louis replied.

"What about the bag jobs?"

Louis shrugged. "Once you cross that street, anything is possible."

CHAPTER

7 ☒

THEY CAME AROUND THE LAST CURVE ON THE HIGH RIDGE AND PULLED over to the curb fifty feet away from Neeley's split-level fieldstone. There was a small army of vehicles parked on both sides of the street fanning out from Neeley's driveway: the morgue ambulance, two black and whites from the Metro Squad, the coroner's lab van, and an unmarked car from Central. Barney thought they were lucky the house was isolated; otherwise, there would have been the usual carnival atmosphere of public crowds and television cameras. The vicarious vultures that swooped down the moment a sudden violent death occurred.

A short, stocky man with a flattened nose and sunken eyes came toward Barney and Louis. The man wore a shield on his shabby blue blazer. He smiled at Barney. It wasn't much of a smile. But Barney figured it was the best the man could do, given the face; he had no lips and bad yellowed teeth.

"Sergeant Espinosa." The man grinned. "Tommy Espinosa. Central."

"Barney Caine and Louis Yosuta. Tactical," Barney replied.

They shook hands. Espinosa spit, wiped his chin with the sleeve of his blazer. "We been expecting you, Lieutenant."

They were walking toward the spiral staircase of the house when Barney noticed the open garage. "I want to look at those cars."

"Sure." Espinosa grinned.

They walked into the open garage. There was a Silver Shadow Rolls-Royce, parked alongside Neeley's Mercedes.

Espinosa said, "The limey car is Mirell's. The kraut car is Neeley's."

"Where's Mirell's chauffeur?" Barney asked.

"Upstairs. On the terrace."

"Anyone talk to him?"

"Yeah, we talked to him, but nothing important. Just name, ID, time of arrival. That crap." Espinosa spit and smiled. "We were saving the important questions for you, Lieutenant."

Barney figured he had to stop Espinosa's arrogance early. "That was smart, Sergeant. Because I'm running this case for the commissioner, and if anyone fucks up, they can start looking for some other way to make a living."

Espinosa's eyes glared at Barney for an instant. Then the smile came back. "Well, that's why we didn't touch nothin' and we didn't ask nothin'. It's all yours, Caine."

Barney stared at Espinosa for a moment, then turned to Louis. "Take the Rolls." Louis went over to the Rolls and opened the left door on the passenger side. The Rolls was built for England; the driver's side was on the right. Barney got into the Mercedes. Espinosa watched silently as the two detectives went through the cars.

Barney pressed the button on the glove compartment, and it fell open. There was a neat collection of manila envelopes wrapped with a red rubber band. Barney slipped the rubber band off and shuffled through the envelopes. There was an owner's registration card dated March 3, 1977, and a "Power-Train" policy that insured the owner against any repairs for five years or fifty thousand miles. There was a Michelin guidebook of the West German Federal Republic, an Automobile Club route map from Berlin to Hamburg, three California road maps, two credit card slips: one from the Hassler Hotel in Rome, and another from the Kempinski Hotel in West Berlin.

Barney put the envelopes aside and looked into the glove compartment. He found a week-old Santa Anita program with the number of a private box on the cover. Barney tucked the German road map, the hotel credit slips, and the Santa Anita program into his inside jacket pocket. He turned to the back seat. It was spotless.

Louis came up to him. "The Rolls is registered to Leo Mirell. There was nothing else except a lady's comb and a program of a Zubin Mehta concert at the Music Center. You get anything?"

"Maybe. We'll see." Barney nodded at Espinosa, and they followed him up the stairs. A uniformed cop at the door saluted them as they went inside.

The living room looked as if it had been put through a blender. The two floor-to-ceiling book-lined walls had been torn apart. The books had been flung across the floor. The shelves were empty. The paintings on the third wall had been pulled from their frames. The twin sofas had been slashed, and the stuffing gutted; the white down lay in scattered heaps like the residue of sheared sheep. The portable bar was smashed. Three leather chairs were decimated by what appeared to be razor slashes. The carpet had been ripped from its moorings and rolled up, exposing the scored wooden floor. A police photographer created intermittent light flashes as he popped away at the wreckage. Two fingerprint men were carefully dusting the fallen books and the barren shelves. The sliding glass door leading out to the terrace was open. Barney could see a man in a chauffeur's uniform sitting in a lounge chair near the pool. Two uniformed cops were chatting and smoking near the chauffeur.

Barney asked Espinosa, "Who are the patrolmen?"

"Cauthen and Meyer. They got here first."

"They always smoke on duty?"

"What the hell do I know?" Espinosa smiled. "I'm with Central. Who knows those guys? They're from West Hollywood."

Louis picked up a leather cushion and ran his finger along the torn edge. "Razor slash. It's too fine to be anything else."

"Check the chauffeur," Barney said. Louis nodded, dropped the cushion, and went out to the terrace. "Where's the body?" Barney asked Espinosa.

"Follow me, Lieutenant."

The bedroom was a large, wide room dominated by a king-sized bed. There was a small terrace off the bedroom, and a single door leading to the bathroom was open. A color television was set into the wall at eye level, directly opposite the bed. There were globelike lamps and Italian phones resting on night tables. A deep-pile red rug covered the floor.

The bedcovers had been pulled down, exposing white, bloodstained sheets. And sprawled on the bed, naked, his arms thrust out in a Christlike pose, was the stiffening body of Thomas Neeley.

There were purple rents in Neeley's body that traveled from a line just above his silver pubic hair all the way up to his forehead. The hole in his forehead was at the bridge of the nose. And resting on Neeley's bloody stomach: a carved black ebony voodoo doll. The doll was a foot long and Barney guessed about three inches wide. A stocky, swarthy, bald-headed man leaned over Neeley's body. He was Chief Medical Examiner Gabriel Torres. He was placing small amounts of tissue, blood, intestinal fluid, and fingernail scrapings onto glass slides. He handed the slides to an assistant, who placed them in glassine envelopes. Torres straightened up and smiled at Barney.

"*Buenos días, teniente.*"

"How are you, Gabby?"

"Muy bien. Como siempre."

They had worked together before, and Barney understood Torres. He knew the coroner was still suspicious of co-workers whose ancestry was not Mexican. Torres masked his distrust of Anglos with a deceptive geniality.

"Nothing like working Sundays, Gabby," Barney said.

"The last time was the naked guy blasted by Metro cops," Gabby agreed. "The guy with the banana."

"Yeah. . . ." Barney sighed. "The naked guy with the banana."

Barney took out a pack of cigarillos and offered one to Torres. The coroner shook his head. "No, *gracias.* I gave it up."

Barney lit the cigarillo and blew some gray smoke over Torres's head. "What can you tell me, *amigo?"*

Torres glanced at the tortured body on the bed. "I'd say he was hit maybe four hours ago. He was shot seven times with a twenty-two long automatic. We found the shells. We'll get the make from ballistics. The shot between the eyes would have killed him instantly. For Neeley's sake I hope it was the first shot. But with all this blood, I doubt it. There was a trace of semen on the tip of his cock. We took a tissue sample."

"You mean he had intercourse before he was hit?"

"It couldn't have been after, *amigo."* Torres smiled. "I found two strands of black hair on the pillow, and. . . ." Torres turned to his assistant. "Let me have that pillow, Jack."

The assistant eased Neeley's head up and slipped the pillow out from under the dead man's head. He tossed the bloody pillow to Torres, who caught it and handed it to Barney. "Smell that, *amigo."*

Barney held the pillow against his nostrils and inhaled. The sweet, cloying odor of a heavy perfume was unmistakable. Barney handed the pillow back to Torres. "Can you make anything out of that?"

"Maybe?"

"What else?"

"Can't say." Torres shrugged. "I need Toxology and Hematology. I need to get his brain in a jar. Of course, there's that voodoo doll on his chest."

"Been dusted?"

"Yeah." Torres nodded. "Dusted. And photographed."

"Okay. I guess he's yours," Barney said.

Torres signaled to his assistant, who nodded and left.

Barney turned to Espinosa, who stood silently in the doorway. "After I talk to Louis, I want everyone out; just a cop at the door, day and night. Now, get me an evidence envelope."

"Right away, Chief." Espinosa left.

Barney didn't like Espinosa's use of the word "Chief" but decided not to make a thing out of it. There were a lot of men on the force like Espinosa, and there wasn't much you could do with them. They were old homicide bulls. They had seen too much and heard too much, their careers had stagnated, and they were waiting for pensions. Torres was packing his medical tray, sliding the trays into their grooves and locking them. Barney went over to the bed and carefully lifted the voodoo doll off Neeley's chest. He looked at the base of the doll and saw the carved words "Port-au-Prince, Haiti."

Two men came in with a stretcher, lifted Neeley's rigid body off the bed, and lowered it into an open black bag. They zippered the bag closed, placed the body on the stretcher, and carried it out. Torres picked up his medical tray and looked at Barney.

"I should have it all for you tomorrow afternoon."

"Thanks, Gabby."

"*De nada, señor.*" Torres smiled. "You ought to quit those cigarillos. Poison, baby." Torres patted Barney on the shoulder and left.

Barney placed the voodoo doll upright on the bamboo end table and stared at the grinning face of the doll for a moment. He then walked slowly around the foot of the bed and went into the bathroom. It was a large blue-tiled room with a standing shower stall and a sunken Roman tub. Drops of water still came out of the shower head. Barney thought he smelled a trace of the heavy perfume. He went to the sink and opened the cosmetic cabinet. It contained the usual mix of medicines, salves, lotions, deodorants, and shaving cream. The only item that jarred the masculinity of the contents was a pair of false eyelashes. They were black. Barney checked the towels hanging over a bar in the tub; one of them was still damp. The piece of pink soap in the shower was soft and damp. Barney went out of the bathroom, walked through the bedroom, and entered the living room. The photographer was gone, but the print men were still at it. Barney surveyed the wreckage for a moment, then walked out onto the terrace.

The smog had cut the view from the terrace to less than half a mile. Louis came up to Barney, and they both stared at the smog-shrouded city below.

"Goddamn smog," Louis muttered.

"Yeah," Barney nodded.

Louis sighed. "Something about that chauffeur doesn't smell right."

"Something he said?" Barney asked.

"No, just a feeling. He says that his boss told him to pick Neeley up at twelve-fifteen. He got to the door, rang a few times, tried the knob, and went in. He saw the wreckage, got scared, went down to his car. Used the car phone and called the Beverly Hills police. They told him to call the West Hollywood Division. He says that's all he knows."

"But you don't feel right about him?"

"I think he knows a hell of a lot more."

Barney sucked in some smoke and exhaled. "Neeley was shot seven times. He had intercourse before he was hit. There were strands of black hair on the pillow. And a voodoo doll on his chest."

"With coke inside?" Louis asked.

"Probably. That's how they get the stuff past customs. And leaving it on his chest is a typical mob hit on a cheating dealer." Barney dropped the cigarillo and stepped on it. "We'll crack the doll open when we're clear."

"What do you make of it?" Louis asked.

"I don't know. There's that stuff I found in Neeley's car."

"What stuff?"

"German road maps. A Michelin guide to West Germany. And paid receipts from a hotel in Rome and a hotel in Berlin."

"Bag trips?" Louis asked.

Barney nodded. "Looks like Tom was carrying hot money for someone."

They turned from the view and walked over to the patrolmen. Barney addressed the tall, thin cop. "What's your name?"

"Patrolman Meyer. This is my partner, Jack Cauthen."

"What time did you arrive?"

"We were dispatched at twelve-thirty-four P.M. and arrived on the scene at twelve-forty-six P.M." Meyer glanced at the chauffeur. "We found him waiting for us."

"Where?"

The short, handsome cop, Cauthen, answered, "He was standing at the garage."

"What else?"

Cauthen shrugged. "Nothing. All we know is what we found. We didn't touch a thing."

"Okay," Barney said. "File a report with Metro, and see that Tactical is copied."

The patrolmen stood there for a moment, neither speaking nor moving.

"That's it, boys," Barney said. "Go get some lunch."

The men saluted quickly and left.

Barney moved a wrought-iron chair over to the lounge and sat down opposite the chauffeur. He opened his shirt collar and turned to Louis. "See if you can find that asshole Espinosa." Barney took out a pack of cigarillos and looked at the chauffeur. "Will this bother you?"

The pale face with the worried hazel eyes and scarred mouth shook his head. Barney lit the cigarillo and blew the smoke directly into the man's face.

"I'm Lieutenant Barney Caine. Tactical Squad. I'm in charge of this case."

"I'll tell you everything I know, Lieutenant."

"Good. Let's start with your name."

"Herbert Glenn."

"And what do you do, Herbert?"

"I'm Mr. Mirell's chauffeur."

"My partner, Sergeant Yosuta, tells me you stumbled onto this mess."

The man's head bobbed up and down rapidly. "Scared hell out of me. I never seen anything like this."

"Did you go in the bedroom?"

"Once the cops got here I did. Jesus Christ, they really hit Tom."

"Tell me, Herbert, why were you sent over here?"

"I was told to pick Mr. Neeley up at twelve-fifteen."

"Where were you supposed to take Mr. Neeley?"

The man shifted his long legs. "To Mr. Mirell's home."

"Where's that?"

"Twenty-two-oh-nine Chalon Road, Bel-Air."

"What was the occasion?"

"What do you mean?"

Barney leaned forward, and his voice took on a hard edge. "I mean Tom Neeley has a beautiful SL Mercedes sitting in his garage. Why does he require a chauffeur? What the hell was the occasion? What was the program of activity at Mirell's house?"

The chauffeur blinked three times, and his voice wavered. "Well, Mr. Mirell likes to send the Rolls for his friends. Nothing more than that. And, uh, well, every Sunday he has friends over. They play tennis. You know, the usual social stuff."

Louis came out onto the terrace with Espinosa, who held a large manila evidence envelope. Espinosa stood behind the chauffeur, and Louis stood alongside Barney. The chauffeur stared up uneasily at the two men. Barney's voice grew gentle; he patted the chauffeur's knee.

"Tell me, Herbert, what do you mean by 'usual stuff'?"

The chauffeur grimaced and chewed on his lower lip for a minute. "Christ, can I stay out of this?" he stammered. "I mean . . . I got to be—"

"The lieutenant knows what you mean," Louis snapped.

"You bet I do, Herbert," Barney said. "Just tell me about the social stuff."

"Well, Mr. Mirell usually has a few friends over every Sunday. There's some tennis. Then everyone turns on. And these broads come over."

"Who are the few friends?" Barney asked gently.

"Well, it changes. But most of the time it would be Neeley, a guy named Clements, and some wop named Maldonado. And sometimes a few celebrity clients of Mr. Mirell's."

"You said they turned on. To what? Booze, grass, heroin. Uppers, downers?"

"Cocaine."

The word hung in the afternoon haze. Magical. Mysterious. And strangely elegant.

"Who provided the coke?" Barney asked.

The pale, sweat-soaked man shook his head. "I don't know."

"I believe you, Mr. Glenn. You know why I believe you?"

The chauffeur shook his head.

"Because, Herbert, you'd put the finger on your mother to get off the hook." Barney looked up at Louis. "Can you think of anything else?"

"Yeah," Louis said. "What did Neeley talk about when you drove him?"

"Nothing. Horses mostly. He liked to talk about horses."

"Racehorses?"

"Yeah. Thoroughbreds." The chauffeur paused, then added, "Last Sunday Neeley gave me a horse belonged to Arthur Clements."

"Who is Arthur Clements?"

The chauffeur shrugged. "A businessman. Playboy. Semiretired. He owns racehorses. It's his hobby."

"How did Mr. Clements's tip turn out?" Barney asked.

"The horse lost . . . ran fifth."

"You're not very lucky, are you, Herbert?" Barney said.

There was a moment of silence as the three detectives stared at the frightened, squirming chauffeur. Then Barney tossed his cigarillo into the swimming pool and asked, "Who were the Sunday broads?"

"Models. From Laura Gregson."

"Hookers?"

"I think so. I think they were paid for."

Barney got to his feet. "Okay, Herbert. You live at the Mirell house?"

"Yeah. In a small cottage behind the tennis courts."

Barney glanced at Espinosa. "Take Mr. Glenn down to Central. Hold him in protective custody, as a material witness. Read him his rights. And run a make on him."

Espinosa walked up to the chauffeur, grabbed him by his jacket, and yanked him to his feet. "Let's go, Herbert."

The chauffeur's lips trembled, and he blurted, "What for? What did I do? What the hell did I do?"

"Nothing," Barney said. "Absolutely nothing."

"Then what are you booking me for?"

"You weren't listening, Herbert. We're not booking you. We're holding you in protective custody."

"What do I need protection for?"

"Well, for starters, you named Maldonado. You know who Victor Maldonado is?"

"A greaseball friend of Mirell's."

Espinosa laughed. Louis smiled, and Barney said: "That greaseball is head of the L.A. mob. Mr. Glenn, you're going to thank me for keeping you out of harm's way. Just for a few days. As soon as we get some answers, you're out."

Espinosa handed the evidence envelope to Louis and propelled the chalk-faced chauffeur toward the living room.

"He'll be out in seventy-two hours," Louis said.

"I know. But it'll give us a chance to see Mirell before Mr. Glenn can get to him."

They walked over to the pool and stared into the clear aquamarine water.

"Tom Neeley lived pretty good," Louis said.

"Not anymore," Barney replied.

The fingerprint men were gone. The front door was open, and a single patrolman stood guard. But the house was empty except for Louis and Barney. They walked through the rubble of the living room and entered the bedroom.

"Okay," Barney said. "Let's start with the drawers, then the end tables, then the closets."

"What about the doll?"

"It'll wait."

"You checked the bathroom?"

"Yeah, but we'll go over it again. I found some false eyelashes."

"I wonder whose?"

"They weren't Neeley's," Barney said.

They searched quietly and methodically for half an hour. Barney sensed a trace of the heavy, sweet perfume. He wondered who the girl was who had shared Neeley's final orgasm. Did she kill him? Or did she set him up for a hit man? Why was the living room the only room that was torn apart? The questions whirled as they went through drawer after drawer. They opened the large closets and went through suit after suit, pocket after pocket. They came up with a small black book full of names of Neeley's former "squeals" and underworld contacts. There was a matchbook from the Oloffson Hotel, Haiti, a raw pornographic color shot from a place called the Sexporium in Hamburg. And in the inside pocket of a velvet tuxedo they found a scrap of paper with carefully printed block letters: "OBERMANN–GENESIS." In the bottom drawer of the bureau they found a photo album of nude models and the name "Laura Gregson."

They placed everything in the manila evidence folder. Barney walked over to the end table and picked up the voodoo doll. They found a claw hammer in the kitchen drawer. Louis carefully spread a newspaper sheet from the calendar section of the L.A. Sunday *Times* on the kitchen counter. He placed the doll on its side and held it fast to the paper. He swung the claw side of the hammer down into the neck of the doll. It broke off on the third swing. Louis turned the doll upside down, and a thin stream of snow-white powder fell silently onto John Travolta's face.

As they left the house, Barney instructed the patrolman at the door to seal the apartment. That no one was permitted entry without a signed order from Tactical. The policeman nodded and asked, "What about them?" The patrolman indicated a mobile television truck across the street. A sound man and a cameraman were talking to a very tall brunette whom Barney recognized instantly. She was a roving reporter for a local television station.

"The Barracuda," Barney sighed. "How the hell does she scoop everyone else?"

"They say she sucks like Picasso paints."

"Well, that's one way to get inside information."

They walked toward the Pontiac as if they had blinkers on, ignoring the presence of the news team. But the tall girl headed them off.

"Remember me, Lieutenant?" She smiled sweetly.

"Sure. How are you, Gloria?"

"I'm fine." She ran the tip of her tongue slowly across her bottom lip. "I've been told that former Police Chief Thomas Neeley was murdered this morning."

"That's correct. Thomas Neeley was found shot to death some time this morning."

"You're assigned to Internal Security, aren't you?" she asked.

"That's right."

"How come you're on this case? Thomas Neeley was a civilian."

"You'll have to ask the police commissioner."

"Yes. I can do that. I know the commissioner."

Barney nodded. "I hear you know a lot of people."

The tall girl smiled. "Is this crime connected in some way with the current investigation into the police killings?"

"Absolutely not."

Barney heard the whirring sound of the camera as the cameraman began to record the interview.

The girl persisted, "If Thomas Neeley's murder is connected to the police killings, will it be made public?"

"The Los Angeles Police Department is not a secret unit. It operates under civilian authority."

"What about the documents related to the police killings that were shredded in the DA's office?"

"You'll have to ask the DA." Barney took a few steps toward the driver's side. Louis went around and got in the passenger side. The girl moved quickly to the door of the Pontiac, the cameraman, still shooting, followed.

"Tell me, Lieutenant," she asked softly. "Was Neeley a bag man for an oil company?"

"No comment."

"Was Neeley involved with Victor Maldonado?"

"Ask Maldonado."

"I'm asking you, Lieutenant."

"Thomas Neeley was a fine policeman who dedicated his entire professional life to the service of the citizens of this city. He was murdered this morning. I think we owe the man a few days before we destroy his memory."

"But my viewers are entitled to the news."

Barney felt the heat rise from his stomach up to his throat. "Fuck your viewers, sweetheart! No business today on dead cops!" He shouldered her aside, opened the door, and slid into the seat.

The tall pretty girl leaned down and in a husky voice said, "You ought to be nice to me, Lieutenant. 'Cause I'd like to be nice to you. Besides, I'll get the story. I promise you that."

Barney turned the engine over and said, "I'm sure of that, Gloria. You've blown the lid off more than one story in this town." He shifted into reverse, U-turned, and started down the steep hill.

CHAPTER

THE GIRL GAZED OUT THE WINDOW OF HER BEVERLY WILSHIRE SUITE. The two men stared at the girl. The younger man imagined the girl naked. The older man thought about Neeley. The girl whispered as if to no one, "A pity. So far. So wrong."

"I offered him a chance," the young one said. "After each shot I offered him a chance."

"Neeley was a professional," the older man said. "He knew you would kill him anyway."

"Perhaps Neeley didn't know about the Swiss," the girl offered. "Perhaps he never made the connection to the Swiss."

The older man replied, "But if he did, Genesis is in jeopardy."

The young man rose and stretched. "I'll say one thing for Neeley: He was tough. Very tough. After I shot him the third time, I asked him again. And he said, 'Fuck you!'"

The girl continued to stare out the window and said, "The question now is whether the cocaine situation was proper."

"It fits American drug-crime patterns," the older man said. "Besides, we simply followed orders."

"It's too obvious," the girl said. "I never liked that."

"Tearing up the living room will help," the young one said. "It's a good deception."

The older man rose, scratched his white hair, and said to the girl, "You must seek permission from Clements for us to see the Neeley woman."

The girl turned to him. "If you see her, you will have to kill her."

The older man shrugged. "Perhaps. But there is no other recourse."

"I do not enjoy the killing," the girl replied.

"No one does," the young man snapped.

"Except you," the girl answered coldly. "You orgasm at the trigger."

"Thinking of you." The young man smiled.

The silver-haired man turned to the girl. "When are you leaving?"

"Tomorrow. National to Miami. Then Pan American to Port-au-Prince."

The swarthy young man walked over to the beautiful girl at the window and smiled through perfectly capped snow-white teeth. "You never told us how Mr. Neeley's last sexual effort was."

The girl's eyes blazed. They were as blue and fiery as a perfect set of sapphires. She spoke fast in German. Her full lips had a curious way of circling each word. She finished and turned her back to the young man.

He responded softly in halting German. It was an apology. But the girl never looked at him again. The young man abruptly left the suite. The older man sat on the sofa in utter silence for five minutes; then he rose and looked at the girl.

"You'll speak with Arthur Clements?"

She nodded, and the man left.

The girl remained at the window, looking down at the traffic on Wilshire Boulevard. She rubbed her arms, using each palm against the opposite arm, but despite the effort, she shuddered as she remembered Neeley's body entwined with hers and him gasping, "Jesus Christ . . . Christ . . . Christ Almighty."

She saw an elderly couple crossing at Wilshire and El Camino, and she thought: The Jews. Then she remembered; they were not to refer to them any longer as "Jews." They were now called Zionists. The word "Jew" had been replaced by "Zionist" in all the avenues of propaganda.

She walked quickly to the phone, dialed room service, and ordered a shrimp cocktail, a rare steak, asparagus tips sautéed in butter, and a bottle of Dom Pérignon. She went into the bedroom, opened her bag, and lit a joint of pure Moroccan hashish. She lay down on the bed, letting her robe fall open. She drew heavily on the strong, sweet-smelling hash. Her body ached for a young man who shared her apartment in the Seventh Arrondissement in Paris.

CHAPTER

THEY TOOK SUNSET BOULEVARD WEST TOWARD THE PACIFIC COAST Highway and stopped for lunch in Brentwood at a small Mexican restaurant. They ordered margaritas and two combination plates of chicken enchiladas, chile rellenos, and refried beans. Barney took his margarita with him as he went to the public phone booth at the rear of the restaurant. He dropped a dime in the slot and dialed the Malibu number. He sipped the margarita as the phone rang. The dime suddenly dropped back into the coin-return chamber, and a female voice dripping with bureaucratic disdain came on, demanding twenty cents for the first three minutes.

Barney dropped a quarter in the slot and in precise, icy cadence was told he would be credited with an extra minute. He thanked the chilly voice politely. The number rang four times, and Barney was about to hang up; but he remembered the beach house at Malibu had a large sun deck, and if Kay was outside, she deserved a few more rings. On the seventh ring an out-of-breath female voice said, "Hello."

"Is this Kay Raines?" Barney used Kay's maiden name.

"Yes. Who's calling?"

"I'm Lieutenant Barney Caine, Tactical Squad. Los Angeles police. You may remember me, Kay. Tom Neeley was a friend of my parents."

There was a long pause.

"Yes. I remember you, and I remember your mother. You visited my house many years ago." There was another pause. "What is it you want, Barney?"

Barney sipped the margarita, took a deep breath, let it out. "Tom was shot to death earlier today."

There was another period of silence, followed by a soft "Oh. . . ."

Barney continued: "I'm in charge of the case. I would like to come out there, Kay, and ask you a few questions."

Before she could respond, the operator's voice cut in: "Deposit another ten cents for the next three minutes."

Barney searched his pockets, found a quarter and a nickel. "Here's a quarter, Operator."

"Thank you." The operator's voice had all the warmth of water falling off an icicle. "We will credit you with an extra three minutes."

"Hello . . . Kay?"

"Yes. I'm still here."

"Would it be all right if I came out now with my partner?"

"When will you be here?"

"We're in Brentwood. I'd say a half hour."

"You have the address?"

"Twenty-two forty-five Malibu Colony Road."

"I'll be waiting, Lieutenant."

The late-afternoon sun painted a shimmering mass of white diamonds into the surface of the Pacific. A few surfers fought for balance on the curving waves that broke on the small stretch of private beach. And beyond the surfers a flotilla of gaily colored sailboats skimmed across the sea, tacking and turning gracefully, like ballerinas warming up for the dance.

Barney turned left off the coast highway and entered the private road on the beach side of Malibu Colony. A security guard at the gate checked their names against a visitors' list and waved them on.

The house was a two-story A-frame, painted white, with a brown shingle roof. There was an open garage off to the right of the entrance. Barney pulled into the garage alongside a blue Lincoln. They went up to the door, and Barney pressed a small button and heard the sound of chimes, followed instantly by the barking of a dog.

Kay Neeley, now Kay Raines, opened the door and led them into the high-ceilinged living room. She said something to the police dog, and he went obediently out onto the terrace.

Kay was in her late fifties; but she was still slim, and her high cheekbones and alert blue eyes belied her age. She was one of those fortunate women whose natural beauty would not be damaged by time. The living room was furnished tastefully but casually. The wooden floor was covered in part by Navaho throw rugs. A sliding glass door led to the outside wooden deck and afforded a marvelous view of the ocean. There was an open kitchen off the living room, and a circular staircase led to the upper floor. A huge piece of driftwood served as a coffee table and separated the two sofas.

Barney introduced Louis, and Kay asked if she could get them something to drink. Barney declined, but Louis asked for a beer.

They watched her walk toward the kitchen. Her hips moved seductively, and the tight-fitting black slacks and loose white blouse complimented her figure. She had a grace and style to her movements that seemed almost calculated. But Barney knew better; some women were simply born with it, and it almost never had anything to do with money. Louis sat on the sofa and picked up a copy of *Vogue* magazine. Barney moved to the glass terrace door. The police dog was on the terrace chewing on a rubber bone, and way out on the horizon a dark smudge of smoke traced the slow progress of a tanker. Barney wondered whether it had begun its voyage in Dubai, or Saudi Arabia, or whether it had come down from Alaska. He thought wherever it had started, its cargo was now the most sought-after commodity in the world. He remembered the oil embargo of '73 and the long lines of motorists waiting impatiently at the pumps, cursing both the Israelis and the Arabs.

Kay came out of the kitchen and handed Louis a bottle of imported Beck's beer and a large tapered glass.

"Thank you." Louis smiled.

Kay lit a cigarette. There was a moment of silence punctuated by the sound of breaking waves. She sat on the sofa opposite Louis and puffed nervously on the cigarette.

Barney sat in a deep leather chair, his back to the glass doors. Kay looked at him. "You're sure I can't get you anything?"

"I'm sure. Thanks, Kay."

There was an awkward moment of silence. Then Kay suddenly blurted, "You know, of course, that Tom and I were divorced five years ago."

"But you're still next of kin. That is, you and your son."

"Roger is in South Africa," Kay said. "Mining business. I get letters regularly, but he and Tom . . ." She paused and crushed the cigarette. "Well, they had no relationship."

"Listen, Kay, before we go any further, I want you to understand something." Barney leaned forward. "My job is to inform you of Tom's death. That's all. But I'd like to ask you some questions, none of which you have to answer without counsel present."

She lit another cigarette.

Barney continued. "You know that time is everything in these things. You crack a murder case in the first seventy-two hours, or usually it drifts into months or even years. It would be helpful if you would answer these questions."

Kay inhaled deeply and blew a stream of smoke that hung in the air between the sofas. "Ask anything you like, Barney," she said softly.

"Would you mind if Louis took notes?"

"Not at all."

Barney nodded at Louis, who took out a small note pad and a black felt pen. Barney looked at Kay. "When was the last time you saw Tom?"

"About fourteen months ago." She crushed the cigarette and wrung her hands, moving them, squeezing them, the fingers of her right hand darting to her breast, brushing some imaginary lint from her white blouse.

"Where did you see him?"

"Tom's house."

"Was anyone else there?"

She arched her back. "A man named Arthur Clements."

"Do you remember what they discussed?"

"It was a long time ago. But I think they talked about breeding racehorses."

"When was the last you spoke to Tom?"

"That was the last time," she replied nervously. "Look, Barney, I know about the cocaine rumors." She rose abruptly. "Excuse me." She went up the spiral staircase to the second floor. They heard a door close.

"You see what I see?" Louis asked.

"Yeah." Barney nodded. "She's terrified of something."

They heard the toilet above flush; then a door opened and closed, and Kay came back down. She looked at Barney and smiled slightly. She went to the wet bar at the far end of the room and fixed a scotch on the rocks. She sipped the drink and took a cigarette out of a tortoiseshell box on the bar and lit it with a silver Dunhill. She spun the ice in the glass.

Barney watched her nervous movements for a moment, then asked, "Have you seen or heard from Victor Maldonado?"

"No." She shook her dark hair.

"Is there anything at all you can tell me about him?"

"There is something. I don't know if it's important."

"Everything you know is important, Kay."

"Maldonado owns Leo Mirell's theatrical agency. Through a company called Seneca."

"How do you know that?"

"Tom mentioned it."

"Anything else?"

Kay shrugged. "There were rumors that Maldonado helped Mirell out of a bad marriage."

"How?"

"I suppose he threatened the woman. I don't know. Victor has a dangerous reputation. But you know that."

"Do you know anything about trips that Tom made to Germany?"

"No." She twirled the ice in her drink.

"To Haiti?"

"No."

"To Italy?"

"No." She blew some smoke, then suddenly blurted, "Wait. That's not right. About eight months ago Tom called me. He was excited. He said he was going to Rome."

"Hold it, Kay," Barney interrupted. "You said that the last time you spoke to Tom was fourteen months ago. Now you say eight months ago."

"Right," she said, and brushed the hot end of the cigarette against the ashtray. "I forgot about this particular call."

"Okay," Barney said reassuringly, and glanced at Louis. They both knew she was lying.

"Tom said he was going to Rome," she continued, "and that through Arthur Clements some important doors were opening."

"What doors?"

Kay came around the bar and walked up to the sofa and sat down. She sipped some scotch and toyed with the ice again. She took a long time to answer. It was as if Barney and Louis were not present, as if she were alone.

"What doors, Kay?" Barney repeated gently.

"Tom said he had made a connection with Adam Steiffel."

"The president of Tidal Oil?" Barney asked.

Kay nodded. "Tom cautioned me never to mention the Steiffel connection to anyone."

"Did he say why?"

"No. And I didn't ask."

Barney got to his feet, looked out the glass doors at the sparkling Pacific. There was a moment of silence. He then turned back to Kay. "Did Tom ever mention Laura Gregson?"

Kay rubbed her right wrist. "Yes. He said that Laura Gregson was

Maldonado's protégée. That her models were professional call girls."

There was a pause, and Barney nodded. "All right, Kay, that's all for now." Louis tucked his note pad into his pocket, sipped the last of his beer, and got to his feet. Barney said, "I really appreciate this, Kay. I know it wasn't easy."

"I had a premonition," she said sadly. "I knew sooner or later Tom would be over his head. I didn't love him or anything. But we had a lot of years together."

Barney said, "There's no need for you to make identification, unless you want to."

"No. I don't want to see him. But I will make the funeral plans. And my attorney will take care of the legal matters." She slowly stood up. Her hands brushed against her breasts, and she followed them toward the front door.

Barney got halfway, stopped, and turned. "Would you know if Tom had been seeing anyone? I mean a lady. A particular lady."

"I used to see his name in the gossip columns with a variety of ladies. But I don't know of any particular girl."

"Do you know who decorated Tom's house?"

"Yes." She smiled. "I did."

"Then you and Tom were friendly?"

"We were always friendly. We just had no marriage."

"Do you own a gun?"

"No. They frighten me."

"Where were you this morning, Kay?"

"On the terrace, reading."

"Can anyone verify that?"

"Only my dog. He was on the beach chasing sandpipers."

"Thanks again, Kay."

Louis had the door open. Kay came up to Barney. "You think I had anything to do with this, Barney?"

"No. But you're frightened of something."

"Why should I be frightened?"

"You tell me."

She stared at Barney for a moment. "I have nothing to tell you."

Barney parked in front of the Tactical Headquarters building and kept the motor running. He asked Louis to store the evidence envelope in the Tactical safe. Louis opened the passenger door and smiled at Barney.

"By the way, do you mind sharing my office?"

"I sure as hell do."

"I figured you would say that. Well, you can have Stillman's. He's in San Diego."

Barney nodded. "You think we ought to have Kay Neeley watched?"

"You're running the case, Barney." Louis got out of the car, slammed the door, leaned in, and said, "She's scared stiff."

Barney stared at Louis for a moment, then shoved the car into reverse, wheeled around, and slipped into the west-bound traffic lane of Wilshire Boulevard.

CHAPTER

10 ⊠

BARNEY DROVE CAREFULLY AROUND THE CURVING RIBBON ROAD. CHALON Road was only minutes from Sunset Boulevard, but it could have been the country; a forest of tall pines mingled with groves of wild palms that shaded the huge pink Spanish estates. Bel-Air reeked of old California money, some of which went back to the Spanish land-grant days. The illuminated sprawling mansions were set back from the road and rose like magenta ghosts out of the night mist that shrouded the hills. The estates were protected by electronic gates and complex security systems.

He reached the crest of Chalon Road, turned left into a private driveway, and traveled another thirty feet to a set of huge gates, fronted by an iron stanchion with an attached speaker box. Barney reached out with his left hand and depressed a red button on the speaker box. He glanced up and saw two small TV cameras rotating slowly above the gates. The cameras zeroed in on his car. A voice came through the speaker, and Barney identified himself. The gates swung quietly and majestically open.

He drove past the gates and up the long, curving driveway toward the brilliantly lit Spanish mansion sitting atop the hill rise. He parked the car near an open garage that held a gray Mercedes sedan and a vintage Bentley. By the time he walked up to the front door it was open, and Alice was waiting.

Barney thought his former wife was still attractive in her "cheerleader" fashion: tiny features; big gray eyes set wide apart; her straight blond hair long and falling to her shoulders; her figure slim and boyish. Alice had the kind of pretty face that gave her a leg up on intelligence.

She wore a lavender-colored gown, and a set of diamond earrings sparkled at her earlobes. "Timmy will be right down." She smiled. "Come in, Barney."

He followed her into a huge high-ceilinged sunken living room. "A drink?" Alice asked.

"No, thanks. We just have time to make the seven o'clock movie."

"I wish you would skip the movie and just do dinner," she said as she fixed a drink. "Timmy has to be up by six-thirty."

"I'll have him home before ten."

Alice raised her glass. "Cheers."

"Good health." Barney smiled.

They stared at each other for a moment; then their attention was drawn to the alcove as a small blond boy was led into the room by a tall, gray-haired, distinguished-looking man. Dr. Leon Lindstrom wore a smile and a velvet tuxedo. He patted Timmy's head. "Say hello to your daddy, Tim."

Timmy ran to his father. Barney leaned down, hugged the boy, and kissed his cheek. "I hope you're hungry, Tim," Barney said.

"For McDonald's."

"McDonald's it is." Barney straightened up and shook hands with the doctor.

"We're going to a Cancer Fund dinner tonight, at the Beverly Wilshire," the doctor sighed. "I would rather be going to McDonald's."

Barney took Timmy's hand, and Alice led them to the front door. She kneeled down and kissed Timmy, then straightened up and looked into Barney's eyes. "The maid will be waiting for you."

Barney enjoyed the film as much as his son did. He was totally caught up in the dazzling special effects and found himself rooting for the good guys to save the threatened galaxy.

After the film, they went to the McDonald's on Westwood Boulevard. The place was jammed with a mix of teenagers, college kids from the nearby campus of UCLA, and a few adults eating alone. Timmy ordered a Big Mac. Barney ordered french fries and two Cokes.

He looked around at the long-haired youths dressed in jeans, and despite himself, Barney thought back to his days in the CIA, when he had been forced to adopt that same costume, when he had been required to infiltrate certain groups to obtain intelligence and in some cases to plant information. He glanced at the napkin dispenser on the table and remembered similar dispensers in Santiago, where "bugs" were planted along with the napkins. All the dirty tricks came back in a sudden rush. Yet, in reflection, Barney bore no real malice for the Agency. He knew the KGB was far worse. It seemed to Barney there had been a decided shift in Soviet policy; the Russians were not as covert now as they had been in the sixties. The roving Cuban military hit team in Africa, moving unchallenged from country to country at the Soviet bidding, would have been unthinkable in past years.

Through a mouthful of Big Mac, Timmy asked, "What did you do today, Daddy?"

"Nothing much," Barney said, pulling his thoughts back to the present.

"Any robbers?"

"No. Just a man who got in trouble."

"What kind of trouble?"

"I suppose he just took too many chances."

"What kind of chances?"

"He took chances with the wrong people. Now finish your hamburger. You're talking with your mouth full."

Timmy took a long drink of Coke, and Barney found himself flashing on Tom Neeley. He remembered how Neeley had greased the skids for Barney's entry into the L.A. Police Department. He recalled a long lunch with Neeley, when Tom went through the rudiments with him, telling Barney what to expect and from whom to expect it. He remembered Neeley's telling him what a great guy Barney's father was—and how saddened he was when the news reached him that Barney's father had been shot down over Germany.

In Barney's early years on the force Tom Neeley had taken an almost fatherly interest in his progress, but time and circumstances had caused their relationship to drift. Still, he had not forgotten Neeley's kindness; and the indignity of Neeley's death bothered Barney: the perforated naked corpse, the semen, the voodoo doll, and the cloying odor of the heavy perfume.

On the drive back to Bel-Air, Timmy asked him if he had a girl friend or if he still loved Alice. Barney was honest with his son. He said he would always love "Mom," but sometimes people who loved each other could not live together. But despite their failed marriage, they were friends, and the relationship was as it should be. And no, he did not have a girl friend. They rode in silence while Timmy thought it over. They entered the Bel-Air gates, and Timmy asked Barney about a boat trip down the Colorado River. Barney had mentioned the trip as a possibility this coming summer. He promised Timmy he would do his best to make it happen.

CHAPTER

11 ⊠

KATHY WAS ASLEEP ON HER SIDE OF THE KING-SIZED BED, THE TOP COVER thrown off, exposing her full breasts as they rose and fell gently with her breathing. Barney undressed quietly and slipped on his robe. He went into the bathroom, washed his face, brushed his teeth, and swallowed three aspirin. When he came back into the bedroom, Kathy had turned in her sleep, and for a moment Barney admired the sensual curve of her back and the firm tone of her buttocks and the graceful line of her legs. He thought about waking her but decided not to. He crossed into the living room, poured a vodka on the rocks, and walked out onto the terrace.

The night air had turned balmy; a sultry wind stirred the palm fronds that lined the boulevard below. And the sky was unusually clear, permitting a rare view of the stars. Barney thought it was a good night for the picture-taking apparatus in the constantly circling Soviet space satellites. The warm air and clear visibility meant that the wind was coming west from the desert. Somewhere in the neon-edged night over Vegas, columns of hot desert air had risen up and mixed with a stalled weather front, heating the entire system and energizing it. It slowly moved west, creeping through the mountain passes, spilling through the canyons, and settling over the city. The weather bureau would call it a Santana condition. The Santana had a strange effect on the populace. The murder rate shot up. Calm, sedate middle-aged folks would go berserk and kill their mates. Strangers would instantly fall into bed. The balmy desert winds seemed to harbor the essential life forces of violence and sensuality.

Barney sipped the cold vodka, turned away from the view, and flicked the knob in the FM radio. An old Bachrach tune came on. He stretched out on the lounge and gazed up at the stars. He thought how vague it all was. Not up there. But right here. About himself and Timmy and Alice and the lost relationships, and the strange girl asleep in his bed. And the dead Tom Neeley, by now dissected, his vital organs filling an array of jars. Barney's reflective needle stopped and repeated, like a stylus caught in a groove: Tom Neeley. The questions and answers began to swirl.

The cocaine connection alone was baffling: Leo Mirell, or Victor Maldonado, or an obscure former squeal of Neeley's, or one of Laura Gregson's girls, or Gregson herself. Then there was Arthur Clements; maybe Neeley had skimmed something off a money drop, or perhaps Neeley had offended the old man, Adam Steiffel.

It would be prudent never to have Adam Steiffel as an enemy. And Kay, lying and frightened. Of what? And what were Neeley's killers after? Barney's mental computations stopped suddenly. He had used the word "killers," plural. Why had he made that assumption? A girl Neeley had been intimate with could easily have made love to him, taken a shower, come back into the bedroom, stood there naked, smiling down at the reclining Neeley, then calmly taken an automatic out of her purse as easily as she would a comb. But then why seven slugs? Why a line of holes from above his genitals all the way to his brain?

All he could figure was the weapon. A .22 long automatic was professional; it was a favorite weapon of the Mafia, the KGB, and Arab terrorists. The weapon would indicate a professional hit man. Or woman. But the way the living room was torn up indicated a team. But then again, that part of it might have been staged, and the voodoo doll might be a plant. Barney looked up at the clear midnight blue sky and tried to shut off the questions. He tried to think of his son. He tried to think of Kathy in the bedroom, but the computer whirled on. Germany: the porno shot taken in Hamburg. The photograph stayed in his mind. He had seen some raw stuff in his time on Vice, but he had never seen anything like what the two girls in the photo were doing. Why had Neeley gone from Berlin to Hamburg? What the hell was Genesis? And Obermann? Barney sucked at the ice cubes through the vodka.

If he had to gamble at this moment, he would bet that Neeley was not killed over cocaine. Barney thought about something Louis had said earlier: "When a good man crosses the street, anything is possible." It was true. Eternally true. No one was above a hustle. Presidents tripped themselves up. Senators. Governors. Men in high places fell victim to the heady combination of sex, greed, and power. He had been tempted once himself. A piece of seemingly innocuous information to the East German consul general. It was a hell of a lot of money. All they wanted was the name of a certain Brazilian intelligence officer. There was no risk to Barney. Why had he refused? He guessed it was just not in the grain. There was a line you did not cross. But hell, those who did could not be condemned. It was the way things were. It was beyond the sophistry of psychology tests. It was that mysterious inner strength that somehow makes the stronger case for self-respect. There are those men, flawed, fucked-up, selfish, egocentric, but they were not for sale. Every man did not have a price.

The Bachrach song drifted into a cut-time version of "Mack the Knife." The Santana wind played with the tips of Barney's hair and carried with it the sounds of distant traffic. Barney sensed, rather than heard, Kathy.

She stood naked at the entrance to the terrace. She smiled at Barney and raised her arms over her head. Stretching, as if trying to reach for the stars. For a moment her whole body arched and curved. Then her arms dropped. She came slowly over to the lounge and sat down on the edge. She stared at Barney with that vacant nymphomaniac stare. She opened his robe and leaned over him. She moved her long blond hair aside, so Barney could watch what her mouth was doing.

CHAPTER

12 ⊠

THE SULTRY SANTANA WINDS HAD BEEN CHASED BACK INTO THE DESERT by a cold gray Pacific storm front. Kay Neeley shivered slightly in her jeans outfit as she walked along the shoreline with Arthur Clements. Her police dog ran up ahead, chasing sandpipers.

Arthur Clements looked like a middle-aged male model that had stepped out of a *Playboy* ad, the kind of ad that features the silver-haired swinger in a maroon Ferrari with a laughing Bunny alongside, posing as living testaments to the joys of the swinging life.

Clements was six feet tall and worked hard at keeping himself trim and tan. He had gray eyes and small features set off by fine silver hair. The only flaw in his otherwise handsome face was a nest of purple veins clustered at both sides of his patrician nose. The purple network was becoming more profound with passing time and made Clements detest his morning shave.

Kay bent down to pick up a small piece of driftwood. She rubbed her hand over its smooth surface for a moment, then tossed it away. They strolled silently, watching the breaking waves. The beach was deserted except for the distant figures of two joggers. Kay put the collar of her denim jacket up against the chill Pacific storm front.

"Yesterday it was July," she said.

"Yes," Clements agreed. "It was beautiful at the track. You could see the mountains."

They looked up as three screaming sea gulls swooped low over their heads.

"A pity about Tom," Clements said.

"It was inevitable." Kay sighed.

They passed a clump of seaweed that held two dead fish.

"You say this Detective Caine knew Tom?"

"Yes," Kay answered, and rubbed her arms against the cold. "Tom knew Caine's father. They were in the Army together, years ago."

"What was Caine's attitude?"

"Professional. Courteous. Nothing special."

"Did he mention Genesis?"

"No."

"Tedesco?"

"No."

"Did he ask about me?"

"Yes. I told him we saw each other at Tom's at a dinner party. A long time ago."

Still in a gentle voice, Clements asked, "What else did you say?"

"Nothing."

"Did Caine mention Adam Steiffel?"

"I can't remember. He may have."

Kay stopped walking and turned to Clements. She searched his expressive gray eyes. "Arthur, who killed Tom?"

Clements touched the purple area around his nose for a second, then shrugged. "I have no idea." He then put his hands on Kay's shoulders and for the first time an ominous tone shadowed his words. "Did Tom travel from Germany to Lausanne?"

"I left Tom in Berlin," Kay said. "I don't know."

Clements squeezed her shoulders. "Kay, there's a three-hundred-billion-dollar industry at stake here. Did Tom have a meeting with a Swiss banker?"

"I've told you all I know about the German trip." Her voice trembled. "You've got to believe me, Arthur."

Clements slowly dropped his hands from her shoulders. "I do believe you, Kay." He traced her cheekbone with his finger.

"I would never lie to you, Arthur," she said.

Clements stared at her for a long time, then nodded and smiled. They began to walk again, slowly, along the shoreline.

Kay's voice trembled. "I went to Germany with Tom because he said he needed me—and you agreed, Arthur." She paused. "You said it was a good idea."

"That's right. I did," Clements replied.

"Then why the questions?" She sighed.

"I'm sorry, Kay," he said gently. "Tom's death has me jittery. I didn't mean to imply you were lying about anything. I came out here because you asked me to."

"I'm frightened, Arthur," she said quickly.

Clements put his right arm around her waist and drew her close. They had not been lovers for a long time, but he still admired her. He wished there was some way he could keep her alive.

CHAPTER

13 ⊠

THE LAURA GREGSON AGENCY WAS LOCATED IN A MAGENTA-COLORED
two-story Art Deco building on Sunset and Holloway. It was built in
1932, when the Sunset Strip glowed with a jaded sort of elegance. The
building had miraculously resisted the degeneration of the Strip. It had
refused to surrender to the massage parlors, punk-rock joints, porno
theaters, sleazy bars, and burger stands.

Barney and Louis entered a large reception room. Black-and-white
blow-ups of models set against exotic backgrounds were displayed on
the walls. The sounds of soft rock came out of a hidden tape system. A
pretty black girl was seated behind a large desk, typing rapidly on an
IBM Selectric. She finished a sentence and swiveled around. "Can I
help you?"

Louis went up to the desk while Barney studied the blow-ups. The
pretty receptionist took Louis's card and smiled. "Oh, yes, Sergeant.
Miss Gregson is expecting you." She stood up. "Follow me, please."

A heavy, sweet-smelling perfume seemed to dominate the air-condi-
tioned room. Laura Gregson was seated at a round table that held a
modern telephone console.

The lighting came from pinspots in the ceiling and was designed for
drama. Thin cones of light struck various parts of the room, leaving the
unlit areas in almost total darkness. Barney thought it was lit like an old
black-and-white Bogart movie.

Laura Gregson was on the phone. She nodded to them and motioned
that she would be only a moment. She indicated a trio of Danish chairs,
but they remained standing.

Barney was surprised by her youth and beauty. He guessed she was
in her early thirties; he had expected someone older. Laura Gregson
had long, straight sand-colored hair whose tips touched her shoulders.

She wore a man's shirt, and her large, firm breasts seemed to be protesting against their confinement. The shirtfront was swollen by two perfectly formed globes punctuated at their centers by clearly visible nipples. She had a small, straight nose, a wide, soft, full mouth, and a pair of startling green eyes.

She spoke in a low, throaty, almost conspiratorial tone. She was reassuring someone that he or she had selected the right model. She oozed her final words through the receiver and hung up. She tossed her long hair, arched her back, and said, "I'm Laura Gregson. How can I help you?"

"Just answer a few questions." Barney smiled.

"Of course. Have a seat, please."

They each took an outside Danish chair, leaving an empty chair between them.

Barney said, "We're investigating the death of Tom Neeley. I believe you knew Tom."

She wet her lower lip with the point of a very pink tongue and smiled. "Tell me, Lieutenant, do you think I ought to have my lawyer present?"

Barney felt a sudden surge of anger; maybe it was Neeley's purple corpse, or maybe Mirell's pimp chauffeur, or maybe it was his growing feeling of disconnection with his own past. His son. His wife. The forty-three police killings. The naked guy with the banana. Barney did not fully understand the force that created the ball of heat in his throat, but he felt himself going and tried to keep the anger out of his voice. "You can certainly have a lawyer," he said. "Of course, we would have to take you into custody right now. That means the detention pen downtown. That means a cold shower and a lot of fingers exploring your private parts and probably all night in a cage with some pretty tough bull dykes. Then sometime tomorrow we can talk to you in the presence of your attorney."

Louis noticed the half-moon scar on Barney's face turning red. He wondered why Barney was getting so rough so soon.

Laura Gregson's smile disappeared. "You're not too subtle, are you, Mr. Caine?"

"Whoever killed Tom was not very subtle either," Barney replied.

The tips of her long, slender fingers drummed on the desk. "All right, go ahead," she said. "Ask your questions."

"My partner here is going to record this."

"Go ahead," she repeated.

Louis took out his note pad and waited.

"You did know Tom Neeley, correct?"

"We met frequently. Mostly at Leo Mirell's."

"Cocaine parties?"

"Some people did coke," she said matter-of-factly.

"Do you know Arthur Clements?"

"I've met him, but I don't know him."

"Did you supply girls to Neeley and Mirell?"

She poured some water from the carafe into a glass and sipped it. "I don't know what you mean."

"Did you supply girls for a price?"

Her green eyes seemed to pick up tiny lights. "I run a modeling agency, Mr. Caine."

"Do you know Victor Maldonado?"

"I've met him."

"Do you supply him with 'models'?"

"I hardly know the man."

Suddenly something Kay Neeley had said triggered a thought, and Barney decided to take a wild shot. "That's very strange, Laura, because Victor Maldonado owns your company."

Her mouth twisted nervously for a second. "That's absurd."

"Are you telling me that your company is not owned by the Seneca Corporation?"

The color went out of her cheeks; she sipped some more water and stared silently into Barney's eyes. It seemed to Barney as if she were looking beyond his eyes, seeking some inner mystery, some clue that would tell her all she wanted to know about the man who was questioning her. It gave Barney an uneasy feeling.

"I don't know who controls Seneca," she said. "I merged my company with Seneca for a large amount of money. There's nothing illegal about that."

"No. But there is a law against prostitution."

"Well, if you think I've violated that law, then by all means arrest me."

"If I did that, Laura, I would have to arrest Maldonado as a conspirator. He might get very angry."

Her fingertips drummed on the desk top as she continued to stare into his eyes. Her voice was flat and mechanical. "I operate a coast-to-coast modeling agency. I receive a commission from my clients. What my girls do on their own time is of no concern to me."

"Did Tom Neeley use some of your models?"

"Yes, an Oriental girl."

"What's her name?"

She shrugged and tossed her long hair. "I'd have to check."

"Do you supply models to women, too?"

"On occasion," she replied curtly, and leaned forward. "Look, I supply models to clients for a price. Now, I can't be any clearer than that."

"I have nothing else." Barney looked over at Louis. "What about you, Sergeant?"

"Just one or two."

"Go ahead," Laura said.

"Where were you between ten and eleven A.M. yesterday?"

"At home."

"Can you prove that?"

"Yes." She bit her lip. "I was with someone."

"Who?"

For the second time her composure seemed to falter, and the careful rhythm of her speech became uneven. "He's married. He's famous." She looked at Barney. "Do we have to drag him in?"

"We're not the Salvation Army. We're not interested in hurting anyone. Tell us who the man is, so we can verify your time. We'll keep the man out of it."

"The man's name"—she sighed—"is Paul Isella."

"The race driver?" Louis asked.

Laura nodded. "He's here, stunt driving or doubling some star for a movie."

"Did Isella know Tom Neeley?" Barney asked.

"Yes. They met at Mirell's."

"Where can we find him?" Louis asked.

"The Ontario Speedway."

They got to their feet, and Barney said, "We'll have to check your files."

"What for?"

"The Oriental girl that Neeley played with."

"You can come tomorrow, anytime after ten." She leaned back in her chair, raising and pointing her jutting breasts to the ceiling.

"By the way," Barney asked, "do you own a gun?"

She shook her head. "No, Lieutenant. I'm old-fashioned. I depend upon the police for protection."

CHAPTER

14 ⊠

BARNEY STARED OUT OF THE WINDOW OF HIS TEMPORARY OFFICE. THE
gray Pacific mist had turned into a light rain. It was late afternoon, but
down below on Wilshire Boulevard, the neon store lights had come on,
and the moving cars had their headlights on. Barney turned from the
window and went to a blackboard and studied the diagram he had
drawn:

TOM NEELEY

KAY NEELEY————————————————————————LEO MIRELL
(Tom's ex-wife)   (Theatrical agent)
                                                        (company owned
                                                            by Seneca)

VICTOR MALDONADO
(Head of Los Angeles Mafia)
(Seneca)

ADAM STEIFFEL(?)————LAURA GREGSON————ARTHUR CLEMENTS
(chairman of   (Model agency)   (Horse breeder)
Tidal Oil)   (company owned by Seneca)   (Board chairman
                                                            various
                                                      corporations)

PAUL ISELLA(?)
(Racing car driver)
(Gregson's lover)

Under the diagram was a breakdown of the Seneca Corporation. It was a New Jersey corporation that had controlling interests in the Gregson Agency, Leo Mirell's Talent International Company, a Las Vegas hotel, a circus, two hotels in Atlantic City, three eastern racetracks, a basketball team, and fifteen nightclubs scattered throughout the country.

Another section of the blackboard was headed "Foreign," and a column listed below:

> Michelin Guide-Germany
> Route map Berlin–Hamburg
> Porno shot–Hamburg
> Kempinski Hotel–Berlin–charge slip
> Hassler Hotel–Rome–charge slip
> Oloffson Hotel–Haiti–matchbook

Then two names with question marks:

> Obermann?
> Genesis?

As Barney carefully studied his chalked breakdown, he stopped at the words "Genesis" and "Obermann." He suddenly remembered he had forgotten to ask Kay about those two words. He bent over the battered desk, picked up the receiver, and dialed the Malibu number. Kay answered on the third ring.

"Hello, Kay. It's Barney Caine."

There was a momentary pause, and she said, "Yes. . . ."

He decided to come at her slowly. "We should have the paperwork processed tomorrow morning."

"Paperwork?"

"To release Tom's body for burial."

"Oh, yes." Her voice sounded distant. "I've decided to let my attorney handle that. His name is Bernard Seeger. He'll be in touch with the coroner's office. Is there anything else?"

"Yes. There is something else. Something I forgot to ask you yesterday." Barney paused. "Does the word 'Genesis' mean anything to you?"

"No."

"Did you ever hear Tom use that word?"

"I don't think so."

Barney wished he could have asked her the questions in person, so that he could have watched her eyes. The eyes were always the give-away.

"All right, Kay. Now, please think carefully, does the word 'Ober-mann' mean anything to you?"

There was a momentary pause, and Barney thought he heard her breath escaping. "No," she finally said.

"Did Tom ever mention the word 'Obermann'?"

"I never heard that name."

"Why did you call it a *name?*" Barney asked. "I said it was a *word.*"

"I just thought it was a name," she said haltingly.

The door opened, and Louis came in. Barney motioned him to be quiet, and Louis walked to the blackboard and studied the diagram.

"Are you positive you never heard either word?" Barney persisted.

"Of course, I've heard of Genesis in the traditional biblical usage. But I never heard of the word or name or place called Obermann."

Barney sighed. "Now, have you made any trips in the last two months?"

"I've been down to the desert, that's all."

"I mean to Europe."

"No."

"I think you're lying, Kay." There was no response, and Barney pressed. "I'm sorry to say that. But I believe it. I know you're fright-ened of something. I can help you if you let me."

The receiver clicked in Barney's hand, and the line went dead.

"They're all covering up," Louis said.

"What's worse," Barney added, "there are no real motives."

Louis moved his head in the direction of the blackboard. "We haven't seen Mirell, Clements, or Maldonado."

"I know. But I don't think the patterns are going to change. They seem to cover each other."

"Conspiracy?"

"Maybe. Or maybe it's coincidental, but they're all locked together, one way or another."

There was a sudden clap of thunder, and the rain beating against the window increased its tempo.

Louis slumped down in the hard-back chair in front of Barney's desk and said, "Did you get the ME's report?"

Barney nodded. "Gabby Torres phoned a half hour ago. The weap-on's been identified. A twenty-two long seven-shot automatic; double-action Walther PPK. German manufacture." Barney paused. "The bastards tortured Tom. Gabby says the last shot fired killed him. The one to the head. The blood loss was from the other wounds."

"Christ . . ." Louis murmured.

"Here's the rest of it." Barney picked up a note pad and read, " 'The pillow case yielded traces of ambergris. A compound made from sperm whale intestines. It's used as a fixative in expensive foreign perfume.' " He looked up. "Now this is interesting, Lou." Barney read again from the pad. " 'The two strands of hair found on the pillow are Oriental in weight, body, and curve. They bore traces of chemical dye and a cleansing agent.' " Barney dropped the pad onto the desk and looked at Louis. "Gabby has seen those strands before—on wigs made in Taiwan."

Louis said, "So we've got a girl who wears wigs and expensive perfume."

"And delivers ninety percent pure Colombian cocaine," Barney added. "In voodoo dolls made in Haiti."

"That's one hell of a picture."

Both men fell silent for a moment, listening to the drumbeats of rain against the window.

Louis asked, "What do you make of it, Barney?"

"I think the cocaine is a cover for something else."

"A cover for what?"

"I don't know."

Barney got to his feet and studied the diagram for a moment. His eyes lingered on the word "Genesis." Then he turned to Louis. "The print guys come up with anything?"

"Not a smudge," Louis replied.

"When do we see Nolan?" Barney asked.

Louis glanced at his watch. "Twenty minutes."

"Come on." Barney sighed. "Let's get some coffee."

CHAPTER

15 ⊠

THE GIRL WATCHED THE BEADS OF RAIN STREAK ACROSS THE WINDOW of the suite. Her long dark hair brushed against the shoulders of her beige silk suit, and the ivory bracelets at her wrist clicked together as she raised her hand to puff on the Gauloise.

The traffic on Wilshire Boulevard had slowed to a crawl as the drivers fought the oil-slick surface. She noticed a cluster of well-dressed women come out of the Brown Derby and dash for the shelter of a nearby awning. The girl was amused by the women of Beverly Hills. She had taken a short stroll earlier up and down Rodeo Drive with its expensive international boutiques. Yasir had called this place the richest triangle in the world. And while it was not yet on their target list, it soon would be. "Their time will come," Yasir had said. But the girl felt no hatred toward these women. How could she? What did they know? What did they feel? What was it they wanted? A new dress? A new diamond? A new lover? One could not hate people who had relegated history and conscience to the back seats of their Mercedes. And these wealthy ladies only reflected the social confusion of the times. The Russian imperialists drank too much vodka, and the American capitalists ate too much bacon, and Brazilian children died of starvation on the elegant beaches of Rio. Commerce always took precedence over morality.

The girl sighed and thought; despite her growing doubts about the violence, and despite her terror-filled nights, and the loneliness and the degradation, one single fact remained pure: She was part of a political movement that represented humanity's last hope for survival. The day would come when the common man would unite in world brotherhood. She desperately clung to that belief. She had to. It was all she had left.

She turned from the window and walked over to the coffee table. There was a silver ice bucket holding a sweating bottle of champagne.

She poured a glass and sat down on the sofa. She thought of the incongruity of sipping expensive champagne and a moment ago thinking about the common man. But the champagne was only a prop, a bottle to do business with.

She was beginning to feel uneasy. She had stayed too long in this city. And the danger of discovery grew with each passing day. She knew that a top-ranking Los Angeles detective had been assigned to the case, and while that was expected, it nevertheless increased the peril to her. She missed Paris. She missed Raoul. And this assignment had been particularly vicious. Neeley had been difficult; it had taken all her tricks to rouse him, to lull him into a state of euphoria. It was horrible, but she had managed.

The doorbell sounded twice. The girl rose, fluffed her dark hair, and opened the third button of her blouse, so that the smooth naked skin showed from her neck all the way down to the rising curve of her breasts. She walked to the door, looked through the peephole, and removed the chain latch.

Arthur Clements dropped his beige raincoat on the chair and smoothed his fine gray hair. He stared at her perfect oval face and her glittering blue eyes. Her smile was strangely suggestive, as if they were not meeting for the first time, as if they shared a familiar past.

"You're late," she said.

Clements thought her accent was Nordic, Danish, or German. He wasn't sure. "I'm sorry," he said. "It was unavoidable." He noticed the champagne and walked over and picked up the bottle. "Dom Pérignon. You live well."

"Why not?" she asked. She handed him a glass, and he poured the cold champagne.

"Cheers."

"Cheers," she repeated.

He studied her figure for a moment and let his eyes roam over the very white skin of the firm breasts that curved upward. "I always thought of terrorists as bearded, sweating men and homely women in need of a bath."

"Do I disappoint you?"

"Not at all." He took out a cigarette case and offered her one.

"No, thank you."

Clements lit the cigarette and sat down on the sofa. The girl remained standing, looking down at him. He began to feel a sensual stirring. He knew her history. Behind that persuasive smile and lovely face there was an accomplished assassin, a professional killer with some spectacular exploits to her credit. But in the room with her now, that history did not seem to matter.

"Your friends made a mess out of Neeley," he said.

"We carried out your instructions."

"No. Not mine," Clements said. "I only transmit instructions. I don't design those instructions."

"The results are the same." She sipped her champagne. "You can't escape responsibility for a killing you ordered."

"Had a hand in, not ordered," he corrected her. The girl was beginning to make him nervous. "I take it Neeley revealed nothing."

She moved to a chair and sat down, staring at him curiously, as if she were examining an artifact. She slumped down slightly and spread her legs. The time had come to start the game.

"He admitted only that he saw Obermann in Berlin," she said. "Neeley was very brave. And very loyal. He would not even admit he knew you."

"Did he mention the formula?"

"I did not stay for all of it. I was told he said nothing." She arched her back, thrusting her breasts out, and moved her forefinger slowly up and down the stem of the glass. She ran the tip of her tongue over her lower lip. She watched him, studying her every move. It was time. She could ask the question. "My comrades would like to visit Kay Neeley."

Clements found himself mesmerized by the girl. The way her soft lips curved over her words as if she sculpted them as she spoke, and the way her finger curled around the stem of the glass and moved slowly up and down. And the strange lights dancing in her blue eyes.

"Kay Neeley knows nothing," he said.

She shrugged and tossed her hair. "Perhaps, but it is necessary to talk with her."

"I won't have Kay hurt."

"Are you her lover?"

"Of course not."

"Then you're being sentimental."

"I'm being sensible."

"No one intends to hurt Kay Neeley."

"Kay has no information."

"What about the Swiss banker?"

"I asked her. She knows nothing about the Swiss," Clements replied.

The girl said, "She may not think she knows anything. But Neeley may have said something to her. A chance remark, an offhand thought that might tell us whether Neeley met with the Swiss and how far he penetrated Genesis."

Clements shook his head. "I can't authorize anything on my own. I have to get approval for a visit to Kay Neeley."

The girl unwound slowly and got to her feet. "But your opinion is highly regarded. You can recommend such a visit."

"I don't know," he murmured.

She never took her eyes from his, even as she tilted her head back and drained the glass. She moved to the sofa and sat down on the armrest. She was very close to him. It was time to play the trump card. "I have ninety percent pure cocaine," she whispered. "It's absolutely heaven."

Clements stared up at her, her jutting breasts just above his mouth. He felt his heart racing, and his temples throbbed. "Get it," he said hoarsely.

"Make the call." She smiled.

He looked at her for a moment. "It's not just the coke I want."

"I understand."

He got up and went to the phone. The girl watched him as he dialed a local number. He spoke in hushed tones, requesting permission from someone on the other end of the line for the Kay Neeley visit. He listened a moment and said, "Tomorrow." He hung up and nodded to the girl.

She rose and smiled. "Get undressed."

"Just like that?" he asked.

"Why not?" she said. "You're not a man who requires the usual ceremony. I hear you function very well with professional girls."

She turned and strode out of the room. Clements walked over to the window. The storm had increased its intensity, and the raindrops hammered against the window.

Clements felt bad about turning them loose on Kay. But her demise was an inevitability. If the goddamned Swiss had not stumbled onto Genesis, if only he hadn't contacted Obermann, Tom Neeley would be alive. Kay would have remained out of harm's way. And the Genesis Formula securely buried in the Nazi past. But the Swiss banker had changed all that. The Swiss represented a consortium with sufficient money and technology to reconstitute the Genesis team and undertake the manufacture of the formula.

Clements could not fault the decision to make the plan operative. He just detested the violence, but there was nothing he could do. He was trapped by choices he had made years ago.

Clements sighed heavily and turned his thoughts to the girl and the almost pure cocaine. He slipped off his jacket and began to unbutton his shirt. He felt heady. His nerve ends already projecting that first delicious snort when the white powder would numb his nasal passages and rush up into his brain, exploding in a great arctic flash, liberating the mind and body, sending it spinning off to a distant planet where all was love.

CHAPTER

16 ⊠

LOUIS STOOD IN FRONT OF THE GLASS WALL WATCHING THE NIGHT SKY drape itself across the city. The late-spring rain was augmented by the rumble of thunder and brilliant flashes of lightning. Barney was seated in front of Nolan's desk, sipping a container of coffee. A dowdy woman, Nolan's longtime executive secretary, served the coffee, explaining that Nolan was in his private bathroom. She further informed them that Chief Nolan had not been feeling well. It was her way of telling the two detectives not to aggravate her boss. She brushed a dandruff snowfall off her shoulders, tried a thin smile, and left.

The steady sound of the sleeting rain against the glass walls was suddenly interrupted by the noisy gurgle of a toilet flushing.

"Hey, partner," Louis said. Barney looked up from the documents. "Think you'll ever have an office with a private can?"

"I did. Eight years ago."

"Where?"

"Madrid. A spacious office with a private bathroom and shower, in an elegant old building near the Plaza de España. Besides the private can, I had a private fund for hookers."

"Hookers?"

"Right. I used to import English call girls and place them into the Russian trade council."

"Did they ever get anything?" Louis asked.

"No secrets. But one of my girls caught a severe case of Siberian clap."

"The hazards of détente." Louis smiled.

The private bathroom door opened, and Nolan entered the office. He wore a well-cut dark pin-striped suit, a blue shirt, blue tie, and there were small gold cuff links at the French cuffs of his shirt. His expensive-looking black shoes were shined brilliantly. But despite the correctness of his dress, he appeared to be sloppy and disheveled. It was the sagging folds of skin in his face, and the dark-circled, fatigued eyes, and the paunchy belly; the clothes could not overcome the ruined body they hung on. Nolan walked slowly toward the big desk and sat down in the high-backed swivel chair.

Louis sat down alongside Barney. They faced Nolan, who stared out at the glass wall, watching the rivulets of rain streaming down its smooth surface.

"I had tickets to the ball game," he mumbled, and watched the rain for another moment, then swiveled around and nodded at Barney. "Okay. What have you got?"

"Well, for openers, Tom Neeley was definitely dealing in high-grade cocaine."

Nolan whispered, "Son of a bitch," then looked at Louis.

"No mistake," Louis confirmed.

Nolan rubbed his hand wearily across his eyes. "What else?"

"Neeley was Leo Mirell's coke connection," Barney continued. "Leo passed the snow to his clients and friends."

"Was Mirell selling it?"

"No. Just keeping the right people supplied."

"Where did Neeley get the coke?"

"I can't prove it, but my guess is Victor Maldonado supplied the coke to Neeley through a courier. And I don't think he used a local courier."

"Why?"

"Because Neeley was a pro. He would certainly be aware that most local dealers are junkies. Addicts. Unreliable. They either get nailed and talk, or they get greedy and try blackmail. Tom was too smart to get involved with the local Mexican Mafia or some independent. Tom wouldn't touch the stuff unless the courier were foreign."

"Colombian?"

Barney shrugged. "The voodoo doll came out of Haiti. The girl that fucked Neeley was probably the courier, but she could have been any nationality."

"So the hit on Neeley came out of Haiti?"

"I don't know," Barney said. "But my instincts tell me Neeley was not killed over cocaine."

"Why?" Nolan asked.

"Neeley was hit by professionals. The MO. The free entrance to the house, the sex before death, the weapon, the wreckage, the voodoo doll left on his chest—everything says Neeley was set up by professionals."

Nolan scratched his face. "Why do you say 'set up'? It's fairly obvious Neeley was a drug hit."

"There's nothing obvious in this case," Barney replied testily. "There are other things involved here, unrelated to cocaine. Things we found that in my mind point to something else."

Nolan leaned back and winced in sudden pain. He opened the desk drawer, took out a bottle of Gelusils, popped two in his mouth, and chased them with a glass of water. He grimaced, then looked at Louis. "What do you think?"

"It could be a drug hit, but then Barney may be right."

"Why?"

"Well, we've got some primary suspects, friends and associates, but we can't nail a motive."

"Who are the suspects?" Nolan asked.

"It's Barney's case," Louis replied.

Nolan sighed and looked at Barney. "Okay, you tell me."

"Maldonado is *numero uno*. But no motive."

"Why not?" Nolan asked. "Suppose he and Tom fell into a dispute over the coke."

"Maldonado would not order a hit on a former top policeman," Barney replied. "The capos back east would never approve of a contract like that. If Tom Neeley proved to be a pain in the ass or untrustworthy, Maldonado would just dry up the coke and find a new dealer."

Barney continued. "Second suspect: Leo Mirell, super-agent. A Svengali-like hold on some of the top talent in show business. Not just films. Rock stars, composers, the recording business, concerts, everything. He's also a cocaine addict. Tom was Mirell's connection. No motive."

"Not on the face of things," Nolan said. "But what if Tom decided to escalate the price?"

"Tom didn't set the price. Maldonado did. Tom collected a piece of the action for dealing. Leo had no motive for killing his dealer. Besides, they were thick right up to the end. Remember Leo had sent his chauffeur to pick Tom up that afternoon."

Nolan swiveled around and peered out at the darkening city. After a long moment he turned back to Barney. "All right. Leo Mirell is clean."

"That brings us to Laura Gregson," Barney said. "Her agency is a blind—a cover for a coast-to-coast pussy-for-sale business under the guise of a model agency. She's smart, curvy, and tight with Maldonado. He bought her company, as well as Leo's agency, through Seneca."

"What the hell is Seneca?" Nolan growled.

"A mob corporation. A holding company: hotels, casinos, offshore Bahama banks, professional sports, racetracks, nightclubs, pornography, the Gregson Agency, and Mirell's Talent International Company. Maldonado is chairman of the board."

"Who are the directors?"

"I don't have that yet. Collins at ISI is running that down. But based on what we have, Laura Gregson had no motive for wanting Tom Neeley dead."

Nolan leaned forward. "But she does run a piss-elegant call girl ring?"

"That's a rhetorical question, John." Barney smiled.

"What?"

"Nothing, forget it."

"Does De Lucca over at Vice know about Gregson?"

"How would I know?"

"I don't trust that prick," Nolan said. "But that's another problem. Go ahead."

"Kay Neeley," Barney said. "She divorced Tom years ago, but they were still friends. She's afraid of something."

"Any ideas?"

"I have a feeling based on nothing that she and Tom were involved in something that tied into Tom's European bag trips."

Nolan's face suddenly reddened. "What bag trips?"

"Give me a chance, and I'll get to it," Barney replied sharply. "Kay Neeley is terrified. She's hiding something. But she had no motive to want Tom dead. They were close."

Nolan belched loudly and gasped. He clutched his stomach with his left hand and grabbed the Gelusil bottle with his right. Louis got up quickly and poured some water from the carafe into the glass. Nolan nodded his appreciation at Louis, gulped three pills, and swallowed the water. He leaned back and mopped some perspiration from his forehead with a tissue.

"You ought to get out of here, John," Louis said.

Nolan shook his head. "No, it'll pass. Doctor said it's going to be worse before it gets better. He said I need to go to an island and fish. Tell me about Neeley's bag trips."

"I'm getting to it. Arthur Clements. Retired. On the board of directors of half a dozen major corporations. Owner and breeder of one of the biggest thoroughbred racing stables in the West. Never married. A quiet kind of playboy. Went to parties at Leo's, was friendly with Kay and Tom Neeley. Used Gregson's pussy and Neeley's coke, through Leo. No motive for wanting Tom dead . . . except, now here's where it gets interesting, Clements arranged bag trips for Neeley. He put Neeley into some action with Adam Steiffel."

Nolan peered at Barney as if he had suddenly seen an apparition. His voice was almost a croak. "Did you say Adam Steiffel?"

"Yes," Barney replied calmly.

Nolan got to his feet, came around his desk, and stood over Barney. "Now you listen to me." His voice trembled and took on a menacing bureaucratic authority. "Adam Steiffel is not to be mentioned! Adam Steiffel *is* Los Angeles: Mr. Music Center, Mr. Museum of Art and Science, one of the largest employers in this state, major contributor to both political parties. There is not a single city commissioner who does not owe Mr. Steiffel a debt of gratitude." He paused, sucked in some air, and said, "You do not at any time go near Adam Steiffel without my approval. You do not mention that man's name to the press or anyone outside this room. Now you got that, Caine?"

Louis looked at Barney. He could see the soft brown eyes glaring and the half-moon scar on Barney's cheek starting to go scarlet. Louis hoped Barney would not explode. Louis knew Nolan. And he liked Nolan. All Nolan wanted to do was to survive to his pension.

Barney got up and stood eyeball to eyeball with Nolan. The tone of Barney's voice had the hollow, ominous calm that resides in the eye of a hurricane. "I'm going to say this only because you don't know me. You have no history with me, so pay attention. My personal life is a vacuum, a zero. There are only two things that matter to me—my work and my son. Nothing else. I've been assigned this case by the commissioner because I have a personal stake in it. Tom Neeley was a friend of my father's, and he sponsored me into this force. Tom was very kind to me. And whatever Tom was, he paid a hell of a price." Barney paused. "And I'm going to track and find his killer if it leads to the fucking White House. The same way I'm going to eventually nail four Metro cops who murdered unarmed civilian suspects. I'll never go outside the department. The same way I would never write or leak or disparage the CIA. But I will go as far as I can with what I know. That's how I operate. Now, I'm sorry you have an ulcer. And I'm sorry you're in pain. And I'm sorry your baseball game was rained out. But your problems, political or personal, haven't got a fucking thing to do with me. I'll see Adam Steiffel or anyone else in the case."

Barney's voice lowered. "Now, you can tell the commissioner if he wants my badge, he can have it. But just remember, there are seven television crews camped in the lobby, and the print press, radio, and wire services. They all want to know what an ex-police chief was doing with cocaine, call girls, and bag trips." Barney lowered his voice even more. "I've kept the lid on so far, but if I give you my badge, they're gonna want to know why the hotshot from ISI, the handpicked choice of the commissioner resigned in the middle of the Neeley case. Now, you tell me how you want it!"

Nolan stared at Barney for a long moment, then went slowly back to his desk and took a long Havana out of the humidor, bit off the end, lit it, and looked at Barney through the flame and smoke. He inhaled the cigar smoke and released it in two thick streams through his nostrils. His voice was matter-of-fact. "Okay, give me the rest of it."

Barney spoke in a toneless, reportlike cadence. "Neeley performed certain tasks for Steiffel. He told Kay that Steiffel represented a major opportunity for him. The service Tom performed for Steiffel took him to Rome. From there he went on to Germany. I think Kay knows why. I think she knows what 'Genesis' means, and I think she knows what 'Obermann' means. I think she went to Germany with Tom."

Nolan said nothing, and Barney walked over to the window. There was a moment of silence in the room underscored by the rain striking the huge glass walls.

Louis broke the silence. "We haven't talked to Maldonado, Mirell, or Clements."

"Why not?" Nolan asked.

Barney turned from the window. "Because it's been my practice to collect as much information as possible before I play any cards with major suspects. Besides, in this case I have the feeling that we're going to end in the same place, no matter who we talk to. We will wind up with a group of suspects linked together by sex, dope, and the Seneca Corporation, with perfect alibis for the time of the killing and no apparent motives for wanting Tom Neeley dead."

"There are some minor figures," Louis added. "An Oriental girl who Neeley was banging. And Paul Isella, the race driver, who is thick with Laura Gregson."

"And that's it?" Nolan asked.

"Up to the moment," Barney replied.

Nolan puffed the cigar, then looked at Barney. "What about Mirell's chauffeur?"

"Release him."

Nolan studied Barney for a moment. "Give us a minute alone, Louis."

Louis started for the door. As he passed Barney, he said, "I'll be in my office."

Nolan came slowly around his desk and walked up to Barney. "I'll bring the commissioner up to date. But I want to tell you something. I'm not your enemy. I believe that you are one of those rare birds that go after the truth and let the chips fall. Some sort of patriot." Nolan sighed. "Well, I can't hate you for that. But this isn't the time of the patriot. Now, I've survived this system a long time. And you can't do that without brains. So just a piece of friendly advice: You stick your hand into the world of Adam Steiffel, and you'll never get that hand back."

"I'll remember that, John," Barney said, then paused. "Good night."

Barney strode quickly to the door.

Nolan went back to his desk and slumped into the big chair. He puffed the cigar and stared out at the rain. There was an explosion of thunder and a streaky flash of lightning, and Nolan muttered, "Fucking rain."

CHAPTER

17 ⊠

By the time Barney pulled into the subterranean garage of the Doheny-Palms the rain had become sporadic; it seemed to start and stop at the command of the thunder and lightning.

Barney parked in his reserved stall and noticed Kathy's adjacent space was empty, meaning she had her Firebird parked at the airline terminal and was still out of town. She was either in the air or in someone's bedroom in Pittsburgh, Cleveland, Chicago, or Albuquerque. Barney greeted the night man at the desk, checked for messages, and went up the express elevator.

He took a TV dinner of fried chicken out of the freezer and placed it in the oven. He went into the bathroom, opened the shower door, turned both taps to full, and set the shower head dial onto a reading that said "Massage." He undressed and stared at his face in the mirror over the sink. He noticed the half-moon scar over his right cheekbone. It seemed to be growing progressively scarlet.

Barney stepped into the shower and let the strong needles of water play across his back and neck. He remembered the junkie who had knifed him. A nice-looking boy. A blond-white boy, who dealt uppers, downers, grass, coke, heroin, and PCP at the Fairfax High School. He had taken the boy into an empty classroom and spoke gently to him. If the boy would name the source, Barney would go to bat for him. The boy cried and seemed totally cooperative and trusting, but as they left the empty office, the crying boy suddenly ripped a razor blade across Barney's arm and up toward his jugular. He missed the neck but caught Barney's cheek. A uniformed cop rushed over and brought his blackjack crashing down onto the boy's skull.

The boy remained in a coma for weeks. His parents never spoke to Barney. The look in their eyes was enough. Their son had been a victim of police brutality. Barney visited the boy daily and saw to it that the entire staff stayed on top of the case. The boy never recovered full use of his brain and was in a semi-autistic state in Atascadero Mental Hospital for the criminally insane. One second of violence and one life reduced to a vegetable. The guilt never left Barney. He blamed himself. He should have listened to Joe Rudolph, who was an old Narco hand. Joe didn't approve of private conferences with suspects. He had warned Barney to let him handcuff the boy first; Barney refused and also neglected to search the youth for a concealed weapon. So Barney's guilt remained.

The same way the guilt remained for Velásquez's assassination in Chile. But in truth he had had no way of knowing his lunch date at the café on the corner of Calle Julio Gutiérrez was a setup for the minister's killing. Barney had followed orders. But logic instead of blind obedience to orders would have pointed to Velásquez's demise. Barney knew the CIA regarded Velásquez as the real financial power behind Allende. He should have smelled it out. And he should have handcuffed the kid at Fairfax High. The guilt, remorse, and recriminations kept running with the shower's jet streams. He should have made more of an effort to keep his marriage together. He should be seeing his son more often. But he always sublimated personal relationships in favor of service to the profession and to those who placed their trust in him. When he no longer could function loyally, he walked away. But no betrayals. And he had leveled with Nolan. A detective on a case was like a pilot flying on radar. There was a sweep hand of green electronic logic rotating through the brain of the aircraft, transmitting all the necessary data to the pilot. The talent was knowing how to interpret that logic and how to act on it.

Barney turned in the shower, and the hard jets of water streamed onto his face. He felt a strange mix of fatigue and challenge. This case stirred in him all his best talents. He would go the distance. He might never bring Tom Neeley's killers to justice, but he would find out who had killed Neeley and why. The *why* was the critical thing. That's where the motive was stored. The logic. The true sense of accomplishment came from the process of discovery itself.

Barney came out of the shower, slipped on his robe, went into the kitchen, and took his TV dinner out of the oven. He placed it on the serving section of the wet bar and poured a vodka on the rocks. He carried the TV tray and the drink back into the bedroom and placed them down on the night table. He stretched out on the bed and leaned back against the headboard. He then picked up a piece of chicken and clicked on the television set. The ten o'clock news was in progress. The newscaster was broadcasting the details of an Israeli armored strike into southern Lebanon.

Barney had a grudging admiration for the tiny state. He had met an Israeli intelligence officer years ago. It was a brief meeting in the Madrid airport. He remembered the Israeli's name, Zvi Barzani. A tall, broad-shouldered former paratrooper, who had fought in the '56 and '67 wars and countless skirmishes in between. Barzani had passed documents to Barney concerning the first Soviet air-to-ground missiles. The Israelis had captured them intact in the '67 war, in the Sinai, just south of El Arish. The documents went from the Israelis to the CIA, to the Pentagon, to State Intelligence. Barney had been impressed with the quiet, unassuming Barzani. He had that special quality, that charismatic sense of strength that made men follow other men in combat. Listening to the news of the Israeli strike, Barney wondered if Barzani had been in the October war of '73 and whether he was still alive. The Israeli film report ended with the blond female reporter ducking reflexively against the concussion of a 175-millimeter cannon roaring behind her.

The face of the local newscaster reappeared instantly, and in a voice designed for melodrama he reported, "A crack team of Tactical Squad detectives are still investigating the brutal murder of former Beverly Hills Police Chief Thomas Neeley, who was reported to be dealing in—" Barney pressed the clicker, turning the set off. It died slowly with a lingering cyan heartbeat.

He went into the living room and put on an old Verve album of Stan Getz bossa nova. The cool, lilting sounds were fixed indelibly in Barney's memory. He had first heard them years ago when he was stationed in Rio. The melody of Jobim's "Girl from Ipanema" recalled a lovely, romantic time with Alice.

The phone on the bar suddenly buzzed. It did not ring. The buzz meant the front desk was calling.

The night man said there was a Laura Gregson in the lobby requesting to see Mr. Caine. Barney thought for a second, sipped some vodka.

"Is she alone?"

"Yes, sir."

"Okay. Send her up." He dropped the receiver onto the cradle and went back into the bedroom, removed his robe, and slipped on a pair of old faded jeans and a blue polo shirt with the word "Ischia" embroidered over the right breast pocket. He did not bother with his loafers. He walked across the deep-pile rug in his bare feet.

The seductive, sweet-smelling perfume hit him as he opened the door; it was reminiscent of the perfume on Neeley's pillowcase, but not as heavy; it was lighter and sharper. Laura permitted a small smile to appear on her full mouth, but she let her husky voice and the vivid emerald eyes do most of the work. Barney helped her off with her light beige raincoat and kicked the door closed with his bare foot.

She walked into the living room, reached the center, and turned to him. "I had to see you." She wore black velvet pants, a red silk blouse, black loafers with gold trim buckles, a pair of gold earrings inset with rubies, and a wide plain gold bracelet around her slim right wrist. Her long sandy hair fell across her shoulders.

"A drink?" Barney asked.

"A drink would be fine." She sat on the barstool and swiveled around to face him as he poured some brandy into a large glass snifter. "I'm sorry to barge in here at this hour, Lieutenant."

"We're not working now. Call me Barney." He placed the glass in front of her. She opened her large bag and took out a pack of Gauloises. "How did you find me?" Barney asked.

"Your Japanese partner."

Barney held a match to her cigarette, and it glowed red as she inhaled. "What did you tell him?"

"That I had to speak to you. He gave me your number. That is, the phone number of the building. Once I had the location, I decided to come over."

"Why didn't you use the phone?"

"I don't trust phones."

"You have any reason to think your phone is tapped?"

"In my business it's a distinct possibility."

"But you must have strong connections at Vice."

"The best," she purred. "But there are other people I wouldn't want listening. Dangerous people. You know what I mean, Barney."

It was the first time she had called him Barney. She sort of floated the "Barney" from between her lips. She was letting him know that whatever excuse she had used to see him, the real reason she had come over was to let him know she was available.

She drew hard on the filterless Gauloise and pivoted slowly around on the barstool. She followed Barney with her eyes as he went to the long white sofa and sat down. The bossa nova disc dropped, and the Bee Gees came on. There was a moment of silence as the Bee Gees had the floor. Laura said, "This is nice."

"Suits me. I don't have to make my bed or do my laundry; it comes with the building."

She inhaled, and the smoke oozed out of the center of her mouth. "I didn't realize you were a bachelor," she said innocently.

"Come off it, Laura. Your friend Maldonado must have run a line on me all the way back to the day I was born."

She smiled. "No girl friend?"

"Yes. There's a girl."

She was turning him on. And she knew it. She was truly beautiful, and there was a natural sensuality to all her moves.

"What's on your mind, Laura?"

Her green eyes stared into his and in that incredibly low voice said, "There's something . . . something I should have mentioned this afternoon. But I was too frightened this afternoon. I had no time to think. I didn't know if I could trust you."

"But you do now?"

"Not exactly. But I sense some"—she paused—"understanding. Besides, we're alone; no one's taking notes." She slid off the barstool and took a few steps toward him. Then she stopped and placed her right foot at a sharp angle to her left, so that her legs were wide apart, like those of a professional model posing for an ad. She touched the tips of her long, silky hair with the fingers of her left hand. Her large, round breasts pressed against the red silk blouse, and the imprint of the hard nipples was pronounced. She wet her lips. "What I neglected to mention was"—she took a quick drag of the Gauloise—"Arthur Clements."

"What about him?"

"Have you spoken to him?"

"I'm going to see him tomorrow morning."

"Well, ask him why he sent Tom Neeley to Germany."

"I understood Clements got Neeley an assignment in Rome through Adam Steiffel."

"The Steiffel thing may have been part of it, but Clements sent Tom to Germany."

"How do you know that, Laura?"

"I don't know it. I think it." She moved to a black leather Danish chair opposite Barney and folded her tall figure down into it. Barney watched her, hoping what she would tell him could be corroborated because if it were true, he had the connection: It was the German thing that had Kay Neeley terrified.

"Why do you think it, Laura?"

"Tom mentioned it to one of my girls."

"Which one?"

"The Vietnamese girl. The girl you wanted to find in my files. Tom was after something in Germany."

"Did Tom tell that to your girl?"

"Tom told her that he was close to something of immense value." She drew some smoke. "He told her it was a fantastic score."

Barney tried to disguise the excitement in his voice. "Were those Tom's exact words?"

"That's what my girl said."

"Did Tom tell her what it was?"

She shook her head. "No."

"Did Tom say that Clements had asked him to go to Germany?"

"No. It's just my own feeling."

"You're a bright girl, Laura. Tell me, if Clements trusted Tom enough to put him into a valuable deal in Germany, why would he want Tom killed?"

She tossed her hair. "Well, human nature being what it is, if Tom had run down this score, perhaps Clements would no longer require the services of a partner."

"You figure that Clements used Tom to run down this mythical score, then set him up like a coke hit?"

She slowly traced the curve of her cheekbone with her left forefinger. "Something like that."

"Does Clements know that you have this information?"

"Yes."

"How?"

"The Oriental girl."

"She gets around."

"Well"—Laura smiled—"she's very good. She's in demand."

"Does Kay Neeley know about Tom's German trip?"

"She might." Laura drained the rest of the brandy.

"What made you come up here and tell me all this?"

"I'm frightened."

"Of what?"

"Clements."

"Why?" Barney asked.

"I can't define it for you, much less myself. It's just a feeling."

"But you're under Victor Maldonado's protection. You're in good shape, Laura." Barney smiled. "The real reason for this visit is because Victor is nervous. He doesn't know why Neeley was hit or by whom, and that worries him. So he sent you up here to find out what I know. Right?"

She stared at him for a moment, then opened her large bag. "Would it bother you if I smoked a joint?"

"Not at all." Barney smiled. "A joint is only a misdemeanor in this state."

She lit the joint and sucked the smoke down deep into her chest. She held it down for a long time, then exhaled through her nose. "It's marvelous grass," she whispered. "Would you like some?" she asked.

"Why not? We're alone. No one's taking notes."

She unwound, rose, and walked slowly over to him. He took it and inhaled deeply, then chased the grass with the cold vodka, and felt an immediate floating sensation that seemed to unlock the tension in his brain. He sucked hard on the joint again, some ash fell to the deep-pile rug, but he didn't bother to brush it away.

He looked up at the beautiful girl. "Sit down, Laura."

She sat on the rug between his legs. He passed the glowing joint to her, and she inhaled deeply.

Barney touched her hair. "It's good stuff."

"Colombian," she murmured. She rested her right hand on his left thigh. She didn't move the hand. She just let it lie there, collecting heat.

"Who sent you up here, Laura?"

She didn't answer. She sat up on her haunches, leaned across him, and dropped the joint into an ashtray on the end table. She then put both hands on his thighs. Her face was very close to his.

"It was Victor Maldonado, wasn't it?" Barney asked.

"What's the difference?" she purred.

Barney leaned into her and brushed his lips against hers and said, "No difference."

He felt as if he were moving in slow motion. He grasped her arms and raised her up as he got to his feet. He pulled her to him, his arms going around her. He crushed her breasts against his chest, and her light, sweet perfume rushed into his senses. Her hair was in his eyes as his lips moved across the side of her throat. She took his face in both her hands and kissed the small half-moon scar on his right cheek, once, twice, three times, then slipped her lips down across his cheek to his mouth. She moved her mouth and tongue over his upper lip, slowly back and forth, at the same time increasing the pressure of her body against his. She slid her mouth down to his lower lip and sucked and nibbled across its curve. Her arms went around his neck, and she pressed her lips full, flush onto his. He let his mouth be taken along by the sweep of her lips. They held each other in a furious dope-inspired embrace. They were accidental players, caught in the fallout of a brutal murder.

A spill of exterior light came through the crack in the bedroom drapes, painting their bodies with a pale luminosity. She was kneeling over him, the tips of her long hair brushing against the inside of his thighs. She shifted her body as her mouth moved over him. Her hands were always working, touching and squeezing.

Barney's eyes were half open. He saw their bodies as surreal figures in an Impressionist painting. He could not lose the feeling of being outside himself, a spectator watching two naked bodies in a pornographic film.

His entire body burned as if consumed by a high-grade fever. He felt as if some beautiful soft thing were nursing at his core. He wanted badly to surrender to the delicious sensation of it. But he could not control the spaceless wandering of his brain. The images began to form way back in his consciousness, a vague light . . . a shiny revolving ball throwing specks of polka-dot lights that spread, then suddenly fused into old familiar images. The handsome face of Jorge Velásquez, sipping espresso in the café. The screech of brakes, and the high stutter of the Uzi machine gun and the screams, and Velásquez's head streaming blood down into the coffee. The images came on, fighting against Laura's mouth sliding up and down his flesh. She increased the tempo as if aware that she was competing with phantoms. But the images were too strong. Barney saw Timmy's wide, innocent eyes looking at the space movie. And the inquisitive black eyes of Louis Yosuta, and Nolan's gray, tired skin. The naked banana man lying on a slab with sixteen slugs in his body. The smiling girls in the Hamburg porno shot. And Mirell's chauffeur's pimp eyes. They came and went like sheets of positive film in the developer; just as the image emerged, they would go opaque and vanish. He saw Tom Neeley trying to speak to him through the smashed bloody hole where his mouth had been, and Barney suddenly cried out. Laura looked up at him and slid her body over his, warming him. She kissed and sucked his nipples, then covered his mouth with hers.

Laura raised herself and looked down at him. Her long hair spilled across his shoulders. He opened his eyes and stared up at her. She seemed to be floating, suspended over him. Her green eyes challenged him to make her feel something. The thing that she had hooked him with, she wanted to know what that was. She wanted him to tell her. He took her shoulders and turned her over. The heart of the girl, the soul of the girl, and the smell of the girl overwhelmed him. He pinned her down with his weight and spread her long hair out on the white pillow in a careful, winglike design. He began to kiss her neck, throat, and then down to her nipples, stiff, erect, and long. He moved his mouth over her flat belly, and she spread her legs. He kissed the inside of her thighs and pressed his mouth and tongue into that pink junction that seemed to be the confluence of all that was evil and all that was exciting.

It went beyond sensuality. It was ceremonial, a religious exploration into her very core. The pussy lady. He kept thinking it as he sucked her. The pussy lady. The queen bee. And she moaned, driving him on. It became for him a seeking of absolution. That deep inside this girl he could lose all the images haunting him. She was thrusting herself up into his mouth in a gentle but ever-increasing tempo. Her eyes were half closed, and her lips were parted. Lines of concentration creased the center of her forehead. Her hands went to the back of his neck, and she thrust and pressed his mouth into her and moaned, *"Now—there—right there—oh, God—right there. . . ."*

Barney could not tell how much time passed as they lay silently on the bed. But suddenly without warning or word, she rose and went into the bathroom. He heard the shower running. But he did not move or speak. He wondered if that was how it had been with Neeley. If he had made love to some dazzling girl and relaxed, waiting for her to come out of the shower and get back into bed with him, only to have her stand at the alcove and reach into her handbag and come out with a .22 automatic and methodically pump seven shots into him. In that moment for Barney, it was not hard to imagine.

Laura came out of the bathroom and smiled slightly. She slipped on her velvet black pants, but before she buttoned the red silk blouse, she took a small atomizer out of her handbag and sprayed the sweet perfume across her chest and under her arms. She then buttoned the blouse and put her jewelry back on. She took a brush out of the bag and with brief, furious strokes brushed her long hair. She walked over to the bed, leaned down, and kissed Barney's cheek.

"I have to go," she said. "Paul Isella. I have to see him now." She started for the bedroom door, reached it, and turned back to him. "I want you to know I enjoyed it. But it was a job. You understand that, don't you?"

He glanced at the green luminous hands on the bedside clock; it was three-fifteen. A moment later he heard the apartment door open, then close softly behind her.

CHAPTER

18 ☒

THE RED RAYS OF THE SUN MELTED THE DAWN MIST, AND THE LEAVES of the pepper trees were beginning to throw their shadows. The green rooftops of the yellow barns fell away, row after row, forming a maze of walkways, where pretty young girls and wiry, mustachioed Mexican grooms hot-walked their thoroughbreds around a carousel-like wheel in a slow, circular motion.

Barney watched the girls whispering and cooing to the wild-eyed thoroughbreds, coaxing them to settle down. There was a warm, fraternal feeling in the stable area, as if somehow the owners, trainers, grooms, workout boys, and stable hands were not in competition with one another, but rather shared a commonality of purpose. The reality was that all their energies and talents were focused on producing a winner, and there could be only one winner in each race.

As Barney strolled through the barns, he soaked up the marvelous fragrance of manure, sweet-smelling hay, and the loamy chocolate-colored earth. He reached the end of the stable area and entered the small tunnel that led out onto the main track. The tunnel was less than two hundred feet long, and through an opening at the other end Barney caught an occasional glimpse of a horse flashing around the rail, going full out in the last furlong of his workout.

In front of the stands an announcer holding a microphone called out the names of the horses to the railbirds, members of the public who were admitted free to watch the morning workouts at Santa Anita. The trainers and owners stood just outside the rail at the top of the stretch, their stopwatches poised, clocking their own horses and those of the opposition. Two ambulances were parked ominously in the shrubbery off to the side, one on the far side of the track and one on the near side.

The sun was just beginning to turn the tall San Gabriel Mountains from purple to scarlet. The mountains towered over the far side of the track and on a clear winter day stood out in snowcapped splendor.

The track announcer's voice boomed out and directed the public's attention to the far side of the track, where an almost pure white horse was prancing toward the five-eighth pole. Barney knew the horse. His name was Snowball, and he was famous for his powerful stride and heart-stopping closing finish. Snowball belonged to Arthur Clements.

Barney saw the dapper silver-haired man standing at the top of the stretch. He wore tan slacks, an open blue sport shirt, and a tweed jacket with leather-trimmed elbows. A pair of powerful binoculars hung from his neck, and his attention was focused on the big white horse moving easily up the far side of the track. There was a noticeable hush from the railbirds as Snowball drew close to the five-eighth pole. Barney found a place on the rail and stared across the track at the big white horse.

Snowball reached the red-striped pole and stopped. Then suddenly the rider flicked his whip twice and seemed to melt into the horse's neck. There was a shout from the railbirds as the horse burst forward. The rider's whip flashed again, and the great white horse poured it on, swinging wide, around the far turn, and coming into the top of the stretch. Barney could now hear the horse's hooves thundering along, sending great clods of earth flying up behind him. The horse had a long, effortless stride that seemed to eat up the track.

Clements watched with a satisfied smile as the horse straightened out and pounded down the thousand-foot-long stretch. Barney heard one of the trainers say, "Christ, he'll do the last quarter in twenty-one flat."

Clements lowered his binoculars and waved to a swarthy-looking heavyset man, who congratulated him on Snowball's performance. But the smile on Clements's face slowly diminished as he saw Barney coming up to him.

They shook hands, and Barney said, "Nice horse."

"Great horse," Clements replied. "His dam was a great horse. So was his sire. Breeding is ninety percent of the game." The big white horse was on his way back, loping up toward them. Clements said, "Excuse me, Lieutenant."

The rider on the white horse reined him in close to Barney and Clements. Barney recognized the rider. He was a famous Panamanian jockey. He looked down at Clements and with a thick Spanish accent said, "I couldn't hold heem."

"Walk him for two miles," Clements suggested.

The rider nodded. "He gonna ween beeg Sunday. Nothin' beat thees horse." He patted the horse's neck. The jockey smiled, exposing two gold teeth. He tugged at the reins, wheeled the white horse around and began walking clockwise on the extreme outside of the track to avoid the traffic patterns of horses still engaged in their morning workouts.

Clements said, "Sometimes they go too fast in the morning. It's what they do in the afternoon that counts."

The sun was appreciably higher and Barney could feel the perspiration beginning to collect under his arms. "Do you own Snowball?" Barney asked.

"No. I'm a principal partner. There's a syndicate of five or six individuals."

"That syndicate wouldn't be a subsidiary of the Seneca Corporation?"

The question did not seem to faze Clements. He merely rubbed the purple cluster of veins at the sides of his nostrils. "As a matter of fact, you're right. My racing interests are owned and operated by Seneca." Clements dropped the cigarette into the loamy earth and said, "How about a cup of coffee?"

"Fine." Barney nodded.

The cafeteria was in the center of the stable area and was busy with trainers, exercise girls, jockeys, and jockeys' agents, owners, press people, veterinarians, and the private security guards who were coming off the night shift.

They were seated at a window toward the rear of the noisy room. Clements sipped his coffee and said, "I've been here since five-thirty this morning, didn't sleep too well last night."

"I suppose Tom's death came as a shock," Barney said.

"Tom Neeley was a close friend," Clements answered somberly. "I can't believe he's gone."

"Do you have any idea who wanted Tom killed?"

"I'm sorry, Lieutenant." Clements shrugged and sipped his coffee. "I can't help you."

Barney felt they had played the overture; it was time the curtain went up. "I know about the coke, and the Gregson hookers, and the bag trips."

At the mention of the bag trips, Clements's eyes clouded somewhat. "Well, Tom wanted things, so I put him in contact with certain situations."

"Nothing wrong with that," Barney said. "You're on the board of Seneca Corporation, right?"

"That's right. Seneca, and eight other national corporations."

"Including Tidal Oil?"

"I've been on the board of directors of Tidal Oil for fourteen years."

Barney studied the handsome, smooth man with the flawed purple discoloration. He knew Clements would be an enigma. He was a man who moved in two diametrically opposed worlds: one of respectable corporations, bankers, insurance executives, the horsey set of millionaire owners and breeders; and on the other side, a consort of professional hookers, board member of a mob-operated company, and cocaine user. Barney tried to marshal his thoughts. He would have to be careful with his questions, or he would come up empty. The coffee helped, but he still felt a sense of light-headedness from last night's encounter with Laura. She had been brutally honest. She was Maldonado's eyes and ears. But the taste of the girl was still in his mouth, and her perfume still permeated some part of his brain.

Barney noticed a very pretty girl with a long blond ponytail talking to a famous jockey at another table.

"Cute, isn't she?" Clements said.

"Very cute," Barney agreed. "Did Tom supply the cocaine?"

"There was always an ample supply of high-grade cocaine at Leo's parties," Clements said matter-of-factly. "I don't know who supplied it. We all assumed it was Tom."

"Did Tom get the coke from Victor Maldonado?"

"That's a question I can't answer."

"Well, here's one you can answer: Victor Maldonado is in fact your partner in the Seneca Corporation?"

"Surely, Lieutenant"—Clements smiled—"you don't expect me to be responsible for all the individuals who belong to the same corporations I'm affiliated with."

Barney felt the warning bells of his anger beginning to sound. The same anger he had felt with the chauffeur and Laura . . . and finally Nolan—an anger born of frustration. But he could not afford to lose his temper with Clements. He had to crack Clements's cool facade with facts, not with threats. He had nothing except Laura's disclosure that Clements might have had a hand in Neeley's German trip. But it was too soon to play that card.

"Did you participate in cocaine and sex parties with Leo Mirell and Victor Maldonado?"

"I was present at Leo Mirell's home when certain people used cocaine and certain other people went into bedrooms. Now what does that have to do with Tom's murder?"

"It proves that you and Maldonado were more than passing acquaintances," Barney stated. "And that you may be in a position to separate rumor from fact."

"Look, Lieutenant," Clements said pleasantly, "I understand your problem. An old-time police officer has been brutally murdered. And I know you have a personal interest in this case, but—"

"How do you know that?" Barney interrupted.

"Just a rumor."

"Okay," Barney said. "While we're dealing with rumors, did Maldonado supply the cocaine to Tom?"

"It's possible. I don't know."

"Did Tom have an Oriental girl friend?"

"I saw him with an Oriental girl on more than one occasion."

"When was the last time?"

"A few weeks ago."

"You know the girl?"

"In passing."

"Did you have sexual relations with her?"

"Once or twice."

The pretty girl with long blond ponytail and tight jeans came up to their table and touched Clements's shoulder. He smiled up at the girl. "Say hello to Mr. Caine, Gloria."

She had a wide white smile and a laughing voice, "Hi, there."

Barney said, "Hi."

The girl looked at Clements. "Do you want me to work the filly tomorrow?"

"Yes. Breeze her three-eighths, but don't push her."

"Gottcha." She smiled at Barney. "Nice meeting you."

The girl swished away. They watched after her for a moment; then Barney asked, "Can you tell me anything about Kay Neeley?"

"Kay is a wonderful woman."

"When was the last time you saw Kay and Tom together?"

"I had dinner with them perhaps a year ago. And, well," he started to say something, then backed away. "Hell, it's not worth repeating."

It was an old signal. He wanted Barney to know something.

"Why not let me be the judge of what's important?"

Clements fingered the purple splotch at his nose, and his voice assumed a tone of confidentiality. "I don't like placing friends of mine in compromising positions."

"Tom Neeley's last position was pretty well compromised," Barney said. "As compromised as you can get." His voice became tough and official. "And you were right. I do have a personal interest in this case."

Clements's eyes narrowed, and fine lines appeared at their corners. "This may or may not mean anything, but I heard that Tom was after something in Germany. Something of extraordinary value."

"When did Tom go to Germany?"

"About two months ago."

"How did you come by this information?"

"The Oriental girl told me."

"When?"

"A couple of weeks ago."

"And that's the first time you heard of Tom's trip to Germany?"

"Yes."

"Well, now, that's strange."

"What do you mean, Lieutenant?"

"I mean it's strange because you sent Tom Neeley to Germany."

Clements stared at him a moment, then looked out the window at a passing horse and rider. He was playing for time. Waiting for Barney to follow up with something, anything that would allow him to duck the issue. But Barney said nothing. The question hung in the air, and as the seconds passed, the question slowly became an accusation.

Finally, in a subdued voice Clements asked, "Did Kay Neeley tell you that?"

And Barney had what he came for. Clements's mention of Kay made the European connection. Clements, Kay, and Tom were in on the German thing together.

"It wasn't Kay," Barney said flatly.

Clements stared at Barney as if he were seeing him for the first time. He had been outmaneuvered. This was no ordinary cop. He would have to be careful.

Clements smiled. "You're playing games, Lieutenant."

"I only play games with friends," Barney said. "By the way, you also introduced Tom to Adam Steiffel, right?"

"That's right. Mr. Steiffel needed someone with a background like Tom's. I didn't ask any questions; I simply put them together."

"Where were you this past Sunday between ten and eleven in the morning?"

"Right here." He paused, then added, "There are at least fifteen people who can attest to that."

"Not necessary. I believe you."

Clements glanced at his expensive wristwatch.

"Did you ever hear Tom use the word 'Genesis'?" Barney asked.

The gray in Clements's eyes seemed to pale suddenly. He murmured,

"Genesis," as if it were the first time he had heard the word; then he shook his head. "No. I can't recall Tom ever using that word."

"How about 'Obermann'?"

"No." This time the response was instantaneous.

"Does the Oloffson Hotel in Haiti mean anything to you?"

"Never heard of it."

"Do you speak German?"

"No."

Barney got to his feet. He was worried about Kay Neeley. The questioning of Clements solidified his premonition that Kay Neeley was in jeopardy. "Thanks for your time, Mr. Clements."

"My pleasure, Lieutenant." Clements smiled. "If you ever want to come out to the races, my box is always available. It's right on the finish line."

"Is that where Tom was two Sundays ago?"

"Yes. Tom liked the races."

Barney nodded. "Tom liked a lot of things."

CHAPTER

19 ☒

BARNEY FLASHED HIS GOLD BADGE AT THE SECURITY GUARD, AND THE old man pressed the lever, raising the wooden barrier to the private beach road.

The street was sunny and quiet. A small boy coasted past Barney on his ten-speed cycle, and two Mexican maids pushing market baskets chattered loudly in Spanish.

Barney turned left off the Malibu Colony Road and took the street that was flush to the beach. He caught quick, glittering glimpses of the Pacific between the narrow alleys separating the expensive beach homes. There was no traffic on the small graveled street, and the occasional cry of sea gulls from the beach side added to the tranquillity. But as Barney drew closer to Kay Neeley's street, his uneasy feeling grew more intense. He suddenly wished Louis were with him. He wondered if he had not made a mistake coming out here alone. But he had no choice; time was running against them. And time was always on the side of the killers.

Barney reached the end of the street, made a U-turn, and parked near the open garage. The big blue Lincoln was still in its stall; it seemed to him that it had not been moved since Sunday.

As Barney walked toward the front door, the sun and fatigue pulled at his legs. He pressed the small pearl button on the white door, and the chimes sounded instantly. Barney looked up the street but saw no one. He thought about lighting a cigarillo but fought the impulse. He pressed the pearl button again, thinking that Kay was probably out on the sun deck. Where the hell was the dog? When they had come to Kay's house on Sunday, the dog had barked as soon as they touched the button. Barney stepped back from the door.

A wave of apprehension began to seep into his chest. Then, reflexively, he thought that Kay might be walking on the beach with the dog. But that didn't hold up. When he had phoned her from the track, she'd said she would be waiting.

Barney reached inside his jacket and removed the .38 service revolver from his shoulder holster. He flicked the cylinder open; all six chambers were loaded. He snapped it closed and pushed the muzzle snug down into his belt.

His footsteps on the crushed gravel made a loud, crunching noise as he walked slowly from the front door to the garage. He stopped just inside the garage and slipped his loafers off, then knelt down and removed his socks. The soles of his feet hurt as he walked silently across the gravel toward the narrow alleyway that separated Kay's house from the big clapboard house on the right. The alleyway had a sand floor and ran the length of the house, ending at the entrance to the beach. The sand felt cold and damp against the soles of his feet as he moved cautiously toward the open beach.

He came out of the alley onto the beach and blinked against the sudden glare of the Pacific. The wooden deck of Kay Neeley's terrace extended eighteen feet out over the beach. Barney moved quickly under the wooden terrace where streaks of sunlight came through the planking, creating zebralike patterns on the dark sand. The beach was deserted except for a group of teenage surfers riding the low waves. And farther down the beach there were two men in black skin diver's wet suits, struggling with a faulty motor on a rubber dinghy.

Barney stood still under the dark shade of the decking, listening for sounds from the terrace above. But there was only silence: no footfalls, no radio, no television, no phone rings, no voices, and no barking or growling. There was, however, an insistent, rhythmic, flapping sound.

He checked the beach again, then stepped out from under the decking and went up the staircase to Kay Neeley's terrace.

There were sections of the Los Angeles *Times* scattered on top of a lounge. A tube of sun-screen cream and a pair of sunglasses lay on the floor at the foot of the lounge. The police dog's water pan was full, and his rubber bone was alongside the pan. The sliding glass door that led from the living room to the terrace was partially open, and the corner of the drape had been sucked out by the wind and whipped back and forth.

Barney took the gun out of his belt, gripped it firmly, and moved cautiously toward the partially open glass door. He reached the door, shoved his left foot against it, and as it slid open, the flapping drape receded . . .

* * *

The dog lay on his side on one of the gaily colored Navaho throw rugs; there were bits and pieces of bone, flesh, and fur where his head had been. Barney stared at the dead animal for a long time. The shock and horror of the bloody remains made him oblivious to the loud dripping sound. He pulled his eyes away from the shattered head of the dog and looked off into the dark interior of the room.

Kay Neeley's nude body was draped head down over the second-floor railing. Her arms were extended, and her hair dangled down, covering her face. A steady stream of blood oozed out of her forehead into her hair, soaking it, then dripping down, loudly, onto the wooden floor.

Barney's mind began to race, adding and subtracting. The killers had not come through the private security gate, unless Kay knew them and had been expecting them. But the profuse bleeding of the dog and her own rag-doll body hanging over the balcony indicated she had been killed only minutes ago. If the killers had come through the security gate, Barney would have passed them on his way in. Logic said the killers had entered from the beach side.

Barney pulled the hammer back on the .38 and walked slowly to the open terrace door. He moved the drape aside and stepped out onto the sunlit terrace.

He squinted against the glare coming off the sea. He was just beginning to realize the full shock of what had happened to Kay. He couldn't bring himself to go up to that second-story balcony. He couldn't look at her. He felt the beads of sweat pouring out of his forehead, and he began to feel queasy; the heavy, sweet smell of blood and the bone and gristle of the dog and the sound of Kay's blood dripping away were starting to make his stomach icy. He stared out to sea and took deep lungfuls of the fresh air. He noticed the kids surfing, and down the beach one of the skin divers still struggled with the dinghy's lanyard. He wondered about the other man in the wet suit when a flash of heat singed his right ear and the glass door behind him shattered.

Barney dropped to the wooden deck, flattened out, and began to crawl toward the beach-side railing of the deck. He did not hear the gun reports, but three sections of the railing suddenly blew apart just above his head. He peered out at the beach but saw no one firing at him. He clenched the .38 in his right hand and steadied it with his left. He thought he heard the low crunch of a silencer as another slug whistled in high, hurtling into the sliding doors behind him and shattering another section of glass. Then, like an apparition, a man in a wet suit holding a gun rose out of the sand about thirty yards from the terrace and, while keeping his eyes on the terrace, started moving backward toward his companion in the dinghy.

Barney raised the .38 and caught the moving black-clad figure in the center of the grooved gunsight. He led the man slightly, trying desperately to remember the correct lead distance. He hadn't fired a weapon in the line of duty in eight years. He slowly increased the pressure on his trigger finger, and there was a loud explosion. His forearm shot up from the concussion of the shot. The man stopped for an instant, as if surprised, then began to run.

Barney aimed again and fired twice. The man's arms went skyward, and he fell heavily to the sand. He lay still for a second, then slowly began to crawl toward his companion in the dinghy. Barney vaulted the railing, dropped to the sand, and broke into a low crouching run. The wounded man turned back, saw Barney coming, squirmed around, and leveled what looked like a Magnum .357 at Barney's oncoming figure. Barney saw the sun bounce off the long barrel of the muzzle and dropped to the sand.

He flattened himself, trying to burrow a hole in the sand, as he heard the low thump of a report and a small cloud of sand blew past his right eye, stinging and burning its way across his forehead. He raised his arms, holding the .38 in his right hand and supporting his grip with his left. He took dead aim on the belly-down figure in the wet suit and fired twice. The first shot hit the man in the right shoulder, and the gun flew out of his hand. Barney's second shot sent an instant fountain of blood spurting out of the man's forehead. At that moment the motor on the dinghy caught and roared to full throttle; the small gray rubber boat made a wide arc away from the beach and sped out to sea.

Barney glanced at the fast-disappearing dinghy, then looked back at the prone figure of the fallen man in the wet suit. He kept the .38 trained on the still figure and cautiously raised himself up on one knee; seeing no movement from the fallen man, Barney stood erect and walked slowly over to the black-clad figure, who lay motionless in the sand.

CHAPTER

20 ⊠

A SMALL SQUARE NEAR THE SURF HAD BEEN ROPED OFF, BUT IT TOOK all the muscle of six state highway troopers to keep the crowd of onlookers away.

The police photographers out of Metro had taken the last series of shots of the dead man in the wet suit. The morgue ambulance had come down a wooden ramp onto the beach, and its flashing blood-red lights seemed to lend a theatrical air to the death site. The noisy crowd fell silent as the morgue attendants placed the skin diver's body in an open black bag, zippered it closed, shoved the body feet first into the vehicle, and slammed the doors. The attendants went around to the front of the ambulance and started the vehicle through the sand back up toward the wooden ramp.

A small army had gathered in front of Kay's house: uniformed Malibu cops, highway patrolmen, five police vehicles, a mobile television remote unit complete with camera crew and the tall brunette reporter who had been the only newscaster to appear at Tom Neeley's house the previous Sunday. The coroner's laboratory vehicle was parked behind the garage, and two fingerprint men were dusting Kay's empty blue Lincoln.

Barney stared at the sea through the shattered glass door. He sipped a brandy and smoked a cigarillo. Behind him, in the living room, Kay Neeley's nude body had been wrapped in a sheet and placed on a sofa. Louis watched Torres as he chewed on an unlit cigar and carefully removed the last specimen of tissue from the gaping hole where Kay's right cheek had been.

Torres placed the tissue onto a glass slide, then sealed the slide in a glassine envelope. The medical examiner's assistants waited patiently as Torres leaned over and closed Kay's staring eyes, then forcefully shut her gaping jaw, stuffing her mouth with cotton. He straightened up and took one final look at Kay's body. There were burn marks all over the white flesh and two purple circles at her wrists. Torres nodded to his assistants, and they lifted the scarred body off the sofa, placed it on a gurney cart, and wheeled it toward the front door. Torres removed his plastic gloves and lit the end of the stubby cigar. He looked over the flame at Louis and said, "Goddamn case has me smoking again."

"How about a brandy?" Louis asked.

"Sure." Gabby nodded. The medical examiner glanced at Barney. Torres knew that Barney blamed himself for Kay's death. He felt sorry for Barney, but he could not understand a cop having empathy for a victim. Victims came with the profession. Louis gave Torres the brandy, then went up to Barney.

"Gabby's finished."

Barney tossed the rest of his brandy down, turned back to the room, and his eyes reflexively went to the dark spot on the Navaho throw rug where the dog had fallen.

"You all right?" Louis asked.

Barney nodded and walked over to a chair and sat down opposite Torres. A state highway patrolman, who looked big enough to play tackle for the Rams, shouldered his way into the room and walked up to Barney.

"They found the dinghy floating off the public beach at Santa Monica. Empty. No witnesses."

"Thanks," Barney said, and the man tossed a salute and left.

Louis said, "We have a team of dicks from Metro hitting the stores that sell those dinghies. They say there are fifteen or twenty outlets in the metropolitan area."

"Won't help us. They could have bought that thing in San Diego and brought it up by van."

"Yeah, they could of," Louis concurred, then added, "The tall TV Lady is outside; she wants a statement. She knows you were involved in the shoot-out."

"Just handle it." Barney sighed.

Louis left, and there was a moment of silence, broken by the rhythmic crash of the waves. The tide was beginning to come in, and the force of the breakers was increasing.

"Go ahead," Barney said to Torres.

"I'll start with the guy on the beach." He sipped some brandy. "Your first shot hit him in the femur bone of his right leg, shattering the leg from the knee down. A hell of a shot, considering you were on the terrace and he was in motion fifty yards away and down angle from you."

"He ran into the shot. I missed the first two."

"Still, a hell of a shot. One in a hundred. Your first shot from the beach level caught him in the right shoulder and shattered his collarbone. The next one killed him instantly, split his forehead. All the way through to the central motor of the brain. There was brain fluid leakage all over the back of the wet suit." Gabby drew on the cigar and made a face. "You know the weapon he used. A twenty-two long automatic with silencer. A PPK Walther. The same weapon that killed Tom Neeley."

"What about the dead guy?"

Torres shrugged. "I'd say he was about thirty. Appeared to be of Latin descent, but not Mexican." He said emphatically, "South American. Maybe Argentinian. There's European blood. He was not pure Indian. Not like me. There was nothing to identify him. He was naked under the wet suit." Torres paused. "Want some more brandy?"

"No."

"You look lousy, *amigo*. Let me get you a refill." Torres got up and went to the wet bar. A bespectacled man in a shiny blue suit came in from the front door and walked up to Barney.

"We have all the prints, Lieutenant. The wet suit guy, Kay Neeley, and the bedroom."

"I want the dead man's prints to go to the feds, CIA and Interpol."

"They'll be on the wire the minute we get in," the man replied.

Torres handed Barney a snifter full of Kay's best brandy and sat down. "The dog was shot once through his right eye and fell to his left side. Probably died in three or four minutes. There was nothing unusual on his claws or teeth to indicate he went up against anything. I think he was shot on sight, and close. There was flash powder on his fur. The dog never had a chance to do anything but die."

Barney could feel the brandy warming him.

"Kay Neeley was tortured," Torres continued. "She was burned by cigarettes over most of her body. We counted fifty-eight burn marks; she was burned on her vagina, nipples, anus, mouth, and eyelids. She was shot once. Through the right cheekbone. High up near the temple."

"How did she get to the balcony?" Barney asked.

"She was tortured and shot in her bedroom. The bullet did not paralyze her. It ruptured the artery. But she was able to drag herself from the bedroom along the balcony floor. She probably tried to stand, then finally fell across the top of the railing, where she bled to death."

"How long was Kay dead before I showed up?"

"She may have been clinically still alive while you were here." Gabby sipped the brandy. "They were in the house only minutes before you got here."

"Okay," Barney said. "So they came in by sea, beached the dinghy. Entered the house. Killed the dog. Grabbed Kay, dragged her upstairs, pinned her arms behind her. Undressed her. Tortured her. For how long we don't know. Then they shot her, went back out to the beach, say a three-minute walk back to the dinghy. Meantime, Kay crawls to the balcony and bleeds to death."

"That's it," Torres said. "My guess is you missed walking in on them by ten minutes, maybe less." Torres got to his feet. "You were lucky, *amigo*. One of them would have killed you." He came over to Barney and touched his shoulder. "Don't blame yourself."

Barney shook his head. "I should have had her watched right from the beginning. I knew she was frightened. I should have had someone on the beach side and someone in front."

"Look, Barney, if they are professionals, one way or another they were gonna get her. For Chrissake, they kill the ex-premier of Italy. They shoot Kennedy in the middle of the day in Dallas. You can't stop a professional."

"That's bullshit, Gabby. You can do something."

"No. You can't do a fucking thing. Now get off the cross. Leave the cross to Jesus." He squeezed Barney's shoulder. "All you can do is go after the bastards who killed her."

Torres picked up his medical tray. "I'll have the whole thing on paper by ten tomorrow morning."

Barney swallowed the rest of the brandy, grimaced, and wiped his mouth with his sleeve. He got to his feet and walked out onto the sun deck.

The crowd had disappeared, the police lines were down, and the late-afternoon sun slid in and out of the low clouds, changing the color of the sea from blue to gray, and way out on the horizon line a big naval vessel, which looked like a carrier, was beginning its long journey from San Diego to Pearl Harbor. Barney took several deep breaths of the sea air. He felt his nervous system calming. The adrenaline flow of the shoot-out had chilled him for a long time, causing his hands to tremble and forming an icy circle in the center of his chest. But time, and the brandy and the sea air, had restored a degree of calm throughout his body.

He thought about the dead man on the beach. He hadn't shot at anyone since he had worked Narcotics briefly eight years ago. And that time was different. He never saw the man he fired at. He had aimed at the sound of footsteps racing down an alley. But the thing on the beach had been eyeball to eyeball. A red bubble had burst out of the man's forehead. The man's brains had seeped into the sand. But he felt no sympathy for the dead man in the wet suit. Only remorse that he had been too late to save Kay.

Louis came out onto the terrace. "The TV Lady is gone."

Barney nodded. "Gabby said I missed by ten minutes."

"What's the difference?" Louis sighed. "Kay was marked."

"I should have come out here yesterday," Barney persisted. "I might have been able to get her to open up. Instead, I got ripped with Laura Gregson and spent the night like a trick."

Barney fell silent, and Louis studied him for a moment. "The Vietnamese hooker confirmed what Laura told you. Tom Neeley was after something in Germany."

"Clements told me the same thing," Barney said. "He asked me if Kay had mentioned the German trip."

"Why would he think Kay told you?" Louis asked.

"Clements obviously knew Kay had been involved with Tom in this German thing," Barney replied.

Louis said, "The Vietnamese girl told me that Tom referred to Genesis. He called it a 'beginning.' "

Barney looked at Louis. "You think she leveled?"

"Absolutely. The girl has been sucking cocks in Saigon since she was six years old. Nothing's going to make a liar out of her; not anymore."

Barney sighed and looked out at the gun-metal surface of the Pacific. "We really kicked open an anthill. You have to wonder about human greed. Jesus Christ, is anything worth winding up like the Neeleys?"

Louis whispered something in Japanese.

"What's that?" Barney asked.

"An old Shinto proverb: 'A nest of vipers is not as deadly as the hunger of one man.' "

"Well, whatever it was the Neeleys hungered for, they paid a hell of a price."

"You said Neeleys plural," Louis offered.

"I told you, I'm positive Kay was involved. I think she knew what Genesis meant and who Obermann is."

"How can you be positive?"

"They wouldn't have killed her otherwise," Barney said. "Her murder had nothing to do with cocaine."

* * *

The presence of the dead woman permeated the small, simply furnished bedroom. There were photographs of Kay Neeley on the bureau and on the two end tables at either side of the bed. The closets were open, and her wardrobe hung in neat rows. A faded photograph of a very young Tom Neeley in the uniform of an OCS candidate was stuck in the inside ridge of a mirror on the bureau.

They took their jackets off and worked silently and methodically, searching through drawers, closets, clothes, hatboxes, shoe boxes, valises, handbags, the bathroom, the medicine chest. They turned the bloodstained mattress over and looked under the bed and between the springs. The air was close, and there was a trace of light perfume and the meaty, heavy odor of drying blood.

After twenty minutes Barney began to perspire; beads of sweat fell out of his armpits; others formed on his forehead and slid down his cheeks, staining his shirt. He went into the bathroom and splashed cold water on his face. Louis came in after him. Barney saw Louis's image in the mirror over the sink. Louis shook his head.

"Nothing."

They crossed the small bloodstained second-floor balcony and entered the small study at the end of the circular balcony.

The study was informal, as were the other rooms in the house. Two large windows faced the sea. The floor was scored redwood, and there were two large sofas flush to the book-lined walls; a color television faced the sofa, and just under the windows were a large desk and chair.

Louis began to go through the bookshelves, taking out the books one by one and turning them upside down. Barney sat at the desk. A profusion of papers and bills were stacked on the right side of the large writing surface. Barney thumbed through them: credit card bills, insurance premiums, magazine subscriptions, gasoline bills, and a letter from her son, Roger, postmarked Johannesburg and dated three weeks ago.

Barney opened the top drawer and found Kay's checkbook and personal stationery. He placed the checkbook on the desk top and then opened a small drawer at the top left side. He found a navy blue bicentennial U.S. passport and, underneath the passport, two documents. One was a travel folder from the Oloffson Hotel, Haiti, with the name "Frank Tedesco" written in block letters at the top of the folder. The Haitian connection instantly clicked into place. Barney knew who Frank Tedesco was. An international thief avoiding extradition to the United States, living in self-imposed exile in Haiti. A man whose connections had once penetrated all the way to the Oval Office.

The other document was a canceled airline ticket that read TWA Los

Angeles–New York–Cologne, with Pan American connecting from Cologne to Berlin.

The date of the German portion of the ticket coincided with the date on the American Express credit card slip from the Kempinski Hotel in Berlin that Barney had found in Tom Neeley's bedroom. Barney clenched his eyes and rubbed his sleeve across the beads of sweat coming out on his forehead. He felt jittery and feverish.

Barney dropped the two documents in his pocket and picked up the passport. The current dates started on page four. There was a West German Federal Republic seal of entry, stamped in Cologne. And on the following page, a Haitian seal of entry, dated two weeks after the German seal, and just below on the same page was a United States customs reentry stamp dated three days after the Haitian seal. The port of reentry was Miami.

Barney turned to Louis. "Forget the books; we found what we were looking for." He rose and handed the documents to Louis, then walked slowly over to the window and stared at the flat gun-metal sea.

The thing he had missed—the clue, or unasked question, or obvious action that had eluded him—was rising to the surface of his consciousness. It was something in Tom Neeley's past, something he had just seen. And like a failing light that glows spasmodically, then surges with power and burns brightly, the missing piece hit Barney with sudden clarity. It was the photograph of the young Tom Neeley in military uniform.

Barney turned to Louis and said, "Lou."

Louis looked up from Kay Neeley's passport.

Barney said, "We've got to get a transcript of Tom Neeley's World War Two military file."

CHAPTER

21 ⊠

THE HUGE GLASS WALL OF THE TRANSIT LOUNGE RATTLED AS THE FORCE
of the tropical wind and rain hammered against it.

The girl stood at the window, staring out at the storm. A half mile
away the tall stand of coconut palms that lined the highway leading to
the airport was barely visible. The storm front had blown in from the
Caribbean and had painted a reddish hue onto the Miami night. The
girl was troubled by the options the storm presented. Her connecting
flight from Miami to Port-au-Prince had been canceled, but there was a
National flight, Miami to Paris nonstop, leaving in two hours. She kept
tossing the pluses and minuses back and forth. The morning flight from
Los Angeles to Miami had not been tiring, and the prospect of another
eleven hours to Paris did not bother her; if she decided against Paris
and stayed with the plan, she would have to go into Miami for the night
and try for a flight to Haiti in the morning. She despised Haiti, and
Frank Tedesco always made her feel uneasy. There was something dangerous underneath his casual elegance. The National flight to Paris was
almost too perfect to resist. She could be in there at nine in the morning, Paris time. She would be in the apartment with Raoul by ten. But
Tedesco was expecting her.

She left the window and walked slowly to the bar. Once again she
carefully studied the people in the lounge; there were a few students,
some business types, three elderly couples, and a cluster of Japanese
men chattering and comparing their cameras. She was certain that there
were no "professionals" in the lounge and that she had not been followed from Los Angeles.

A pall of blue cigarette smoke rose up over the bar and disappeared
into the tiny pinspots embedded in the ceiling. Two overweight and

half-drunk American businessmen sat at the bar, and Frank Sinatra's "I've Got the World on a String" came out of the Muzak system.

She sat on a barstool opposite the businessmen and ordered a vodka on the rocks. She took a cigarette out of her gold case, lit it, and drew hard on the strong Algerian tobacco. An ash fell on the thigh of her white Cardin suit, and she carefully flicked it off without smudging the expensive fabric. The businessmen began stealing glances at her and whispering comments to one another.

But her thoughts were not about the businessmen, the bar, or the moment. She was thinking about Haiti, about Port-au-Prince, about the garbage-strewn streets and the begging children squatting in their own feces. It was a sweltering, fetid hell, where just staying alive was an act of vengeance. The smell of the city made her ill. It was an offensive mix of human waste and carbon monoxide that hung like a putrid blanket over the endless alleys of tin-roofed shacks, with their voodoo symbols clamped over the doorways.

She sipped the cold vodka and thought: The Oloffson Hotel was not that bad. It did have character and kept one close to the sea, away from the tangle of poverty and filth. Still, just to be there and go through a meeting with Tedesco when she could be in Paris. She felt the cold vodka sliding down her throat, slipping through her chest, and circling and warming her flat stomach. She began to feel slightly heady. She guessed it was the vodka mixing with the Moroccan hash she had smoked in the first-class toilet of the 747.

Then suddenly the image of Tom Neeley's tortured flesh crashed its way into her consciousness. She shuddered reflexively as she thought of him moaning in ecstasy and twenty minutes later groaning in the agony of his death throes, while Primo methodically pumped bullet after bullet into him. She quickly drained the glass and motioned to the bartender for a refill. She thought about the purple lines around Clements's nose and his eyes watering as he snorted the coke. The revulsion she had felt when she had taken him in her mouth and squeezed and curved and nursed him to a climax. She wondered how long she could continue. She knew that she could never get out. She had sworn her life to the cause that torchlit night in the camp on the Mediterranean, outside Sidon. But that was a long time ago, before the doubts, before the ghosts, before the nightmares.

She lifted the glass and stared at the liquid veins of vodka circling around the ice cubes. She thought: It would have to end soon. When she reached the breaking point, she would go to Yasir, and ask to be removed from the field. Yasir was reasonable. He would understand. Besides, if she managed this task, it would be enough. It was, after all, the most vital assignment in the history of the organization. If they failed, the resources of the organization would be crippled, the financial under-pinnings would be gone. The ultimate weapon, oil, would no longer exist.

When they had summoned her to Beirut, she had committed herself to this assignment without reservation. She had felt a surge of courage and pride. She had done more than her share, from the beginning, from Munich.

She would phone Tedesco, tell him her flight was canceled, and say that the weather in Los Angeles had been cloudy but a break was possible, or some such guarded code, and that she would be in Paris and would give him a full report through a local operative.

The two pulpwood salesmen watched the girl as she slid off the bar-stool and walked slowly to the bank of public phones. The salesmen were in awe of their own carnal fantasies of what they could do with the dark-haired beauty in the expensive white pantsuit.

CHAPTER

22 ⊠

THE SAN BERNARDINO FREEWAY WAS A TEN-LANE RIVER OF CONCRETE flowing between an endless chain of dreary shopping centers. It was early afternoon, and the traffic was light. Louis held the speedometer needle steady at sixty.

Barney leaned back in the passenger seat; his eyes were closed, but he was not asleep. He was trying to place the events of the last forty-eight hours in some logical perspective. He thought of the bitter irony of Kay and Tom Neeley, divorced in life, but reunited in death. They had been buried side by side in the Catholic section of Forest Lawn Cemetery.

Their attorney, Bernard Seeger, had carried out the funeral arrangements according to Kay's wishes. He had also notified the Neeleys' son, Roger, in Johannesburg and received a cabled reply expressing gratitude to Seeger for taking care of the legalities.

The funeral had been something of a media event. All the local channels had sent their crack camera and reporting crews to cover the funeral. The city-side reporters from the *Herald-Examiner* and Los Angeles *Times* were present with their still photographers. There were also reporters from the local radio stations.

In a curious way the funeral had reminded Barney of his mother. She had been about the same age as Kay Neeley when she died. And she had the same good bones, the same angular features. The kind of structured beauty that resisted the ravages of time. His mother had been a soft-spoken, quiet woman with old-fashioned principles. When Barney had stood at the Neeley grave site, listening to the priest's flat incantations, he felt a deep sadness for Kay.

They had gone to the funeral to screen those in attendance. But there had been no surprises. None of the prominent figures in the case had attended. Only a few members of Kay Neeley's church group and some old-line police officers who had served years ago with Tom Neeley.

Barney heard the blare of a horn and felt the sudden swerve.

Louis muttered, "Son of a bitch!" Barney knew someone had made a dangerous lane change. He smiled at the thought of what the press would do if he and Louis got wiped out on the freeway. The journalists would never accept two officers on a major case getting killed in an ordinary freeway accident.

The newspapers had been treating the twin killings of the Neeleys as the initial violence in a Mafia-controlled drug war. The tall TV reporter with the solid connections in the police department had gone further. She related the killings to a huge coast-to-coast sex-for-sale operation, and she promised her viewers some glamorous names in future reports.

All the pressures and collective heat from the press, the commissioner, and the district attorney's office had fallen heavily on the sagging shoulders of John Nolan. Barney felt a tinge of sympathy for the gray-faced bureaucrat with the perforated stomach wall. But so far Nolan had stood the test; despite all the pressures, he had not succumbed to entreaties from the district attorney's office to put a large team of Metro detectives on the case. Nolan was going down the line with Barney.

The diagram of names on the blackboard in Barney's office had grown a new arterial branch: "Frank Tedesco." Tedesco was a celebrity criminal who had pyramided an offshore Bahamian bank into a worldwide holding company, which had stolen more than three hundred million from its gullible stockholders. How much of the three hundred million had found its way into Tedesco's private Swiss account was a matter of speculation among authorities in eight European nations where his company had operated. Tedesco was also a key figure in laundered dollars that had figured prominently in the Watergate scandal. Tedesco lived in luxurious exile, in a villa high up in the mountains of Pétionville above Port-au-Prince. And if, in fact, the plot to kill Tom Neeley was hatched in Haiti, it was certain that Tedesco was part of it.

Barney rubbed his hand across his eyes and peered through the poisonous amber haze at the bleak sprawl of housing projects that sat on high ridges overlooking the shopping centers. He wondered what Tedesco's name was doing on a travel folder in Kay Neeley's possession. Why had she gone to Haiti? Why had she accompanied Tom to Germany? Why hadn't Tom gone with her to Haiti? What the hell were they after in Germany?

"Christ." The word hissed through his teeth.

"What?" Louis asked.

"Nothing." Barney sat up. "Just running the same goddamn questions."

"If we get a make on the guy in the wet suit, we'll be a little smarter," Louis offered.

"What about Neeley's military service file?" Barney asked.

"On the way, from National Personnel Record Center in St. Louis. I spoke to a Colonel Frank Merlo," Louis said. "They're treating it top priority."

Barney nodded, leaned forward, and turned on the radio. The "all news" station was broadcasting the local headline news: The state assembly in Sacramento had rejected a bill to permit the construction of a huge nuclear power plant called Sun Desert. The plant would have the kilowatt capacity to provide five percent of the state's electric power requirements. The bill had been beaten by a strong environmentalist lobby. The proponents of the bill warned that California would be in a severe energy shortage by 1985, but the governor had countered that California could rely on its constant sunshine for its future energy requirements.

They rode in silence for a moment, listening to the radio; then Louis turned it down. "I told my wife last night I didn't think I'd make it to retirement."

"Sure you will. You're on a downer. So am I. It's this fucking case."

"Maybe, I don't know. My uncle's got this vineyard up in Salinas. Wine business is booming. Might be good for me. And my son. I don't know if I'm doing any good being a cop. Maybe it's Tactical. The nature of it is political. When I was on the streets, when I worked Little Tokyo, I knew I was doing some good. Now, shit, I don't know."

"It's the case, Lou," Barney insisted. "You'd go nuts squeezing grapes in Salinas."

He turned the radio dial to an obscure AM station that played the music of the big band era. Woody Herman's "Woodchopper's Ball" was into the final chorus. The big band era was over long before Barney's time, but he found it soothing at times to listen to the old arrangements. He liked the way they clung to the melody line; even though the individual sidemen cut into the line for solos, they would always swing back, ensemble, into the main melody line. It was like police work. No matter the variations, the mutations, you followed the melody line.

CHAPTER

23 ☒

PAUL ISELLA STOOD IN THE PIT ALONGSIDE A GLEAMING RED FERRARI. Two men were adjusting the spoiler fin that jutted up from the rear of the car. Another man bent over the air scoop in front and blasted what looked like an air-pressure hose into the mouth of the scoop. The equipment of the film crew was scattered at various points around the track. They had augmented the hazy sunlight with huge carbon-burning lights.

Isella was talking to a bearded man dressed in safari jacket and khaki pants. Behind them, in the stands, a forty-foot-high camera platform had been erected, and a crew of six men were up on the platform standing by. There were other similar platforms at various points around the saucerlike track. A man at the base of each camera platform with a walkie-talkie waited to transmit directions from the director to the camera crews.

A red and yellow Lotus whirled around the high-banked curve at the far end of the track and came shooting past Isella and the director. They straightened up, waiting for the car to pass; it was impossible to be heard over the thunderous roar of the Lotus. Barney and Louis were in the stands just behind the pit area. They felt the heat and slight concussion as the low-slung car whizzed past them. The driver of the Lotus looked like a toy figure inside the glass bubble of the cockpit.

The slim young man in jeans who had identified himself to Barney and Louis as being the first assistant director had reached the pit area and was relaying Barney's message to Paul Isella.

Isella nodded at the young man and said something to the bearded director, then started toward Barney and Louis.

Isella was a stocky man with dark Mediterranean features. As he drew close, Barney could see his features in detail. He had a large, thick nose, which was flattened like the battered nose of a prizefighter. He had a wide, thin mouth and dark, recessed eyes. His hair was almost gone, but a patch of black clung to the sides of his head. His hands were large, but his fingers were slim and long. Isella walked stiffly, his neck bent slightly to the left.

Isella did not smile at them, nor did he offer any greeting. Louis took care of the introductions, and they showed their IDs. Isella just grunted and with undisguised annoyance said, "They're shooting the Lotus. I'm up next. You got five minutes."

"This won't take long," Louis said. "Laura Gregson told us she was with you the morning Tom Neeley was killed."

"That's right."

"Did you know Neeley?"

"I met Neeley once or twice at Leo Mirell's."

"Do you remember the girl Tom was with?"

"No. The place was full of cunt."

"When did you see Tom last?" Louis asked.

"A couple of weeks ago," Isella said. "He came out here. Asked me some questions and left."

"What kind of questions?"

Isella looked off at the red and yellow Lotus snaking around the high-banked curve on the far side of the track. "Look at that prick. He's turning fifteen thousand RPMs on the curve, never stabilize that in a race, not with jet streams coming back in his face."

"Tell us what Neeley asked you," Louis pressed.

"He wanted to know what kind of fuel we use."

Barney and Louis glanced at each other.

"That's all?" Louis asked.

"More or less. Now look, I got to get back there. That faggot director is paying me three grand a day."

"What kind of fuel do you use?" Barney asked.

"What the hell has that got to do with Neeley's murder?"

"Just answer my question!" Barney snapped.

"Methanol. That's a combination of alcohol and methane gas."

"What's the difference between that and regular gasoline?" Barney asked.

"Methanol has a cooling effect on the internal parts of the engine. If we used regular gasoline, we'd burn the engine up in minutes." Isella spit a dark blue lunger into one of the grandstand seats. "Can I go back to work now?"

"In a minute," Barney said. "What else did Tom ask you?"

"He asked if a regular car, a passenger car, could run on methanol, and I told him that any volatile fuel can be worked into an internal-combustion engine. It's a question of spark, lead, and octane rating. At what point the plugs fire." He scratched the stubble on his cheeks. "You can make gas with grain alcohol, or liquid oxygen, or even shit."

"Shit?" Barney asked.

"Yeah, take garbage, layer on layer of garbage creates methane gas. That's why garbage dumps and grain elevators explode."

"Do you have any idea why Tom was interested in the fuel?" Louis asked.

Isella shook his head. "No."

The director's voice boomed out over an amplifier. "We need you, Paul!"

Isella turned and waved at the bearded man, then looked at Barney. "Is that it?"

"Did Tom mention the word 'Genesis'?"

"No."

"What about 'Obermann'?"

"No. No Genesis. No Obermann." Isella's dark cheeks reddened, and his sunken eyes glared at Louis. "Now, how about taking a walk? You guys got nothing better to do. But I'm working, now fuck off!"

"You're not a very pleasant fellow," Louis said.

"Up yours, Tojo!" Isella sneered, turned, and took two steps before Louis spun him around and hit him twice in the solar plexus. Isella grabbed the pit of his stomach and fell to his knees, gasping for breath. He stared up at Louis, waiting for his breath to return, crouching like a wounded animal deciding whether to strike back.

Louis watched him, his almond-shaped eyes dead calm.

"I wouldn't do it if I were you," Barney said to Isella.

Isella slowly got to his feet, rubbed his stomach. "Aah, you fucking cops. A nickel a bunch!" He turned and lumbered back toward the waiting camera crew.

"I shouldn't have hit him," Louis said.

"Why not?"

"Race drivers don't live too long."

"That's got nothing to do with it."

Louis shook his head. "I shouldn't have hit him. I was wrong."

"Come on, Louis, we'll get caught in the rush hour."

CHAPTER

24 ⊠

THE DRAPES WERE DRAWN, ENCLOSING THE FOUR GLASS WALLS OF LEO Mirell's office. Leo Mirell sat behind a long L-shaped desk, crowded with papers and dominated by a large green console. His tie was off, and his collar was open at the throat. A cigarette burned in a ceramic ashtray.

The powerhouse agent looked tired and distraught. His regular features were betrayed by faded gray eyes rimmed with dark circles. He got to his feet, extended his hand to Barney, and indicated the chair in front of his desk. "Sit down, Lieutenant." He went back behind his desk, pulled the drape aside, peered at the city for a moment, then turned to Barney. "Christ. What a thing. Kay and Tom."

"Yeah," Barney agreed.

Leo sank down in the big high-backed chair, looked up at the ceiling, then leaned forward and picked up the burning cigarette. He took a deep lungful of smoke. "Forgive me if I'm direct," he said, "but I know you discussed certain aspects of this case with my chauffeur."

"Yes. Herbert was very cooperative."

"He told you the truth," Leo said. "Tom supplied coke. Laura supplied girls. There were parties at my home. I liked Tom. I liked Kay. I have no idea who killed them, much less any idea of why they were killed."

"You may know more than you think you know."

"I doubt it."

"Let's try. You know that Victor supplied Tom with cocaine."

"That was rumored."

"Did you supply your friends with cocaine?"

Leo smiled. "Would you really expect me to say yes to that?"

"Look." Barney sighed and leaned forward. "I'm not working Narcotics. If I was, I could book every suspect in this case for felonious use of drugs or being in the presence of drugs. I'm leveling with you, Leo. I am only interested in finding the killer or killers of Tom and Kay Neeley."

Leo rubbed his eyes wearily. "All right, let's say cocaine was around at my parties. Let's say I have certain clients who look to me for a snort once in a while. But I don't deal cocaine. I'm a very rich man. I don't peddle drugs."

"Did Arthur Clements use coke?"

Leo snuffed out his cigarette and exhaled the last of the smoke. "That's a question for Clements, isn't it?"

"Are you afraid of Clements?"

"I can't nail people on innuendos and rumors."

"Okay, simple question. Did Clements arrange trips for Tom? Bag trips? The transporting of hot money?"

Leo looked at Barney, then poured some water from a carafe into a small glass. "That was around. I heard it. I don't know if it's a fact."

"Did Tom ever mention the word 'Genesis'?"

"No."

"Did Kay ever mention it?"

"Not to me."

"How about 'Obermann'? Did either of them ever mention 'Obermann'?"

"No. Never heard of it."

"You're sure?"

"Come on, Lieutenant." Leo sighed. "Let's be honest. You've checked me out. And if you had anything, you would have seen me days ago. You know I'm not involved in these killings. You also know that I can't implicate other people."

Barney looked into Leo's eyes for a long time, then nodded and got to his feet. "You're right. But the thing is, Leo, that whoever killed the Neeleys may be going down a list."

Leo lit a fresh cigarette, and Barney noticed dark rings of perspiration under the armpits of his blue shirt. "You think there's a list?"

"Why would that bother you? You're not a man with enemies. You've got nothing on your conscience."

Leo got to his feet and paced the length of the wall behind his desk, then stopped suddenly and walked up to Barney. "The safest course of action for me is to keep my mouth shut. I'm sorry, but that's how I see things. Now, it's three in the morning in London, and I have a million-dollar director sitting in the Dorchester Hotel waiting for me to return his call. So if there's nothing else . . ."

"There is one last thing," Barney said. "Frank Tedesco."

Leo puffed nervously on the cigarette, and Barney detected a slight quiver in his fingers.

"What about him?" Leo asked softly.

"Did you ever hear Neeley or Victor Maldonado mention Frank Tedesco?"

Leo seemed to pale. He walked quickly back to his desk and poured some water, drank it, and dropped into his chair.

"I think the meeting is over, Lieutenant."

"Okay," Barney said. "But whatever is frightening you probably is the same thing that terrified Kay. And if she had leveled with me, I might have saved her. Thanks for your time."

Barney turned and started for the door. His hand was on the knob when Leo's voice stopped him. "Wait!"

Barney turned; Leo had taken a Kleenex from the desk drawer and was dabbing at the beads of perspiration on his forehead. He took another long swallow of water.

"Tedesco supplied the cocaine directly to Tom through a courier."

"How do you know that?"

"Tom told me."

"Did Maldonado approve or set up the operation?"

"I don't know."

"If you were me, would you make that assumption?"

Leo swallowed, and his teeth chewed his lower lip; then he nodded. "Yes, if I were in your place, I would assume Victor was connected."

"Did you ever meet the courier?"

"No."

"Did Tom ever mention the courier?"

"Yes."

Barney could feel the adrenaline starting to roll. "This is critical, Leo. Try and remember exactly what Tom said."

"He said she was a fantasy."

"She?" Barney repeated.

"Yes. The courier was a girl."

"And he called her a fantasy?"

"I think he said she was *like* a fantasy."

"Did he describe her?"

"No."

"Okay, Leo. We'll talk again."

"Lieutenant!"

Barney turned back to the sweating man.

"Do you think I'm safe?"

"No one's safe, Leo. You have a connected group of people, like an organism. Then suddenly a cell goes crazy, people start to die. Tom Neeley, a hungry ex-cop, gets seven slugs, one at a time, from his cock up to his brain. His wife gets a red-hot cigarette stuck up her insides and all over her body, and then they blow the side of her face away. Someone is looking for something. Something the Neeleys were after in Germany. Something called Genesis, and until I know what that is, no one is safe."

CHAPTER

25 ⊠

BARNEY EXAMINED THE DOCUMENTS RAY COLLINS AT ISI HAD SENT over. The top sheet contained the names of the board of directors of the Seneca Corporation. Frank Tedesco was on the list, with Clements, Maldonado, and twelve other names that ISI had no criminal file on. Barney assumed the other names belonged to men and women whose companies had merged with Seneca for legitimate business reasons.

There was another batch of stapled Xerox sheets containing a variety of articles on Adam Steiffel: a *Who's Who Biography;* a Los Angeles *Times* feature article written in 1963; a *Time* magazine cover story; *Newsweek; Forbes; Business Week; Fortune; Esquire;* and two English newspapers: the *Observer* and *Guardian.* Barney thumbed through them quickly, then placed them in a manila folder.

He got up and walked over to a steel cabinet, opened the top drawer, dropped the file in, took out a bottle of Bushmills, poured a drink, and went to the window. The late-afternoon sun managed a yellow glare that burned through the photochemical haze hanging over the city.

He thought about Paul Isella and the baffling questions Neeley had asked of Isella. Why had Tom been interested in the chemical composition of the racing fuel? The Isella question turned his thoughts to Laura Gregson. He could still see her face on the pillow in that streaky light, with her eyes half closed, and that low, hoarse, desperate whisper: *"There. Right there!"*

He wanted to see her again. He knew she regarded him as a trick. She called it business. But it made no difference to Barney.

The door opened, and Louis came in, looking tired.

"A drink?" Barney asked, and Louis nodded.

Barney poured the Bushmills. "I got the corporate makeup on Seneca. Frank Tedesco is on the board." He handed Louis the glass.

"That ties Tedesco to the mob," Louis said.

"That's right. Even the Senate Subcommittee on Organized Crime couldn't do that." Both men sipped the amber-colored whiskey. Barney said, "Mirell is frightened. Just like Kay Neeley. He confirmed the cocaine came from Tedesco."

Barney tossed the brandy down, walked over to the diagram on the blackboard, and, with a piece of red chalk, drew a line connecting the names Tedesco, Clements, and Steiffel. "How does that strike you, Lou?"

"You can't make that connection."

"Why not?"

"Adam Steiffel is an industrial aristocrat. He's the goddamn American dream. How can you tie him to the mob?"

"They're all part of the same dream. You remember those rumors about the attorney general using the CIA to recruit Giancana and Rosselli to kill Castro?"

"So what?"

"So if the judicial branch of government and the CIA and the Mafia have contacts, don't you think they connect with the powers of American industry? Listen, make no mistake, ITT called some shots in Chile." Barney turned from the blackboard. "Everyone's heard of the underworld, but what about the overworld? Big business. Big government. Big banking. Big oil. Communications. Insurance. Mafia. OPEC. And here"—Barney tapped the blackboard—"you can begin to see the overworld pattern. Believe me, Lou, I know. We used to make these charts at Langley."

"What does it tell you?" Louis asked.

"That there's some common interest between Clements, Steiffel, and Tedesco. The Neeleys were killed because they threatened those interests."

"The overworld is a handle," Louis persisted. "Another name for power, but what the hell does it prove? We're still dealing with pieces that don't make a picture."

Barney slumped down into his chair and began to tap a long yellow pencil against the surface of the desk. "Why was Tom interested in the racing fuel?"

"Suppose he was onto a new type engine, an engine that could run on methanol," Louis offered.

"Why would Tom be into that?" Barney asked.

"Remember what Isella said," Louis replied. "An alcohol-based fuel cools the engine. Meaning the engine parts would last long beyond their present life. A passenger car whose engine ran on methanol would be revolutionary."

"But how does Tom Neeley figure in that?" Barney asked.

"Maybe he stumbled onto something in Germany," Louis replied.

"Tom wasn't into exotic fuels and racing cars. He liked dope and women," Barney said.

"And money."

"Yeah. And money," Barney concurred.

The door opened, and a uniformed cop named Pete Schroeder who worked in Communications came in. "We got something coming in on the telex. It may be about the dead guy in the wet suit."

Tactical Communications was a windowless room with a huge push-button console and two telex machines. Barney, Louis, and Schroeder stood in a semicircle around the seated officer who operated the telex. They watched expectantly as the keys moved in involuntary bursts, printing combinations of unintelligible words. Then the keys fell silent. The machine whirred and clicked, but nothing happened.

"Trouble?" Barney asked the operator.

"Maybe. I sent them a 'ready to receive,' but nothing's come back."

"Send it again," Barney snapped.

The operator punched the keys, and they flew up at the cylindrical paper:

LAPD-TACTICAL-LA-TELEX #167432 to PARIS INTER-POL—#333878: WE RECEIVED YOUR "STANDBY" AND ACKNOWLEDGE AND WAITING. PLEASE ADVISE. IS LINE OPERATIVE?

The machine sputtered, whirred, and clicked, but nothing appeared on the glassed-in paper.

Without looking away from the machine, the operator offered, "Sometimes there's a sudden line break."

"What do we do?" Louis asked.

"We wait," the operator said.

Sergeant Schroeder went over to a small coffee machine. "You guys want some coffee? It's fresh."

Louis shook his head, and Barney said, "No, thanks."

They stood quietly staring at the sputtering machine. After the better part of three minutes the keys of the telex machine suddenly flew across the paper:

INTER-PARIS TO #167432 LAPD-TACTICAL. READY
NOW. ACKNOWLEDGE.

The operator pressed a sending key and punched: "LA #167432
READY." He then depressed the send button and pressed a key
marked "Receive." There was a flurry of whirring electric current and a
hail of clicking, followed by a furious battering of the keys pounding
the message from Paris across the paper:

HAVE MADE POSITIVE ID ON YOUR SUSPECT—PER
YOUR REQUEST 3/16. PRINTS BELONG TO PRIMO SAN-
TIAGO. AGE 34 CITIZEN CALI, COLOMBIA. PASSPORT
#666222. ALSO HAS AKA-PRIMO SANCHEZ DE OBRE-
GON. SUSPECT ALSO CARRIED HAITIAN PASSPORT
#(98657). ARRESTED ORLY AIRPORT 6/8/75 SMUG-
GLING COCAINE. RELEASED AND EXTRADITED TO CO-
LOMBIA PER REQUEST COLOMBIAN AMBASSADOR
PARIS: SUSPECT WANTED IN BOGOTA FOR QUESTION-
ING IN HOMICIDE CASE. MORE.

The keys stopped printing. The machine hummed and clicked. They
watched in awe, as if the telex machine were the most miraculous invention since Cro-Magnon man had rubbed his stones together and produced a spark.
    The keys suddenly flew against the paper:

FOLLOWING FROM OUR DEUXIEME BUREAU: SUSPECT
WAS A COMPANION OF "ANTONELLA GRIMALDI"
MEMBER ITALIAN RED BRIGADES. END MESSAGE.
PLEASE ACKNOWLEDGE.

The keys fell silent, and the operator pressed the send lever and
punched out:

LA ACKNOWLEDGES. RECEIVED AND UNDERSTOOD.
PLEASE WAIT.

The operator looked up at Barney. "Anything else?"
"Ask him if he has a location on Antonella Grimaldi."
The operator punched the message up on the line, then pressed the

receive lever and waited. There was a delay of less than a minute; then the keys hit the paper:

ANTONELLA GRIMALDI KILLED IN ATTEMPTED BOMB-ING OF FIAT FACTORY—MILAN—5/6/77.

The keys fell silent, and Barney said, "Give them our thanks."

The operator hit the keys, exchanging salutations with his unseen colleague six thousand miles away. The operator then opened the glass receptacle and tore off the message and handed it back to Barney.

Back in his office, Barney chalked the name Primo Santiago into the diagram. He then stepped back and examined the names.

TOM NEELEY

KAY NEELEY————————————————————————————LEO MIRELL

ARTHUR CLEMENTS

ADAM STEIFFEL—————LAURA GREGSON————VICTOR MALDONADO

PAUL ISELLA

PRIMO SANTIAGO   FRANK TEDESCO

There was a total of ten names. Louis came in and said he had spoken with the Colombian consul general in San Francisco and advised him that they were holding the unclaimed body of a Colombian national in the L.A. County Morgue.

Barney nodded and picked up the file on Adam Steiffel. Behind him the exterior yellow daylight was beginning to go blue.

Louis said, "The Interpol report tends to confirm the cocaine link. The guy was a convicted cocaine smuggler."

"Yeah," Barney said. "The Neeleys may have gotten someone angry. Someone on the cocaine pipeline."

"You don't believe that for a minute, do you?" Louis smiled.

"No, I don't. This dead guy in the wet suit had terrorist connections," Barney said. " 'Genesis' might be a code name for some terrorist operation. Maybe it was tied into one of Neeley's bag trips. Kidnapping is a major industry in Europe."

"You're reaching, Barney. It's dope."

"Maybe you're right, Lou." Barney sighed. "Maybe it's all just cocaine."

CHAPTER

26 ☒

THE GIRL CAME UP THE ESCALATOR AT THE LOUVRE STOP ON THE Métro and walked out into the special blue light that belongs exclusively to twilight in Paris. She loved the city. Paris had always been her place. The affinity she felt for it had nothing to do with Raoul or any of her past lovers. It was the city itself. In an otherwise ugly antiseptic world of glass and steel, Paris remained beautiful, eternal, and indestructible.

She passed the Meurice Hotel, and the uniformed doorman tipped his cap. She was glad that the Hôtel du Bac had been chosen for her rendezvous because it permitted her to walk along the turn-of-the-century elegance of the Rue de Rivoli. She reached the corner and crossed into the manicured beauty of the Tuileries Gardens. The lights had just come on, illuminating the flower-lined walkways.

The evening was balmy, and she strolled casually through the splashes of vivid red roses and lavender-colored lilacs. She passed small children playing with tiny boats in the luminous fountains of the gardens. The nannies of the children were blond au-pairs from Germany. The girl had no trouble recognizing their cheap Hamburg accents.

She came out of the park and crossed over to the Pont Royal Bridge. She noticed some old men fishing along both banks of the Seine. The fishermen were not bothered by the gaily lit boats that moved leisurely up the ancient river. The image of the old men fishing in the twilight reminded her of a Sisley canvas in the Jeu de Paume Museum.

There was a strong, briny smell coming off the Seine, and she breathed it in deeply. She felt fine. She was over her jet lag. Raoul had met her at the futuristic tunnel of Charles De Gaulle Airport and driven her home. She slept for seven hours and woke up hungry. Raoul fixed her steak and *pommes-frites,* and they drank two bottles of Mouton-

Cadet 1974. They smoked two long Thai sticks of hash and made love furiously for the better part of the night.

But something disturbing had occurred. She had not been able to reach orgasm. It was the first time that had happened with Raoul. She thought it might have been fatigue; but she had rested, and Raoul had done all the things she liked. All the things she had taught him to do with the same abandon, the same lack of restraint. None of it worked. She faked the right sounds and motions. She didn't want him to know that she had been unable to reach a climax. Perhaps it was only temporary.

She knew better, though. It was part of a pattern that had started after the first killing. The one in Copenhagen. The Israeli military attaché they had machine-gunned to death in the café off Helmstrom plads. When she saw the man fall, spurting that dark arterial blood, that's when it began. She was sleeping with Klaus in those days, and that night —the night of the killing—she had felt nothing when they made love.

She would try again with Raoul tonight. It would be all right. Raoul was special. He was beautiful and gifted and never asked questions. He believed her or at least wanted to believe her when she had told him she traveled for a cosmetic firm. Raoul was a medical student at the Sorbonne. And up to now they had been very good together.

The sudden image of Tom Neeley's shuddering death throes broke through the surface of her consciousness, forcing her to stop for a moment. She rested her elbows on the railing of the Pont Royal and gulped the sharp, fresh bite of the Seine.

The Rue du Bac was a quiet residential street with a few small hotels run by private families. The street traffic was light, and only a handful of pedestrians waited patiently at the corner for the St.-Germain bus.

The girl walked up the steps of the Hôtel du Bac and entered the small lobby. She smiled at the Algerian boy behind the desk and turned sharply left and entered the bar.

Seated at a table at the far end of the bar, his back to the wall, was the man whose photograph she had been given. The man called Antonio. He had a long, thin nose from which a thin stream of cigarette smoke poured. He was reading Le Figaro and sipping coffee. He looked up as she entered, and his thin lips pulled back into a semblance of a smile. He rose and kissed her on both cheeks. She sat down alongside, and he signaled the bartender for another coffee.

They talked about a current film until the bartender came over with the coffee and went back behind the bar to his racing form. Antonio spoke English that was heavily laced with a northern Italian accent.

"Comrade Tedesco is upset with you." He spoke without a trace of emotion.

She sipped the strong coffee and shrugged. "It was a judgment I had to make. I thought it safer to come directly to Paris than spend a night in Miami."

"You had no right to think. The practice of terrorism requires the sublimation of all individual thought."

The quote was pure Dr. Habash. She was dealing with a robot. A cold clinical theoretician, the kind of revolutionary she despised. "Spare me your philosophical horseshit, Comrade," she said angrily. "Do you want my report or not?"

"Actually, no," he said icily. "We are current with all the events in Los Angeles."

She wasn't surprised, but it bothered her that the thin-faced, pale man knew more than she did. She lit a Gauloise and asked, "Did they see the woman Kay Neeley?"

"Yes. The woman was eliminated. She knew nothing. She merely accompanied her former husband."

"How can you be certain of that?" the girl asked.

"The method of torture employed by Primo was not terribly sophisticated," he replied. "If the Neeley woman had been aware of any contact between her former husband and the Swiss, she would have said so." Antonio picked at the yellow of a pimple on his chin. "She admitted her former husband had contacted Obermann. Nothing more."

He lifted his coffee cup, and she detected a slight feminine movement he made with his wrist. She wondered why so many of them in the movement were homosexuals. It was true of the women as well. She remembered a Czechoslovakian girl who had accompanied her to a meeting in Tripoli. And that night the Czech girl had pleaded with her.

The man crushed his Gitane cigarette and matter-of-factly said, "Primo is dead."

"When?" she asked.

"A week ago. At the Neeley woman's beach house. They were having trouble with the rubber boat. They saw a man enter the beach house minutes after the killing. Primo went after him. The man was a Los Angeles detective. He killed Primo on the beach."

"And Kerem?" she asked.

"Got away."

"Thank God." She sighed. She admired the older man and believed his dedication was genuine. So many of them were adventurers. "Where is Kerem?"

"Kerem was eliminated yesterday. In Port-au-Prince."

"Eliminated?" she said fearfully. "Why? By whom?"

"In Tedesco's opinion Comrade Kerem had become unnecessary."

There was nothing more to say. She waited for Antonio to give her the orders.

He signaled for the check. The bartender came over, and Antonio dropped a ten-franc note. The man thanked him and left. Antonio turned to her, and his breath carried a strong odor of tobacco. "For the moment you will stay in the Paris apartment." He rose, kissed the top of her dark hair, and softly said, "Take care, *chérie.*"

The night sky had turned a brilliant blue. But the girl no longer felt the beauty of the city. She was thinking of Frank Tedesco, and with him came images of the black, swollen bellies of the Haitian children, squatting in the streets that ran with raw sewage. She wondered if revolution and terror would change things. If men like Tedesco and Yasir in Beirut really cared to change life for the children, or was it power? Were they all the same man: those they killed and those who ordered the killings? The Soviet imperialists. Castro. And her own hero, Klaus, in Munich. Were they all the same person? And in the end would nothing change? She had once believed in freedom, but they said that only through blind obedience could the revolutionary victory be reached. That would be the day of universal brotherhood. It was not a goal to be questioned, and one could try only to effect the change—by whatever means. Yes, that was it. For the moment, for this time in history, terror was the only philosophy worth practicing. Terror brought chaos, and with the chaos came the vacuum. The revolution would fill the vacuum. Violence and the temporary loss of freedom were a small price to pay for the realization of universal brotherhood.

CHAPTER

27 ☒

BARNEY, DRESSED IN GRAY SLACKS AND LIGHT BLUE TURTLENECK, sipped a vodka on the rocks and read the file on Adam Steiffel. Kathy had left a note at the desk. She had flown to Denver.

Barney was not upset by her absence. Since Kay's death he could not accommodate Kathy's inane in-flight stories, and their sexual activity had become a performance. They both knew the relationship was at an end.

Barney read from the *Forbes* magazine piece dated June 1973. Adam Steiffel's father had crossed the Great Divide and come west in a caravan of settlers, battling the elements and the Indians, grinding their way toward the Oklahoma Territory. He had brought in the first oil gusher in the state of Oklahoma and organized his fellow wildcatters into paramilitary squads to protect their wells from the hired thugs of John D. Rockefeller. Steiffel's father was also politically astute and backed the right state candidates with hard cash. The governor of Oklahoma was a bourbon-sipping friend, as were both senators from the new state.

Young Steiffel was sent to military schools in the East and, after graduating and through his father's political connections, was one of two students nominated by both Oklahoma senators for admission to the West Point Military Academy. Adam Steiffel graduated third in the class of 1922. He traveled abroad for two years, then returned and attended Harvard University, where he was awarded a master's degree in business administration.

Barney shifted from the *Forbes* piece to the *Time* magazine cover story on Steiffel. In the summer of 1935, at the height of the Great Depression, Adam's father was killed in the crash of a small private plane at Midland, Texas. The landing attempt was made in a howling dust storm, and the plane hit a tin-roofed repair shed at the edge of the field and blew up. There was nothing left of his father for Adam to bury. A simple memorial tablet was erected in the Lutheran Cemetery outside Tulsa.

Adam assumed control of Tidal Oil. He carefully analyzed all areas of the company's activities. He engaged expert geologists to survey the productivity factor of the original oil fields at Red Sands. The report was gloomy. The geologists estimated that the fields would run dry in fifteen years at the current rate of pumping. Adam began to move Tidal's operations away from drilling and exploration. He concentrated the company's efforts toward the acquisition of refineries and the transportation of crude. He purchased a fleet of oil trucks and seagoing tankers and organized a coast-to-coast chain of gas stations. The new focus of activity required all the ongoing revenue from the oil fields, plus a hefty loan from an old Harvard chum who was highly placed at the Chase Manhattan Bank in New York.

Over the years the company acquired controlling interests in distilleries, fertilizer plants, coal mines, pharmaceuticals, agricultural land, bull semen, and vast holdings in grain and cattle.

The gross revenue of Tidal Oil went from eighteen million in 1935 to three billion in 1975. The company had more than a hundred thirty thousand employees and six million stockholders. Tidal Oil had never missed a dividend and was regarded as one of the bluest blue chips on the Big Board.

Adam Steiffel was the first major American industrialist to do business with Red China. When asked by the *Time* magazine interviewer if he had any qualms about doing business with the giant communist nation, Adam replied with his now-famous slogan: "When money talks, people listen."

Barney began to feel the numbing effect of the vodka and the tension release that came with it.

He closed his eyes and saw Kay Neeley after Torres had clamped her jaws together; a strange grin had formed on the dead woman's face.

Barney shook off the nightmare image of Kay, sipped some more cold vodka, and went back to the *Time* article. Steiffel's current wife was his fourth; they had married in 1950. Loretta Steiffel was thirty years younger than her husband and, according to the photograph in the *Time* article, a handsome woman. She was socially prominent and a leading figure in the cultural aspects of city life. An invitation to one of Loretta Steiffel's private dinner parties was an indication of one's lofty social and financial standing in the community.

Steiffel himself was a man of taste, style, and ruthless intelligence.

According to the *Time* article, Steiffel had known Hoover, Roosevelt, the Rockefellers, Henry Ford, John L. Lewis, Adolf Hitler, Benito Mussolini, Eisenhower, Truman, the Kennedys, Nixon, Kissinger, Faisal, and the shah of Iran. He was a major contributor to candidates of both political parties, and some of the most renowned figures in the House and Senate were among Steiffel's personal friends.

In the winter of 1973, during the Arab oil embargo, Steiffel was unanimously appointed chairman of the National Petroleum Council by his colleagues. The *Time* article called him the "godfather" of the American oil industry. He was a collector of Impressionist art, and the National Gallery in Washington had an entire wing of Steiffel-donated paintings. The Sloan-Kettering Institute in New York had been the beneficiary of a huge cancer research grant from the old man, and there was an open-end scholarship program at UCLA, USC, and Cal State for underprivileged students of merit.

Barney got up, went into the kitchen, fixed a cup of hot tea, took a few bites of the cold roast beef sandwich, but had no appetite.

The phone on the wet bar rang. It was Louis. His voice was tense. "Victor Maldonado, along with his bodyguard and chauffeur, was blown up thirty minutes ago."

Barney sucked in his breath, let it out slowly. "Where did it happen?"

"In the parking lot of the Stardust Hotel in Las Vegas."

"Christ," Barney murmured.

There was a moment of silence, and Louis asked, "What do you think?"

"I think it's unrelated. But I'm guessing," Barney said. "Listen, Lou, first thing in the morning call St. Louis and find out what the hell happened to Neeley's military records."

"Okay," Louis replied.

Barney hung up, went into the bedroom, undressed, and took a long hot shower. He came out, toweled off briskly, slipped on his robe, and went back into the living room. He poured a fresh vodka and spun the ice with his forefinger.

Barney considered the lack of imagination of Maldonado's killers. Their method was very old, but still held in high esteem. Two sticks of eighty percent TNT wired to the ignition.

The phone rang. It was Laura Gregson. "Did I wake you?" she asked.

"No. What is it, Laura?"

"I assume you've heard about Victor?" Her voice was calm and flat.

"Yes. A few minutes ago," Barney replied.

"Do you think someone's going down a list, killing Tom Neeley's friends and relatives?"

"No, I don't think Victor's death is related to the Neeleys. He probably skimmed some money that didn't belong to him." Barney paused, then asked, "Where are you, Laura?"

"In bed," she purred.

"Alone?"

"Alone. In bed, wearing a drop of Joy."

He could feel himself getting aroused and knew there was no immediate future in that. "What did you want, Laura?"

"I wanted your opinion about Victor's death."

"Well, you have it. Of course, I may be wrong."

"I'd like to see you, Barney."

"When?"

"Whenever," she said.

"I'll call you."

"Do that," she whispered.

He hung up, wondering why she had called him, and what had happened to her affair with Paul Isella, and what she knew about Victor Maldonado's execution.

Maldonado's death made one thing a certainty: Another chalked name on the diagram could be marked "deceased," bringing the total to four: Tom Neeley, Kay Neeley, Primo Santiago, Victor Maldonado.

Barney drained the chilled vodka, went over to the sofa, stretched out, and picked up the thick file on Adam Steiffel.

CHAPTER

28 ⊠

THE TIDAL OIL BUILDING WAS ONLY FIVE BLOCKS EAST OF TACTICAL, on Wilshire. The building was something of an architectural celebrity. It was concave and looked like a towering glass wave about to break over Wilshire Boulevard. The glass had a mirrorlike reflective quality, and when the clouds were right, it appeared as if the sky were drifting over the upper floors. It was a vivid illusion which gave the building a remarkable dreamlike appearance.

The lobby was a giant atrium whose glass ceiling rose five floors. There were two live coconut palm trees growing on either side of the slim shaft of steel and glass that contained the six elevators. A waterfall cascaded down from the top of the atrium through a staggered marble spillway. The force of the waterfall threw a cool breeze across the dazzling interior. Barney thought the design of the lobby was calculated to place the visitor in instant awe and subliminally set up the power and importance of the executives who resided in the floors above.

Barney walked to the elevator marked "Express 18th Floor." The doors were open, and two young women holding containers of coffee were talking about the diseases of their respective children. They rode up the eighteen floors in fewer than ten seconds.

Three walls of Adam Steiffel's outer office were green Italian marble; the fourth was darkly tinted glass. There was only one decoration on the wall behind the secretary; it was a sepia-colored photograph of a sandy hillside covered with old-fashioned oil derrick rigs. A caption under its wooden frame read: "RED SANDS—1923."

Steiffel's executive secretary was a middle-aged, pleasant-looking woman who sat behind a large mahogany desk. "You're the Detective Caine who phoned?"

"That's right."

"May I see your identification?"

Barney gave her his leather ID case. She jotted his badge number on a piece of notepaper and handed the case back to him.

"Thank you." She lifted the receiver on the phone console, pressed a button. She said nothing but held the receiver to her ear a brief moment. She hung up, looked at Barney, and indicated a blond oak door set into the marble wall to her left. "In there, Mr. Caine." She pressed a button on the desk, which set off a clicking sound from the lock mechanism in the door.

Barney walked quickly to the door, opened it, and entered the office. The door swung shut behind him. The room was deep, wide, and dimly lit. Its windows were draped, cloaking the room in semidarkness. Barney stood still just inside the door, trying to adjust his eyes to the gloom. It seemed to be more of a study than an office. A small wooden plaque on the far wall bore the inscription *"When Money Talks, People Listen."* The room was expertly soundproofed, and the silence was finite, like the silence of a tomb.

Barney saw the thin, solitary figure sitting on a sofa, spooning yogurt out of a paper container. Adam Steiffel was staring at him. Barney did not move or speak. The old man put the paper container down, touched a napkin delicately to his lips, and the grave voice floated across the room. "They tell me you were with the CIA."

"That's right."

The old man fell silent for a moment, but his eyes never left Barney. "Have a seat, Mr. Caine."

Barney walked across the blood-red carpet and sat down opposite Adam Steiffel.

The hooded eyes peered at Barney again. "You must forgive me this lighting. But my eyes object to concentrated light."

Barney could see the old man's face in detail. His skin was taut and cracked by severe lines; it reminded Barney of wet cardboard that had been left to dry in the sun. Steiffel's eyes were small and very blue, and there was something accusatory about them. His nose was thin and large, but not ugly, and his mouth was small and full with curvy lips like those of a child. It was a face of disharmony that was somehow pulled together by the bright blue eyes. But the one outstanding feature that gave the old man majesty and authority was a long, thick mane of glowing silver hair. It framed his face like a mantle of white purity. The backs of his hands were covered with liver spots, and the knuckle on his right hand was disfigured.

But his fingers had the long, thin, sensitive appearance of a concert violinist. He opened a humidor. "Cigar, Mr. Caine?"

The raspy, ghostlike quality of Steiffel's voice was contagious, and Barney found himself whispering involuntarily. "No, thank you."

The old man used a gold cutter to slice the end off his cigar. He picked up a leather-bound lighter and lit the cigar, carefully turning its end slowly through the flame. He sucked the smoke in, inhaling the cigar.

"Is it true you speak Spanish?"

"Yes," Barney replied.

"I'm always in awe of Americans who have mastered foreign languages. We are a people who tend to disregard the fact that there are other languages spoken on this planet."

Barney did not answer, and the old man stared at him for a moment, then spoke in that thin, hollow voice.

"You were stationed in Spanish-speaking countries while you served in the CIA." It was not posed as a question; it was a statement of fact.

"Yes."

Steiffel leaned back and studied Barney. Neither man spoke for what seemed a long time. The accusatory blue eyes made Barney nervous. The old man knocked his cigar ash into a large black enamel ashtray. "They tell me you're divorced and that you have a son."

"What else do they tell you?"

"Well, they tell me you want to inquire about Tom Neeley's activities on my behalf."

"In principle," Barney replied.

Adam Steiffel got to his feet. He was more than six feet tall, and his neat blue suit hung perfectly on his narrow shoulders. He pressed a button on the fieldstone wall, and the drapes swung open, exposing a wall of tinted glass that faced out over the city. The light that entered the room had a blue cast to it and lit their faces with a cyan tone.

The old man peered out at the city for a moment. "California was something fifty years ago. Orange groves all the way from the North Valley to the Pacific." He turned from the window and took a few steps toward Barney, puffing on the cigar and inhaling the smoke. "You know when the first oil well was drilled in this country?"

Steiffel did not wait for an answer. "The first strike was in Pennsylvania in 1859. And old J. D. Rockefeller and his thugs closed in fast. And by 1905 ten percent of U.S. energy ran on oil." Steiffel stood in the center of the room, like a soldier at attention. "My father brought in the first well in Oklahoma, between the Red River and the Kansas border.

Hell, in those days, the oil just poured out of eastern Oklahoma. Then came Texas and California. By 1925 the U.S.A. produced seventy percent of the world's oil." He paced a few quick steps. "You have any idea what a barrel of oil sold for in 1930?" Barney shook his head, and the old man smiled. "Ten cents. That's a fact. A barrel of oil sold for one thin dime; up to 1953 we supplied half the oil for the world. And now"—he sighed heavily—"we produce less than twenty percent of our own requirements."

Adam Steiffel paused and almost reflectively said, "The trouble with Americans is their divine belief in technology." He thrust the cigar out at Barney. "By 1985 the price of Arabian crude will triple. The standard of living of every American citizen will plunge. The industrial nations will be in a fierce battle for the remaining oil. Old alliances will shatter; it will be every man for himself. You were in the CIA. You must be aware of their 1975 report that projects global chaos by 1987: runaway inflation; industrial shutdowns; catastrophic unemployment; worthless paper money, like Germany in 1930. And we know what happened there. The vacuum of chaos is always filled by a man on a white horse. It will be the end of Western democracy." The old man brushed his brilliant silver hair. "The lights will slowly flicker out; farms will be abandoned; schools will be dark. The sick will die in frigid hospitals. The cars and planes will stand idle. Millions will be destitute." He took a few steps toward Barney, inhaling deeply on the cigar. He spoke in a low, confidential voice. "Myself and my colleagues stand in the breach, between salvation and obliteration. Our responsibility is the realm of megabodies. If we cannot provide energy for two hundred fifty million Americans in 1985, what in God's name will happen to them and this great Republic?"

Barney shrugged. "I have no idea."

The old man sat down opposite Barney. "But you must have an opinion. You must care. You would not have spent time in dangerous government service if you were a man without conviction."

Barney realized Steiffel had maneuvered him into an ambient state of being less than caring and intellectually inferior when measured against the magnitude of the old man's responsibilities.

Barney sighed. "I have no convictions about geopolitical energy problems. I'm just a cop, Mr. Steiffel."

The old man smiled. "Well, don't ever be anything but proud. Being a police officer is a fine and noble occupation. And perhaps I paint too hopeless a picture. Remember one thing, son: When money talks, people listen. And we still have a few cards to play."

"Who's we?" Barney asked.

"Myself and my colleagues. OPEC is a dagger aimed at the heart of the free world, but so far we have outmaneuvered those hot-handed Arabs. We have them holding eighty billion in U.S. currency, and if we go down, their holdings are reduced to worthless paper. In a sense you might say OPEC is our invention." He sucked at the cigar and continued.

"They have to be considerate of what happens to the old U.S.A. It cost those Arabs thirty cents a barrel to get the oil out of the sand, and they charge us anywhere from fourteen to twenty dollars a barrel, and it's going higher every day, son. That's over forty times the cost of production. But they have to take our dollars. And we send them military hardware. Of course, we have to do business their way. Their goddamn middlemen have to be bought."

"Which brings us to Tom Neeley," Barney said.

"I guess it does."

"How did you meet Tom?"

"Through my good friend Arthur Clements. I needed someone like Tom. Someone I could trust. Someone who was hungry but not starving. Someone well schooled in police methods."

"Yes, I can see where Tom would have been the perfect bag man."

"I dislike that term," the old man said. "I would say Tom was a pragmatist. I think Tom understood that life is a struggle of civilized people to sustain themselves against the forces of atheism and tyranny."

Barney got up, went over to the coffee table, and poured some water out of a carafe. He drank it all and turned back to the old man. The bright blue, birdlike eyes were fastened on his own. Barney realized the old man had led him along a pseudopatriotic line that contained a veiled threat in almost every passage: that thing about worthless dollars, and no oil by 1987. And megabodies. And the global cataclysm. And how distasteful, but necessary, it was to grease the Arabs in the name of American survival. And the delicate balance of it all. Barney decided it was time to test the waters.

"I have to admit," he said, "that all of what you say may be over my head. But I don't see how buying off Arab middlemen helps a fading American morality. Or how maintaining the price of oil at a four hundred percent markup protects us from atheism. I think you're all a bunch of highwaymen, Mr. Steiffel."

The old man glared at him, then placed the cigar in the ashtray. "You're a patriot, son. A true patriot. I know all about you. So I forgive your ignorance." Then Steiffel's voice trembled, and the words came in a slow-motion cadence. "But don't you ever again accuse me of being a highwayman."

Barney felt the unmistakable dimension of evil, the kind of evil that is nourished by incredible power. Barney knew he had made a mistake. He should not have questioned Steiffel's dedication or honesty.

"I'm not your enemy, Mr. Steiffel," he said gently. "You must understand my position. I'm here only because you may shed some light on two brutal homicides."

"I do understand, son. Now sit down. I dislike looking up. It bothers the sciatic nerve in my neck. I'll answer all your questions."

Barney came over and sat down opposite Steiffel. "When did Tom make the last trip for you?"

"Two months ago. He carried half a million dollars to Yussef Kaladi, in his villa in the EUR section of Rome."

"Who's Kaladi?" Barney asked.

"A Saudi agent, a payoff man."

"And Kaladi is in Rome?"

"That's where he lives. That's where Tom dropped the money."

"And you never sent Tom to Germany?" Barney asked.

"Never."

"Did Tom ever mention the word 'Genesis' to you?"

Steiffel's eyes blinked twice; then he shook his head. "No."

"What about 'Obermann'?"

"No."

"What is your connection to Arthur Clements?"

"Business. He's on our board of directors."

"Do you know or have you ever met Frank Tedesco?"

"You mean the exiled thief?"

"Yes."

"Never."

"Do you know or have you ever met Victor Maldonado?"

"Wonderful group of people you hang out with, son. No, I never met the late Victor Maldonado."

"Did you know that Clements, Tedesco, and Maldonado served together on the board of directors of a Mafia-operated company known as the Seneca Corporation?"

The old man shrugged his shoulders. "We have fifty-six men and women on the board of Tidal Oil. These people serve on the boards of other corporations as well. I can't possibly be aware of all their various interlocking relationships, now, can I?"

"I guess not," Barney agreed. "Did Tom Neeley ever express any interest in certain fuels or exotic energy sources?"

"I don't understand your question."

"Was Tom interested in the chemical or organic composition of fuel?"

"Tom never asked any questions about anything," the old man said flatly. "Tom was a delivery boy. A good one. He made his trips and kept his mouth shut."

"Who carries the hot money now?"

Steiffel glowered at Barney for a brief moment; then his eyes softened. "Why do you ask?"

"Just curious," Barney offered.

"One day the bribes will end," the old man replied, and moved away from the window toward Barney. "Last Sunday I flew across Europe in Yussef Kaladi's private 747, sipping champagne and eating Iranian caviar. I watched Kaladi and his entourage being entertained by young boys and blond English whores. They were smoking hashish and playing their games at thirty-five thousand feet. I watched them with a smile on my face. But I was thinking: In time I will destroy this man and his colleagues. I will see those Satanic Muslim robes of his burn in hell. The day of the bribes and the time of the Arabs will end." The old man's hand touched Barney's arm, and the long, sensitive fingers squeezed with surprising strength.

"One day their oil fields will burn. We will not need oil. We will—" He stopped suddenly and lowered his voice. "The interview is over, Mr. Caine." He steered Barney toward the door and knocked. The knock was followed by the electronic clicking as the secretary in the outer office pressed the release button. "I wish you well, Mr. Caine. I hope you find Tom Neeley's killer."

Barney opened the door, and the clicking ceased. "Thank you for your time, Mr. Steiffel."

They shook hands, and Steiffel smiled. "Take care of that son of yours. A growing boy needs his father."

CHAPTER

29 ⊠

BARNEY MET LOUIS AT TACTICAL AND FILLED LOUIS IN ON HIS INTER-view with Steiffel right up to the old man's reference to Barney's son.

"Did it come down like a threat?" Louis asked.

Barney shrugged. "Everything he says sounds like a threat. You really understand what power is all about just being in his presence. And yet there's some truth in what he says."

"Maybe Nolan's right. Maybe you just don't get involved with men like Steiffel."

The door opened, and a uniformed Metro cop came in, carrying a manila envelope. "Who's Caine?" he asked.

"I'm Barney Caine."

"This just came into Communications." He handed Barney the envelope. It was sealed with an address label that read: "National Personnel Record Center: Military Division, 9700 Page Boulevard, St. Louis, Mo." There was a red stamp marked: "Approved LAPD Tactical, Col. Frank Merlo."

Barney said, "Thanks." The man saluted and left. Louis watched Barney as he slit the envelope open, removed a single Xerox page, and began to read.

Thomas Neeley enlisted USAF: March 14, 1941. Basic Infantry Training, Fort Jackson, South Carolina. Attached to: D Company —4th Battalion—2nd Brigade—27th Infantry Division. August 23, 1941: T. Neeley to OCS: Ft. Monmouth, N.J. February 4, 1942: T. Neeley to USAF pilot training: Heavy Bomber wing 8th AF Command—Langley Field, Va.

COMMENT: Subject failed to pass flight requirements. Subject transferred to U.S. Army Intelligence: G-2, Rokeby, England.

May 17, 1942. Due to fluency in German, subject assigned: SHAEF—Command: Intelligence Section: Reims, France, November 3, 1944.

FINAL ASSIGNMENT: April 26, 1945. Subject assigned command escort of truck convoy containing captured secret German documents. Destination convoy British Intelligence M-1: Hamburg, Germany. Subject remained attached to British through August 23, 1945. Captured German documents code named: GENESIS.

Louis saw the color go out of Barney's cheeks. "What is it?" he asked.

Barney handed him the sheet. "Read the last part. 'Final Assignment.'"

Louis sat down and carefully read the cryptic paragraph. There was a pause, and he looked up at Barney. "Jesus Christ."

"I felt it in my guts," Barney said. "I knew the pivot of the case was in Neeley's past." Barney rose and looked out the window.

Louis said, "But we still don't know what Genesis is."

"I've got to see Nolan." Barney paused, and his voice was dead calm. "The answers are in Germany. I've got to get Nolan to send me there."

"What can you do in Germany?" Louis asked. "You can't make an arrest. You can't carry a weapon. You have no authority to conduct an investigation."

"I have connections," Barney replied. "The chief of the West Berlin police is Hans Lehmans. I met him when Willy Brandt visited L.A. I worked security with Lehmans."

"But you'd be operating like a private eye. And in the dark. You still don't know what you're after."

"Maybe, but whatever Genesis is, it's still in Germany."

"How do you know that?" Louis asked.

"Because if it wasn't, Tom and Kay Neeley would still be alive."

CHAPTER

30 ☒

JOHN NOLAN SWALLOWED SOME BUTTERMILK AND GRIMACED. "ALL YOU have is a group of people tied together, loosely tied together, by sex and cocaine."

"And Genesis," Barney added.

"All right, so thirty-three years ago Tom Neeley took a convoy of secret German documents to the British in Hamburg. What the hell has that got to do with the current events? Look, I've let you run the case, and under considerable pressure. I've backed you up all the way, Barney."

"I know that, John."

Nolan waved his hand in disgust. "Ah. What do you know? You have no idea of what I'm going through. The press has nailed Neeley and the department to the cross: a former career officer up to his badge in cocaine and call girls. His ex-wife tortured and killed, and Maldonado blown up. The commissioner came down on me like a thunderclap. *'How are we protecting the good name of the department?'* What the hell can I say?"

"You can tell him the case has nothing to do with sex or dope."

"That's a fucking theory," Nolan shouted. "The goddamn case is classic: a rogue cop dealing coke; a pussy-for-sale operation; a Mafia tie-in, and a hotshot show-business agent. All the things that will sell newspapers and keep people watching the six o'clock news. The department is catching hell every day. Besides that TV cocksucker knows you were investigating the cop killings before you took this on, and she somehow ties all the Neeley stuff into those forty-three police killings. So that sore had been dredged up, too. We need a suspect. And you talk about going off to Germany to run down some mythical thing called

Genesis. It doesn't add up, Barney. You don't have anything!" Nolan went back to his desk and sipped the buttermilk.

"I can't give you hard evidence," Barney said patiently, "but I can give you facts that raise questions. Questions that are unanswerable. Questions that in my experience take this case out of a cocaine hit. Questions that indicate Tom Neeley was onto something valuable or volatile enough to warrant four killings in less than two weeks."

"Where do you get four?"

"The Neeleys, Maldonado, and the guy on the beach."

"You tie Maldonado and that spic into this Genesis thing?"

"Maldonado may not have been aware of the German thing; but he was part of it, and so was the Colombian citizen I nailed."

"That spic was a known cocaine smuggler," Nolan snapped.

"Among other things," Barney replied.

Nolan sat down heavily and drained the last of his buttermilk. "Look, Barney, I know you have this overworld theory in your head, and maybe you're right; but that's in the realm of international power politics. I can't relate the facts in this case with that theory. I know that you and Louis have performed professionally. You haven't missed a thing. You've gone down every open alley and some that were blind. But I can't justify sending you to Germany based on what you have."

Barney took a few steps toward Nolan. "I disagree. I think there's enough for us to go to the commissioner. Let me run this down for you. The same way I'd run it down for the commissioner."

Nolan bit off the end of a long dark cigar. "Okay."

"We start with Tom, set up for the killers by some female, probably foreign and probably the coke courier. She was certainly someone Neeley knew and trusted. We find the voodoo doll and the coke, classic mob hit on a cheating dealer. Too classic. Now we find Tom went to Germany. Tom's holding a slip with 'Genesis' and 'Obermann.' A week before he's killed he tells some slope hooker that Genesis is a big score. Kay Neeley was afraid to tell me she accompanied Tom to Germany. *Why?* Kay Neeley went to Haiti. The voodoo doll is from Haiti. Tedesco is in exile in Haiti. Kay, tortured and brutally wasted, by two foreign hit men. *Why?* The late Mafioso Victor Maldonado supplies Neeley with coke and is a chairman of the board of Seneca, where oddly enough Arthur Clements and Frank Tedesco show up. Clements introduces Tom Neeley to Adam Steiffel, who recruits Tom as a bag man. Tom transports hot money to some Arab in Rome named Yussef Kaladi. Steiffel's business is oil."

Barney walked up to Nolan's desk. "Tom goes out of his way to ask Paul Isella about racing fuels? *Why?*"

"How the hell would I know?" Nolan shrugged.

"Isn't it conceivable that 'Genesis' was a Nazi code name for some new or exotic energy source the Germans had developed?"

Nolan leaned forward. "And Neeley stumbled back into it thirty-three years later?"

"Right." Barney nodded; he placed his hands on Nolan's desk and stared into the tired eyes. "You have any idea what that would be worth?" Barney asked. "You have any idea of what a new energy source would do to the geopolitical structure in the world? Whatever Neeley uncovered about Genesis represents one hell of a threat to somebody."

Barney went over to the window and lit a cigarillo. Nolan leaned back and stared up at the ceiling. He puffed thoughtfully on his cigar. There was a moment of silence in the office, broken only by the muffled sound of phones ringing in the outer office.

Barney turned from the window. "Well? What do you say? Can we go to the commissioner?"

"I'm thinking."

"What have you got to lose, John?"

"My pension."

Barney nodded. "All right. Let's examine my request from a purely political viewpoint. If I'm wrong and get nowhere in Germany, you're out my time and expenses. And while I'm gone, Louis can still keep hassling the local suspects. But if I'm right, John, if I can prove that the Neeleys were killed over something totally alien to his former police activities, the department is off the hook. Everyone's clean. And like it or not, there is no other way we're going to come out clean."

Nolan stared at Barney for a moment, then got to his feet, went over to the small Frigidaire set in the wall, and poured a half glass of buttermilk. He drained it in one long swallow. Nolan then looked at Barney and softly said, "Let's go see the commissioner."

Francis X. Lambert was regarded as something of an intellectual and his office was more like a judge's chamber than the traditional police commissioner's office. The furnishings were subdued but rich and elegant. There was a smell of leather polish in the room. The walls were lined with lawbooks and volumes chronicling the great military strategists of all time, dating back to Alexander the Great and continuing through to Mao, Rommel, Patton, MacArthur, Giap, and Dayan.

They had consumed the better part of a bottle of scotch while Barney ran the case down. He had taken his time, skipping nothing. He scrupulously analyzed every angle, every tangent, every facet. The commissioner neither questioned, nor interrupted, nor betrayed any emotion. He listened with the kind of attention that a scholar pays to his professor.

Barney finished by stating that the interlocking relationships indicated the presence of what he termed the overworld. The commissioner nodded, and Barney fell silent.

Nolan had not uttered a word since the initial salutations. He chewed nervously on the dead cigar. Barney sat back in the comfortable easy chair and waited.

The commissioner's fingers began to drum on the polished heavy oak desk. After a long moment he cleared his throat. "You have not established an evidential basis for Germany." He paused and rubbed the edge of the scotch glass against his cheek. "Facts in any complex case spawn conjecture which almost always bears investigation. But to send you off to a foreign country without authority, without a clear picture as to what it is you're seeking, seems to be a risk that transcends the conjecture."

Nolan glanced at Barney and saw the telltale sign of rising anger; the small half-moon scar on his cheek was beginning to go red. There was a pause, and Barney got to his feet.

"Well"—Barney swallowed twice—"I walked out of the CIA, I can walk out of this."

The commissioner stared at Barney's angry brown eyes and in a flat, calm voice said, "Sit down, Lieutenant."

Barney slowly sank back into the deep leather chair. The commissioner's fingers drummed again on the desk top.

"I said, the risk *seems* to transcend the conjecture." He paused, pursed his lips between his hands. "This feeling you have that the truth of this case lies somewhere in Neeley's past, somewhere in Germany. When did this feeling become apparent?"

"From the beginning," Barney said without hesitation. "That Sunday afternoon at Tom Neeley's home. When I found the German road maps and the hotel expense stubs, the West German Michelin guide, the slip with 'Genesis' and 'Obermann.' The porno shot from the Hamburg sex club. Kay Neeley's murder just confirmed what I sensed. That the answers were in Neeley's past. That he and Kay were killed over something much more valuable and profoundly more complex than cocaine dealing." Barney paused. "Now we find out Tom Neeley was in charge of a convoy containing secret German documents, code named Genesis."

"What about Obermann?" the commissioner asked.

"I don't know. But I'd guess Obermann is a German citizen who Neeley contacted on his German trip."

The commissioner stared at Barney for a long moment, then got to his feet and slowly walked to the long wall and examined the titles on the books. Nolan could feel a pocket of gas building up in his intestinal tract; he wanted to break wind but restrained himself. The gas pocket was turning into a hard knot of pain. He regretted coming to the commissioner. He wished the handsome graying man would speak, would dismiss them. Barney watched the commissioner impassively. He had done all he could. There was nothing more to say.

The commissioner turned to Nolan. Nolan's pain and nervousness triggered a rush of words. "I'm sorry we took up your time, Francis, but with all the heat on the department I—I, well, since this would be a classified case, I felt it should be your decision. I felt I had to come to you."

The commissioner said, "You could do no less. And I appreciate it." Nolan seemed to relax but said nothing. The commissioner then turned to Barney. "You say you have a police connection in Germany?"

"Yes. The prefect of police in West Berlin is Hans Lehmans. I'm certain that with the proper letter of authorization from the department he will do whatever he can for me."

"That may not be much."

"I know that."

"You'll be operating alone."

"I've done it before."

The commissioner nodded imperceptibly, and his gray eyes fastened themselves on Barney. The tone of his voice was still soft, but the slow cadence and finality of the words made it a command. "Go ahead. As soon as possible." He then turned to Nolan. "I want the tickets and expenses to come out of Tactical. You can charge it back to ISI when the case is terminated."

The commissioner turned back to Barney. "You'll make any contacts through Sergeant Louis Yosuta. At his home number. And make them from a safe phone. I want those communications minimal. I want you not to violate any German law. You operate by *their* book. Understand?"

"Yes, sir."

"And, Barney, if you're right, if Genesis does indeed involve a new energy source, you know better than I, the higher the stakes, the greater the personal risk."

"I understand the risks," Barney replied.

The commissioner placed his manicured hands on the desk and said, "The meeting's over, gentlemen." The commissioner walked up to Barney and grasped his right hand. "Good luck."

Barney thanked him and followed Nolan out. For a long moment the commissioner watched them go down the hallway.

BOOK II

"GENESIS"

CHAPTER

31 ⌧

THE HUGE 747 LANDED SMOOTHLY AT FRANKFURT AIRPORT, ARRIVING only two minutes late. Barney walked through a series of seemingly endless tunnels, following signs that indicated "In Transit-Connecting Flights." The canvas shoulder bag slung over his left shoulder felt a lot heavier than it had sixteen hours ago in Los Angeles. The jet lag pulled at his legs, and his fatigue made him feel heady, almost stoned. It made the moment seem like a time out of nowhere, and the endless tunnels were dreamlike.

He passed blue and white illuminated signs that advertised the delights of Frankfurt: hotels, restaurants, Schultheiss Beer, Frankenwein, and sex clubs that guaranteed satisfaction in English, French, and Arabic. The fact that the sex club signs were in Arabic lent final testimony to the ascendancy of Islam.

A throaty, sirenic female voice oozed out of the unseen public-address speakers. The voice announced the final departure of a Lufthansa flight to Tel Aviv. The message was repeated in English and German. The tone of the girl's voice was incredibly sensual, and Barney remembered that same intonation in every foreign airport he had ever been in. It was as if there were a central casting office for airport paging somewhere in Europe and the same girl always got the job. The voice called an Iberia flight to Ibiza, then repeated the call for the Tel Aviv flight, and once again Barney thought of the Israeli paratroop colonel Zvi Barzani, the man who passed the Soviet missile systems to him in the Madrid airport years ago.

The big terminal was not busy but nevertheless was heavily patrolled by young German men in uniform, carrying automatic weapons. Barney had almost forgotten the reign of terror that had gripped Germany since the days of the Olympic massacre in Munich. There was a large crowd milling around Gate 35; those who had been checked in were seated in multicolored plastic chairs behind the check-in counter. The other passengers were standing in line in front of the check-in counter. Barney took his place on line. A woman in front of him turned and frowned at his cigarillo but said nothing. A small child vomited on the shoe tops of the elderly Japanese who had been on Barney's flight from New York. The mother of the child apologized in German; the Japanese merely bowed and smiled. The old allies were still compatible.

The security check before boarding was thorough and included a body frisk; people with cameras were asked to snap the shutter control, and every piece of carry-on luggage was X-rayed and examined. Barney was impressed by the attention to detail and the professionalism of the security people. He thought that they could give lessons to their counterparts in the American airports.

The Pan Am plane was a small 727 and left precisely on time. They flew along the carefully prescribed air corridor laid out by the East Germans and their Soviet masters. Barney thought about other men who had flown over this same countryside forty years ago, men who had touched switches that released tons of bombs out of the Flying Fortresses that had blackened the German skies. Men like his own father. Men who fought and died in this same sky, over this same blood-soaked country.

They arrived at Tegel Airfield in the French sector of Berlin. The terminal was small and almost deserted. The luggage came off the belt fast. Barney collected his one piece and walked through the customs control. The guard did not ask him to open anything. He reached the curb and pulled up the collar on his suede jacket. It was sunny but cool. He blinked in the sunlight for a moment; then he heard his name called and saw the smiling face of Hans Lehmans coming toward him.

Lehmans grabbed Barney's hand and shook it twice, then signaled to a black Mercedes, which instantly glided toward them. The driver got out, and Lehmans said something in German to him. The man nodded and hefted Barney's suitcase toward the luggage compartment.

"How was the trip?" Lehmans asked.

"What trip?" Barney smiled.

"Come. Get in. You must be exhausted."

Barney touched Lehmans's sleeve. "Before we begin, I want to thank you, Hans."

Lehmans's gray eyes studied Barney. "You would do no less for me."

Barney thought the gray eyes were a lot older than he had remembered, and the regular features had begun to sag and there were severe lines around the kind mouth. Barney guessed any high German police official must have been through hell since Munich and the Baader-Meinhof reign of terror. The big sedan pulled gracefully away from the curb and picked up a two-lane highway. Lehmans took out a pack of Marlboros and offered one to Barney, who declined.

"Have you stopped?" Lehmans asked.

"No. I go through about ten cigarillos a day."

"You find them less harmful?"

"No. Less addictive."

"I followed your instructions and booked you into the Kempinski."

"That's fine," Barney said.

"Yes and no. It's a fine hotel. But incredibly expensive." Lehmans added, "The dollar doesn't buy much in Germany."

"So I've heard."

"Perhaps you should think of staying in a pension."

"Not a chance. If a crooked cop could stay in the Kempinski, so can an honest one."

Lehmans shot Barney a curious glance. And Barney knew he had blundered out of fatigue. He had violated a very old professional code. You never mentioned crooked cops. They didn't exist in the fraternal order of police.

"That's not the real reason," Barney said, trying to make amends. "I derive a certain satisfaction from sticking it to my boss. They told me not to worry, just use my charge cards, and that doesn't happen too often."

Lehmans nodded but did not respond. Barney looked out the window. They were approaching a small arched bridge that spanned what appeared to be a lake. There were people boating on the lake and picnicking along its grassy banks. Lehmans touched Barney's sleeve. "You know, at the very end of the war, I helped defend this bridge." Lehmans's voice sounded sad and old. "I was only fifteen at the time. We were children, trying to hold this bridge, waiting for General Wenck's Twelfth Army." He paused. "The Twelfth Army never came."

"You mean you held this particular bridge?"

"Yes." Lehmans exhaled, then tossed the cigarette out the window. "Of course, this bridge has been rebuilt. We destroyed the original. We blew it up at the last moment, with Russian shells from their T-Thirty-four tanks falling everywhere. I was one of five boys out of two hundred who survived. This whole area was reduced to rubble, along with the entire city of Berlin. It was all just a sea of ruins."

The two-lane highway fed into a six-lane autobahn. They passed a huge Siemens factory and a football stadium. There were signs to Spandau, Moabit, and Charlottenburg. They kept going straight ahead toward Charlottenburg. Vast housing developments lined either side of the highway. They were designed like building blocks of glass and cement cubes, layer upon layer. Barney noticed a cluster of small dwellings sandwiched between the developments whose roofs were red-tiled and gabled. They appeared totally alien in style to the huge cement cubes that surrounded them.

Barney indicated the gabled houses to Lehmans. "Are they original?"

"Yes." Lehmans nodded. "Now and then you see a few. A prewar building in Berlin is like an archaeological artifact."

The car moved in swift silence, passing through the suburbs of Berlin. Barney was too tired to talk, and Lehmans seemed to be locked in preoccupied silence. They crossed Kaiserdamm-Bismarckstrasse and swung onto the Kurfürstendamm and entered the heart of the city.

"I've spoken with the manager of the Kempinski, Helmut Bergen," Lehmans said. "He will have the records of Neeley's visit available to us in the morning. He only insists on being present when we go through them."

"What about Obermann?"

Lehmans shrugged. "We don't know who he is, or if he exists at all, and in what city. Obermann is not an uncommon name. We can only hope that the data in Neeley's hotel file provide us with a lead."

"Why wait till tomorrow?"

"We must give the hotel manager time to assemble the records, and besides, I think it best that you get some sleep at least until five or six this afternoon. Then take a sauna. It's good for the nervous system. Bergen will be on duty later; you can introduce yourself. There is a very good, inexpensive restaurant and outdoor garden across the Kurfürstendamm from the hotel. Try to stay up until ten our time; then go to bed. You will accommodate your body to our time cycle. I'll be in the lobby at nine in the morning. And we begin."

Barney felt relieved. It was exactly what he wanted Lehmans to say. He had offered to begin working that night only out of professional courtesy.

As they started up the wide boulevard, Barney saw the ruins of the Kaiser Wilhelm Church. The West German government had left the medieval church as it was after the war. A reminder to the Berliners of the destruction that had occurred almost four decades ago. There was a new tall, graceful modern church made out of marble and stained glass attached to the ruins of the old church. The structures were surrounded by an island of cement. A permanent plaza of remembrance to what had been. In the distance off to the east Barney saw a huge needle that seemed to be well over a thousand feet high. The sun glinted off a round ball at the point of the needle creating a perfectly shaped cross.

"What the hell is that?" Barney asked.

"It's the East Berlin television tower. Three hundred and sixty-five meters high, with revolving restaurant. A symbol to West Berliners of Communist technical prowess."

"It didn't work out too well," Barney said, "not with that cross shining on its top."

"Yes." Lehmans smiled. "An ironic phenomenon. They have been unable so far to control the rays of the sun."

They passed a glass and steel shopping complex dominated by a huge office building with a sign "EUROPA CENTER." At the top of the skyscraper the symbol of Mercedes-Benz, a huge tristar, revolved slowly.

"We are now at the Times Square of Berlin," Lehmans said.

It seemed to Barney a good analogy. The Kurfürstendamm was lined on either side by sleazy-looking shops and arcades advertising sex shows. There were sidewalk pushcart vendors who appeared to be Arabs. The colors orange and blue were everywhere. At the corner of Meineckestrasse a fifty-foot-high billboard featured the naked back and large white ass of a blond girl. The marquee sign under the girl's ass read: "Blue Movie." Below the sign there was an arcade with flashing blue and orange bulbs that advertised "The Café der Western." On the opposite corner there was a large billboard with Sean Connery's smiling face. His right hand held an automatic pistol, and the numbers 007 stenciled across in red. Alongside the Connery poster was a smaller, forlorn-looking poster advertising the last film of the Italian director Piero Pasolini.

Barney noticed a two-story red-brick building with a red-tiled gable roof and tall, narrow oblong windows that made the building unmistakably prewar. A simple sign over the entrance said "Kabarett." It was an incongruous remnant of *I Am a Camera,* of Brecht, Weill, and Mann and the rest of pre-Nazi Berlin. But there was no charm in its survival. It reminded Barney that the neon of the sex shops and the Pina Colada stands and the Arab peddlers were built on a huge cemetery. Barney imagined the unseen presence of millions of dead screaming under the pavement. But it was all beginning to blur; he was eighteen hours off-time. He barely nodded when Lehmans said, "I know you will find it hard to believe, but this was once the Fifth Avenue of Berlin."

They reached the corner of Fasanenstrasse, and the pervasive blue and orange marmalade came to an abrupt end, as if there were an invisible border. The rest of the Kurfürstendamm seemed to be taken up with stately apartment buildings that had been rebuilt in their former prewar style. The Mercedes turned right into Fasanenstrasse, which was occupied in almost its entirety by the Kempinski Hotel.

The lobby of the Kempinski was wide and low-ceilinged. Its decor struggled between Louis XVI elegance and space-age glitter. It was as if the decorator had been unable to decide which century he was working in.

The check-in procedure was fast and efficient. Barney said good-bye to Lehmans, thanking him again. His room was on the fourth floor, facing Fasanenstrasse. The room was large and comfortable with a king-sized bed and a huge bathroom. There was a small Frigidaire in a corner that contained mineral water and a wide range of alcoholic beverages. He tipped the bellboy four marks, the equivalent of two dollars. The boy said, *"Danke,"* and left. Barney called the operator and asked her to give him a wake-up call in five hours. He did not bother to unpack. He undressed, pulled the drapes and slid between the cool white linen sheets. It was ten minutes after twelve, Berlin time, when Barney fell into a deep sleep.

CHAPTER

32 ⊠

AT THAT MOMENT IN ROME IT WAS ONE HOUR LATER AND TWENTY-FIVE degrees warmer. The girl came slowly down the majestic beige marble of the Spanish Steps. She moved carefully from step to step, picking her way through the tourists and the backpackers, ignoring the obscene shouts of the Italian men who hustled the steps. She wore oversized sunglasses that were tinted blue and deflected the sun's rays. Her dark hair, startling features and tall, curvy figure made heads turn. She wore a wide, full black linen skirt and sheer linen blouse and carried a canvas leather satchel. She had flown into Fiumicino from Paris that morning. She was tired. The Roman heat was getting to her, and the two hundred thousand dollars in Swiss francs tucked into the compartments of the money belt around her hips rubbed against her flesh, causing rivulets of sweat to run down her thighs.

She disliked being used as bag lady and she had only disdain for Yussef Kaladi, the Saudi go-between who waited for her delivery.

The sexual problems she experienced with Raoul had not gone away. If anything, they had become more profound. Desire itself eluded her. Two nights ago, in the Paris flat, she had bolted upright in bed, screaming out of the horror of her nightmare. The images of the nightmare had been vivid.

The blood spurting out of Tom Neeley's mouth had somehow superimposed itself over the hollow eye of an Iraqi they had killed five years ago in Soho. The grotesque faces of those they had murdered were alive in her nights. She would have to speak with Yasir in Beirut. She would continue to serve the cause. Yes. Always. But not in the action cells. Not anymore. Perhaps the propaganda section. Propaganda was vital. And they were winning the propaganda war. The oil money had given them control of major Western publications and broadcast media. It was Yasir who said that once the propaganda victory had been achieved the real war could begin. Once and for all they would eliminate the Zionist state. Yes, the propaganda section was critical, and she was well qualified; she was fluent in six languages.

But what if they refused? Well, she could work with the children in the refugee camp near Sidon, or assist the guerrilla movements in Mozambique or Angola or even the rising movement in Mexico. There were many possibilities. But this would be her last action assignment.

She was suddenly shoved hard by a heavyset man who was coming down the steps in a hurry. She cursed him in German, but the man did not respond. A wave of depression washed over her. What if Yasir did not agree to her request? Well, what could they do? She shuddered despite the heat. She knew very well what they could do. There had been others who had refused assignments. She remembered the words of Carlos: "Shit is thicker than blood. Make shit out of them." She straightened her shoulders and rationalized her own fears. They would not eliminate her. She was too important. The very fact that she was Western made her more valuable to them than their own kind. Besides, she was dedicated, and her record was spotless.

She had been one of the few who had managed to penetrate Israeli Intelligence. She had arrived in Haifa on a cruise ship, carrying a French passport and accompanied by an Italian comrade posing as her husband. During the four days of the ship's stay they had photographed the huge oil refineries and the key installations of the port. Yes, Haifa had been a singular triumph. But that was before the killings. Before the movement had succumbed to those thin-lipped theoreticians, those nightclub firebrands who sent others out to die.

The girl crossed the busy traffic off the Piazza di Spagna and entered the Via Condotti. She walked on the left side of the expensive street. The shade side. She remembered her return from Haifa. Yasir himself met her on the pier in Marseilles. They celebrated on the Mistral, the crack train that ran from Marseilles to Paris. They were drinking a very dry vintage Moët in the superb dining car, with the French countryside flashing by, when she suddenly thought of a group of Israeli children she had seen playing in a park in Haifa. The children had been between the ages of five and eight. Innocent. And lovely. *Could they be the enemy?* The question had ruined her moment of triumph. Even as she touched her glass to Yasir's, she saw the faces of the Israeli children. *Would the photographs of Haifa she took one day help kill those children?* The question had been unanswerable then, and now it was no longer a question. It was a self-imposed accusation. Like all the other questions of late.

She reached the corner, went into the café and ordered an iced coffee. She shoved the dark glasses up on top of her head and lit a Gauloise. A handsome man sitting alone at a white-topped Formica table stared at her.

She felt naked, as if the man could see through her linen dress all the way to the money belt. Her thighs were wet, and she longed for a cold shower. At precisely 12:35 P.M. the Fiat sedan pulled up in front of the café. The girl placed three hundred lire in coins on the counter, walked out into the brilliant sunshine, and got into the passenger side of the Fiat, alongside the dark-skinned driver.

It took them thirty-five minutes to arrive at Yussef Kaladi's villa. They made a sharp right turn off Via Pacifica, into an alleylike entrance that ended abruptly in front of two huge iron gates. The girl noticed three miniature television cameras atop a fifteen-foot-high wall. They rotated slowly, covering the entrance from all angles. The driver picked up a small electronic device, pressed a button, and the gates swung open. They drove up a curving driveway through a forest of tall pines for half a mile. At the top of the slope the driveway curved sharply, and the two-story fieldstone and glass villa appeared. The girl thought the exterior of the villa was strangely reminiscent of Neeley's hillside home.

The Fiat came to a stop at the entrance. Two black men dressed in dark brown suits appeared out of nowhere. The girl was startled by the color of their skin; their flesh tones were blue-black. Their eyes were light brown and seemed to be floating in a reddish fluid. Their features were alike: flat noses and thin, cruel lips, set off by very high, fine cheekbones. She guessed they were Sudanese, and from the same tribe. Sudanese were favorite bodyguards of the oil sheikhs.

The girl got out of the car, and one of the men came up to her. His companion on the other side was already frisking the driver. The Sudanese motioned to the girl to raise her arms. He ran his hands from her armpits down her thighs. He knelt down and motioned her to raise her skirt. She did, exposing herself all the way up to a brief pair of silk panties. The Sudanese unfastened the money belt, straightened up, and motioned her to lower her hands. He gave the money belt back to her and took her handbag and carefully examined the contents, then returned it to her. The other black bodyguard and the driver of the Fiat had disappeared around the corner of the villa. The girl followed the Sudanese to the door and waited while he spoke in a strange Arabic dialect into a speaker alongside the door. There was a moment's pause, followed by a loud buzzing. The Sudanese twisted the lion's-head knob and opened the huge polished oak door.

The girl stood in the large portico whose floor, walls, and ceiling were black-and-white squares of marble. A spiral staircase led to an upper floor and, directly ahead were a pair of tall oak doors. The African opened the doors for the girl. The living room was brutally modern, with chrome tables and black leather furniture resting on the black-and-white marble floor.

The far wall was glass, and through the gauze of the beige drapes the girl could see an exterior patio area dominated by an Olympic-sized swimming pool. The Sudanese motioned her to be seated. She moved to a couch and sat down. The black man stood behind her. She held the money belt in her lap. In the silence the girl thought she heard the sound of feminine laughter coming from the pool. There was another long moment of silence that was suddenly shattered by a burst of laughter and the sound of voices speaking Arabic. The girl turned in time to see Sheikh Yussef Kaladi enter the room.

Kaladi was a small man with friendly brown eyes, a generous nose, black hair, and a carefully barbered goatee. He was immaculately dressed in a double-breasted pearl gray suit, blue silk shirt, and dark blue tie. Kaladi was flanked by two older, bearded men in flowing caftans, wearing the traditional Arab headdress. The men in robes glanced quickly at the girl, said something to Kaladi, who laughed, and then proceeded out through the sliding glass doors to the patio.

Kaladi came up to the girl, took her hand, bowed slightly, and kissed the back of her hand, then straightened up and smiled. "Would you care for some champagne?" He spoke with a pronounced British accent.

The girl shook her head. "I would like a cigarette."

"Of course." Kaladi opened a platinum case and offered her an English cigarette.

"Thank you." She took the cigarette, and Kaladi pressed a button at the top of the case and a small blue flame appeared. He held the light for her, and she inhaled deeply.

The sheikh walked briskly over to a chrome table and brought an ashtray back to the girl. She thanked him and blew some smoke at his face, then handed him the money belt. Kaladi took it and flicked his fingers at the Sudanese, who came around the sofa and took the belt over to the chrome table and began the tedious process of counting the Swiss currency. Kaladi smiled at the girl. "You are certainly far more attractive than the previous courier."

"You mean Neeley. The American," she said.

"Yes. The American. I was saddened by his death. I rather liked him." Kaladi sat down slowly in a chair close to the girl. "We are having some lunch at the pool," he offered. "Perhaps you would care to join us."

She shook her dark hair. "I'm returning to Paris on the three o'clock flight."

"Well, perhaps another time." Kaladi smiled.

They sat in silence. The sheikh studied her striking beauty, feature by feature, as if he were viewing a painting. But he sensed something was wrong. Her eyes were not seeing so much as they were staring. A thin stream of smoke escaped from her lips, but her eyes never left Kaladi's. He shifted uneasily under her relentless gaze and finally forced himself to speak. "I take it the Americans are with us in this Genesis business."

"Why?" She asked the one-word question only to torment the elegant Saudi.

"Come, come, my dear." Kaladi smiled. "Tedesco's involvement is an American involvement."

"Why?" she repeated.

Kaladi fumbled in his jacket for the platinum cigarette case. The girl enjoyed his uneasiness. She detested the dapper Saudi who flew in a private 747, drank vintage wine, ate hundred-dollar-an-ounce Beluga caviar, and fucked English call girls. This bloodsucking professional pimp was as far away from the soul of the cause as were those hashish-smoking revolutionaries who displayed their courage in the nightclubs of Beirut. She could have killed Kaladi without a second thought. She thought how cruel and complex was the web she moved in that this pirate, this leech, was an ally, and the Israeli children playing in the Haifa park were the enemy. *How could that be right!* It was right because the Saudis provided the money. And the means always justified the end.

Kaladi was having trouble with the lighter button on his cigarette case. She smiled inwardly at his nervousness. The flame caught, and two thick streams of smoke rushed out of his nostrils. "You realize it is not so easy to answer one-word questions," he said.

It was too delicious to resist. "Why?" she asked.

Kaladi sighed. "Frank Tedesco is an American. He works for them."

"Tedesco is an exile from his own country," she said coldly.

"Then I take it you mistrust the Americans?"

"I trust only the positions people are forced to take," she replied.

Kaladi was beginning to perceive the hatred in the cold, staring eyes.

His uneasiness forced him into an area of conversation he hadn't planned to enter. "Suppose we obtained the formula?" he asked.

"We don't require a formula," she countered.

"Now that, my dear, is indisputable." He smiled. "Our oil comes pure and natural from the sands of my country. A gift from Allah. We have no need for chemical substitutes or complex formulas." He waited for a response, but she remained silent; her piercing gaze held painfully steady. He crushed the cigarette and said, "I understand things did not go well in California."

"That's a question you should direct to Comrade Tedesco."

"I have," he said. "Tedesco informed me that five people have already died: the Neeleys and another American and two of our own people. He also told me that the American detective is en route to Berlin pursuing the Obermann connection."

"I know nothing of Obermann," she said, crushing the cigarette. "Or the American detective."

The Sudanese finished counting the Swiss currency and spoke to Kaladi in Arabic. Kaladi nodded, and the black man stuffed the packets of money into a leather pouch and left the room.

Kaladi smiled to the girl. "You're certain you would not care for some champagne?"

Before the girl could reply, the glass patio doors slid open violently, slamming against their retaining grooves. A very tall naked girl, with long red hair, stood just inside the living room. She was swaying slightly and grinning. She held a magnum of champagne in her arms and was obviously drunk. She giggled, looked at Kaladi, and shouted in a cheap cockney accent, "Yussef! Yussef! You bloody little fucker! When are you coming out?" The naked redhead's grin slowly disappeared as she saw the girl sitting on the sofa. Her voice dropped as she murmured, "Oh!" Kaladi glared at her and got to his feet.

"Not to worry," the naked girl exclaimed. "I had no idea you were conducting"—she paused—"business." She turned quickly and went out, slamming the sliding doors as she left.

Kaladi spoke to the girl, and his voice was apologetic. "You must forgive me. These—these girls are for those Syrian gentlemen. I am obliged at times to provide certain entertainments for my colleagues. It is distasteful but"—he shrugged—"necessary."

The girl rose. "I would appreciate your driver taking me to the airport."

"Yes. Of course. Immediately."

Kaladi strode quickly to the oak door and held it open for the girl.

The two blue-black Sudanese appeared in the marble entryway. Kaladi spoke to the one who had counted the money. The man nodded, and Kaladi turned to the girl. "The car has been waiting for you."

The Sudanese opened the front door, and a single beam of sunlight entered the dark portico, bouncing harshly off the black-and-white marble squares. Kaladi touched the girl's arm.

"Who will bring the next payment?"

"Didn't Tedesco tell you?" she asked.

"No. He did not."

"It will be the American. Clements."

The girl stepped out of the cool marble portico into the hot Roman sun.

CHAPTER

33 ☒

BARNEY CAINE WOKE UP WITHOUT BENEFIT OF THE CALL FROM THE operator. He glanced at the electric clock on the night table; it read 5:23 P.M. He had slept for five and a half hours.

He went into the large tiled bathroom and took a long shower, alternating the taps between hot and cold. He then shaved and swallowed two vitamin C tablets. He felt rested, but there was a dull ache in his neck and shoulders that spread throughout his back. A residual stiffness from the long flight.

He came out of the bathroom and impulsively decided to try some push-ups. He got to fifteen and collapsed on the rug. He shook his head and remembered he had not kept his promise; he never did get to his health club. He unpacked and hung up his pants and jackets, leaving the shirts, underwear, and socks in the suitcase. He put on a pair of beige slacks, a dark blue turtleneck, and his suede jacket. He closed the door and checked it to be certain the automatic lock was working. It was, and he started down the long corridor to the elevator.

The lobby was quiet, only a few tourists asking questions of a bellman . . . and a small man in a black chesterfield overcoat sitting at the rear of the lobby, reading a German newspaper.

Barney walked up to the reception desk, gave the clerk his name, and asked for Mr. Helmut Bergen. Barney could hear a piano playing an old Rodgers and Hart standard in the Bristol Bar. He felt like having a drink, but decided to take Lehmans's advice about a sauna. His bones ached, and the dry rock steam would be better than booze. The door behind the reception counter opened, and the clerk came out followed by an older man.

Helmut Bergen was a tall, gaunt man in his late fifties. He had the kind of face that made it difficult for him to smile. His eyes had the grave countenance of a diplomat who has come to a critical negotiation without any cards to play. He reached the counter and tried a smile that never quite happened. "I've been expecting you, Mr. Caine." He thrust his right hand out. Barney shook it and said, "Hans Lehmans told me to introduce myself."

Bergen nodded. "Is everything satisfactory?"

"Perfect."

"Good. I will have all the records of Mr. Neeley's visit for you in the morning."

"I know. I just wanted to say hello and"—Barney smiled—"find out how I get to the sauna."

"Of course. At once." Bergen snapped his fingers at a bellboy. "Escort Mr. Caine to the sauna and see that he has everything he requires."

"Thank you," Barney said.

Again Bergen tried to smile and failed. "A pleasure, Mr. Caine."

The sauna and swimming pool were on the basement floor. A white-clad attendant sat at a booth at the entrance. Behind him was a good-sized bar and, beyond the bar, a swimming pool.

"It is almost closing time," the attendant said. "You have perhaps twenty minutes."

"That's enough," Barney replied.

"Very well." The attendant handed Barney two towels and a locker key and directed him through a small brown door.

The heat coming off the rocks stunned Barney as he entered the room. He stood in the dimly lit room for a moment, peering at the naked shapes on the benches. The three tiers of benches on the right side were all occupied. The top tier was taken up by the prone naked body of a man with a huge sweating belly. There were two naked girls on the bunks immediately below the fat man. One was brunette and the other blond. Blond all over.

They were not particularly pretty but had nice figures and were sweating profusely. The fat man said something in German that evoked mild laughter from the naked girls. Barney was embarrassed by the presence of the girls and nodded sheepishly at them. He went to the opposite side of the sauna, spread his towels on the top bunk, climbed up, and stretched out.

He tried to forget about the fat man and the girls. He closed his eyes and relaxed as the intense heat slowly forced his pores open, and the rivulets of sweat began to run. After a while his curiosity got the best of him, and he began to steal glances at the naked girls. The blond girl caught his eyes and smiled, and Barney smiled back. The dull pain in his neck and shoulders was diminishing. The intense heat was beginning to sting his face, and he turned over onto his stomach.

Barney turned his collar up against the night chill, as he walked slowly up the Kurfürstendamm. The garish neon lights blazed and blinked, providing a vicious illumination of the avenue's daytime sleaze. He had walked four long blocks down the Kurfürstendamm since leaving the hotel and was approaching the memorial plaza of the Kaiser Wilhelm Church.

Barney reached Meineckestrasse and remembered that Lehmans had said there was a good, inexpensive open-air restaurant in that street. He turned left into the treelined street, whose stateliness was a relief from the glare and glitter of the Kurfürstendamm. Halfway down the street he saw the sign, "Pariser Café."

The restaurant was a collection of tables scattered throughout a large garden that was part of a private home. Waiters streamed in and out of the house, carrying trays of food to the people at the tables. The majority of the tables were occupied by young couples, sitting under strings of soft blue lightbulbs. They were eating sandwiches, sipping wine and drinking from big mugs of draft beer. And from speakers attached to the trees, the Bee Gees were singing "More Than a Woman."

Barney sat down at a vacant table and motioned to the waiter. The man spoke English, and Barney ordered a rare hamburger and a draft beer. He lit a cigarillo and suddenly felt a wave of loneliness wash over him. The melodic disco rock of the Bee Gees seemed to him a profoundly American sound and amplified his solitude. He thought about his last day in Los Angeles, spent with his son. They had gone to the beach, and after a long swim they strolled along the surf. Timmy suddenly broke into a run, his blond hair gleaming in the sun, his feet kicking up the surf. A big stray dog came out of nowhere and ran alongside the boy. At that moment the boy and the dog, and the swooping gulls, and the foaming surf were like a frieze of lost innocence. Later that night Timmy placed his head on Barney's chest and cried, "Don't go, Daddy." In a life where the real values always got away, the cry of his son was real. Now, alone and disconnected, Barney felt like Hemingway's leopard, wondering what the hell it was that had driven him to this place: *Berlin*. The word itself conjured up demons; mythological gods—Siegfried and the Valkyrie—and klieg-lit masses screaming, *"Sieg heil,"* and millions of bleached bones, and not more than four miles away was the grass-covered mound of Hitler's bunker.

The waiter brought the hamburger and a stein of beer, and Barney ate in hungry silence. He was sipping the last of his beer when he noticed a man sitting alone at a table near the entrance. The man was smoking a cigarette through a long holder and reading a German magazine. He looked vaguely familiar, but Barney could not place him.

The Bee Gees were replaced by Carly Simon, and the waiter brought the check; the hamburger and beer came to eighteen marks, or nine dollars. Barney shook his head. Lehmans had said the restaurant was inexpensive. Barney gave the waiter twenty marks, got up, and walked through the garden out into Meineckestrasse.

He walked slowly up the treelined street, passing a Chinese restaurant and a lesbian sex bar with a window poster display of two young girls in passionate embrace. The buildings on the street were residential and appeared to be prewar. Barney guessed they had been rebuilt in their former style. He still had the feeling of detachment that came with fatigue, but the food and beer had given him a lift.

He reached the corner, lit a cigarillo, and glanced back up Meineckestrasse. Halfway up the street he noticed a small man in a chesterfield overcoat, wearing a homburg. The man had stopped in front of a store and seemed to be interested in something on display in the window. He was the same man who had been in the restaurant smoking and reading a magazine. Barney's right hand reflexively went to his left shoulder, but the familiar bulge of the snub-nose .38 was missing. He suddenly remembered Louis's words: "You'd be operating like a private eye." And then the commissioner's words: "The higher the stakes, the greater the personal risk."

Barney turned the corner and walked leisurely toward the corner of Fasanenstrasse. He glanced back before he turned into the street. The little man could not be seen. Barney entered Fasanenstrasse.

It was a long street with small shops whose windows were dark. Barney did not look back, but midway up the street, he ducked into the alcove of an Agfa camera shop. Its windows reflected the shapes of oncoming cars, and Barney stood at a point in the alcove where the side window gave him a perfect visual angle, like a rearview mirror on a car.

He dropped the cigarillo and waited. The lights of two cars loomed up in the window, flared and passed. There were no pedestrians, and Barney could hear the sounds of heavy traffic coming from the Kurfürstendamm. The reflected image of the little man suddenly appeared in the window. His hands were deep inside his overcoat, and he no longer seemed interested in the passing windows. His pace was leisurely. His attention focused directly ahead.

Barney knew better than to let the man's small size fool him. Hit men were not built like linebackers, they didn't come king-sized, and it did not require much strength to pull the trigger of a .22 automatic. He took a few steps farther back in the alcove, unbuttoned his suede jacket, and flexed the fingers on both hands. The reflected image of the man in the homburg was now only twenty feet away. Barney could hear the sound of the man's leather heels, striking the pavement.

Barney took a deep breath and let it out. And repeated it. The man was ten feet away from the storefront. Barney thought if the man were a professional hit man, he would reach the alcove, spin, and fire; if he were not, if he were just shadowing, he would go past the alcove and keep walking to the corner. The oncoming image in the glass was large now, and the sound of the man's footsteps were like drumbeats. He was only five feet from the alcove. Barney counted the remaining steps: four . . . three . . . two. . . . The little man took the last step, stopped, turned and peered into the dark recess of the alcove.

The little man's eyeglasses picked up the light of a streetlamp. His right hand started out of his coat, and he smiled. *"Guten Abend."* Barney felt the pumping rush of the adrenaline shoot through his chest up to his brain. He took three running steps and sprung at the little man. His right fist preceded his body and crashed into the little man's cheek, knocking his eyeglasses off. Barney's body hit the man seconds after his right cross, and he went down with Barney on top of him. Barney had his knees and full body weight resting on the man's back. He pulled the man's head up with both hands in a closing vise that would ultimately snap his neck. The man groaned, "Please . . . please . . . I . . . I can explain. I can explain to you."

Barney eased the pressure on the man's neck, grabbed his right arm, turned him over, and felt his pockets for a gun, but the man was unarmed. Barney yanked him to his feet and shoved him violently back into the alcove, pinning him to the front door of the camera shop.

"Take my wallet." The little man's voice trembled. "I give it to you. Please do not hurt me." His right cheek had already started to swell, and there was a trickle of blood where the skin had broken.

Barney relaxed his grip and gasped, "Who the hell are you?"

"My name is Ernest Hoess."

"Why were you following me?"

The man rubbed his cheek. "I saw you in the hotel. And later alone, walking on the Kurfürstendamm. I thought you might desire a woman."

The incongruity of the little man's words sent Barney into an insane gale of laughter.

"May I go?" the little man asked.

Barney nodded, unable to speak. The little man walked shakily up to the alcove's entrance and bent down to pick up his glasses. He carefully put them back on and rubbed his swollen cheek. He stared ruefully at Barney, who panted, catching his breath between bursts of laughter.

"Are you a madman?" the little man asked.

Barney lost control again and went into another hysterical spasm. He could not speak.

"You must be mad," the man sputtered. "There was no need for violence." He turned and walked swiftly toward the glare of the Kurfürstendamm.

Barney walked off the hysteria and the adrenaline and got back to the Kempinski twenty minutes later. He showered again, directing the thrust of the hot spray between his shoulder blades. After the shower he took a cold beer out of the small Frigidaire, doused the bedroom lights, and stood in front of the large window. He stared at the Mercedes emblem high atop the Europa Building, towering above the city. Its three-pointed emblem illuminated in blue neon, revolved slowly, majestically. Barney thought the sign displayed an exotic disdain for the past, a fitting replacement for the swastika, an indestructible symbol in glass and neon, proving the ancient truth that money never lost a war.

CHAPTER

34 ⊠

IT WAS PRECISELY 9:00 A.M. WHEN BARNEY STEPPED OUT OF THE ELE-
vator. Hans Lehmans was waiting for him. The men shook hands, and
Lehmans said, "You feel rested?"

"I feel fine. Took your advice. Slept till late afternoon. Then introduced myself to Bergen. Had a sauna, took a stroll. Ate in the outdoor
café and went to sleep."

"Well, you'll be tired again this evening," Lehmans said. "It takes a
few days."

Helmut Bergen sat behind an enormous desk. Its size was exagger-
ated by the tiny room. The manager's face was even grimmer in the
morning than it had been at night. They exchanged "good mornings,"
and Lehmans thanked Bergen for taking care of Barney. Bergen nodded
and glanced at him. "Did you enjoy the sauna, Mr. Caine?"

"It was fine."

"Good. Please sit down." Bergen indicated the small chairs in front
of his desk and asked, "Coffee?" They declined. "All right," Bergen
said, "then we begin." He opened a thick manila file. "First, the registration card. We keep these for seven years." He moved a white five-by-
seven card across the desk to Barney.

Bergen said, "You will note the card is broken down into six categories: the name of the guest; the month, date, and time of arrival; the
home address of the guest; the room number; the time and date of departure; and the forwarding address."

The card showed that Neeley had registered as Mr. and Mrs. on January 3, 1978. Neeley had listed his Los Angeles address as city of origin
and had registered at 2:15 P.M. Their room number had been 436.

Their departure date had been January 9, at 10:25 A.M. Their forwarding address was the Atlantic Hotel in Hamburg.

Barney handed the card back to Bergen. "We'll need a copy of this."

"Of course," Bergen replied as he took the card and set it aside. He then removed a thick sheaf of odd-sized papers from the manila folder. He slid them across the desk to Barney. "There you have the soul of any client's stay: the bill. It is broken down into telexes, newspaper charges, car rentals, swimming pool or sauna, sight-seeing, postage stamps, room service, and bar."

Barney thumbed through the slips. There were charges for the daily *International Tribune, Playboy, Time* and *Newsweek,* and a German magazine, *Der Stern.* There was a charge from the beauty salon signed by Kay Neeley on January 5. There were two telexes both dated January 8; both had been sent as night letters. The first telex was addressed to Arthur Clements at his Century City office, and read:

MADE CONTACT OBER AND DIESTEL. GOING TO HAMBURG ATLANTIC HOTEL. WILL ADVISE.

Barney handed the cable to Lehmans and read the second one:

Y. KALADI—300 VIA PACIFICA. EUR-ROME, ITALY. GENESIS EXISTS. ADVISE TED.

"I wonder who the hell Diestel is?" Barney said.

Lehmans shrugged. "It's not an uncommon name. What about Kaladi and Ted?"

"Kaladi is a Saudi grease man," Barney replied. "Takes bribe money from U.S. oil companies, for private use of oil sheikhs. Ted is Frank Tedesco."

Barney handed the second cable to Lehmans, who read it and returned both cables to Bergen. "Copies," Lehmans said.

Bergen nodded and placed them on top of the registration card.

"You have Neeley's phone calls?" Barney asked.

Bergen took a stapled sheaf of long, narrow white and green slips and shoved them across to Barney. It was a computerized readout. The headings were in multiple categories and all in German. Lehmans leaned over Barney's shoulder and interpreted.

"The first box is the trunk line used. The next is the number dialed, then unit cost, then room number charged to; the last three headings are the date and time of call."

Bergen added, "The slips are in chronological order. And the data contained are absolutely accurate. Our phone system is operated by a Siemens T-one-hundred computer."

Barney gave half the slips to Lehmans. "Look for any number that repeats."

Bergen rose. "While you examine those slips, I'll have these copied."

Barney was on the fifth slip when the first number repeated itself. The number on the fifth slip matched that of the first slip, the first call Neeley had made on the day he checked in. The number was a West Berlin area code and read: "871094." The same number reappeared on the ninth slip. Lehmans finished checking his half of the phone records and had placed two slips aside. "These two repeat." He handed Barney the slips; the numbers read "871094," making a total of five calls to the same number spread over four days.

Bergen came back with copies of the telexes and the registration card. Barney picked up the five phone slips containing the repeated number and looked at Lehmans.

"What do you think?"

"Try it," Lehmans said.

Barney handed one of the slips to Bergen. "Mr. Bergen, would you be kind enough to dial this number?"

"Who am I calling?"

"We'll see," Barney replied.

Bergen's hand trembled slightly as he picked up the receiver and dialed the number on his private line. There was a brief moment while the phone rang; then Bergen tensed and spoke into the phone in German. He paused again, listening, then said, *"Eine Minute, bitte."* He cupped the receiver with his palm. "It's the Berlin Power and Light company."

Barney glanced at Lehmans for a second, then turned to Bergen. "Ask for a Mr. Obermann."

Bergen uncupped the speaker and spoke into the phone, *"Ist dort ein Herr Obermann angestellt?"* There was another brief pause, and Bergen said, *"Eine Minute."* He cupped the speaker again and said, "Paul Obermann is the chief engineer."

Barney had to fight to keep the excitement out of his voice. "Ask the operator to ring his office. And give me the phone when you get him." Barney rose, went around the desk, and stood alongside Bergen.

"He may not speak English," Lehmans said.

"Neeley spoke to him," Barney replied.

"Perhaps Neeley spoke German," Lehmans suggested.

Barney nodded and looked down at the nervous manager. "If you get Obermann, ask him if he speaks English."

Bergen asked the operator to ring through to Mr. Obermann's office. He then spoke to a secretary. There was another pause, and Bergen's voice tensed. "Herr Obermann?" There was a brief exchange in German that ended with Bergen's question *"Herr Obermann, sprechen sie englisch?"*

Bergen listened, then looked up at Barney, nodded, and handed the receiver to him. Barney took a deep breath, exhaled, and said, "Mr. Obermann, my name is Barney Caine. I'm an American police officer investigating the murder of two American citizens." There was no response, and Barney continued. "The victims were Kay Neeley and Thomas Neeley. I have reason to believe you were in contact with Mr. Neeley in January of this year. I would like to see you."

A tired voice answered in heavily accented but grammatically correct English. "I cannot help you or see you." The line clicked off.

Barney held the dead phone for a moment, then gently placed the receiver back on the cradle. "He hung up."

"I'll talk to him," Lehmans said, and took out his Marlboros, lit one, got to his feet, and went to the phone. "I can have him subpoenaed to appear at the Berlin Hall of Justice."

"You mean a court order?" Barney asked.

"Exactly. You furnish the questions, and a judge puts them to Obermann." Lehmans completed dialing the number and, after a brief exchange with the operator and Obermann's secretary, got through to Obermann. Lehmans spoke politely but with authority, and Barney understood the gist of his words.

Lehman identified himself as an inspector in the Bunderskriminalsamt. Lehmans listened to Obermann's response, his cheeks slowly reddened, and when he spoke again, there was unmistakable anger in his voice. *"Herr Obermann, ich werde in zehn Minuten bei Ihnen im Büro sein!"* He slammed the receiver down. "Let's go, Barney."

"Where to?"

"To see Herr Obermann."

They thanked the chalk-faced manager who nodded but did not answer. Bergen sipped some water, thinking the day was starting off badly.

The Berlin Power and Light Company was at number 40 Birkbuschestrasse. It was a complex of red-brick buildings that sat on the banks of a canal. The central building was a cathedral-like medieval structure with huge oblong windows and a sloping gray-gabled roof. Two white smokestacks towered over the entire complex.

They followed a young man wearing a gray smock down a long alley paved with black cobblestones and surrounded on all sides by low red-brick buildings connected by snaking overhead steam pipes. The loud whine of generators reverberated through the alley. They approached a two-story wooden barracks-like structure, and the young man turned to Lehmans. *"Hier ist das Büro von Direktor Obermann."*

Lehmans introduced himself to Obermann's secretary, an overweight middle-aged woman with thinning orange-colored hair. She eyed the men uneasily, then motioned them to enter the door to the inner office.

Paul Obermann looked like his office: old, neat, and reliable. He was a slim, balding man with steady brown eyes, a large, straight nose, and a small mouth that did not go too well with the rest of his face. By the lines at his eyes and mouth Barney figured Obermann had to be in his early sixties. He was well dressed, in a dark blue suit, white shirt, and maroon tie. He stared up at the two men but remained silent. He did not offer a chair or greet them in any way. Lehmans took out his ID and motioned Barney to do the same. Obermann examined both cards carefully, each in its turn.

"Let us conduct this business in English," Lehmans said.

"As you wish, Inspector."

"Thank you," Lehmans said. "I am confirming what you already know. My colleague, Mr. Caine, is a detective with the Los Angeles police. He is interested in asking you questions pertaining to the murder of Mr. and Mrs. Thomas Neeley."

Obermann leaned back in his swivel chair. He did not answer for a long moment; then, as if choosing his words carefully from a wide possibility, he asked Barney, "Why do you come to me?"

"Because your name was found in Tom Neeley's home. And we know that he called you here at least five times between January third and January ninth of this year."

Obermann cleared his throat. "Mr. Neeley may have had the general number of this plant, but there are over six hundred people working here on three different shifts. Why do you assume he spoke with me?"

Lehmans answered, "He had your name and this number. Are you saying that is a coincidence?"

Obermann did not respond. There was a pause; then Barney said gently, "Please believe me, Mr. Obermann, I'm not trying to implicate you in this case. And I have no desire to cause you any trouble. It would help me if you would consent to answer a few questions."

"I'm sorry, I cannot help you."

"In that case," Lehmans snapped, "I want officially to inform you, Herr Obermann, that I will proceed at once to compel your appearance in court."

Obermann pushed a button on a console, and his orange-haired secretary appeared in the doorway. "Good-bye, gentlemen."

Barney stopped halfway to the door, then turned to Obermann. "Tom and Kay Neeley were brutally murdered two weeks ago in Los Angeles. I know you and the Neeleys were involved in Genesis." Barney paused. "I think your life may be in danger. If you should change your mind, I'm at the Kempinski."

Obermann stared at the closed door. He was overcome by fear and remorse. He sensed that in some way the Neeley killings were connected with his own visit to the Swiss industrialist eight months ago. The Swiss had been after the Genesis Formula, and so had Neeley. And now there was the American detective to deal with.

Obermann looked up at the ceiling as if some elusive answer hid in the peeling white paint. Fortunately he did not have to choose any course of action. He would do what he had always done. He would follow orders. He lifted the receiver and dialed the number of Friedrich Diestel.

CHAPTER

35 ⊠

THE BERLIN PREFECTURE OF POLICE WAS A FOUR-STORY GRAY-STUCCO building in the suburb of Tempelhof. During the war years it had been a military record center for the Wehrmacht. Barney noticed two huge crows sculpted onto the sides of the building above the entrance. "Why crows?" he asked.

"After the war the Nazi eagles had to be removed from all the buildings. No one knew what to put in their place." Lehmans smiled. "It was finally decided that crows would be safe."

Barney followed Lehmans up the steps past a sign that read: "DER POLIZEIPRÄSIDENT BERLIN." Lehmans's secretary was a pleasant-looking girl who spoke English fluently. Lehmans dictated the order compelling Obermann's appearance in court. He also asked her to request a background check on Paul Obermann from Federal Police Headquarters in Wiesbaden. He gave the secretary the eleven remaining slips of Neeley's phone calls made from the Kempinski and asked her to phone each number and determine the place or person called. The secretary left, and Lehmans said, "Come on. I'll buy you lunch at the Berlin Museum."

"A museum for lunch?" Barney asked.

"The museum is ordinary. But the restaurant is fantastic."

The entrance to Lehmans's office was suddenly filled by a huge, muscular man who had a cigarette dangling from his lips. Lehmans looked up at him and said something in German. The man responded, and the color suddenly went out of Lehmans's face. The big man left, and Lehmans leaned back in his chair and rubbed his hand wearily over his eyes. There was a universal language about police activities, and Barney knew the big man had brought bad news.

"What is it, Hans?" he asked.

"Two terrorists just escaped Moabit Prison."

"How?"

"We don't have the details. Only that they're killers. A man and a woman." He lit a cigarette, then looked at it with disdain. "You've been fortunate in America. You haven't been hit by organized terrorism."

Lehmans rose and went to the window. He looked out for a moment, then blew a cloud of smoke against the glass pane and turned to Barney. "The woman who escaped. I questioned her on and off for over a year. Her psychological profile fits the terrorist pattern perfectly. Age thirty-one. Upper middle class. University student. A love-hate relationship with a strong father figure. Her ideological and political interest gradually overwhelmed by the gratification of violent criminal action. Trained in Beirut."

"Beirut?"

Lehmans nodded. "All the terror groups are internationally related." Lehmans walked up to his desk and crushed the cigarette. "The Red Brigades and NAP in Italy are trained in Havana and Damascus. The Red Army here in Germany is trained in Tripoli by Habash's group. That connection became apparent at Entebbe and confirmed at Mogadishu. The Basque separatists in Spain and the terror groups in Argentina and the IRA are financed by the KGB. The PLO is financed by the Saudis and the oil sheikhdoms."

"That's a hell of a parlay: Arab royalty and the KGB both financing the same terrorist groups."

"Money dictates its own allegiance," Lehmans replied.

"You know, the guy I nailed on the beach at Malibu was a companion of an Italian girl, a member of the Brigati Rosse."

"I know." Lehmans sighed. "I saw that in your report. Come on, Barney. Let's get out of here."

Lehmans had been right; the Berlin Museum wasn't much except for a few wonderful German Expressionist paintings. He was also right about the small restaurant tucked away in one of the cavernous halls of the baroque building. The restaurant was done in the prewar style of a German country inn, and the food was superb.

They ate with the kind of hunger that is fed by tension. They started with three different kinds of smoked fish, followed by a cold beet soup and large steins of draft beer. The main course consisted of veal sausages cooked in a mustard sauce and served with a tasty potato salad. Barney took a piece of black bread, spread some mustard sauce on it, and wrapped it around the last piece of sausage. He washed it down with the cold beer and pushed the plate away.

"Christ. That's good."

"The best in the city," Lehmans said, finishing the last of his potato salad. He drank some beer, took out the omnipresent red and white Marlboros and offered one to Barney.

"Why not?" Barney sighed. Encouraged by the older man's bravado, Barney inhaled deeply and luxuriously. They listened to the chatter from the other tables and a Mozart concerto drifting out of speakers in the corners of the high-ceilinged baronial room. "Do you have any ideas about Genesis?" Barney asked.

"The Nazis often used code names based on Greek gods, German mythological gods, and biblical names and places," Lehmans offered.

"What would 'Genesis' indicate?"

Lehmans shrugged. "Could be anything from a biological weapon, to rocketry, to electronic sensory devices, or something so revolutionary it wasn't even labeled. In my opinion, the portion of your report concerning Neeley's questions to Isella, the race driver, supports the exotic fuel theory."

The waiter brought two coffees and a small dish of assorted pastries. Barney crushed the cigarette and bit into a chocolate-covered cream puff. He shook his head, thinking of the calories, but ate it all anyway. Lehmans sipped his coffee and said, "Let's assume that Genesis was a Nazi secret that had something to do with energy. Obermann is a chief engineer of a power and light company. Neeley was in American Intelligence during the war. There is a certain thread of logic that would indicate they knew each other."

On the way out they strolled leisurely through the Hall of German Expressionists. Lehmans told Barney the paintings had been recovered from Göring's private collection. After the war the Allies had returned them to the West German government.

Outside the pink building the cool air had warmed slightly. The sun shone sporadically as it ducked in and out of high, fleecy clouds.

Lehmans said, "This prison break will demand some of my time. Do you mind taking a taxi back to the hotel?"

"No problem."

"There's nothing more you can do anyway, not until I obtain the court order. Get some rest. Enjoy Berlin."

They walked up to a parked taxi. At the door of the car, Lehmans put his hand on Barney's shoulder. "Don't get restless. Don't do anything on your own."

"What are you saying, Hans?"

"I'm telling you not to be a hero."

CHAPTER

36 ⊠

BARNEY CAME DOWN THE LONG FOURTH-FLOOR CORRIDOR AND PASSED a homely young girl pushing the cleaning cart. *"Guten Tag."* Barney tried the German greeting, but the girl answered him with a thick Irish brogue. "Good afternoon, sir." Barney was surprised by the brogue and wondered what an Irish girl was doing working as a day maid in a Berlin hotel. He remembered seeing some street cleaners who appeared to be Turks or Arabs, and he guessed that the menial tasks in West Germany were performed by foreign laborers. Even without Hitler, the Germans still believed that biology was destiny.

His room had been made up, and through the windows Barney could see the TV needle from East Berlin with its curious sun-made gold cross blazing off the round ball at the top. He draped his jacket over a chair and went to the phone on the night table. He checked his watch and calculated the time differential. It would be a little after 6:00 A.M. in Los Angeles. He asked the operator to place a person-to-person call to Louis Yosuta. He spelled Yosuta for the operator and gave her Louis's home number. The operator told him to hang up, she would call right back.

Barney stretched out on the bed and picked up the newspaper: President Carter was still trying to pass an energy bill; the dollar continued to decline in Western Europe and Japan. The Soviets had condemned two dissidents to Siberian concentration camps; both dissidents were Jews. The Israelis announced a new electronic antimissile system they had developed at the Technion Institute in Haifa. Barney turned to the sports section. Pete Rose was on a record-setting consecutive hitting streak, and the first pro football contract disputes were already under way. The phone rang sharply. Barney picked up the receiver, and the operator said, "Your party's on the line."

"Hello, Louis?"

"How are you, Barney?"

Barney felt a rush of reassurance from the friendly voice, seven thousand miles away. "I'm fine. Stalled for the moment, but fine." Barney explained the Obermann situation then said, "Neeley sent a telex to Clements telling him that he had located Obermann and someone named Diestel. The telex is in the mail to you."

"Who's Diestel?" Louis asked.

"Beats me. There was another telex to the Arab payoff man in Rome. Kaladi. You remember?"

"Yes," Louis said. "Neeley's hot money drop for Steiffel."

"Right. He telexed Kaladi saying that Genesis exists, and advise Ted." Barney paused. "Ted is Tedesco."

"What do you want me to do?" Louis asked.

"Wait till you get the copy of Neeley's telex, then see Clements." Barney added, "Put some muscle on him. Threaten to book him."

"He's too smart for that, Barney. All we have is a thin business link between him and Neeley. Clements has already admitted to that. We have no grounds to book him."

"Well, hassle him. Put some guys on him. Have him tailed. Try and get an okay from Nolan to put a tap on his phone."

"Where does Tedesco fit in?" Louis asked.

"Tedesco is Mafia," Barney said. "Beyond the cocaine, I can't figure his connection. The one weak link in the chain, the one man we have the most information on is Clements. I want you to put the heat on him."

"I'll do my best."

"I know you will." Barney paused. "What's going on back there?"

"Three murders up in the hills," Louis said. "A crazy. Killing teenage hookers and draining their blood. Papers and TV are having a field day. 'Vampire Killer Loose in Hollywood Hills.' It's bigger than the Hillside Strangler."

"Have you seen Laura Gregson?"

"No. But I have some Metro guys watching her."

"Thanks, Louis."

"Take care of yourself, Barney."

Barney hung up slowly; talking to Louis accented his loneliness. He got up and lit a cigarillo, went to the small Frigidaire, took out a bottle of mineral water, popped the cap, and was about to search for a glass when the phone rang.

"Hello?" Barney said.

"Mr. Caine?" The English was heavily accented, and the tense voice had a familiar ring.

"Yes?"

"This is Paul Obermann."

Barney felt the rush of excitement; he cradled the phone and sat down on the bed.

"Are you in a position to speak freely?" Obermann asked.

"Yes. I'm alone."

"I am prepared to discuss the matter of Tom Neeley."

"What changed your mind?"

"What does it matter?"

"I'm a professional, Mr. Obermann. This kind of abrupt turnaround makes me ask questions."

"You are a foreigner. Unfamiliar with German political life. One does not bring the police into private matters."

"I understand."

"Now, Mr. Caine, if you promise to come alone, I will agree to meet with you. If you violate my wishes, I will not say a word. Understood?"

"You have my word." Barney inhaled deeply on the cigarillo, wishing it were a cigarette.

"I cannot risk any exposure to the police."

"I've given you my word," Barney said. "You'll have to trust me."

"So long as we understand each other," Obermann repeated.

"We do," Barney replied.

"Meet me at the zoo at five-fifty-five. Second floor of the Aquarium. There is a bamboo bridge. You will see it."

"Why the zoo?"

"It is safe. Children, tour groups, guards, and at closing time the crowds are thin."

"I'll be there," Barney said.

"Five-fifty-five. Sharp." The line clicked off, and the connection went dead.

Barney hung up and puffed thoughtfully on the cigarillo. If he met Obermann alone, he would be violating Lehmans's instructions; on the other hand, by Lehmans's own admission, the police were a liability.

But the risks of playing into something he did not fully understand, in a foreign city, worried Barney. Obermann could be setting him up. Yet his reason for the zoo seemed plausible. And his reasons for not cooperating earlier also had the ring of truth.

Barney went into the bathroom, tossed the cigarillo into the toilet bowl, and flushed the toilet. He then went to the sink and splashed cold water over his face. He straightened up, staring at his image in the mirror above the sink. There were dark circles under his eyes, and the tan of his last day at the beach with Timmy had faded. The small scar on his cheek stood out in its reddish hue against his pale skin. He would have to see Obermann. He had no real choice. Obermann was the key that could break the case open. He would have to go with the risk and violate Lehmans's instructions.

There was a young, darkly handsome man on duty who smiled at Barney as he approached the reception desk. "What can you tell me about the Berlin zoo?" Barney asked.

"Quite a lot," the young man said. "A moment, please." The clerk went to a compartmented shelf that held transportation and sight-seeing brochures. He shuffled the colorful pamphlets and handed Barney a folder that had the picture of a lion cub on the cover. "Our Berlin zoo is a legend, Mr. Caine. In 1939 the Berlin zoo contained the most important collection of animals in the world." He continued with pride. "Our zoo was also the first in the world to employ open-air enclosures for its animals."

"I'm really interested in marine exhibits," Barney said. "Do you know where the Aquarium is located?"

"On the second floor of the Administration Building. You enter on Budapester Street."

"I'm meeting someone there, at the bamboo bridge."

"Yes. The bamboo bridge is in the Crocodile Hall. One of the most famous exhibits."

Barney tucked the brochure into his pocket. "Thank you."

The clerk spread his hands. "Please don't expect too much."

Barney smiled. "You said it was the best in the world."

"Up to 1939," the clerk explained. "In just a few hours in 1943 and again in the great Allied raids of 1944, the zoo was largely destroyed. The work of a hundred years was obliterated. But the coup de grâce took place in the last days of April 1945." The clerk's voice was genuinely sad. "The zoo became the final battleground. A fanatic battalion of SS held out against the Russian tanks. The zoo was a funeral pyre. Animals running wild amongst the firing of soldiers. Zebras dashing into the tanks. Building after building, exhibit after exhibit blown to pieces." The clerk sighed. "The Reich came to an end in the zoo."

"I'm sure after all these years it's been restored," Barney said.

"Yes. It has. But it will never be the same."

Barney spoke quickly. "Well, thank you. I appreciate your help." He started away, then turned back. "If anyone asks for me, I'll be in the bar."

Barney ordered a scotch and soda and thought again about the wisdom of meeting Obermann alone. He didn't want to cause Lehmans any trouble. Lehmans had enough on his hands.

Barney stared into the scotch and moved the ice cubes around with his forefinger. He remembered watching Kay Neeley do the same thing when they went out to question her the first time. The Sunday Tom Neeley was shot to death.

"Are you Mr. Caine?" Her voice was smoky, and the German accent gave it mystery. He found himself looking into a pair of very light blue eyes. Her cheekbones were high and dramatic and curved symmetrically down to a small, patrician nose and a full, soft mouth. Her face was framed by long pale hair. It was the kind of natural blond color that was not for sale on cosmetic counters. She was tall and thin with full, swelling breasts and a narrow waist. She held her wide shoulders straight. And a sweet, heady perfume circled her presence.

He cleared his throat. "Yes. I'm Barney Caine."

She moved closer to him and he could see a pinwheel of topaz-colored lines running out from the light blue irises. "I am Lisa Obermann. May I join you a moment?"

"Please." Barney rose and pulled the barstool out for her. She wore a grape-colored dress and carried a black cape over her arm. "Would you like a drink?" he asked.

"Perhaps a glass of dry white wine."

Barney ordered the wine and glanced back toward the alcove of the bar. No one else had come in with her. The same businessmen were in the same booths. There were no new faces.

The girl opened her large beige bag and took out a pack of German cigarettes. Barney picked up a pack of matches and struck one. Her fingers touched his hand while he held the match to her cigarette. She inhaled deeply and smiled "thank you." She had the kind of delicate beauty that comes to all things that have been created artfully, but there was a quality of strength in her pale blue eyes and high cheekbones and the determined way she carried her shoulders.

The bartender served the wine and she raised her glass. "Good health," she whispered.

"Cheers." He smiled.

She sipped the wine and turned to him. "I introduced myself to you as Lisa Obermann. But my legal name, that is to say, my professional name, is Spangler. I'm a photographic model. Spangler was the name of my natural parents." She tossed her pale hair. My mother gave birth to me in a military hospital in Zossen just before it was overrun by the Soviets."

He thought it was curious that she said "Soviets" rather than Russians.

She puffed gently at the cigarette. "My mother was killed when they shelled the hospital. She died three days after I was born."

Barney wondered why she was telling him her history but decided not to ask.

As if reading his mind, she said, "I know I'm trying your patience, but it will all be quite clear to you in a moment." She sipped the wine and continued, "I was taken with a group of orphans from Zossen to a hospital not far from Hamburg. The hospital authorities contacted Paul Obermann. He was my mother's brother. He took care of me after the war. I consider him my stepfather. He raised me. You can't imagine how fortunate I was. And how few of us survived." She toyed with the stem of the wineglass and then looked at Barney. "Now you know who I am."

"But not why you're here."

"I'm here because my stepfather phoned me a short while ago. He said that you had attempted to see him about a Los Angeles crime you're investigating. That it involved an American man named Neeley. And that he was going to meet you at the zoo."

"That's strange. He swore me to secrecy. Why would he tell you?"

"Because he's frightened. And I'm the only family he has. He wanted me to know where he would be." She paused and stared into Barney's eyes. "And who he would be with."

"What is he frightened of?"

"My stepfather was involved in highly sensitive work during the war."

"What kind of work?"

"I don't know. Only that it was secret and sensitive."

"How do you know that?" Barney pressed.

She crushed her cigarette and brushed her long pale hair away from the sides of her face. She swung around in the chair so she faced him directly. "About eight months ago a Swiss man came to see Paul. An industrialist. Whatever they discussed had to do with Paul's work during the war. The meeting with this Swiss frightened him."

Barney nodded and glanced at her cigarette. "Do you mind?"

"Help yourself, Mr. Caine."

"Barney." He smiled and took one of her cigarettes and lit it. "Tell me, do you know anyone named Diestel?"

She shook her head. "No. What has that to do with Paul?"

"Maybe nothing. Have you ever heard your stepfather mention the word 'Genesis'?"

"No. Never."

"Do you think his activities during the war may have been connected with war crimes?"

She smiled sadly. "Why do Americans always think the entire German population was involved with war crimes?"

"Well." Barney shrugged. "What else would frighten a man thirty-three years after the war?"

"There were many valuable secrets during the reign of the Nazis," she replied.

"So you believe he might know something valuable enough to place his life in jeopardy."

"Yes. That's why I'm here. I am convinced my stepfather is in that kind of danger." Lisa stared into Barney's eyes and moved her face close to his, and her lips closed slowly over her words. "Please, leave Paul alone. I came here to ask this favor of you." The blue eyes roamed across his face, ending on his mouth.

"I'm a professional policeman," Barney said. "I have reason to believe your stepfather can help me. I have to see him. I have no choice."

Lisa nodded, rose slowly, unwinding in a feline fashion, the smell of her perfume strong and heady as she leaned close to him. "Mr. Caine, I hold you personally responsible for the safety of my stepfather."

She started away, but Barney grabbed her right wrist. "Where can I get in touch with you?"

"Why do you ask?"

"Because I might have to."

"I'm in the Berlin directory," she replied with a curious sense of triumph.

CHAPTER

37 ☒

BARNEY GOT OUT OF THE TAXI AT THE BUDAPESTERSTRASSE ENTRANCE to the zoo. The sky had darkened, and a cold northern wind chilled the city. He tossed his cigarillo away and walked up to the steps into the grim cement building.

The ground-floor lobby was bisected by a dark U-shaped tunnel that housed illuminated glass tanks of marine exhibits. There were groups of schoolchildren and clusters of adults going through the gloomy tunnels. Barney glanced at his watch; he had eight minutes to kill. He entered the mouth of the tunnel and walked slowly past the evil-eyed grotesqueries gliding through the murky green water. The schoolchildren watched the hideous marine creatures with a mixture of curiosity and dread.

Barney came out of the opposite end of the U-shaped tunnel and started up the stairs to the second-floor serpentarium. A brilliantly colored Christ in stained glass rose up behind the staircase making an incongruous theological connection between the evil-looking monsters in their watery cases below and the coiled serpents in their glass cases on the floor above.

The U-shaped tunnel on the second floor was bisected in its center by a thirty-foot-high and fifty-foot-wide glass atrium. A sign over the atrium said: "Krokodilhalle." Barney could see a profusion of tall green flora growing inside the atrium, and spanning the width of the atrium was the bamboo bridge. Barney entered the tunnel, and walked slowly past a variety of coiled serpents.

Thirty feet into the tunnel, he entered the crocodile atrium, and was instantly assaulted by a blanket of moist, fetid heat.

He stepped out onto the bamboo bridge; it was only four feet high and suspended over a large circular moat. A bank of muddy earth circled a pool of yellow-green stagnant water, and a nest of gray coils wallowed in the mud. They were fifteen feet long with gray, spiked skin, tapered serpentine tails, and hooded, bulging eyes; a few had their huge jaws open, exposing rows of murderous-looking teeth. They were entwined, sleeping, watching, occasionally whipping their tails.

There was a small child with his mother on the far side of the bridge. The woman held the boy's hand as she spoke to him. Barney shook his head, wondering how the authorities could have permitted the low bridge; one curious, energetic child making one miscalculation, and it would be over.

The heat, the humidity, the dark green foliage, the dank smell, and the gray monsters began to grate against Barney's nerves. He felt sweaty and queasy. He checked his watch. Obermann was two minutes late. Barney opened his suede jacket. He could feel drops of perspiration forming under his arms, and the wool turtleneck sweater was beginning to itch. He looked around at dark tunnels of serpents to his right and left. He was standing in the center of the U directly under the only bright light on the entire floor. A professional gunman firing a weapon from the darkness of the tunnels on either side could not miss.

He wondered why Obermann was late. He knew he had taken a hell of a chance coming alone. He rubbed the sleeve of his jacket against the beads of perspiration beginning to ooze out of his forehead. The little boy and his mother left the atrium.

It was very still, with only the occasional sound of footfalls coming from the dark tunnels. He decided to give Obermann two more minutes.

There was a sudden, violent movement from the moat below that shook the jungle foliage. Barney looked down, and on the mud bank a huge crocodile thrashed its ten-foot-long tail, snarling open-mouthed, teeth bared, face to face with an equally large monster. The tail stopped thrashing, and they stared at each other, motionless.

Then one of them turned abruptly, its four small legs churning up the mud as it slithered beneath the brackish water.

Barney checked his watch, then looked up and saw Paul Obermann crossing toward him from the opposite side of the bridge. He wore a dark topcoat and a gray felt hat. His eyeglasses were slightly tinted. He seemed unnaturally calm, but his steady brown eyes of the morning were nervously shifting from point to point. He reached Barney and removed his hat. He did not greet Barney or acknowledge his presence in any way. He simply stood there, staring down at the gray monsters in the pit below.

After a long moment Obermann said, "Do not look at me or appear familiar. We are strangers discussing an exhibit in the zoo. We have only a few minutes. Now what is it you wish to know?"

"Did you meet with Tom Neeley here in Berlin in early January?"

"Yes."

"How did you know Tom Neeley?"

"We met many years ago."

"Where?"

"Hamburg."

Obermann stepped back slightly from the low rail of the bamboo bridge, and Barney watched him carefully; it would not take much to throw a man over that low rail. Obermann stared at Barney through the misting lenses of his glasses. He then removed them, took out a tissue, and began to clean the lenses.

"How did you and Neeley come to meet one another?" Barney asked.

Obermann held the lenses up to the light. "In April 1945 I was taken prisoner by the British in Hamburg. Thomas Neeley was there on temporary assignment with British Intelligence." Obermann replaced his glasses.

"What was the nature of Neeley's assignment?"

"I don't know. But he was very kind to me. I was engaged in translation of certain secret documents."

"Pertaining to what?"

"Genesis."

Barney felt a surge of exhilaration that always comes with a major break in a complex case. "What did 'Genesis' stand for?"

"Genesis was a code name for hydrogenation: a chemical process by which lubricants and fuel are manufactured synthetically from organic matter, principally coal."

Barney wiped his face with his sleeve and felt the perspiration running from his armpits down his rib cage. "When you say 'fuel,' you mean gasoline?"

Obermann nodded. "Yes. Also propane, methane, ethylene, natural gas, crude oil, all manner of thick lubricants, and even butter."

"Butter from coal?" Barney asked incredulously.

"Yes. What you Americans call margarine. I was employed in a hydrogenation plant in Nordenstadt that produced eight hundred tons of butter a month, primarily for use by the Africa Corps." Obermann turned to Barney. "You see, the synthetic butter did not turn rancid in the desert."

"But this synthetic fuel, was it made in great quantities?" Barney asked.

Obermann looked back down into the pit. "For those times you could call the quantities great. We had fifteen hydrogenation plants throughout the Reich. The entire war machine ran on synthetic fuel. We even produced jet fuel at the end of the war."

"Why jet fuel?"

"We had developed the world's first jet fighter, the ME-262. The fuel requirements were different from that of regular piston aircraft. Of course, the Führer waited too long to approve mass production of this plane, so it had no bearing on the outcome of the conflict. But we also made the fuel for the big rockets. The A-four and A-nine. They were fueled with grain alcohol."

"And all of this work was under the code name Genesis?"

Obermann nodded. "Yes."

A uniformed guard came out onto the bridge. *"Wir schliessen in zwei Minuten."*

Obermann waved at the man, then turned to Barney. "Come, let's walk. They are closing in two minutes."

They crossed the bridge and entered the cool dark tunnel and walked slowy past the illuminated cases of serpents.

"What was it that Neeley wanted of you?" Barney asked.

"The Genesis Formula."

"Why would anyone want the formula? I mean, after all these years how can the process still be secret?"

"The general process is well known. The secret is the metal catalyst that makes the process viable," Obermann continued. "The catalyst is not well known. It is incredibly complex. You might say the catalyst is the 'black box.' It is the heart of the whole process. At the end of the war it was rumored that we had developed a remarkable catalyst. A catalyst that reduced the quantity of hydrogen and water, lowering the tremendous heat necessary to crack the coal. It also produced a great rise in the coal-to-oil ratio: from sixty percent to over ninety percent."

"Would such a catalyst be regarded as secret today?"

"Without question."

"Just how valuable would that formula be?"

"Whoever had that formula would need only technology and coal to be self-sufficient in fuel." Obermann paused. "The value of the formula cannot be calculated."

They passed a huge case where a black and green python was beginning to uncoil. "Then it would follow," Barney continued, "that certain petroleum interests would not be overjoyed with the mass production of synthetic fuel?"

"You are now beginning to understand my reluctance to discuss this matter. The formula would represent a distinct threat to a three-hundred-billion-dollar industry."

They were moving toward the end of the tunnel. "Did you meet Neeley's wife, Kay, in January?"

"Yes. We had dinner one evening."

"Did you ever hear the name 'Frank Tedesco' mentioned?"

"Yes. Kay Neeley said she was going to Haiti to meet this man Tedesco."

"Did the Neeleys mention a man named Arthur Clements?"

"Yes. I believe it was Clements who suggested she go to Haiti."

The perspiration was beginning to dry and turn cold on Barney's rib cage. "Do you know anyone named Diestel?"

"No."

They were approaching the final exhibit at the end of the tunnel. "What can you tell me about the Swiss industrialist who approached you eight months ago?"

Obermann stopped and looked at Barney in consternation. They were directly in front of a glass case holding a king cobra that had risen up on its tail, its head fanned out. Its body swaying back and forth measuring the two men on the other side of the glass.

"How did you know about the Swiss?" Obermann inquired.

"Lisa Spangler came to see me a few hours ago."

For a flashing second Obermann seemed perplexed; he chewed on his lower lip. And Barney said, "She was concerned with your safety."

Obermann nodded. "She always has been."

The weaving cobra behind Obermann was unnerving Barney. He touched Obermann's arm, and they resumed walking. "Tell me about the Swiss," Barney said.

"He wanted information pertaining to the formula. I told him I knew nothing."

"Can you explain how Tom Neeley tracked you down after all these years?" Barney asked.

"Neeley was a high police official. He was no stranger to police procedures. And I have not been in hiding. I have been quite visible. I am, after all, a man in some position."

"Who was in charge of the Genesis program during the war?"

"The man at the top was Hermann Göring."

"But who was the chief scientist specifically in charge of the hydrogenation plants and production?"

"I don't recall. There were thousands of scientists employed in the process."

"Do you know why Neeley went to Hamburg this past January?"

Obermann shrugged. "I have no idea."

They reached the end of the tunnel, and two guards were herding the last of a group of schoolchildren down the stairs. Obermann put on his gray felt hat, and Barney said, "I appreciate your time and help."

Obermann nodded. "Please permit me two minutes. I wish to leave the building alone."

"Why? There are two exits. You take one. I'll take the other."

"No. The Budapester Street entrance is closed. We must take the West Gate."

"All right," Barney agreed. "Go ahead. I'll wait."

"Thank you." Obermann put his hand out. "I wish you luck, Mr. Caine. Tom was very kind to me . . . many years ago." Obermann turned and went down the marble staircase shrouded by its huge, ornate stained glass wall.

Barney checked his watch. It was eight minutes after six. The wetness around his rib cage had dried to his skin, sending a chill through him. He glanced back at the crocodile atrium. The interior lights had been extinguished, leaving only one overhead ceiling light shining down on the deserted bamboo bridge. He tried to assimilate the facts he had obtained from Obermann, but the facts ran together. He thought about the butter made from coal for the Africa Corps, and the fact that Germany had been self-sufficient in synthetic fuel almost forty years ago. And the probable existence of an ultimate catalyst that made the entire process economically feasible. And how Tom Neeley had met Obermann in Hamburg and tracked him down again, thirty-three years later.

Barney started down the stairs, descending into the splash of red and blue light thrown by the stained glass wall. He reached the ground level and looked around. There were no tourists left, only a uniformed guard at each door. The guard opened the door for Barney and smiled, saying, *"Guten Abend."*

Barney stood on the stone terrace that faced the open exhibits of the zoo. He remembered what the hotel clerk had said: The final battle had been fought in this place. The vivid image of zebras dashing madly against the Russian tanks came alive for an instant. Then the lights on the park's walkways suddenly came on, and the mad imagery of the

Last Battle went out of Barney's mind. The night chill had a winter bite, and he turned his collar up against it.

A thin stream of stragglers were making their way toward the West Gate exit. A bank of spotlights came on, illuminating a giant stone iguanodon to Barney's left at the base of the terrace steps. The grotesque figure of the huge prehistoric iguana rose forty feet up from its base. Its colossal body was in a standing position, poised on great clawed feet. Barney's eyes traveled slowly down the monster's body. At the base of the statue a dark, spreading pool of blood leaked out of a gaping hole in Paul Obermann's head.

Barney felt paralyzed, as if he were caught in a nightmare. His legs refused the repeated command of his brain. He finally felt himself moving toward the fallen figure that lay at the base of the prehistoric monster. Barney knelt down and gently turned the body over. The right side of Obermann's head had been blown away, and there was another gaping wound in his chest, soaking his shirt with blood.

Barney looked around. The remaining tourists were still headed for the gate, unaware of the dead man only forty feet away. Whoever shot Obermann had used a silencer. Barney looked down at Obermann's glazed eyes and felt a rush of compassion for the dead man. Barney understood just how much courage it had taken for Obermann to meet with him. Lisa Spangler's words had been prophetic. He wished now he had listened to her. He reached into Obermann's jacket pocket and removed his wallet. It contained an identity card, a few credit cards, a library card, and sticking out between a fold of paper money was a white slip of paper. Barney lifted the paper, tilting it toward the light, and printed on it he saw the name "Friedrich Diestel," followed by the number "83 45 67." Barney quickly tucked the note into his own pocket and put the wallet back in Obermann's jacket.

There was a sudden flat "crump" of sound, and a chip of cement flew out of the iguanodon's leg only six inches from Barney's right eye. He instantly flattened his body to the pavement. He heard a woman scream and saw a tall figure wearing a ski mask standing in the shrubbery near the West Gate. The man held an automatic in his hand, pointed at Barney. The man methodically squeezed off shots between the running, screaming tourists. Their cries were joined by the roar of the lions that were out in their open enclosure some fifty yards away. Barney began to crawl back toward the terrace of the Administration Building. Another cement chip flew out of the stairs as he snaked his way up the five steps. He heard the shatter of glass, followed instantly by a sharp decrease in light. A spotlight near the base of the statue had been hit. The loss of light helped shadow Barney's movements. He crawled up onto the flat surface of the terrace and inched his way toward the door of the Administration Building. He reached his hand up to the knob, and the glass panel in the door shattered, sending shards of glass cascading down onto the back of his head. He dropped his hand reflexively just as the door opened and two uniformed guards rushed out. Barney heard the shrill blast of a whistle over the screams of the panicked tourists and the thunderous roars of the aroused lions.

He crawled inside the open doorway as three more guards came racing down the steps from the second floor. Two of them ran past Barney. The other man helped Barney to his feet and asked, *"Sind Sie in Ordnung?"*

Barney gasped, *"Nicht sprechen.* I don't understand. *Nicht sprechen deutsch."*

A guard stuck his head inside and shouted, *"Rufen Sie die Polizei an!"*

The guard standing with Barney went for the phone at the far end of the lobby.

CHAPTER

38 ⊠

THE BREATH OF THE MEN VAPORIZED IN THE GLARE OF THE HOT LIGHTS. Barney lounged against the side of a police car and sipped lukewarm coffee from a container. He was impressed by the universality of police procedure in the aftermath of homicide. Two detectives were searching through the shrubbery with flashlights, hoping to find a shell casing. The coroner and his white-clad attendants were standing over the corpse of Paul Obermann. The coroner, a tall, handsome man, reviewed his notes against a list on a clipboard held by his assistant. He finally nodded at the assistant, who handed him the clipboard. The attendants placed the body on a standing mobile stretcher and slid it into the waiting morgue van. The coroner went over to Hans Lehmans and spoke to him briefly, then went back to the van and signaled the men to leave.

The police photographer flashed a final exposure of the chalked out-line that marked the position of the body. Lehmans checked some point with one of the detectives, then walked slowly over to Barney.

He took out a pack of cigarettes and offered one to Barney. Lehmans cupped his hands around the flame against the night wind. Barney drew hard on the cigarette, preparing himself for the verbal assault. Lehmans said nothing; he just smoked and looked out over the murder site. There was only one spotlight still on at the base of the giant iguanodon. It slashed up toward the sculpted head, giving the stone monster a shad-owed reality, as if at any moment it would move.

Lehmans looked tired; the lines at his eyes were deeply etched, and the kind mouth was drawn back into a thin line. He took a deep drag and said, "You disappoint me, Barney." Barney did not respond, and Lehmans continued. "Now I have to deal with the homicide of a Ger-man citizen, along with the criticism leveled at me for this afternoon's terrorist breakout. I asked you to do nothing alone."

Barney sighed. "It was impossible for me to see Obermann on any other basis. He wouldn't talk in the presence of police. What the hell was I supposed to do?"

"You have to respect my problems," Lehmans replied.

"What if you were in my place?" Barney argued. "Obermann is the only link. You're in Los Angeles faced with the same situation. What would you do?"

Lehmans shook his head. "Not the same, and you know it. You're into something that goes back in time almost thirty-five years, in a country where the past may involve individual actions so horrific they'll go to any lengths to keep that past sealed. And you're probing that past with no legal status, no arms, and no protection." Lehmans turned to Barney. "I don't want you going against my instructions. That's not a request. That's an order."

Barney thought about the slip of paper in his pocket. The slip of paper he had taken from Obermann's wallet with Friedrich Diestel's phone number. He anguished over whether to mention it. And decided not to.

A detective carrying a plastic bag with five shell casings came up to Lehmans.

Lehmans took one of the shell casings out of the bag, examined its base for a moment, then handed it to Barney. "A twenty-two long. They found it in that clump of shrubs."

Barney handed the casing back to the detective. Lehmans said something in German to the plainclothesman, and the man went back over to the detectives who were still questioning the zoo guards. Lehmans dropped his cigarette and stepped on it. "Is there anything else Obermann said that I should know?"

Barney shook his head.

Then in a weary voice Lehmans said, "I suppose we'd better have a look at Obermann's apartment."

"We ought to call his stepdaughter," Barney suggested.

"Yes, you're right. I've forgotten her name."

"Lisa Spangler. She's in the Berlin book."

They took a last look at the chalked tracing outlining the final position of Obermann's body.

"Hell of a place to die," Barney said softly.

"Death is no stranger to this place," Lehmans said.

Obermann's apartment was located on Sperlingstrasse. It was a small street of quaint rebuilt three-story dwellings. A peaceful residential neighborhood in the British sector of the divided city.

The landlady was a toothless, heavyset woman, with stringy gray hair and angry brown eyes. She refused to give Lehmans the passkey to Obermann's flat and insisted on opening it herself.

The old woman carried on a bitter monologue all the way up the three flights. She opened the door to Apartment 3B and flicked on the lights. Lehmans tried a few questions, but the landlady did not permit him to interrupt her diatribe. Lehmans finally moved her out and in a soothing voice kept repeating, *"Danke. Danke schön . . . mein Lieb."* But her voice continued protesting even after Lehmans had closed the door.

"What was that all about?" Barney asked.

"She complains that her pension check is too small and arrives too late."

"But why tell you?"

"These old people connect anyone in an official capacity with their pension problems. She said her husband and two sons were killed fighting for the old Reich. And now she is being destroyed by the masters of the new Reich." Lehmans sighed heavily. "We're a nation of fifty-three million scars."

They walked slowly through the small apartment, which consisted of a living room, a small bedroom, a surprisingly large, modern kitchen, and a good-sized bathroom. The design of the apartment focused on food and its elimination. The furniture was old but comfortable. A few lithographs on the walls depicted snow scenes of the Bavarian Alps. There was a framed photograph of a much younger Obermann standing beside a tall, distinguished-looking man, and another framed photograph showed Lisa Spangler standing on what appeared to be a university campus.

After determining the layout of the apartment, Barney and Lehmans began the laborious task of searching it. They went through bureaus, closets, suits, luggage, moving methodically from room to room. They were thorough and precise, skipping nothing, ignoring nothing. A half hour later the two men had collected a few scraps of pertinent documents: a savings and checking account, a pile of federal tax payments in chronological order dating back to February 1956. There was a letter from a woman dating back to late 1957, and another from a Professor Wolf Siebold dated October 25, 1956, and postmarked Brownsville, Texas; and a current West German passport with a single stamped entry for Zurich, Switzerland, July 19, 1977. The rest of the papers were a collection of current bills and salary stubs from the Power and Light Company.

Barney said, "It's as if his life began in 1956."

Lehmans reread the letter from Professor Siebold and stuffed it in his pocket. "This Professor Siebold was apparently a section chief of Genesis. He says in the letter that he is working with American petroleum experts on a pilot synthetic fuel plant in Brownsville, Texas, but that the project is being abandoned after eight years of research, and he is returning to Germany and looking forward to seeing his old assistant, Herr Obermann."

"Then Obermann lied to me," Barney said. "He claimed he was not involved with synthetic fuel; only the manufacture of synthetic butter. Why would he lie about that?"

"For the same reason he was killed. He lied to protect the surviving Genesis scientists."

"Then it would follow that this Professor Siebold is still alive."

"That would be my assumption," Lehmans agreed.

Barney walked to the mantelpiece and studied the photograph of Obermann and the tall, distinguished-looking man. After a moment he turned to Lehmans. "What would a German scientist be doing in Brownsville, Texas?"

Lehmans placed all the slips of paper in a brown bag. "After the war the Americans, British, French, and Russians took thousands of captured German scientists back to their own countries."

"Why would the Americans cancel a synthetic fuel project after eight years of research?"

Lehmans shrugged. "You'll have to ask Professor Siebold."

They heard a loud knocking at the door and the raucous, complaining monologue of the landlady. Lehmans opened the door, and the landlady moved her enormous girth aside to permit Lisa Spangler entry to the apartment. The old lady had shifted her angry comments to the detective and the uniformed policeman standing beside her in the alcove of the doorway. Lehmans nodded at her and closed the door.

Lisa Spangler stood just inside the living room. Her pale blue eyes were red-rimmed, and they darted back and forth from Lehmans to Barney.

Barney said softly, "I'm sorry it turned out this way."

She glared at Barney but did not respond. Lehmans said, "Mr. Caine followed police procedure, common to any investigation. He is in no way responsible for your stepfather's death. Paul Obermann was a man living in fear of something. Something that killed him. And you may be in a position to help us determine what that was."

"I have no interest in helping you," she said flatly.

"You have no choice, Miss Spangler. I am conducting an official investigation into the homicide of a German citizen. I can compel your appearance in court to answer my questions, or you can cooperate and answer our questions now, privately, in this room."

She stared at both men for a moment, then walked slowly over to an easy chair and sat down. "There's a bottle of brandy in the kitchen. In the cabinet over the sink. Would you be kind enough to give me a drink?"

Lehmans nodded and went out of the room. Barney sat down wearily on the sofa. The jet lag was beginning to hit him hard. He felt the nine-hour gap in time, and the events of the evening were taking their toll of his nerves. Lisa opened her large handbag, took out a package of cigarettes, and lit one. The smoke curled up out of her lips.

"I don't understand men like you, Mr. Caine," she said. "What in God's name can be so important that you endanger the life of an innocent man?"

"I can't operate on the assumption of violence and death," Barney replied. "I did what my professional code dictated."

Lehmans came in carrying the brandy and three glasses. He handed Lisa a glass and poured a hefty shot. He repeated the process for Barney and himself. Lisa took a mouthful of brandy and shivered. She drew hard on the cigarette, exhaled, and with resignation said, "All right, Inspector, ask your questions."

Lehmans took out a note pad and a ball-point pen. "Where do you work?"

"Lemendorf Agency. In the Europa Building."

"Your occupation?"

"Model."

"When did you last see Paul Obermann?"

"Several months ago."

"You don't recall the exact date?"

"No. It was before I left for an assignment in Paris. Sometime in March."

"What happened?"

"When?"

"When you last saw Obermann."

"Nothing really." She sipped some brandy. "We had lunch at the lakeside restaurant in the Tiergarten. He loved that place. He loved its tranquillity." She glanced off toward the photograph of the young Obermann. "All his friends were dead. I was the only one he had."

"What about his fellow workers at the power company?"

"Paul did not make friends easily."

"Why not?"

She shrugged. "There was something about his past that made him keep to himself."

"Did he ever marry?"

"Yes. When I attended the Berlin University. He married a woman from Westphalia. I think it was in 1958. The woman was aristocratic. Very cold."

"Where is this woman now?"

"Dead. She suffered a stroke a year or so after they were married."

There was a pause, and Lehmans looked at Barney and nodded. Barney leaned forward and placed the glass of brandy on the coffee table. "Would you mind if I asked you a few questions?"

She shook her head.

"Did Obermann ever mention a man named Wolf Siebold?"

"No."

Barney then indicated the photograph on the mantelpiece. "Do you know who that tall, bearded man is?"

"Some friend from the past, I imagine."

"Why did you believe Obermann was in danger?"

"When the Swiss industrialist contacted him, Paul came to see me. He was frightened. I knew then it was related to his past activities. But I told you that this afternoon."

"Yes, that's right—you did."

Lehmans handed her his card. "If you will call me in the early morning, you can claim the body and arrange the funeral."

She took the card and got to her feet. "There will be no funeral. There is no one left to attend a funeral. I will have Paul cremated and spread the ashes in the Tiergartensee. You see, for him the lake was a place of remembered beauty."

"What about his belongings?" Lehmans asked.

"I will leave everything to the old woman downstairs. I want nothing except my photograph. May I have it?"

"Of course."

She moved to the mantelpiece and picked up her framed photograph. She looked at Obermann's photo for a moment, then turned abruptly and strode to the door.

"Wait a minute!" Barney stopped her.

"Yes?"

"I would like to pay my last respects to your stepfather."

She looked at Barney for a moment. "As you wish," she said and went out.

Barney looked at Lehmans. "Some girl."

Lehmans nodded. "She has that cold, magnetic beauty you find in northern women. Those born in Helgoland. It's as if their beauty were beaten into them."

"Where is Zossen?" Barney asked.

"A small city, perhaps twenty kilometers southeast of Berlin. In East Germany. Why do you ask?"

"She told me she was born in a military hospital there in 1945."

"It's possible," Lehmans said. "At the end, civilians were admitted to military hospitals and Zossen was OKW headquarters. But she looks northern to me."

"She said the Soviets shelled the hospital. Her mother was killed a day or so after she was born."

Lehmans picked up his topcoat. "Again, it's possible. It was a time of total chaos. But I'll run a check on our Miss Spangler. Come. I'll drop you at the hotel."

Lehmans drove swiftly through the city, slowing down on the busy Kurfürstendamm and turning into Fasanenstrasse. He pulled up to the entrance of the Kempinski and waved the doorman away. "You can meet me at eight in the morning in the autopsy room. The morgue and pathology unit is in my building."

"I think I'll pass on that one," Barney replied.

"Then I'll phone you at ten," Lehmans offered.

Barney nodded and rubbed his hand wearily across his eyes.

"What is it, Barney?"

"Just tired."

"No. It's more than fatigue. I sensed something else, since the zoo. Do you feel responsible for Obermann's death?"

Barney sighed heavily. "No. It's not that." He turned to Lehmans. "I'm going to give you something, and then I want a favor." Barney reached into his pocket and handed Lehmans the note with Friedrich Diestel's name and phone number. "I found this in Obermann's wallet."

Lehmans studied the note. "You have a copy of this?"

"Yes."

Lehmans dropped the note in the bag containing the rest of the Obermann papers. "What's the favor, Barney?"

"I want you to let me see Diestel alone."

"I can't do that."

"I'll only see him at his place of business. I'll phone you first, so you'll know exactly where and when."

"How do you know he has a place of business?"

"One of the guards at the zoo phoned for me while we waited for you. A night service answered."

Lehmans said nothing, and Barney pressed his point.

"Let me see Diestel alone. Then he's yours."

There was a moment of silence, accented by the distant traffic of the Kurfürstendamm.

"All right." Lehmans sighed. "You let me know where and when. You also let me know when the meeting is over."

Barney nodded. "We can use this procedure all the way."

"What do you mean?"

"Let me operate alone. But you'll know exactly where I am all the time. In other words you'll always be able to cover my action."

"We'll try it," Lehmans said. "Now get some rest."

Barney got out of the car and came around to the driver's side and bent down close to Lehmans. "I'm sorry about the zoo business."

"What are you sorry about?" Lehmans smiled. "I would have done the same thing in your place."

Barney stood at the window of his room watching the blue neon Mercedes tristar revolving slowly atop the Europa Building. He tried to assimilate the information that he now possessed covering almost forty years of Tom Neeley's life. He thought of the young Tom Neeley that long-ago April 1945 in command of a sealed convoy transporting the Genesis file from Reims to Hamburg. A barrage of questions hammered at Barney: Had Neeley known what Genesis meant? Did the Genesis Formula contain the ultimate catalyst that Obermann had described? Why had the Americans turned the Genesis Formula over to the British? And what happened to it? Had Neeley worked with Obermann on the Genesis file? How did Neeley rediscover the Genesis Formula thirty-three years later? And what had been the purpose of that convoy of German military secrets? Perhaps they were moving their most sensitive documents to a safer location. But the reason for the movement of those documents was not critical to Barney's case. It was Neeley's involvement that was vital. Everything came down to that; from the beginning, all roads began and ended with Tom Neeley.

Barney took a split of Moselle wine out of the Frigidaire, opened it, and went into the bathroom. He took a Seconal capsule out of a small vial and washed it down with the red wine. He looked at his face in the mirror above the sink. The dark circles under his eyes were more pronounced and the color of his skin was gray. He snapped the bathroom light off and got into bed.

Twenty minutes later the combination of wine, Seconal, and jet lag put his tired brain to rest, and his body followed into the sanctuary of sleep. In the dim recess of his slumber he thought he heard the phone ring, but the sound was surreal, like a dream.

CHAPTER

39 ⊠

BARNEY WOKE UP HUNGRY. HE ORDERED JUICE, FRIED EGGS, SAUSAGE, English muffins, and a large pot of coffee. After breakfast he phoned Friedrich Diestel. A secretary with a cultured British accent answered. Barney identified himself and was told to hold.

A moment passed, and then Diestel's voice came on. Barney was careful to explain that there was no legal basis for Diestel to grant the interview, but that it was either Barney or the police. Diestel's voice was bathed in gentility. "If I can be of any assistance, you have only to ask." Diestel paused. "How is eleven-fifteen this morning?"

"Eleven-fifteen is fine," Barney replied.

"Good," Diestel said. "I look forward to seeing you."

Barney hung up and placed a call to Hans Lehmans and told him where and when he was meeting Diestel.

Lehmans thanked Barney for letting him know and said, "The autopsy showed Obermann was hit twice in the chest and once in the head. Any one of the three shots would have killed him. The shots were fired from a PPK Walther twenty-two long automatic."

They made plans to meet later in the day. Lehmans said, "My secretary checked the other phone calls Neeley made from the Kempinski."

"Anything?" Barney asked.

"No. They were an assortment of calls to airlines, restaurants, nightclubs, the Pergamon Museum in East Berlin, and three calls to the Atlantic Hotel in Hamburg, and one to Friedrich Diestel."

"When will you have the federal file on Obermann?" Barney asked.

"Three or four days. It comes from Wiesbaden, and they have to dig. The records relating to events before 1945 are scattered throughout West Germany."

"What about the girl?"

"She checks out to this extent. She attended Berlin University for two years. She is a model and works principally for the Lemendorf Agency. She holds a valid West German passport. She has no criminal record."

"What about her birth records?"

"As I told you, Zossen fell to the Russians. There are thousands of children who grew up with no birth records. Those records went up in smoke along with the Third Reich. Let me know what happens with Diestel."

"I will."

"Take care, Barney."

There were two blond secretaries seated at desks on opposite sides of a large room. A huge glass wall behind them afforded a panoramic view of the city. Barney chose the girl on the right. She was a homely girl with great dark eyes that seemed to be in constant mourning.

"I'm Barney Caine. I have an appointment with Mr. Diestel."

Her warm, generous smile fought against the sad eyes. "Go right in, Mr. Caine, through that door. Mr. Diestel is expecting you."

Diestel's office was large and richly furnished. All four walls were glass. And through the center pane Barney could see the East Berlin television needle with its gold ball.

Friedrich Diestel rose from behind his large desk and came around with a smile. Diestel appeared to be in his late fifties. He was slim and of medium height. He had regular features set off by yellow hair that was going gray. His only unpleasant feature was a thin, almost lipless mouth. He was dressed in a dark conservative double-breasted suit. They shook hands, and Diestel indicated a chair.

"Sit down, please."

They sat in black leather chairs facing each other.

"Some coffee?" Diestel asked.

"No. Thank you."

"A cigar?"

"No."

"You're certain? They're Havanas."

"No, thanks."

Diestel took a small dark cigar out of a humidor and bit off a piece, which he carefully placed in an ashtray. He struck a match, drew on the cigar, and said, "Go ahead, Mr. Caine."

"How did you know Paul Obermann?" Barney asked.

"I first met the poor fellow in the summer of 1939 when all the chief operating scientists in the Genesis program were placed under the authority of SS supervisors." He paused and leaned forward. "I was one of those SS supervisors. Paul Obermann was employed at the Hoesch-Treibstoffwerk hydrogenation plant in Dortmund. It was there that we met, in the late summer of 1939. A fateful summer, you might say."

"What was Obermann's specific function?"

"He was a chemist."

"Who was Obermann's superior?"

"A Professor Wolf Siebold was in charge of the Dortmund facility and also chief coordinator of the other fourteen hydrogenation plants."

"How did the chain of command work?"

"What do you mean?"

"Suppose Siebold requested materials or manpower. How was that request acted upon?"

"Well, assume it was a request for labor. That was actually my province. You see, outside of the German scientists, the unskilled labor were Jews."

"Jews?" Barney asked incredulously.

"Yes. Does it surprise you? I thought since Nuremberg there were no more surprises. We used slave labor recruited from the thirteen killing centers throughout Eastern Europe."

Diestel's casual reference to "killing centers" shocked Barney.

Diestel cleared his throat and smiled. "Forgive me if I offend you, Mr. Caine. But history is immutable. We cannot hide from it."

"Tell me about the chain of command."

"Do you have something to write with?" Diestel asked.

"No."

Diestel rose, went to his desk, picked up a pad and a black pen, came back, and handed them to Barney. "I don't understand the point in recording these names. It was after all, almost forty years ago."

"There probably is no point," Barney said. "But cases of multiple homicide demand a certain thoroughness."

Diestel walked up to the glass wall and peered out over the city for a moment then turned back to Barney. His voice changed; there was no longer any syrupy warmth. It was cold, clipped. Precise. "The request for labor would come to me from Siebold. I would pass it on to Keppler. That's spelled with two *p*'s. Keppler would make his recommendation, then forward the request to Pohl." Diestel spelled Pohl for Barney and continued. "Pohl would relay the request to Krouch"—he spelled Krouch—"and from him it went to Göring. I trust you can spell Göring."

Barney ignored the sarcasm. "What would Göring do with it?"

Diestel examined his nails for a moment. "Field Marshal Göring would call in Dr. Abraham Esau, chief of the Genesis program."

"How do I spell it?"

"E-S-A-U. Like the Bible."

"What happened after Esau was consulted?"

"Dr. Esau would take the request to I. G. Farben."

Barney put the pad down. "Why Farben?"

"Farben was the industrial heartbeat of the Reich. All matters of armaments and research ultimately were decided either by Hitler or Farben." Diestel walked toward Barney and stood with his arms pressing down on the back of the leather chair. "People like myself and Siebold and Obermann were just small cogs in a vast machine. By late 1943 the Farben empire stretched from the Arctic to Africa and all of continental Europe."

"Using slave labor?"

"Of course. There was a huge Farben synthetic fuel plant at Auschwitz. Over thirty thousand inmates died working in that plant."

Barney got to his feet. He felt the anger rising and an insane urge to smash Diestel's face. "You make it sound like an achievement," he said angrily.

"Please don't play the sanctimonious American, Mr. Caine. Because your country's hands are far from clean. Without the help of Standard Oil of New Jersey in the summer of 1938 we would not have been able to go to war. The blitzkrieg would probably have been postponed. Do you know what tetraethyl is?"

"No."

"It's a lead additive used to advance gasoline octane. Without that additive our planes could not fly. In July 1938 the Genesis scientists had still not solved this chemical synthetically. Standard Oil not only supplied I. G. Farben with the chemical itself but also furnished the formula for its manufacture. So by September 1939 we were ready for the invasion of Poland—the blitzkrieg was a reality—thanks in part to American technology. Just so you understand, the allegiance of the cartel is only to itself. There is nothing to apologize about. Business is business. Now, Mr. Caine, if you have any other questions, please ask them. I am backing into another appointment."

"Can you tell me why Obermann denied he knew you?"

"No. As a matter of fact, we do business with the Power and Light Company on a regular basis. I spoke with Paul only last week."

"When did you see him last?"

"I think it was at a business lunch with ten or fifteen executives, perhaps eight months ago."

"Do you know why anyone would want Obermann dead?"

"Absolutely not. Obermann was a professional man. He did his job and tended to his own affairs."

"Do you know his stepdaughter, Lisa Spangler?"

"Not personally. But Obermann spoke of her."

Barney looked out of the window. He had been saving this for the last. He had hoped to puncture the smiling, cool veneer of Diestel, but he had no more time to try. He had to go with the question. He turned from the window and faced Diestel. "Did you see Tom Neeley in January of this year?"

"Yes. Obermann sent him to me."

"What did Neeley want?"

"He wanted information concerning the Genesis Formula. I obviously could not help him with that. He then asked about Professor Siebold."

"What did you tell him?"

"Pretty much what I've told you. That I met Siebold years ago at Dortmund. That Siebold was rumored to have been taken prisoner by the Americans after the war."

"Do you know anyone who had a motive to kill Tom Neeley?"

"No. Is there anything else, Mr. Caine?"

Barney nodded. "Where would a man begin to look for Siebold and Esau?"

The smile was back on Diestel's thin mouth. "Your friend Neeley asked me the same question. And I give you the same answer. You would go to the Documentation Center in Zehlendorf. It's a suburb of Berlin, open only to Americans. Qualified Americans. Journalists, researchers, or in your case police officials."

Barney started for the door, and Diestel went with him. "If you should decide to go to Zehlendorf, I can provide one of my English secretaries to translate the documents."

"Thanks. I'll manage."

Diestel opened the door. "A pity you are so preoccupied, there are many relaxing activities available here in Berlin. We are truly the epitome of capitalistic achievement. We have reached that golden age where insanity is a greater problem than hunger. I personally always preferred National Socialism."

"Well, maybe you'll get another chance. But you might have to find a new source of labor next time."

"On the contrary, Mr. Caine, we will always have our Jews."

CHAPTER

40 ⊠

THE MAN OF SORROW LOOKED BENIGNLY DOWN FROM HIS STAINED GLASS prison. There were two sprays of roses on either side of the open pine casket, and several benches placed in rows in the center of the room. The benches faced a red-bricked wall that had a huge circular iron lid in its center. The lid was open, lending a one-eyed Cyclopean appearance.

Lisa Spangler stood alongside the open casket, gazing down at Paul Obermann in repose. A piece of sealing wax and other expert makeup touches had disguised the head wound. Barney stood on the opposite side of the casket, but he was not looking at Obermann. He was studying the German girl with the long pale hair and the light blue eyes. She wore a plain black dress, and a single strand of small pearls circled her neck. Barney could smell the girl's perfume as it drifted across the open casket. A door opened, and two grave-looking men entered. Lisa crossed herself. The men came forward, and one of them spoke softly to Lisa. She answered, then turned to Barney. "They will bring the ashes to the anteroom. Do you still wish to go to the park with me?"

Barney nodded. She glanced at the casket for a last brief look, then turned away. Barney followed her out of the oppressive room.

The thick green forest crept up to the banks of the lake, and the tall trees filtered the sunlight, making it dance across the placid surface. Flocks of ducks paddled by in straight lines. Two regal white swans glided majestically close to the curving shoreline.

The Tiergartensee restaurant came right up to the edge of the lake, and gaily colored umbrellas topped each table. A few Berliners, along with a scattering of tourists, were lunching at the red-checkered tables. No one took notice of the blond girl carrying the blue enamel jar and her male companion as they moved through the tables toward the small boats at the edge of the lake.

Lisa spoke to the young boy in charge of the rowboats. The boy said the charge was six marks for one hour, and Barney paid him. The boy shoved one of the boats off the muddy bank, out into the water. He held the boat with a line and helped Lisa into the prow. Barney followed her into the boat, sat on the center plank, and raised the oars. The boy cast the boat off, and Barney dipped the oars, rowing easily out into the soft gray light.

They reached a bend in the lake which took them out of sight of the restaurant. Lisa opened the enamel jar and held it out over the water. She glanced at Barney for a brief instant, then turned the jar upside down, and a fine white ash spilled onto the shimmering surface of the water. They drifted silently for a while, watching the white ash disappear. She then dropped the jar into the water and watched it sink below the surface. She turned to Barney. "There's a path through the trees. I would like to walk for a while."

They returned the boat and set out through the narrow footpath. The dappled sunlight coming through the tops of the trees splashed across them, creating camouflage patterns of light and shadow. The forest was silent, and they could hear their own footfalls. She walked slightly ahead of Barney with her head tilted up and the light breeze playing with the tips of her hair. They walked for a long time before she took a fork in the pathway that led back to the lakeside. She stood on the bank, staring off at the still water. After a moment she whispered, "We can go now."

They took a table near the entrance of the restaurant. She ordered a green salad and a white Frankenwein. Barney asked the waiter to bring him the same thing.

"It was kind of you to come," she said.

"It was the least I could do."

The waiter placed the wine in a silver bucket of ice, and from a hidden speaker system the sounds of a Chopin nocturne drifted across the terrace. Lisa sipped the wine and said, "I had this feeling for a long time—a feeling that Paul was a marked man."

"It's fairly obvious they were waiting for him," Barney replied.

"The question is: Who are they?" she asked.

"Did you tell anyone else that we were meeting at the zoo?"

She shook her head.

"Then he was followed. Or he mentioned the meeting to someone," Barney offered.

Lisa toyed with the stem of the glass. "What do you do now, Mr. Caine?" she asked.

"Keep searching."

"Where?"

"The past. The next place is Zehlendorf. There are files there. Official Nazi files that may be helpful."

"Those files will be in German. How will you read them?"

"I'll have to hire someone."

"Can you trust just anyone?"

"I don't have much choice."

The waiter brought their salads, and they ate in silence, watching a group of children shouting and chasing the swans near the bank of the lake. By the time the coffee arrived they had finished the last of the wine. Her cheeks were flushed, and the wine seemed to revive her spirits.

She lit a cigarette and said, "He really paints, doesn't he?"

"Who?" Barney asked.

"Chopin," she replied. "There are lots of colors in his music, don't you think?"

"Yes." He found himself staring at her.

"What is it you want with me?" she asked suddenly.

Barney was startled by the directness of her question. "What do you mean?"

"You spent the last two hours with me. You're in the middle of a critical investigation. Why do you take this time with me?"

"The truth is I did want to pay my respects to Paul Obermann. And the truth also is that I want a favor."

"What sort of favor?"

Barney indicated her cigarettes. "May I have one of those?"

"Of course." She slid the pack over to him.

He lit one, exhaled, and said, "I think your stepfather was a name on a killing list. A list that began with the Neeleys. I have no idea who's behind these killings. But I do know the roots are in the Nazi past and connect with the work your stepfather performed during the war."

"How do you know that?"

He told her about the long-ago German truck convoy carrying the secret documents and how Neeley met Obermann at British Intelligence Headquarters in Hamburg. That Genesis was a code name for synthetic fuel. That the formula disappeared in 1945 and that its value today was incalculable. That whoever killed the Neeleys and Obermann was after the formula.

She crushed her cigarette out. "But what is it you want of me?"

"I need someone I can trust. I need someone who is not connected with the police."

"To do what?"

"To locate and translate documents and work with me."

"Why do you ask me?"

"Because you have the purest motives and you are personally involved. The man who raised you, who took care of you, was shot down in cold blood."

She leaned back and stared at the lake. She took her time before answering. "When would you need me?"

"Now. Today. I would like you to go to Zehlendorf with me."

"And afterward?"

"Wherever the case leads. I'll take care of all the expenses."

She smiled. "I probably make more money in one week than you earn in a month. I'm quite a famous model. Very well paid."

"Almost everyone makes more money than cops. But I'll still take care of the expenses."

Once again she stared at the gray light spilling onto the surface of the lake. After a moment she turned back to him and stared into his eyes. "Pay the bill, Mr. Caine. It's a long way to Zehlendorf."

The Documentation Center was a compound of wooden barracks enclosed by a high wall topped with barbed wire. There was a sign at the entrance that read: "HALT! U.S. MISSION—DOCUMENTATION CENTER." The gate was flanked by two sentry booths manned by two MPs. Barney walked up to one of the soldiers and presented his ID card and passport. He identified Lisa as his secretary and translator, assigned to him by the West German police. The MP took Barney's documents, went into the sentry booth, and phoned the information to someone inside the compound.

A middle-aged woman with a midwestern accent escorted them into a huge windowless storeroom crammed with steel filing cabinets. There were overhead fluorescents that bathed everything in a harsh white light. As they moved through the gymnasium-sized room, their footsteps echoed off the wooden floor. It seemed to Barney that the ghosts of those SS men whose criminal files resided in the cabinets hung over the building. And there was an ominous quality to the dead, musky air. The bright fluorescent light was as incongruous as floodlights in a cemetery.

They passed through and out of the huge storeroom and entered a smaller room with windows and scattered plastic furniture. The room was dominated by a concave computer console. A staff sergeant was seated at its control panel. He was a thin-faced, bespectacled youth, absorbed with the current month's centerfold. He reluctantly dropped the magazine and listened to the middle-aged woman with a bored civility. His eyes carefully took in all of Lisa's natural attributes. He hardly noticed Barney. The woman concluded the introductions, and the sergeant drawled, "What can I do for you all?"

"I'd like the file on a German scientist named Wolf Siebold and the SS file on a Friedrich Diestel. And—"

The sergeant held up his hand. "Hold it." He picked up a pen and said, "Okay. Now give me the names and spell them." Barney went through the names given to him by Diestel. "Is that it?" the sergeant asked.

"That's it," Barney replied.

The sergeant spun around in his swivel chair and began punching names up on a computer keyboard. The names and serial numbers and file codes appeared almost instantly on a TV screen mounted on the console. After each name, the sergeant jotted down the file code. The entire process took less than three minutes.

The woman librarian looked at Barney. "It will take a few minutes to bring the files. If you will come with me."

She led them into another room that looked like a reading room in a library. There were long wooden tables with note pads and pencils and small lamps with dark green shades. The woman managed a small smile. "Just be seated. The sergeant will be right in."

Barney thanked her, and she left.

They worked in silence. Lisa sampled the files, discarding some and translating others, handing her notes to Barney, who reconstructed them in chronological order. There were numerous pages of SS correspondence complete with the Nazi eagle letterhead.

Time crept by silently. The documents absorbed their attention, isolating them, moving them through the recorded history of a blurred nightmare. There were long periods when Barney had to wait for Lisa to digest a series of documents before deciding whether they were worth translating. In those moments Barney found himself inexorably drawn to the girl. He stared at her perfect profile. The way her pale gold hair parted in the center and fell suddenly down both sides of her face. And the sweet aroma of her perfume.

She handed him her final notes on Siebold, and he added them to his fact sheet on the professor and studied the chronology.

PROFESSOR WOLF SIEBOLD: Born in Neustadt, Schwarzwald 10/3/1905. Graduate Berlin University 1929. Master's degree: physics, chemistry, and biochemistry. Chief assistant to Franz Fischer in research and development of Fischer-Tropsch process, specializing in the hydrogenation of coal to fuel.

May 8, 1938, ordered by Dr. Abraham Esau to take charge of the Darmstadt Hydrogenation Facility. Siebold pioneered the research on middle-pressure synthesis utilizing a new platinum and cobalt catalyst. Recipient of "Führer Citation" for overseeing production of seven million metric tons of synthetic fuel in June 1944, despite heavy Allied bombing.

Barney had listed the final item under the heading of "ADDENDUM":

Professor Wolf Siebold captured by units of U.S. 7th Army, June 8, 1945. Siebold transferred to ALSO control Brownsville, Texas. Returned Germany 11/56. Employed by Saarbrücken Gemeinschaft. Joined teaching staff Chemistry Department, University Berlin 10/67. Left university 8/7/76. Present location: unknown.

Barney then examined his annotations on Dr. Esau.

DR. ABRAHAM ESAU: Born 1/8/1900—Hamburg. Attended University Heidelberg, doctorate in physics and chemistry. Instituted first hydrogenation facility at the Leuna Works in 1927. Used first direct process of synthesized gas from pit coal in generators. Developed network of fifteen hydrogenation plants. Associated with Siebold on catalysts research conducted at Kaiser Wilhelm Institute in Mülheim. Inventor of "symbol"—a fuel composed of alcohol and synthetic oil. Appointed Chief of Reich "Energy and Research" in March 1937. Dr. Esau succeeded in obtaining funding from Göring for continuous research and expansion of hydrogenation programs. Instituted I. G. Farben plant at Auschwitz in 1942. ADDENDUM: Captured by elements of First White Russian Army, May 30, 1945. Released by Soviets in July 1956. Whereabouts: unknown.

The SS supervisory chain was unimportant. Diestel had been right: Keppler, Pohl, and Krouch were all dead. The file on Diestel was brief:

Born: 10/27/1918. Accepted for membership in SS 6/15/38. Assigned Genesis program 7/14/39.

They rode back into the city in silence. It was impossible to shake off the sense of doom brought on by rummaging through the history of a nation gone mad.

As they passed the telephone building on Kaiser-Wilhelm-strasse, Lisa asked, "Where are we going?"

"The Kempinski. I have a call to make and one I would like you to make."

"To whom?"

"The Berlin University, Personnel Department, see if they have a location on Wolf Siebold."

She nodded. "It's curious that of all those SS men attached to Genesis, the only one who survived is Friedrich Diestel."

"I'd bet on good old Friedrich," Barney said sarcastically.

"You know him?"

"I saw him this morning."

"How did you locate him?"

"Your stepfather had his number. For some reason he denied he knew Diestel."

"I never heard him mention that name." She looked at Barney. "Do you find it strange that my stepfather's name was not listed in the files?"

"Maybe he wasn't important enough."

"Perhaps," she said softly. "But he was important enough to be killed."

There were two messages at the desk. Louis Yosuta had called at 11:15 A.M., and Hans Lehmans had called a half hour ago.

They walked down the long fourth-floor corridor, passing the Irish day maid. "Good afternoon, sir," she said in her thick brogue.

"Good afternoon." Barney smiled.

The room had been made up and was spotless; Barney thought: German or Irish, the result couldn't be faulted. He tossed his jacket on the bed, unbuttoned his shirt collar, and loosened his tie.

"Would you like a drink?" Barney asked Lisa.

"A beer. If you have it."

Barney went to the Frigidaire and took out two bottles, opened them, and poured a glass of the foaming brew for Lisa. "Would you make that call for me?"

"Now?"

"Yes."

"But you have two messages to return."

"They can wait."

Lisa sat down on the edge of the bed. Barney slumped in an easy chair opposite her. Lisa asked the hotel operator to get information for the number of the Berlin University. She stared curiously at Barney while he sucked the beer from the mouth of the dark bottle. She jotted a number down and dialed. There was a pause, and she asked, *"Personalbüro, bitte."* She swung her right leg up and down while she waited; then the leg grew still. *"Ja. . . . Können Sie mir bitte sagen wo Herr Professor Wolf Siebold wohnt?"* She paused and cradled the phone in the crook of her neck and shoulder and reached into her bag for a cigarette.

Barney got up and helped her with the cigarette. He struck a match, and she closed her fingers around his hand. He looked down at her as her lips circled the cigarette and drew a red glow into its tip.

She glanced up at him for a second, and in that brief moment both of them knew something inevitable had passed between them.

Lisa spoke into the phone, *"Ja."* She wrote something on the pad and said, *"Danke schön,"* and hung up. "The forwarding address for Professor Siebold is the Institute of Advanced Technology in Hamburg."

The Bristol Bar was beginning to fill up with tourists returning from the day's excursions and foreign businessmen having a drink before dinner. The piano player displayed the same bemused smile that was common to all salon pianists. His fingers were tripping down memory lane with "You Are My Lucky Star."

They were seated in a comfortable wide booth at the far end of the room. There was a bottle of scotch on the table and two small green Perrier bottles. Barney had decided to postpone calling Louis; it would be a little after five in the morning in L.A.

Lisa toyed with her drink and mentioned that she had posed for a Perrier layout only last week. The piano player skipped forty years and played the theme from *A Man and A Woman.* Lisa glanced at the piano player for a moment, then said, "That's a lovely melody. Do you remember the film?"

Barney nodded. "I saw it three times, with a girl I had a terrible crush on."

"What do you mean, 'crush'?"

"When you think you're in love with someone for no real reason."

"We call that *vernarrt sein*. It isn't exactly the same. It means being foolish."

"That's close enough," Barney said.

She stared at him for an instant, then looked down into the scotch. She held the glass in the palms of her hands and gazed into it as if it contained answers to all the universal mysteries. "Do you want me to go to Hamburg with you?" she asked.

Barney nodded. "I meant what I said this afternoon. I'll need you all the way."

She turned to him. "All the way to where?"

"I hope all the way to Dr. Esau."

"Why?"

"Because Esau would have had the final Genesis Formula."

"Why do you suppose the Americans would have sent such a valuable secret to the British?"

"In 1945 the United States had plenty of oil. It was only two dollars a barrel. The British had to import all their oil, even then. My guess is the Americans were accommodating a legitimate British interest in synthetic fuel."

"And to the Americans the Genesis Formula was simply a curiosity?" she asked.

"Something like that. You can't blame them. No one was predicting a world crisis in oil in 1945. Besides, synthetic fuel was probably too expensive to manufacture in those days."

"But the Germans made it."

"Yes. With slave labor."

She turned away, looking off into some other zone of time. There was an understated melancholy to the girl that Barney had perceived the first time he saw her. He felt a strong urge to put his arms around her, to embrace the mystery of her cool beauty. He looked away from Lisa in time to see Hans Lehmans enter the salon.

The tired gray-faced inspector sat down next to Barney. He greeted Lisa in German, and she responded in German.

"What would you like?" Barney asked.

"I'll do it," Lehmans said.

Lehmans placed some ice in a glass and poured a large dose of scotch over the ice, added some Perrier, raised his glass, and said,

"*Prosit.*" He took a long swallow and asked Lisa, "Can you join us for dinner?"

"No. I have to settle things with the landlady and notify my agency . . . and pack some things."

Lehmans's eyes narrowed. "Where are you going?"

"Hamburg"—she paused—"with Mr. Caine."

She picked up her bag and got to her feet. The men tried to rise but she said, "No. Sit, please." She looked at Barney. "I'll meet you here at ten. You will arrange the flight?"

Barney smiled. "The tickets. The hotel. Everything. You're a guest of the Los Angeles taxpayers."

She nodded and looked at Lehmans. "*Auf wiedersehen,* Inspector."

"*Auf wiedersehen,* Fräulein Spangler."

Lehmans took Barney to a Hungarian restaurant on Perlberger-strasse. The place was small and crowded. The clientele were all Berliners. And the food was good. They were served a spicy eggplant salad sprinkled with paprika. The salad was served with a strong red cognac and preceded the traditional black bread and goulash.

Barney related the day's events and concluded by saying, "Diestel was a new experience for me. I've been in with homicidal maniacs and junkies who would sell their children for a fix. But I've never seen a businessman discuss 'killing centers' with such nonchalance."

Lehmans did not respond but took a big swallow of red cognac.

Barney said, "Why do you suppose he told me about Farben and slave labor and Auschwitz?"

"So you would tell me."

"To what purpose?"

"To demonstrate his lack of guilt and that he has nothing to hide."

"You haven't seen Diestel yet?"

Lehmans shook his head. "I have an appointment with him tomorrow morning." Lehmans dipped his bread in gravy and chewed slowly, savoring its flavor. He then drank some of the red-colored brandy. "We caught the man who posed as an attorney. The man who managed the escape of the terrorists."

"That's a major break!" Barney exclaimed.

Lehmans shrugged. "The man says they went to Zurich. We alerted the Swiss federal police. We'll see. Tell me about your arrangement with the girl."

Barney followed Lehmans's example and dipped his bread into the thick dark gravy and spoke while he chewed. "I asked her to help. I said it was a chance for her to avenge the death of her stepfather, that I needed someone I could trust. Someone not connected with the police."

"And she agreed?"

Barney nodded, drank some cognac, and asked, "Will you try and get to Siebold for me?"

"Yes. I'll try and set a meeting for you." Lehmans pushed his plate away and lit a cigarette. "You know, of course, you're playing with Siebold's life. Not to mention your own." Lehmans drained the last of his cognac. "I'll give you the name of a colleague of mine in Hamburg. You keep him informed. Where you are. Who you see."

"Okay," Barney replied.

"Where will you be staying?" Lehmans asked.

"Same place Neeley stayed. The Atlantic."

"Good place. Good section. On Lake Alster." Lehmans paused. "Very romantic."

"I booked separate rooms." Barney smiled.

"That's nice."

"You said she checked out," Barney offered.

"To a point: She's unmarried. She attended the University of Berlin. She has no criminal record. She is a model." Lehmans inhaled deeply. "But we cannot confirm the fact that she is or was Obermann's stepdaughter."

Barney said, "When I mentioned Lisa to Obermann, he knew her, and her photograph was in his apartment."

Lehmans nodded. "I'll still feel better about Miss Spangler when I have the federal file on Obermann."

"What bothers you about her?"

Lehmans shrugged. "I can't define it. A feeling, nothing more."

In his villa on Lake Havel, in the Berlin suburb of Wannsee, Friedrich Diestel sipped the last of his Armagnac brandy. His British secretary with the large sad eyes was upstairs in the master bedroom, along with a Dutch girl she had recruited for the evening. Diestel lit an expensive Upmann cigar, rolled in a special Cuban leaf. He studied the somber tones of a Breughel that hung high up on the rose-colored wall of the baronial living room. He walked slowly over to the painting and for a moment examined the extraordinary brushwork. The painting had been a gift from Göring, and it had taken some brilliant machinations for Diestel to hold onto it.

He turned abruptly and walked quickly to an ornate antique desk and lifted the receiver of an ultramodern phone and dialed Professor Wolf Siebold in Hamburg.

The professor answered on the third ring. *"Ja?"*

"Guten Abend, mein lieber Professor." Diestel smiled.

Siebold recognized the smooth voice at once. *"Guten Abend, Herr Oberst."*

Diestel said, *"Ich möcht dass Sie dem Amerikaner alles erklaeren."* Siebold asked, *"Auch über Reimeck?"*

"Ja," Diestel replied.

"In Ordnung, Herr Oberst," Siebold replied. Then asked, *"Was ist wirklich mit Obermann passiert?"*

And with a cold finality Diestel replied, *"Obermann hat nichts mit dir zu tun . . . auf wiedersehen, Herr Professor."* Diestel hung up, satisfied Siebold would lead the American detective along the carefully prescribed path. He had reacted rather curtly to the professor's concern over Obermann's demise, telling him it was none of his affair. He disliked being abrupt, but he had to maintain authority. The war may have been lost, but not the SS authority. The *Kameradschaft,* the great Fraternal Order, was as closely knit as ever.

Diestel thought about the waiting girls upstairs, and a small ball of heat warmed his testicles. He moved back to the long mahogany dinner table and poured another Armagnac. He had one more call to make. He went back to the desk and placed a direct call to the Hassler Hotel in Rome. It was twelve minutes after midnight, Rome time. Frank Tedesco would be in his suite waiting for the call.

Barney thumbed through the *Time* magazine as he waited for the call to Louis to go through. It was early morning in Los Angeles. Louis would still be at home. There was a feature story in the magazine about current Middle East peace negotiations. The phone rang loudly, and Barney picked up the receiver.

"How you doing, Barney?" The sound of Louis's voice gave Barney a lift. He proceeded to fill Louis in step by step. He told Louis about Obermann's murder. And his own meeting with Diestel. That he was in effect retracing Neeley's footsteps. That he was going to Hamburg to see Professor Wolf Siebold, who was a principal scientist in the Genesis program.

Louis sighed audibly. "It's too big, Barney. You ought to turn it over to the feds."

"No chance," Barney replied and asked, "Did you question Clements?"

"He's out of the country. On his way to Rome."

"Shit. Did you get the copy of my telex?"

"Yeah."

"Show Nolan a copy of that telex," Barney said. "Tell him it proves the Genesis connection between Neeley and Clements. That when Clements returns, he should be booked as an accessory before and after the fact of homicide. And fill Nolan in on everything I've given you."

"Okay. Anything else?"

"No," Barney said, and thought about mentioning Lisa Spangler, but instead asked, "How's the wife and kid?"

"Fine. Next time marry a Japanese girl, Barney. Nothing like it."

"I'll try and remember. Well, you know where I'll be starting tomorrow."

"Atlantic Hotel, Hamburg," Louis confirmed. "Think about turning it over to the feds, Barney."

Barney said, "Take care, Lou." He hung up and tossed Louis's advice around; it was well meant, but naïve. The forces behind Genesis controlled and funded the feds and the CIA. And in particular State Department Intelligence. There was no one to turn it over to. In the old days, in the Agency, the control officers would call this kind of case Solitaire. You played the hand out alone—to the last card.

CHAPTER

41 ☒

Lisa waited in the lobby while Barney spoke to Helmut Bergen. He told the grave-looking manager he'd be back in a few days and offered to pay his bill. Bergen said it would remain in abeyance pending Barney's return.

They got into a Mercedes taxi which was parked behind a chauffeur-driven limousine. The license plate of the limousine had no national identity and only the letters *CD* and three numerals. They pulled away from the curb.

Barney asked Lisa, "Did you happen to notice the license plate on that limousine?"

She shook her head. "No."

"Ask the driver what CD plates stand for."

Lisa spoke to the driver in German, and to her surprise he replied in English. "They stand for Corps Diplomatique. They belong to official foreign missions, which means they can go anywhere without being challenged."

"Including East Berlin?" Barney asked.

"They can go anywhere," the driver repeated.

"What country did that limousine belong to?"

The driver shrugged. "You cannot tell from the plates. You have to ask."

They swung onto the autobahn and followed the big blue and white signs to Tegel Airport.

"I gave everything to the landlady," Lisa said.

"That must have cheered her day."

"I don't know. She complained all the time I was there about her pension checks. She thinks I'm with the police."

"You are."

"Am I?" She smiled.

Barney gently said, "I want you to know, I appreciate this help."

"I'm not doing it for you, Barney." It was the first time she used his given name.

They arrived at the Atlantic Hotel three and a half hours later. The hotel was all white and six stories high. It reminded Barney of a wedding cake. There were lacy wrought-iron terraces facing the lake. And way out on the Alster Lake, gaily colored sailboats heeled and tacked in the cool breeze. A treelined path circled the perimeter of the huge lake, and stately mansions hugged its curving shore.

They were checked in quickly and efficiently. The concierge gave Barney two messages: one from Lehmans and one from an Inspector Peter Baumer, Lehmans's man in Hamburg. They were assigned adjoining rooms, 316 and 317, on the lakefront side.

His room was spacious, with a high vaulted ceiling and large French windows that opened onto the terrace. Barney tipped the bellboy and glanced at the pink message slips. Lehmans had contacted Siebold, and the professor was expecting a call from Barney. Lehmans listed Siebold's office and home numbers. The other message was from Peter Baumer, welcoming Barney to Hamburg, and listed phone numbers at Police Central and Baumer's home.

Barney walked over to the French windows, opened them, and stepped out onto the terrace. The sun slid in and out of low clouds, turning the surface of the lake into a shimmering sheet of gun metal.

There was a soft knock at the door, and Barney turned and shouted, "It's open!" Lisa came into the room. She had changed to French jeans and a white silk shirt. Barney walked up to her. "How's your room?"

"Lovely."

"Care for a drink?"

She shook her head. "Actually, I'm starved."

"Well, make this call for me and we'll get some lunch." He handed her the slip with Siebold's numbers. She went over to the bed and sat on the edge. She glanced at the note, then looked at Barney.

"Which number shall I try?"

"It's early afternoon. Try the institute."

Lisa got through to a secretary and was told to hold. After a moment a cultured male voice came on and Lisa asked, "*Ist Professor Wolf Siebold?*" Lisa nodded at Barney, then asked the professor, "*Sprechen Sie englisch?*" The professor replied that he did speak English. And added the word "fluently." Lisa smiled. "*Eine Minute, bitte.*" She handed the phone to Barney and went up to the French windows and stepped out onto the terrace. Barney took the receiver and identified himself to Siebold as the American detective Inspector Lehmans had mentioned.

Siebold replied in lightly accented English, "Yes, Mr. Caine, I have been expecting your call. Do you suppose you could come to my home this evening at eight?"

"This evening will be fine," Barney answered.

"Will you be alone?" the professor inquired.

"No," Barney said. "I have Lisa Spangler with me. She is the step-daughter of your former colleague, Paul Obermann."

There was a pause. Then the professor cleared his throat. "All right. I have no objection to Miss Spangler. I am just across the lake from your hotel. You get off the public boat at the Uhlenhurst landing. My home is down the street from the landing: number thirty-eight Schöne Aussicht."

The line went dead. Barney depressed the button on the phone and dialed Lehmans's associate Peter Baumer. He advised Baumer of his forthcoming meeting with Professor Siebold. Baumer thanked him and asked Barney to keep him informed.

Barney walked out onto the small terrace and stood beside Lisa. The fading sun cast a pale winter light on the lake. A chilly wind had risen, chasing the distant sailboats toward the shore. It seemed to Barney that the dark clouds and cool wind belonged to another season.

CHAPTER

42 ☒

IT WAS SUNSET, AND THE NIGHT WIND COMING UP FROM THE SEA AT Fregene cooled the heat of the Roman day. The domes and spires of the eternal city were backlit by the red sun, and their shapes seemed almost arabesque. At the top of the Spanish Steps, Frank Tedesco placed his leather attaché case down and leaned on the marble balustrade.

The tropical Haitian sun had painted his face a permanent copper color, and his thick, wavy brown hair had only lately shown flecks of gray. His black eyes were clear and alert. He had a friendly mouth, free of the cruel lines that come with age. Tedesco was just over six feet tall. His trim figure reflected his cautious diet. And his tennis game was better at fifty-four than it had been at forty-four.

He checked his three-thousand-dollar Patek Philippe watch; it was 6:48 P.M. He still had a few minutes and was reluctant to surrender the rose-colored view. Tedesco had a special fondness for Rome. He and the city were alike. They were both whores. Rome sucked you in, and for the right price it would spit you out.

The Roman emperors had been entrepreneurs, show-business shills, mesmerizing and manipulating the citizens to solidify their own power. They were hustlers. Like himself.

Frank Tedesco had shot every trick in the book from the day he stepped out of a cold-water tenement onto the brutal streets of south Brooklyn in the early thirties. He learned the hustlers' code of survival quickly: "Greed was the easiest and surest mark of all." The code went all the way back to Eve reaching for the apple; the brains in the Garden of Eden definitely belonged to the snake.

The young Tedesco took to the streets the way a basking shark takes to a school of fish. At the age of sixteen he ran a large network of policy slips and was a layoff man for the top bookmaker in Brooklyn.

Tedesco possessed a genius for mathematical equations and advised the bookmaker what bets to hold and what bets to lay off. He could commit more than fifty separate horse bets to memory. His reputation grew, and in 1937 the mob's auditors put him in charge of a national wire service that transmitted the odds on all races at the six major tracks from New York to California.

He ducked service in World War II because of a chronic case of clap that defied all known remedy. He moved into international money circles: hot money; money that needed laundering; important money that had to elude the Internal Revenue Service. After the war he set up a huge off-shore Bahamian stock corporation that eventually bled its greedy and gullible investors of more than three hundred million; most of which went into the coffers of the mob. He sailed through the fifties and sixties becoming a multimillionaire.

He had made only one mistake. In the presidential election campaign of 1972, he agreed to launder half a million in campaign funds for one of the presidential candidates. The scam blew up with Watergate, and Tedesco was forced into exile. But he nevertheless maintained a pivotal role between the Mafia and the CIA and the industrial cartels. Tedesco was a power broker: moving cocaine, hot money, hiring hit men, and occasionally making a money drop. Like now. Like today. He managed at times to leave Haiti for the capitals of Europe. But in his heart, he missed America. There was no action in the world like America. But hell, he had over five million stashed away in Diestel's bank, Ghelen A.G., in Bern, Switzerland. And while he truly longed for America, he knew no one had it all. The essence of life was knowing when to surrender, when to compromise. That was the difference between professionals and suckers. The professional never pressed bad luck.

Tedesco took a deep breath of air; it tasted faintly of the sea, but mixed with it was the taste of carbon monoxide. The sulfurous smell of fuel hung over the city. It was everywhere. In every city. The smell of oil. That black precious fluid, the last great hustle. And he, the exile, the Brooklyn numbers man, was the broker for the oil cartel. He played many roles for them: courier, enforcer, and even counselor. They were the sharks, but he was their pilot fish. He cleaned their bodies, for a price.

He picked up the attaché case, which contained fifty hundred-dollar bills spread across the surface of fifty stacks of phony 1861 Confederate fifty-dollar bills. Tedesco smiled. The Confederate money was a poetic touch.

He turned from the view and glanced across the small piazza, at the gleaming Rolls Corniche parked in front of the Hassler Hotel. A uniformed chauffeur sat behind the wheel, reading something he held in his lap. Tedesco checked the crease in his English slacks and brushed some lint off his hand-tailored blue blazer. He took a small Binaca spray out of his pocket and sprayed the sharp, tingling fluid into his mouth. He then walked casually over to the Rolls Corniche.

The chauffeur stared in hypnotic fascination at the magazine photo of a spectacular redhead sprawled naked on the tiger-skin rug. Her legs were wide apart, and the forefinger of her left hand touched her Vasolined clitoris. Her right forefinger was inserted in her smiling mouth. The chauffeur's body jumped as he heard Tedesco cough. It was an occupational reflex brought on by years of servitude. He got out of the car, opened the rear door and bowed nervously to Tedesco. *"Scusa, signore, per favore."*

He ignored the man's apology and got into the back seat. The chauffeur closed the rear door and went back behind the wheel. Tedesco settled into the soft, luxurious leather, adjusted the air conditioning, and turned on the FM radio. He then opened the small refrigerator built into the divider wall and removed a split of open white wine and poured some into a frosted glass.

"Where does the *signore* wish to go?" the driver asked.

"Piazza del Popolo," Tedesco replied, curtly.

They rolled silently through the Parco Dei Principi and Tedesco's thoughts turned to the Genesis Formula. The stakes were incredible. It was tempting to play a little crisscross on this one. The formula contained the ultimate catalyst and would endow its owner with supreme power. Tedesco sipped the wine and tossed the thought away. He had been too long in the game to pull a cross on this bunch. Only an amateur or a goddamn fool would try to swindle the cartel. They were worse than the mob. Hell, the mob took orders from them. The cartel ran the world. And no one who still cared about living played games with that kind of power. Neeley should have known better. But he was old and driven and infected with that fatal suckers' disease: greed. The cocaine hadn't been enough for Neeley; he had to take on the cartel. In a strange way, Tedesco felt some sympathy for Neeley. Neeley had always been straight with him. But, Christ, Neeley should never have told that piss-elegant asshole Clements about Genesis. The cop in Neeley should have warned him about Clements.

He sipped some more wine and watched the African trees go by as they descended the slope of Trinità de Monti. Tedesco felt pleased with himself. This Genesis thing had been his biggest assignment, and all things considered, it was going well. The girl had fingered Neeley. And the two terrorists that hit both Neeleys had themselves been hit. Obermann had been iced. And that bright boy, that hotshot L.A. cop, Caine, was exactly in place. And Diestel followed orders to the letter. That's what those fucking krauts were famous for, following orders. But Tedesco did not dislike Diestel; after all, his five million resided in the vaults of Diestel's Swiss bank.

The big maroon Rolls-Royce came down the slope and turned into the picturesque piazza.

"Where to, *signore?*" the driver asked.

"Park at the church."

The car rolled slowly across the width of the piazza and parked at the side of the columned church. Tedesco placed the attaché case upright on his lap. He moved a small numbered combination wheel at its top, setting it on the number eight. He depressed the wheel, heard a click, and spun the wheel three times. He set the attaché case down on the back seat, got out of the car, and walked up to the driver.

"Wait here for Signore Francovelli; take him to Kaladi. *Capisci?*"

"*Si, capisco.*"

Tedesco strolled across the ancient piazza toward Rosati's. He found a sidewalk table and ordered a Campari and tonic. Rosati's was busy with its regular clientele of actresses, actors, screenwriters, and the usual plainclothesmen working out of the Ministero dell' Interno's Anti-terrorist Division. Tedesco could always smell a cop. But the two secret policemen were not interested in the dapper American; they were looking for a notorious female member of the *Brigati Rosse*. For the next ten minutes Tedesco sipped his drink, munched on macadamia nuts, and flirted with a homely Italian actress. At precisely seven-thirty he saw the familiar figure enter the piazza.

Arthur Clements walked slowly toward the Rolls-Royce. The chauffeur leaped out, opened the rear door, and said, "*Buona sera,* Signore Francovelli." Clements nodded and got into the car.

They were passing the illuminated ruins of the Roman Forum, but Clements saw no beauty in them or any significance to their history. His disdain was not confined to Italy; he despised Europe. Clements never understood the desire of Americans to visit this archaic, blood-soaked continent. He would deliver the money and go directly back to the airport.

He was booked on a nine o'clock Air France flight to Paris. He would sleep at De Gaulle Airport and take the morning Concorde to

New York. They were running the Suburban Handicap at Belmont on Sunday. And nothing was going to prevent him from seeing that race. His own champion, Snowball, was going in the Cinema Handicap at Hollywood Park the following week. He loved the white horse. It was the only living thing that Clements did love. He could see the great white horse flying in the stretch, overtaking horses as if they were stationary. And Snowball was honest. He'd break his heart to win. Honesty was the key. The courage of the great thoroughbred in that final turn for home was the last honest action in Clements's world.

Yussef Kaladi greeted Clements warmly, apologizing for the body search by the Sudanese guards. Kaladi did not fail to notice the purple lines spreading out of the sides of Clements's aquiline nose. They had grown thicker and more vivid in the six months since he had last seen the American.

Kaladi motioned to the blue-skinned Sudanese, who instantly removed the green bottle from the ice bucket and served the men champagne. "To good health." Kaladi smiled.

"Cheers." Clements drank, then said, "Please don't think me rude, Yussef, but I'm booked on a nine o'clock flight to Paris."

"Yes, of course." Kaladi placed the glass down. "I had something special planned, Swiss twins, only eighteen and totally uninhibited. But no matter. Another time." He spoke two words in Arabic to the Sudanese. The blue man picked up the attaché case and placed it on a chrome table.

Kaladi stood over the case, and Clements said, "Two-eighteen, twice."

Kaladi placed the attaché case in an upright position. And put his finger on the small combination wheel. He moved the wheel carefully: 2 . . . 18 . . . 2 . . . 18. He pressed the brass buttons at either end of the case, and the gleaming latches flew open. Kaladi set the case on its side and opened the lid. He fingered the top layer of hundred-dollar bills; then his eyes narrowed as he saw something alien, something that shocked him. He quickly cleared the top layers of hundreds and found himself staring down at neat rows of strange currency, bearing the image of someone named Jefferson Davis. It was the last thing that Yussef Kaladi would ever see.

There was an ear-shattering roar and a bright red-orange ball of flame. Kaladi's rib cage imploded, driving shards of bone through his lungs and up through his throat. A fountain of dark blood shot out of the hole in his face where his mouth had been. The top of his head blew off in one piece. The concussion ring picked his body up and hurled it through the big glass wall out into the pool some fifty feet away. Clements's heart burst instantly, and his stomach opened, spilling his steaming intestines onto the priceless Persian carpet. His arms were wrenched from their sockets and flew across the room, banging hard against the splintered oak doors. The Sudanese was lucky. He never felt the sheet of glass that sliced him cleanly in half. The concussion ring circled the walls, pushing them out and down; then it moved vertically, blowing up the ceiling and causing a circular bed to come hurtling down into the smoking rubble of the living room.

Two passing carabinieri had twelve seconds to wonder about the explosive thunderclap before their Fiat was hurled twenty-five feet up onto the sidewalk of the Via Pacifica. They were shaken, but unhurt. The luckiest of all were the Swiss twins who had decided to get stoned before keeping their appointment at Kaladi's villa. At the time of the explosion they were in a bar in Trastevere, trying to score some coke.

Several hours later Frank Tedesco was in bed in his suite at the Hassler, watching the news bulletin describe the killings of Sheikh Yussef Kaladi and the American businessman Arthur Clements and the still unidentified remains of a black man. The newscaster went on to say that worthless, counterfeit currency dating back to the American Civil War was strewn about the rubble of the once-elegant villa. And operatives of the Ministero dell' Interno were investigating. Their preliminary findings indicated the work of rival Arab terrorist groups.

Tedesco snapped off the set and placed a call to an unlisted number in Palos Verdes, California.

CHAPTER

43 ⊠

A COLD MIST HUNG OVER THE ALSTER LAKE, DIFFUSING THE LIGHTS OF the villas that rimmed its shoreline. The public boat chugged its way across the southern edge of the lake toward the Uhlenhurst landing. Barney and Lisa sat on the wooden benches in the brightly lit cabin listening to the mournful wail of tugboats coming from the port of Hamburg.

Barney studied the lovely reflection of Lisa's face in the glass wall of the cabin. She had taken him to lunch in a section of the city called Karolinen. It was an ancient quarter. A favorite place of the German Expressionist painters in the early 1900s. The streets were winding, narrow cobblestones with small two-story structures whose sides were decorated with three-dimensional paintings that projected an illusion of the wall opening into another narrow street. There were small plazas in the section with cafés, antique shops, and bookstores.

They ate in a cozy café called the Fürsthof, which specialized in thick delicious hamburgers and pitchers of a local rosé wine. The Fürsthof was a favorite haunt of college students, and the speaker system played contemporary disco rock. The male students paid due attention to Lisa, and Barney felt a curious pride, almost a macho satisfaction that the beautiful pale blond girl belonged to him. It was a feeling he had not experienced since his college days. The warmth and conviviality of the place picked up their spirits. For a while they forgot Obermann and the coming meeting with Professor Siebold.

They talked about lost times and stolen moments. She told him about an Italian man she had met by chance on the "Blue train" from Milan to Rome and how they both changed their plans and got off in Venice. They went to the Lido, and made love, and swam, and sunned and gambled in the casino, and took moonlight gondola rides drifting through the Renaissance beauty of the magical city. Three days later it was over. They never saw each other again.

She asked Barney if he agreed that chance meetings, the unplanned, were not the best times. Barney replied that it worked only if each party understood it was a transient thing. She said she had always wanted to visit Mexico. That in her mind there was something exotic about Mexico. And two winters ago she had almost gone. It was a modeling assignment in Acapulco, but at the last moment another girl was chosen. Barney listened and wondered what an Acapulco tan would do to those light blue eyes and pale gold hair. After lunch they strolled the narrow streets arm in arm, like lovers on a holiday.

The throb of the boat's engines decreased, and the conductor announced, "Uhlenhurst." They left the cabin and went up on deck. The public boat was approaching the landing, and on either side of the long pier, small sailboats showing their night lights bobbed and rocked in their moorings.

The boat was made fast to the pier, and they got off with half a dozen other passengers.

When they reached the street, Lisa asked a woman for directions to number 38 Schöne Aussicht. The woman said it was just two blocks ahead on the lakefront.

They walked past the dignified two-story homes, and Lisa explained that the entire section had been devastated by British bombs. But as he looked at it now, it was impossible for Barney to imagine these tranquil streets in ruins.

They reached the corner, waited for the light, and started to cross. Barney glanced down the street to his left and suddenly froze. He saw a small man in a black coat wearing a homburg. Lisa asked, "What is it?"

But Barney didn't answer. He shouted at the figure of the man. "Hey! You! Stop!"

The man turned back, and even in the dim streetlight Barney could see it was not the Berlin pimp. This man had a Vandyke beard and wore no glasses and seemed to have heavier features than the man who had accosted him that night on Meineckestrasse. The man stared curiously at them for a moment, then turned and proceeded up the street. Barney took Lisa's arm and crossed the street.

"Why did you call out to him?" she asked.

"I thought I knew him. I was mistaken."

Number 38 Schöne Aussicht was a two-story gabled house with a flower-filled wooden balcony protruding from the second floor. There was a brick walkway that bisected the lawn and led up to the front door. A stout gray-haired woman wearing a white maid's uniform cracked the door open and asked, *"Ja, bitte?"*

"Fräulein Spangler *und* Herr Caine," Lisa answered.

"Ein Moment, bitte."

The woman closed the door, and they waited for what seemed a long time before she reappeared. This time she opened the door wide, flooding the steps in light. *"Kommen Sie bitte."* She smiled.

The professor's study was a cluttered, comfortable room. There were bookshelves and honorary degrees framed in glass on the wall, and between the degrees was a wooden plaque with an inscribed brass plate.

Professor Wolf Siebold was seated behind a battered wooden desk. He was the same man who had appeared in the photograph in Obermann's apartment. He was thin and appeared to be tall. He wore his white hair long and had a magnificent full white beard. His features were regular, almost handsome, and his dark eyes were alert and inquisitive.

He glanced up at them. "I'll be just a moment." The professor was carefully writing musical notes on a page of sheet music. He completed a passage of notes, studied what he had just written, then, satisfied, put the pen down and got to his feet. He was well over six feet tall. He came around the desk, shook hands with them, and directed them to a pair of velvet chairs. The professor sat on the sofa facing them.

"Well, as you can see, I am a composer of sorts. I play the flute in a chamber group with some of my colleagues from the institute. We are performing a concert this coming Sunday evening in the park." He looked at Lisa. "I was deeply saddened by your stepfather's death. Paul and I were old friends." He then glanced at Barney. "I understand you have reason to believe that I too am in danger."

"It's a possibility."

The professor smiled. "And you're in a position to save me, eh?"

Barney ignored the gentle sarcasm and asked, "What can you tell me about the Genesis program?"

The professor leaned back and looked up at the ceiling, as if trying to find the proper beginning. He then looked at Barney. "Genesis was one unit in a vast research and development section. The goal of the Genesis scientists was the production of synthetic fuel and petrochemical by-products through hydrogenation. You must understand that the manufacture of synthetic fuel was not a new idea for the Reich. It was first discovered by a German scientist named Bergius in 1913 and was perfected and refined during the ensuing years." Siebold continued in a voice that seemed to be enjoying its own sound. "On December fourteenth, 1933, Hitler guaranteed I. G. Farben a nonrefundable loan of two hundred and fifty million dollars to build a plant with a capacity to manufacture three hundred and fifty million barrels of synthetic fuel per annum. This plant became known as the Leuna Works. The cracking and liquefying of hard coal into petrol was one of the highest priorities in the Reich's scientific research program."

The professor started to say something else, but there was a knock at the door. The maid entered and placed a tray of tea and three cups on the coffee table. She looked at the professor, who nodded, and she left.

"Please join me," the professor said. "This tea is made from special herbs. You'll find it quite refreshing." He proceeded to pour the tea for them, serving himself last.

Barney asked, "Can you explain in layman's terms how the process of hydrogenation works?"

The professor smiled. "I'll try. One combines hydrogen, water, and oxygen with coal, preferably hard coal. It is then heated and pressurized over and through a metal catalyst, producing a wide variety of fuels: benzene, kerosene, methane, methanol, and all manner of thick lubricants, including what you Americans call natural gas." Siebold paused and added another cube of sugar to his tea. "It is quite complex and requires great precision. The so-called Fischer-Tropsch process was a great advancement and led directly to the establishment of the fifteen hydrogenation plants that provided the Reich with energy all through the war." The professor indicated the plaque on the wall. "That plaque is a commendation to me from Albert Speer. It is dated April twenty-ninth, 1944, and compliments me for producing seven million metric tons of fuel, despite the continuous Allied bombing."

"Weren't the fuel plants hit?" Barney asked.

"Only sporadically. I have always wondered why your bombers squandered their explosives in our streets. If they had concentrated their efforts on our hydrogenation plants, the war would have been over in 1943. Curious, don't you think?"

He smiled and sipped his tea and looked at them with a sense of satisfaction, of accomplishment, as if he alone had outwitted the British and American generals. "How is your tea?" he asked Lisa.

"Fine," she said.

Barney said, "Paul Obermann told me that the catalyst was the key to the process. He called it the black box."

"That's correct," the professor agreed. "The catalyst is like the conductor of an orchestra controlling the tonal force of the composition."

"What sort of catalyst did you use during the war?"

"Cobalt and magnesium oxide. Later on we added thorium and copper."

"Was that the final catalyst?"

"No. We tested one at the very end of the war." The professor put his cup down. "It was truly remarkable. We called it the Mangan catalyst. It contained a combination of manganese, platinum, and iridium. In the pilot project, it lasted for over one hundred million tons of coal and produced a ninety percent yield of nonsulfurous fuel. A purer oil than Arabian light crude."

Lisa asked, "Do you mind if I smoke?"

"No. Not at all."

Barney lit her cigarette and asked Siebold, "In your opinion, would this final Mangan catalyst be considered secret today?"

"Without question."

"Do you have any idea of what happened to that final formula?"

"In late April 1945 I received an order from Dr. Abraham Esau to turn over all our files to Oberkommander SS Pohl for transport of the formula to OKW headquarters in Zossen."

"For what purpose?"

The professor shrugged. "The rumor was that it would be part of a convoy of secret documents to be used as barter in negotiations with the Americans."

"And Genesis was a part of that convoy?"

"Yes."

"Were you ever approached by a Swiss industrialist concerning the Genesis Formula?"

The professor nodded. "It was after the Arab oil embargo in 1973. He asked if I could reconstitute the Genesis team. He also asked about the Mangan catalyst. I told him I was not interested."

Barney glanced at Lisa, then asked, "Did he offer you any money?"

"Quite a lot."

"Then why did you dismiss him?"

"I'm seventy-three years old, Mr. Caine. I have finally found serenity, in my teaching and in my music. I enjoy life. I have no desire to conquer any new worlds."

Barney rose and went over to the wall and examined the brass plaque. He studied the Nazi eagle with its claws holding the swastika. And without looking at Siebold, he asked, "Do you know a man named Friedrich Diestel?"

"No."

"Did you see an American named Thomas Neeley in early January of this year?"

"He phoned me repeatedly, but I refused to see him."

"Why?" Barney asked.

"He had no credentials. And the past is not something I enjoy exploring." Siebold sighed heavily. "We used slave labor in all our plants. It is not something I am proud of. Besides, many German scientists were murdered by SS men to still their voices."

"What happened to you after the war?"

"I was captured by the Americans and taken to Brownsville, Texas. I worked with experts from various American oil companies and instituted a pilot synthetic fuel plant. The operation was terminated in 1956." Siebold lifted the teapot and asked Lisa, "Would you care for some?"

"Yes. Thank you."

The professor refilled her cup, then his own. "This tea is quite good, don't you think?"

"An unusual flavor," Lisa remarked.

Barney paced for a moment, stopped, and asked, "Why was the pilot project terminated?"

"I can't say." The professor rose, carrying his tea, and went back behind his desk. He glanced down at the sheet music, then looked at Barney. "I really must be getting back to my music."

"Just a few more questions," Barney said. "Tell me, in your opinion can synthetic fuel be manufactured economically in today's marketplace?"

The professor rubbed his beard. "Absolutely. With OPEC's price at almost fourteen dollars a barrel and going higher. And with the enormous American reserves of coal, I would say that pure, nonsulfuric synthetic fuel can be produced in great quantity for about ninety cents a gallon. Furthermore, if it contained an alcohol base, it would shake the entire automotive industry to its roots. The engine would last for over two hundred thousand miles." The professor paused to sip his tea. "Alcohol has a tremendous cooling effect; that's why it's used in racing cars."

Barney recalled Paul Isella's words: *If we used regular gasoline, we'd burn the engine up in minutes.* Barney asked, "Is there any technical reason why the United States is not making synthetic fuel?"

"Technical?" The professor shook his head. "No. They have the know-how. The money. And the coal."

Lisa suddenly spoke. "But they don't have the catalyst."

Siebold nodded. "The Mangan catalyst would make the process instantly feasible," the professor explained. "But they nevertheless have enough information to begin, and in great quantity, of course, it requires an enormous investment to start. Perhaps as much as five billion. But that is not unreasonable when one considers that America would be self-sufficient in energy for hundreds of years."

"Do you think," Barney asked, "that there is a conspiracy to keep synthetic fuel from being manufactured?"

The professor smiled. "I am a chemist, not a geopolitical theoretician."

Barney got to his feet. "Do you know the whereabouts of Dr. Esau?"

"I know only that he was taken prisoner by the Soviets in late 1945. Years later he was exchanged for a Soviet spy. Dr. Esau returned to Germany a broken man."

"Do you know if he's alive?"

"I have no idea."

"Do you know anyone that was close to Esau?"

The professor rose and came around the desk and faced Barney. "There is a man named Manfred Reimeck. He was Dr. Esau's adjutant. He lived with Esau day and night. If anyone is in touch with Dr. Esau, it would be Reimeck."

"Where would I find Reimeck?"

"He is one of the curators of the Deutsches Museum in Munich. Now I must insist we conclude. I am tired, and I have an early class tomorrow."

Lisa rose and stood alongside Barney. "One final question. Do you know anyone who had a motive to kill Paul Obermann?"

Siebold shrugged and sighed. "The past contains elements of danger for all of us who worked on Genesis."

CHAPTER

44 ☒

THE PUBLIC BOAT LEFT THE UHLENHURST LANDING AT 9:25 P.M. THE gray mist had been dispelled by a cold night wind coming off the Atlantic. The lights of the city were in sharp focus. They were up on deck, leaning on the rail. The cold salty air hitting their faces felt refreshing after the closeness of Professor Wolf Siebold's study.

Barney noticed a narrow strip of blazing lights coming from a section of the city just beyond the eastern edge of the lake. "What are those?" he asked.

"Where?"

Barney pointed toward the line of distant lights. "Those lights. There. Follow my finger."

"Oh," Lisa said. "That's St. Pauli. In the Reeperbahn. It's a small district with clubs that have pornographic shows."

Barney remembered the photograph he found in Neeley's home. The one with two smiling girls. "It's all legal, I suppose."

"Yes," Lisa replied. "It's the most famous tourist attraction in Hamburg. Perhaps in all of Germany. Would you like to see one of the shows?"

"I don't think so."

"Why not?"

"I never got much of a thrill watching other people." He turned to her. "Why do you ask?"

She shrugged. "I just thought you'd like to see it. Most men would."

"Most men haven't spent five years working Vice in Los Angeles."

Her eyes smiled. "I keep forgetting you're a policeman."

"In Germany I'm just another tourist."

"Yes, a tourist who gets shot at," she said softly. "A tourist who sees terror in the shape of a small man in a dark overcoat."

* * *

Barney checked for messages at the desk, but there was none. They picked up their keys and started for the elevator. Then as an afterthought he asked, "Would you like a drink?"

She shook her head. "I don't think so."

They rode up to the third floor in silence, walked down the long corridor, and stopped at Lisa's door.

"I'll make the arrangements for Munich," Barney said. "We'll try to leave around noon."

She nodded and stared at him. Her light blue eyes were cloudy, almost misty.

"Is there anything wrong?" he asked.

"No. Just tired." She made no move to open her door. She held his eyes with her own, and suddenly she seemed very fragile.

Barney cupped her face in the palms of his hands and gently brushed his lips against hers. Lisa neither responded nor resisted. She turned abruptly and opened her door. Then she looked back at him for a brief instant. It was a startling look, as if she were seeing him for the first time.

Barney showered and stretched out naked on the king-sized bed. The darkness of the room was relieved sporadically by the revolving red light thrown by a distant neon sign. He could still taste Lisa's lipstick and smell the heady perfume that seemed to come out of her pale hair. He wished he knew what it was that haunted her.

Barney snapped the night table light on and picked up the pad and pencil. He wrote in column order:

Call: Lehmans, fill him in on Siebold. Have him phone and run
      a check on Reimeck.
Call: P. Baumer, fill him in.
Call: Reimeck at Deutsches Museum.
Call: Louis, fill him in.

Barney snapped off the light and leaned back on the down pillow. He thought of Professor Siebold's words: "The Mangan catalyst would make the process instantly feasible." The forces arrayed against the mass production of synthetic fuel were awesome: OPEC, Bil Oil, Big Banking, and, if an alcohol fuel was used, Big Auto.

And if America became self-sufficient in oil, OPEC's power would dissolve overnight; its chokehold on the Western democracies would be gone. Israel would no longer be trading its blood for oil. Barney felt a sudden surge of euphoria. If any force on earth would benefit from the manufacture of synthetic fuel, it would be Israel. And in that moment, Barney realized there was a way to hedge his bet. A way to stay alive.

He tossed and turned for an hour. The pillow burned his cheek. The image of the little man in the black coat came alive in the darkness of the room. Was he the same man who had shadowed him that first night in Berlin? There was no answer, only the increasing pounding at his temples. Barney looked up and watched the red glow move across the ceiling, then vanish, then reappear.

There was a soft knock at the door, but it sounded to Barney like a gunshot. Jolting him. He lay still for a moment; then the knock repeated. He got off the bed and went to the door. "Who is it?" he said hoarsely.

"It's me. Lisa."

He lifted his robe off the chair, slipped it on, and opened the door. She came in, and Barney went over to the night table and snapped the light on.

"Leave it off," she said.

Barney looked at her.

"Please," she whispered.

He put the light out and sat on the edge of the bed. He watched her, standing there in the dark, staring at him, her figure periodically illuminated by the red glow of distant neon.

She took off her blouse and unfastened the zipper at the side of her skirt. It fell to her feet. She stepped out of the skirt and removed her shoes. She was naked except for a pair of brief blue panties. She walked up to the bed and stood over Barney.

He slipped off his robe and looked up at her. Their eyes locked. His hands went to her narrow waist, and he moved the panties down over her hips, down her thighs, all the way down to her ankles. And she stepped out of them. He moved off the bed and went down to his knees and pulled her to him, kissing the smooth white skin of her flat stomach.

The strong, heady aroma of her perfume went from his mouth to his throat and up to his brain. It was intoxicating and exhilarating. His mouth, tongue, and lips seemed to take on a life of their own as they moved over her, caressing her, tasting her. He glanced up at her once, and her eyes glinted strangely. Her body was arched into him. And she began to murmur in German, *"Bitte . . . bitte. . . ."* Then crossed to English: "Oh. Please . . . please."

He moved Lisa onto the bed, and she lay back, spreading her legs. Barney bent over her and stared at the symmetry of her body. Again she whispered, "Please." He placed his cheek against the inside of her thigh and began to kiss the smooth skin. He covered her belly and thighs with kisses, moving his mouth from place to place, and her body began to pump. And she groaned. *"Bitte . . . bitte. . . ."* And when he could no longer resist, he pressed his lips into the moist sensual core of the girl. His hands were underneath her, pulling her up, crushing her against his mouth, bruising his lips. His temples throbbed, and beads of sweat oozed out of his forehead and coursed down his face. His mouth became part of her. Her hands went around the back of his neck, pulling him into her. He felt himself slipping into a bizarre fantasy. She was the great Valkyrian bitch goddess. The Nordic myth. Naked and fierce, a giantess. A queen warrior out of the ancient Teutonic tribes, and she was at his mercy, moaning and pleading, while he swallowed the holy water of the Aryan myth.

She was coming up to meet his madness. Low moans escaped her parted lips, and her hands clenched into small fists beating on the pillows. Her stomach was throbbing, pulsing, and her body arched, coming up off the bed. Her hands began to open and close rapidly. She moaned loudly and dug her nails into his shoulders. Her entire body convulsed and shuddered violently, over and over in one long, continuous spasm. Her lips drew back over her teeth, and two severe lines of concentration snaked down her forehead.

She was crossing that ultimate sensual threshold where pleasure and pain meet, and ignite, and take possession of the mind and body. Barney was gone, obsessed by the myth and the moment.

She was at the crest of a long spasm and screamed, "You must stop! Stop now! Please! You must!" But her pleading only fueled his obsession. She had to use all her strength to push his head away and pull her legs together. Barney raised himself up; he was on all fours. The room was spinning. He stared down at her still convulsing, sweat-soaked body. He gasped for breath, then moved up, covering her body with his. He held her face in his hands and pressed his mouth into hers. She opened her legs, and he slid easily inside her. A wave of warmth radiated up to his stomach and spread through his chest. She locked her legs around him and ran her hands from his waist up to his shoulders, up and down, never still. Their mouths were joined together, as they rocked toward the outer edges of orgasm. They were one. A single unit of throbbing flesh, trapped by an excruciating passion neither understood. It was a passion fired by the purest sensual connection of all. A transient connection that held no past. No future. Only the moment.

CHAPTER

45 ⊠

BARNEY SAT UP IN BED, WATCHING THE MORNING LIGHT FILTER THROUGH the drapes. They had awakened at a little after eight. Lisa drew him to her. They made love again. But it was different. Silent, and methodical, but fulfilling and in a curious way, reassuring. Its daylight normality validated the madness of the night. Afterward she kissed him, got up and went into the bathroom. He could hear the shower running now.

He was still amazed by the force of their lovemaking. He could not remember ever feeling so completely fulfilled. He was surprised by the fantasies that had overwhelmed him, by the intensity of emotion they had transmitted to each other. For Barney it was unique. He could not remember anything in his life that had come close to it.

There was a knock at the door, and Barney slipped his robe on as a blond youth in a white uniform wheeled in the breakfast table. There were two large pots of coffee, platters of eggs and sausages, toast, rolls, jams, and a plate of sliced oranges. The waiter asked if everything was all right. Barney said it was and tipped him. The boy left, and Barney poured himself a coffee, feeling the relief as the caffeine hit him.

He sat down and opened the morning paper. It was in German. He scanned the front page and saw a photograph that kept his arm from bringing the coffee up to his mouth.

The bathroom door opened, and Lisa came out with a large white towel wrapped around her body. Her long hair was still damp and hung down to her shoulders. She came up to the table and poured some coffee. She noticed Barney's eyes riveted to the front page of the paper. She knew he could not read German and wondered what it was that held his attention. She sat down, and he handed her the paper and indicated the captioned photograph. "What does it say?"

She studied the photograph and caption. Her face seemed to tense, and she bit down on her lower lip. Then she handed the paper back to Barney. "Three men were killed yesterday in a suburb of Rome. A villa belonging to a Saudi, named Yussef Kaladi. The other man was an American." She paused. "His name was Arthur Clements. The third man is an unidentified black."

She had confirmed what he guessed the German caption meant. He thought: Two more had been hit. Arthur Clements. He had been counting on cracking Clements. The one man he could tie directly to the Genesis conspiracy. That was probably why Clements was hit. But why Kaladi? Kaladi was on the perimeter of Genesis. It was true he had been sent the cable by Neeley. But Kaladi's principal grift was the bribes he took down from the American oil companies. Why would Kaladi get involved with Genesis?

He put the paper down, picked up a piece of toast, and dipped its edge into the yolk of his fried egg. Lisa watched his face screw up in a frowning concentration.

"Is that incident in Rome connected to Genesis?" she asked.

"Yes."

"Does it have anything to do with the death of Paul Obermann?"

"I'm not sure. There's an article alongside the photo. Would you read it to me?"

She picked up the paper. But this time she read without a trace of tension. "It says Kaladi was a highly placed official in the Saudi Investment Fund, and that Clements was an American businessman. They were killed by a charge of high explosives detonated from an attaché case." She paused and sipped some coffee. "The Italian police found bits and pieces of false currency dating back to the American Civil War." She moved her lips slightly as she read on. "The notes were fifty-dollar bills with the photograph of Jefferson Davis." She looked at Barney. "Can that be right?"

"Yeah, that's right. Good old Jeff Davis. Christ, what a touch."

"Did you know these men?"

"I knew the American."

"And the Arab? Do you know anything about him?"

"He was a middleman. He took large sums of money, bribes from the American oil companies, and deposited the money in Swiss accounts for the royal Saudi family. Tom Neeley was the bag man."

"What do you mean 'bag man'?"

"Someone who transports illegal funds."

Barney mopped up the last of his eggs, swallowed the remains of his third cup of coffee, got to his feet and started for the bathroom.

"Barney," she called to him.

He stopped, and she came to him. Her arms went around his neck. She kissed him lightly and whispered, "I want to thank you for last night. For asking no questions. For accepting what I wanted."

He kissed her long and deeply and tasted toothpaste and coffee. He had forgotten the tastes of morning romance. He held her for a moment and then said, "You better pack. We have to leave at eleven."

She nodded. "I want you to promise me something."

"Sure."

"Promise me that no matter how it ends for us, you will remember how it was." He started to speak, but she placed her forefinger against his lips. "Don't say anything. Just remember."

Professor Wolf Siebold concluded his class in the modern laboratory. The subject of the morning sessions had been hydrocarbons, and the professor was pleased. The dissertations of his small elite group of students had been brilliant. The professor glanced at his watch. It was a little after ten, time for his morning break. He went to his large desk on the raised platform and lit an American cigarette. He inhaled deeply, luxuriating in the dangerous indulgence. The smoke made him slightly heady and euphoric.

And why not? He had performed his prescribed duty; his meeting with the American and his female companion had presented no problems. He would report to Diestel, then have a coffee and spend the balance of the morning composing his flute part for Sunday's concert.

He took another deep lungful of smoke and dialed Friedrich Diestel's private office number in Berlin. Diestel answered on the first ring. They exchanged greetings, and the professor said, *"Ich habe den Amerikaner mit dem Mädchen Gestern Abend gesehn."*

Diestel grunted his acknowledgment, and the professor continued, *"Ja, ich habe sie zu Reimeck geschickt."*

"Gut, Herr Professor," Diestel replied.

The professor said, *"Zu Ihren diensten, Herr Oberst. Auf wiedersehen."*

"Auf wiedersehen," Diestel replied, and hung up.

Diestel walked to the huge center section of the glass wall and looked out over the divided city. He could clearly see the top of the East Berlin television tower. Diestel's thoughts were always the same when he looked east: What a monumental tragedy that insane Austrian had committed on the German people. That astrologer, that drug addict had lacked even the capacity to negotiate a proper surrender. Diestel remembered a cold, bleak day in November 1944 when a heartbroken SS general, Felix Steiner, addressed them, telling them the Führer had rejected his plan. Steiner had proposed that all the forces of the Wehrmacht be shifted to the eastern front. That their struggle against the British and Americans be abandoned. That the Western Allies be permitted entry to the Reich while the entire might of their own forces be used against the Soviets and their Mongol hordes.

A negotiated settlement with the West would then be possible, and the German nation would be saved. The Führer had not only angrily rejected the proposal, but ordered a full-scale attack on the American salient near the Belgian village of Bastogne.

Diestel sighed heavily, and turned from the window. He sat down behind the gleaming desk. Well, he thought, at least the cartel had survived. No Führer could prevent that. The cartel always survived. And prospered. He glanced at his watch, the one given to him by the distinguished Dr. Abraham Esau. It was time to phone Tedesco. This time there was no need to make an international call. Tedesco was only a few miles away, at the Berliner Hotel in East Berlin. He would report to Tedesco that Professor Siebold had followed orders and sent the American to Reimeck. Diestel leaned back in his leather chair. He admired the genius of the plan. It was in a way a privilege to be part of it. And while he was far from the master of this chess game, he was certainly not a pawn. In this game he was at least a castle. No. In this game he was a knight. Yes. That was more accurate.

After all, he played an intricate role in the strategy. Diestel admired the master strategist, the designer of the Genesis ploy, who resided at the top of the cartel. So far the moves had been precise, brilliant, and protected. And above all, it had order at its core. And more than anything else, Diestel admired order. Order was an end unto itself. Order permitted progress and security for the individual, the state, and, ultimately, the cartel.

CHAPTER

46 ⊠

THE ISRAELI CONSUL GENERAL WAS LOCATED IN THE EPPENDORF SECtion of Hamburg. Barney came around the T-shaped hallway and started for the office at the end of the hall. He slowed his walk as he saw the two blue-uniformed federal police standing on either side of the glass doors. They were armed with deadly-looking machine pistols. They motioned Barney to halt. The stocky man stopped Barney while the taller one covered him; the snout of the machine pistol pointed to a spot just above Barney's eyes. Barney showed the stocky man his ID card and mentioned Hans Lehmans's name. The man passed Barney's card to his tall companion, who examined it and said, "Passport, please."

Barney handed him his passport. The man checked it carefully, taking his time. The man then handed the ID and passport back to his partner, who returned them to Barney. The stocky man then knelt down and gave Barney a fast and thorough body check. He straightened up and nodded to his partner, who asked Barney, "Who do you wish to see?"

"The consul general."

The tall guard took out a small walkie-talkie and said something in German into the device. There was a pause, followed by a woman's voice responding in German. The tall guard motioned Barney to walk in front of them. When they reached the glass door, the stocky guard pressed a button on the side of the door; it was followed by a buzzing sound from the door lock. He opened the door, and the buzzing ceased.

Barney found himself standing in a wide, well lit, sparsely furnished office. There was a plain-looking middle-aged woman seated behind a desk. Behind her on either side, were the flags of the State of Israel and of the West German Federal Republic. The woman glanced up at Barney. "Why do you wish to see the consul, Mr. Caine?"

"I am here in Germany on official business. There are certain aspects of the case I'm investigating that I believe will be of interest to the State of Israel."

The woman studied him a moment. "Why do you come here? Our embassy is in Bonn."

"Because I have no time to go to Bonn. I have a simple request. I want to place a phone call to an old Israeli colleague of mine."

"But why come here?" the woman asked. "Why not simply phone him?"

"I don't know where he is. I last saw the man in Madrid in 1968. At that time I was with the CIA and he was with Mossad."

The woman's soft brown eyes grew interested. She stared at Barney for a moment, then nodded at the German policeman, who left. The woman picked up the receiver and pressed a button at the base of the phone. She paused for a second, then spoke rapidly in Hebrew. She then cupped the phone and looked up at Barney. "What was the name of this Israeli friend of yours?"

"Zvi Barzani."

She spoke hurriedly into the phone and hung up. "Come with me, Mr. Caine."

The consul general was a slightly built, handsome man with black eyes and prematurely gray hair. Barney guessed him to be in his late thirties, maybe younger. The consul came around his cluttered desk and shook hands with Barney. He smiled and indicated a chair. "Sit down, please, Mr. Caine." Barney sat in the chair facing the desk. The consul took a pack of cigarettes off his desk and offered one to Barney, who declined. The consul lit his cigarette and remained standing. He then sat on the edge of his desk. "When did you last see Barzani?"

"It was in the fall of '68. In Madrid, at the Barajas Airport. He passed documents to me detailing Soviet ground-to-air missiles."

"I see." He puffed calmly on the cigarette. "Do you remember the code name of that operation?"

Barney was surprised by the question. "Hell, it was a long time ago."

"Yes. I know. But try to remember. We have time."

Barney searched his memory and said, "I'll have one of those cigarettes."

The consul gave him one and lit it for him. Barney looked up at the ceiling, then got to his feet and walked across the green carpet and looked out of the windows. He tried to restructure that long-ago meeting in the Iberia lounge in Madrid. He detailed the lounge in his mind and remembered a pair of large silver wings on the wall . . . and he felt a surge of excitement. He turned from the window. "It had something to do with air, with flying."

"Take your time," the consul said.

Barney paced for a moment, then walked up to the consul. "It was a Hebrew word. I know that. The operation had a Hebrew code."

"What was its meaning in English?"

Barney sat down. "I—I think the Hebrew is coming back. It was *nahir*. Or *sharir*. Wait, wait! I have the English equivalent! It was 'Eagle'! It was *neshre* in Hebrew!"

The consul's black eyes smiled. "That's close enough. The word is *Neshir*." He went back behind his desk. "Barzani is now deputy director of Mossad." The consul took out a small notebook, thumbed through the pages, and stopped on a certain page. He looked at the number and dialed it directly on his private line. He waited a moment, then spoke into the phone in Hebrew. He wrote a new number down on a scrap of paper and said a final word that sounded like *Bakashah*. He hung up, redialed, and glanced at Barney. "Barzani is in Jerusalem." The consul's face tensed, then blossomed into a smile, and he spoke into the phone. "*Zvikah! Areil Aloni. Tov . . . Ken . . . Hamburg . . . Ken.*" He then switched to English. "I have an old colleague of yours here in my office. An American policeman named Barney Caine. He remembers you from the Madrid airport in '68. Operation Neshir." The consul waved Barney to the phone.

In his tiny office tucked away in the inner recesses of a produce market in East Jerusalem, the six-foot-three Barzani rested his legs on a battered desk. His dark, tough good looks were betrayed by melancholy eyes that had witnessed a lifetime of intrigue and violence.

He glanced up at the red sword and red shield fixed to a plaque on the wall. Barzani kept the insidious symbol of the KGB in a prominent place as a constant reminder to himself and his staff of the true face of the enemy. He pressed a button on a tape device attached to the phone and tried to place Barney's face. He remembered the meeting in Barajas, and slowly Barney's features came into focus. He recalled the face was regular, typically white American Protestant. And Caine had been honest. He had kept his end of the bargain. In return for the Soviet missile blueprints, Israel had received ten Hawk missile units. Barney was already repeating his "hellos" into the phone and Barzani replied, "Hello, Caine."

Barney stood over the consul, holding the receiver.

"Long time, Zvi."

"Yes. How are you, Barney?"

"I'm on a case."

"How can I help you?" Barzani asked.

Barney said, "I may have occasion to send you an envelope, and if that happens, take the envelope by hand to the chief scientist at the Technion Institute in Haifa."

Barzani took his feet off the desk and leaned forward. "I would like more. But if you can't, I understand."

"No. I can tell you. The envelope will contain data on a secret formula for the manufacture of synthetic fuel."

The muscles in Barzani's jaw tensed. "Send the envelope to the following address."

"Just a minute." Barney cupped the phone and asked the consul, "Can you write this down?" The consul nodded, and Barney spoke into the phone. "Okay, go ahead."

Barzani spoke carefully and slowly, "Albert Yaacov." He spelled "Yaacov" and continued. "Number sixty-three Hayarkon, Tel Aviv, four-three-eight-five."

Barney repeated the name and address.

Barzani said, "Do not mail it to Israel from Germany. There's leakage, and stoppage. They are infested by KGB and East German intelligence."

"I understand," Barney said.

"You must mail it from America," Barzani added. "And do not mail it registered or special delivery. Simply normal airmail."

"Okay," Barney replied. "Now remember, this may never happen."

"I understand. If you send it, I assure you it will be placed in the proper hands."

"Zvi!" Barney said.

"Yes?"

"I'm glad you're still around."

Barzani smiled. "You were worried, eh?"

"Well . . . Yes. The October war worried me."

"I was in the Golan with my boys," Barzani replied.

"That's what I figured," Barney said.

Zvi thought he detected something strained in Barney's voice. "Can I help you?" Barzani offered.

"No. This game is called Solitaire. You know what I mean."

"Yes. Very well. Stay alive, because one day you must come and visit the Holy Land."

"One day, I will."

"*Shalom,* Barney."

The consul general walked Barney to the office door. Barney turned to the consul. "When I came in here, the German officer outside spoke into a walkie-talkie to this lady."

The woman looked up and said, "What of it?"

"Suppose those policemen were overwhelmed and someone else picked up that walkie-talkie?" Barney asked.

The woman smiled, and the consul answered, "The German officer speaks to my assistant in a prearranged code. The code is changed three times a day."

Barney shook his head. "That shows you how long I've been out of the spook business."

"*Shalom,* Mr. Caine. And good luck."

CHAPTER

47 ☒

THE GRAY MERCEDES TAXI ENTERED THE CITY OF MUNICH ON VAN-DER-Tannstrasse, passed under the Doric-columned memorial arch, and rolled through the narrow streets of Schwabing.

The outdoor cafés were crowded with young people sitting in the warm Bavarian sunshine, smoking, chatting, reading, and drinking beer out of large enameled steins.

The taxi turned into Königsplatz and crossed a stone bridge that spanned a fast-flowing green river. They came off the bridge and onto a cobblestone drive that led to the massive gray walls of the Deutsches Museum.

The taxi pulled up at the main entrance, just as two yellow and red buses unloaded a group of schoolchildren. Barney asked Lisa to find out what the driver would charge to wait for them.

"For how long?"

"Say, a half hour."

Lisa spoke to the driver, who thought for a moment. *"Ungefähr zwanzig mark."*

"He wants twenty marks," Lisa said.

"That's ten bucks." Barney sighed. "Well, okay."

The exhibit hall was awesome and breathtaking. It was the size of several football fields. The center of the hall was taken up by a restored 1895 sailing vessel. The hull resided in a deep well; its mast soared a hundred feet high, almost reaching the second tier of the museum, where World War I and World War II planes, suspended on cables, appeared to be flying in formation.

At the far end of the hall, beyond the sailboat, were gleaming locomotives. A group of children surrounded one of them, watching a man in a white smock operate an engine, setting its wheels in motion and blowing its whistle.

A museum guard went over to the man in the white smock, said something to him, and pointed toward Barney and Lisa. The man nodded and pulled a lever stopping the engine to the accompanying groans of the children. The man then moved through the crowds, passed the sailboat, and approached Barney and Lisa.

Manfred Reimeck was a small, wiry man whose face was marred by a flattened nose common to prizefighters. He extended a large hand and smiled. "Manfred Reimeck."

Barney shook his hand. "Barney Caine and Lisa Spangler."

He smiled at Lisa and said, "Come. We go to my office."

They squeezed their way onto an elevator jammed with children and a sprinkling of adults. The doors closed, and the big elevator began a slow ascent. A small child started to cry as his ice cream fell out of its cone onto the floor of the elevator. Reimeck patted the boy's head and gave him some coins, telling him to buy another but to be careful not to drop it.

Reimeck's office was cluttered with documents, and there were Xeroxed copies of technical data tacked up on the corkboards attached to the walls. Reimeck shoved some papers aside, sat down at his desk, and motioned them to be seated. "I have no secretary, so forgive the disorder. Now, what is it you wish to see me about?"

"Did you receive a call from Inspector Hans Lehmans?" Barney asked.

"Yes. Early this morning." Reimeck rubbed his flat nose. "He requested that I see you. Nothing more. So I am in the dark."

"I'm here because Professor Wolf Siebold said you might know the whereabouts of Dr. Abraham Esau."

Reimeck studied Lisa for a moment, then looked at Barney. "Why do you wish to know that?"

"I'm investigating a crime that took place in Los Angeles. The tangents of that crime—"

Reimeck cut him off. "I'm sorry. I don't understand that word."

"What word?"

"Tangents."

Lisa translated. "*Umstände.*"

"Ah," Reimeck said, "circumstances."

Barney nodded. "This case involves the Genesis program."

Reimeck walked to the window and looked down at the green river flowing past the museum. The sun was very high and losing its light to a profusion of white, fleecy clouds. He said nothing for a moment, then turned to Barney. "I know very little about Genesis. I was a test driver for Porsche. When the synthetic fuel, a diesel fuel, based with alcohol, was tested in the new Tiger tank in March 1944, Dr. Esau and other high officials of armaments and research came to the test grounds near Stuttgart. I test-drove that tank. There was an octane problem with the fuel. In the following weeks I found myself working closely with Dr. Esau. After the octane problem was solved, Dr. Esau requested me to be his driver and personal adjutant. I was transferred to the Kaiser Wilhelm Institute in Berlin."

"Did you know about the final Genesis Formula, the one that contained the Mangan catalyst?"

Reimeck walked back to his desk. "Yes, we all knew. It had performed magnificently in Siebold's test projects."

Reimeck sat down, and Barney asked, "When you say, 'we all knew,' who do you mean by 'we'?"

"The highest people in the program: Krouch, Keppler, Pohl, and ultimately Göring."

"What about Friedrich Diestel?"

Reimeck rubbed his nose nervously. "I assume so. But Diestel was not directly involved in the science of Genesis."

"What was his function?"

Reimeck sighed. "Diestel provided slave labor for the hydrogenation plants."

"Including the Farben plant at Auschwitz?"

Reimeck looked surprised, then shrugged. "I don't know."

Barney got to his feet and took a few steps to the window. He lit a cigarillo and blew the blue smoke against the windowpane and without looking at Reimeck said, "Have you seen or spoken with Diestel recently?"

"No, I have not."

"Did you know Paul Obermann?"

Reimeck glanced at Lisa. "No."

Barney turned away from the window and walked toward Reimeck. "All right, you were in Berlin with Esau. You knew about the Mangan catalyst. It had successfully been tested. What happened to it?"

"One morning in late April 1945—I don't recall the date—Dr. Esau was summoned to a secret meeting at the Adlon Hotel."

"Summoned by whom?"

"Brigadier General Walter Schellenberg. He was Himmler's minister of foreign affairs. There were other civilian heads of armaments and research present. And an SS Panzer general, Kladen. A famous Panzer officer."

Barney crushed his cigarillo out in a paper-clip dish on Reimeck's desk. "Were you at that meeting?" he asked.

"No. I drove Dr. Esau there." Reimeck paused. "It took over an hour to travel the two kilometers."

"What took place at the meeting?" Barney asked.

"Dr. Esau ordered the release of all secret documents pertaining to synthetics, not just fuel, but rubber, plastics, magnetic tapes, everything in our control. These documents were part of a truck convoy under the command of Panzer General Kladen."

"Was the Mangan catalyst part of the Genesis Formula?"

"Yes."

"Do you know what happened to that convoy?"

"We heard that it was intercepted by units of the Third American Army."

"Did Dr. Esau have a copy of that final formula?"

"Yes."

"What happened to it?"

Reimeck shrugged. "I don't know. In late May the Soviet tanks of Konev's army broke into Berlin. Dr. Esau was taken. I escaped to the West." He paused and glared at Barney; beads of sweat were beginning to appear on his forehead. "In 1956 Esau was returned to East Berlin in an exchange for a spy, by agreement with the Soviets."

"Who arranged the exchange?"

"The Americans."

Barney paced for a moment. "Where is Dr. Esau now?"

Reimeck stared at Barney, then shifted his gaze to Lisa. The scream of a low-flying jet invaded the silence of the room.

In a calm, cold voice Barney said, "I asked you a question."

"I heard your question." Reimeck's voice rose. "I must remind you that you have no official position here! I granted this interview out of courtesy. Nothing more!"

Barney felt the heat come out of his chest and rush up into his throat. He moved quickly around the desk and grabbed the lapels of Reimeck's smock and yanked him to his feet and slammed him against the wall. Barney's face was florid, and the small crimson scar was livid. Lisa tried to move Barney's arm from Reimeck. He shoved her aside violently, keeping Reimeck pinned to the wall. "Now you listen to me, you son of a bitch. I've had two friends of mine tortured and shot to death. And this young lady's stepfather was gunned down in cold blood. And I've been on a seven-thousand-mile trail that I promise you isn't going to end in this office. I'm sick to death of you bastards. You and Diestel and Siebold and all the other 'innocent' scientists. You had a hand in the deaths of thousands, and all your fucking ice-cream handouts to children aren't going to change that. Now listen carefully, I'll stay on top of you from now on. Until you tell me what I need to know. No court. No legal red tape. No Lehmans. Me. Just me!"

Barney shoved him back down into his chair. Lisa watched from the window. She hadn't realized Barney was capable of such rage. Reimeck opened his shirt collar and rubbed at his throat.

"You're quite a paradox, Mr. Caine. You raise the specter of my alleged criminal activities, and yet you come in here and use Gestapo tactics. It seems justice always depends upon the convenience of one's point of view." Reimeck paused. "Dr. Abraham Esau is terminally ill. He has perhaps three months to live. He resides in a private sanitarium in Baden-Baden, called Kessenger Haus."

"Phone him," Barney snapped.

"You understand Dr. Esau is eighty-three years old. He is under heavy sedation and constant care. I may not be able to speak directly to him."

"He has a nurse, doesn't he?"

"Always."

"Then call. And be careful with the German."

"I'm aware Miss Spangler speaks German." Reimeck dialed nine digits and waited. Barney could feel his nerve ends pulsing the tension of the entire case fusing into this moment. Reimeck spoke in rapid but polite German to someone on the end of the phone. Barney heard his own name and that of Lisa's used in the stream of German. Reimeck cupped the phone and asked Barney, "When will you present yourself to Dr. Esau?"

"We'll phone in the morning. Before noon."

Reimeck translated into the phone, hung up, scribbled the number on a pad, and said, "He has a male nurse: Karl Plieger." Reimeck handed the note to Barney. "You have the phone number and the address in Baden-Baden."

Barney took Lisa's arm and started for the door.

"Mr. Caine!" Reimeck called. Barney turned. Reimeck rose from behind his desk. "You should keep in mind. You are stepping on the toes of people who have survived great difficulties. People who know very well how to take care of themselves."

* * *

Barney and Lisa caught the Mozart Express to Baden-Baden. The porter showed them to their first-class compartment and hefted Lisa's bag up onto the overhead luggage rack. There were reading lights, pillows, and blankets. Barney tipped the porter and asked when the dining car opened. The man replied, "Dining car one hour. Bar opens in *zwei Minuten.*"

They ran through a long tunnel for two minutes, then burst out of the darkness into the late-afternoon sun. Lisa stared up from her magazine at Barney. His face was lit in stuttered flashes of sunlight. They were rushing past a small suburban station just outside Munich, and Barney saw the sign on the station. "Dachau." He shook his head; the screams of the past were inescapable.

"Come on," Barney said. "Let's get a drink."

The club car was not crowded. A few businessmen were seated at tables doing their homework. And two stunning women were drinking champagne and staring into each other's eyes. Barney found a window table diagonally across from the two women. They ordered scotch and watched the Mozart Express knife its way through rolling cultivated fields, climbing slowly toward the distant snow-topped Alps. The drinks came and they touched glasses. They watched the passing green fields and grazing cattle and the line of tractors working the land, turning over a rich, dark, loamy soil. They were silent for what seemed a long time; then Barney asked, "What are you thinking?"

She raised the glass to her lips and tossed her long hair. "Oh. Foolish thoughts."

"Like what?"

"That it will end well for us."

"What's foolish about that?"

She shrugged. "I no longer believe in happy endings."

"Maybe it won't end at all."

"Of course it will. It must. We may as well be from different galaxies." She looked out the window at the white peaks of the Alps. And there were tiny lights in her eyes when she turned to him. "Do you ski?" she asked.

"Years ago. In Chile. I wasn't very good."

"There's no sport quite like it," she said. "There's a purity to it, even a poetry. To be alone, coming down a great slope, late in the day, rushing into that silent white world. The snow flying up and the trees flashing by. It's a test of nerve, skill and defiance. It's like the moment Hemingway describes at the end of the bullfight. It's a moment of great personal truth."

The conductor announced, "Augsburg." The two elegant women eyed Lisa boldly as she and Barney left the club car. The women were on their second bottle of champagne and were now holding hands. The German businessmen did not bother to look up from their papers as the train pulled into Augsburg. No one noticed a small man, with a trim beard, carrying a dark coat and a homburg hat. He walked to the end of the bar, sat down, and ordered a beer.

CHAPTER

48 ⊠

THE VILLAGE OF BADEN-BADEN SAT IN A SMALL VALLEY SURROUNDED by pine-covered mountains. The town itself seemed to have been hollowed out of a forest. There were parks with streams running through them and bandstands erected for public concerts. Turn-of-the-century streetlamps illuminated the winding streets with their terraced buildings and gabled red-shingled roofs. The taxi rolled past the ornate Greco-Roman casino.

There was little traffic, and the pedestrians strolling the streets were a mix of the very old and the middle-aged.

The Park Hotel was a four-story structure with terraced balconies and large French windows. It was situated in a large park and had its own private driveway. Lisa had suggested the hotel, and Barney had phoned the reservation from Munich.

A doorman escorted them into the lobby. There was a salon off the lobby, and a piano played "Mack the Knife" in slow tempo. There were several middle-aged couples in evening clothes changing money at the desk and asking the concierge for directions to the casino.

The concierge was a gray-haired man with pleasant features that were marred by a faded whitish scar that curved from the edge of his right eye down to the corner of his mouth. He wore a static smile that seemed to be permanently pasted to his face. His smile widened slightly as he greeted them. "We have a large double, Mr. Caine. It faces the pines. Quite nice." Barney thanked him and registered as Mr. and Mrs. Barney Caine.

The room was large, luxurious, and cold. The Alpine chill came through the French windows that opened onto the pine forest. The bell-man closed the windows and adjusted a thermostat. "It will warm up quickly," he said. Barney tipped him, and the man smiled. *"Danke. Guten Abend."*

Barney picked up a brochure from the writing desk and leafed through the colorful photographs. He glanced at Lisa. "Listen to this." He began to read from the brochure. "For two thousand years the natural hot springs of Baden-Baden have been used for healing purposes. The baths were first used by Roman soldiers of the Fifth Legion. The waters cure damaged locomotory systems, rheumatism, metabolic disorders, and. . . ." He looked at her and smiled. "The waters are said to have an aphrodisiac effect and stimulate those who suffer from sexual dysfunction." He tossed the brochure back onto the bed. "Now you know," Barney said, "why the Romans were so sexually turned on. It was the goddamn baths."

He went over to the bed and stretched out. Lisa came over and sat on the edge; she touched his face, tracing the curve of his cheek with her finger. "You don't need any baths."

"Not with you, kiddo."

"But I do." She smiled and rose. "What time do the baths close?"

Barney looked at the brochure. "Nine-thirty."

"Good. That gives me an hour."

"You really going?" Barney asked.

"Why not?"

"Because I'm ready for dinner."

"But we ate on the train."

"That was three hours ago."

"Give me an hour," Lisa said.

"Okay."

She went into the bathroom. Barney dialed the hotel operator and asked her to place a call to Hans Lehmans. He held the phone while the call went through. It was answered by a woman, and an exchange in German followed between Lehmans's wife and the hotel operator. The operator asked Mrs. Lehmans to hold and switched to English. "Mr. Lehmans is not at home. His wife wishes to know if you will speak with her."

"I can't speak German. Ask her to please have her husband phone me."

The operator translated, then cut the Berlin connection. Barney asked her to place a call to Louis Yosuta in Los Angeles. But she said, "I'm sorry, Mr. Caine, there is a two-hour delay on all calls to the States." Barney thanked her and said he'd try later.

Lisa came out of the bathroom wearing a white terry-cloth robe. Bar-

ney put his arms around her and kissed her hair. "Nine sharp, okay?"
She nodded and whispered, "Okay."

Barney undressed and went into the large tiled bathroom. He turned
the tap on the tub to the hot side, went over to the sink, and laid his
cosmetics out on the glass shelf. He glanced up at his reflected image in
the mirror. The circles under his eyes had deepened, and there were
minuscule red lines running from the whites of his eyes into the brown
pupils. But he did not feel the same depression that had afflicted him in
Berlin. He was beginning to feel a sense of accomplishment.

While he still had no idea of who the master puppeteer was, the
shape of the case was crystallizing. The killings of the Neeleys, Kaladi,
Clements, and Obermann were all motivated and strung together by
their involvement in Genesis. And contrary to the theory put forth by
the Italian police, it was Kaladi who was the victim of circumstance.
The hit had been on Clements. And whoever it was that called the shots
was motivated by the need to possess the formula or keep the formula
from falling into alien hands. Where Tedesco fitted in was still mystify-
ing. Barney speculated that Tedesco was an intermediary between the
overworld and the underworld.

Barney knew he would ultimately have to nail Tedesco to reach the
top man. But that was on the horizon. The case was breaking. He
turned from the mirror. The sunken tub was almost full. He turned the
tap off and settled into the steaming water. He leaned back into the
curve of the tub and luxuriated in the liquid heat that folded over his
tired body. The scent of Lisa's perfume still lingered in the room.

He could have made love to her in that small compartment on the
train. Now he was sorry he hadn't. It would have been one of life's
memorable moments: making it on the Mozart Express. Barney smiled.
It sounded like a great song title.

His pleasant thoughts were ruptured by the sharp ringing of the bedroom phone. He sighed and hoisted himself out of the tub, wrapped a
body towel around his waist, and went into the bedroom. He sat down
on the edge of the bed and picked up the receiver.

"Barney?" Lehmans asked.

"Yes. Hello, Hans."

"Are you free to speak?" Lehmans asked.

"I'm alone," Barney answered with a sense of foreboding.

"Your girl is a plant," Lehmans declared. The words struck Barney
with a devastating force, crippling all emotion and shocking him into
stunned silence.

There was a long pause, and Lehmans asked, "You with me?"

Barney cleared his throat, and managed to say, "Yeah. Go on."

"Paul Obermann was captured by the British in May '45. He was taken to England in July '46. He spent six years in England working with British chemists on a formula for synthetic fuel. They went so far as to construct a pilot plant. Another item: Obermann had no sister named Spangler. He was in no way related to Lisa Spangler and could not possibly have raised her." Lehmans paused, expecting Barney to comment, but Barney said nothing. He just felt cold and empty.

He found himself finally asking, "Is that it?"

"No," Lehmans said. "There's more. We searched her Berlin apartment. We found a forged French passport with an entry stamped at the Miami International Airport and dated the week immediately preceding the killing of Tom and Kay Neeley. The French passport also contains entry stamps for Beirut, Damascus, Tripoli, and Port-au-Prince, Haiti."

Barney fell silent, awed by the long arm of the cabal whose machinations had been seeded with cocaine and ended with synthetic fuel.

"You still there?" Lehmans asked.

"Yeah, I'm here," Barney said.

"Your blond German girl friend and the mysterious Los Angeles brunette are one in the same. She's either PLO or connected to some splinter group. But she's a terrorist, recruited by someone who wants to keep the Genesis Formula off the market. The Arabs would obviously have similar interests."

Barney's response was calm and shaded by utter desolation. "I guess that's the ball game."

"Not quite. We found Diestel's private phone number in Lisa Spangler's apartment. Which means she was planted by Diestel."

"What the hell for?" Barney asked.

"To have minute-by-minute knowledge of your progress. Remember Diestel still controls the surviving members of the Genesis team. It's the strong arm of the *Kameradschaft*."

"The what?" Barney asked.

"The Fraternal Order of SS," Lehmans replied.

"Which means Diestel ordered Obermann and Siebold to see me," Barney offered.

"And to direct you to Esau," Lehmans added. "It also proves that Diestel knew you were coming to Berlin and that you had Obermann's name in your possession."

"How do you figure that?"

"Diestel had to have advance information," Lehmans replied, "in order to plant the girl. Diestel put her in with Obermann before you ever arrived. Like it or not, Barney, someone in Los Angeles tipped Diestel before you ever left."

"You're suggesting it was someone in the department?"

"No. I said 'someone.'"

Barney sighed. "What it means is that Diestel wanted me to rediscover the surviving Genesis team of scientists."

"Yes, that becomes quite apparent," Lehmans replied.

"Why?"

"I don't know."

"Who gives Diestel his orders?" Barney asked.

"The answer to that question cracks the case," Lehmans said. "I'm going to pick up Diestel as a material witness in Obermann's death. And I'm going to book Lisa Spangler as an accessory to the murder of Paul Obermann. I want her in custody, along with Siebold and Reimeck. I want them all. I'll question them around the clock. Someone will crack."

"How long can you hold them?"

"I'll book them on our new codes relating to terrorists. I can hold them almost indefinitely."

Barney thought about that for a moment. "I'd rather you didn't do that."

"Why not?"

"Because," Barney explained, "it's a gamble that might never pay off. They're all seasoned. Diestel is SS. A killer. So is the girl. And Siebold and Reimeck fear the Fraternal Order more than the police."

There was a pause, and Lehmans asked, "What do you suggest?"

"Let me play it out with the girl. I want Tedesco. The girl can lead me to him."

"I can't do that," Lehmans said cautiously. "The L.A. killings are your problem. The German homicide is mine."

All of Barney's tensions suddenly fused, and he exploded, "Goddammit, Hans. Don't get technical with me. I've come too fucking far. I want forty-eight hours. If I fall on my ass, the girl is yours. The Fraternal Order is yours. The whole goddamn case is yours."

There was a long pause, and Lehmans's voice was bruised and subdued. "I don't think I deserve that."

Barney sucked a mouthful of air. "You're right." He sighed. "Forgive me. I'm sorry."

There was another pause; then Lehmans spoke. "I'll go along with you to this extent. You have forty-eight hours. Call me after you see Esau."

"Thanks, Hans."

"Be careful. You have no experience with terrorists. You may be fucking her, but she'd kill you in a minute."

Barney hung up and slumped onto the bed, stretching out. He thought about the cool, fragile beauty of the girl. The same girl who had left two strands of black hair on Neeley's pillow.

An ominous pervasive thought crept into his consciousness, keeping him awake. He wondered if the trail he'd been on since that fateful Sunday at Tom Neeley's had been programmed.

The Genesis note. The Obermann note. The charge slip from the Kempinski. The Lufthansa stub. Bits and pieces. Subtle clues, direction finders, pointing the way to Germany. And to the past. Then Berlin, and Obermann suddenly agreeing to the zoo meeting. Then Diestel, smiling, cooperative. And Siebold with his flute music. And Reimeck aiming the flange of the arrow toward Esau, the eighty-three-year-old father of Genesis. The man who had last possessed the final formula. Had this Byzantine trail been carefully prescribed? And if so, by whom? And was Lisa just another arrow along the way?

No. It wasn't possible. He was drifting from logic to paranoia. The idea that someone had designed the sequence of events from Los Angeles to Baden-Baden was inconceivable. It was simply the way the case broke. No different from the bizarre twists and turns of any complex case.

CHAPTER

49 ⊠

THE BAVARIAN NIGHT WAS COOL AND LACED WITH A VERY LIGHT RAIN. They walked through the grounds of the hotel, crossing a wooden bridge over a rushing, bubbling stream. Barney had revealed nothing at dinner. He discussed plans for the coming meeting with Dr. Esau. But Lisa had been strangely quiet.

And ironically, as if she had read his mind, she said, "There's a quotation from Goethe that keeps running through my head."

"What is it?" he asked.

"Even in desperate situations, where everything hangs in the balance, one goes on living as though nothing were wrong."

He circled her waist with his arm. "What made you think of that?"

She shrugged. "I don't know. Perhaps it's this tranquillity. And knowing it can't last."

As they walked, he studied the beauty of her profile and, despite himself, wondered how many she had killed or had a hand in killing. And what did she feel? And how did she deal with the ghosts of those they killed? What kind of armor protected her from the violent images? He knew that under certain circumstances almost anyone could be trained to kill. But he had seen the most bestial killers crack. Only recently a Bulgarian exile who had carried out five assassinations for the KGB had blown his brains out in the Grosvenor House in London.

Lisa was a new experience for Barney. This sensual, vibrant girl at the apex of her life, devoting herself to the ordered executions of strangers, was a distortion he could not fathom. He had no frame of reference for her motives or dedication.

They recrossed the bridge and circled the terrace of the hotel. The tinkling sounds of the piano coming from the salon drifted out into the cool dampness of the night.

She glanced at him and said, "You remember those documents at Zehlendorf?"

"What about them?"

"They were written in the most primitive German, almost childish. Most of them were ego protests over bureaucratic authority. It's horrible to think those men were regarded by my parents' generation as gods."

Barney said, "Given the right circumstances, any people can invent false gods."

She shook her head. "Germany had enough gods. What it needed was conscience."

He stared at her for a moment, thinking of something to say, but her face was suddenly animated by something she noticed on the terrace.

"Look, Barney!"

He glanced up at the terrace, and in the spill of light coming from the salon, he saw neat rows of five-foot-high chess figures. They were lined up in formation: white on one side; black on the other. The tall chess figures standing alone in the night reminded Barney of a surreal scene in a Fellini film.

"Do you play?" she asked.

"Not since college."

"Come. I'll make you checkmate in six moves." She grabbed his hand, and they went up to the terrace.

The tall plastic figures rested on black-and-white squares of marble. Lisa went behind the white, and Barney took the black. And they began to play. Two silhouetted figures in a spill of light, under a thin veil of May rain, with the sound of Jacques Brel's "If You Go Away" drifting in from the salon. They carried the tall plastic chess pieces, placing them down, advancing and retreating. They were only slightly taller than the pawns, knights, and castles they moved. Barney maneuvered his pawns so he could bring his queen into play quickly, vaguely recalling a strategy from his college days called the Spanish Attack.

But she blocked his advance by clever use of her pawns, and after ten moves she had his queen trapped by her pawn and castle. She smiled. "Do you concede?"

"Nope."

"You should. It's quite hopeless."

"We'll see."

She left his queen in a static position and moved her bishop, taking another pawn and placing his castle in jeopardy. Barney was faced with losing the queen or the castle. He retreated with the queen, and she captured his castle. She then forced him to take her knight with his king, placing his king in checkmate from her queen.

"Surrender?" she asked.

"Unconditionally." He smiled.

She laughed, and they placed the plastic figures back in starting formation.

"Come on, I'll buy you a drink," he offered.

She took his arm and her eyes sparkled, her long hair glistened in the rain, and she whispered, "Let's have some champagne in the room."

As they strolled arm in arm, Barney thought she was probably all the things Lehmans said she was. But hell, if you lived long enough and had seen enough, the truth was never objective. In the end, the truth was what you wanted it to be.

They undressed in the dark, and Barney took a bottle of Moët Chandon out of the refrigerator, popped the cork, and poured two glasses. He handed her a glass and got in bed with her. They sat side by side, resting against the headboard.

"Put on some music, please," she said.

Barney leaned over and fiddled with the radio. He tried a few stations and found one that played classical music. "How's that?"

"Lovely." She paused. "I love Mahler."

They listened in silence to the graceful ebb and flow of the composition. The melodic line was warm and emotional, and its subthemes were sensual and stirring. She drank her champagne quickly, and he refilled her glass.

She kissed him lightly and said, "You're a terrible chess player."

"I know. Let's talk about something important."

"Like what?"

He kissed her throat. "Like what the hell is that perfume called?"

"Quelque Chose. It means 'something.'"

"It certainly is." He smiled.

They opened another bottle of Moët, and Barney stroked her hair. He felt like a man in a vise, inexorably drawn to the girl, obsessed with her, yet she stood for everything he despised.

He was beginning to feel heady from the wine and aroused sexually. He felt her warm breath on his cheek, and she asked, "Who else is there, Barney?"

"What do you mean?"

"I mean women."

"No one important."

She placed her glass down and crawled up on top of him and began to kiss him, slowly, lightly. She kissed his forehead, the bump at the ridge of his nose, and the scar on his cheek. Then her mouth found a soft place in his neck, and she nibbled at it, drew on it. The same place over and over again. Her mouth roamed down his body, kissing all the places as she moved. She took him in her mouth, sucking gently and moaning softly as he grew hard.

He waited until he couldn't stand her slow nursing any longer. He turned her over and entered her. And they made love soundlessly, slowly, savoring the moments as they came up to the edge of orgasm together.

They prolonged the ecstasy until neither one could summon the willpower to hold back any longer. She whispered, "Now!" And they moved in a rush, legs locked, bodies arching and thrusting with total abandon. Their fingers digging into each other's flesh. Their mouths pressed together, their tongues entwined as their bodies shuddered.

It was just before dawn when Lisa stirred in her sleep. A slight opacity penetrated the darkness, and she saw an image form. It was the face of Yasir, smiling at her, and she heard the sound of train wheels clicking against tracks. She was in a dining car, seated opposite Yasir. He wore his red-checkered kaffiyeh, and he was smiling at her, and unseen voices were speaking French. Then she found herself in a playground, and there was a flagpole in the playground, and the blue-and-white flag with the Star of David flew from its mast. Children were dancing in a circle and singing a Hebrew song, and Arthur Clements rode around the flagpole on a stunning white horse. There was a scream and a red flash, followed by a shattering explosion. And she was naked, bleeding, on her knees, staring up at the dapper Yussef Kaladi; only he had no face. But it was Kaladi, and dark blood pumped out of his neck, and a naked English girl screamed at Kaladi's gushing neck, "Yussef, Yussef, you bloody little fucker!"

Then she was back on the train, and Yasir was speaking to her softly in Arabic . . . and suddenly the other passengers screamed as Tom Neeley came down the aisle between the tables, his body leaking blood from his groin to his temple, and Neeley fell across their table. And she stared in horror across Neeley's body at Yasir. But it was no longer Yasir. It was the Iraqi. The one they had killed in Soho, and he was drinking champagne. But a small nest of white maggots crawled out of the hole where his eye had been.

Lisa tried to scream. Over and over again, but the scream would not come. She tried desperately to force air into her lungs. Then she managed a low grotesque moan, then a growl, then finally her lungs responded, and she screamed, an unending scream of terror.

Barney came instantly awake. His eyes started at what he saw. Lisa was sitting up, her arms flaying, her face contorted. Her eyes wide in terror. He grabbed her shoulders and shouted, "Lisa! Lisa! I'm here! I'm here!"

But she was encapsulated in the lingering horror of her nightmare. Barney slapped her face, back and forth, and the screams began to subside, and the look of terror in her eyes began to fade.

He put his arms around her shivering, sweat-soaked body and held her tightly, kissing her face and murmuring over and over, "It's all right. It's all right. . . ."

CHAPTER

50 ⊠

THE OPAQUE SUN PAINTED AN INFINITY OF TINY FLASHING MIRRORS INTO the rippling surface of Lake Alster, and in the distance sailboats heeled over, tacking in the early-morning breeze.

On the Atlantic Hotel side of the lake, a young boy and his father were fly casting off the muddy bank. A family of brown ducks with green bills waddled near the shoreline, squawking their annoyance at the public boat that chugged its way toward the Atlantic landing.

Professor Wolf Siebold was enjoying his morning constitutional. He walked briskly along the lakefront path, humming the melodic line of the concerto he and his colleagues were to perform that evening. The professor paused as he noticed the small boy and his father casting their lines. Siebold wondered if the pike and cod had returned to the lake. He remembered how years ago, before the war, the lake had teemed with fish. But that was before the refinery at the estuary had leaked its oily residue into the lake. The professor took comfort in the fact that people were once again fishing in the Alster. He took a deep breath of the tangy morning air and continued his walk.

There were ten passengers in the wide cabin of the public boat. A young couple and three small children in the care of their nannies were seated on the forward bench alongside an elderly couple. The old man was forced to shout at his wife, who was hard of hearing, and the small children amused themselves by imitating the old man.

In the rear seat of the cabin, staring out of the open window, toward the fantail, was a well-dressed, mild-looking man wearing a beige topcoat. The man's face was oddly tense as he surveyed the tranquil shoreline. His slate gray eyes narrowed as he saw the tall, distinguished professor striding briskly along the path, not more then twenty meters away from the moving boat.

Professor Siebold and the public boat were approaching each other from opposite directions. The gray-eyed man in the rear of the boat calculated twenty seconds before their paths would cross. He slipped the blue-steel Ingram Mac-10 9-millimeter Parabellum out of his coat. The automatic was only slightly larger than a .45, even with its three-inch silencer. The difference between the Ingram and the .45 was in load and velocity. The Ingram took a clip of fifteen bullets and fired the entire clip in less than two seconds, without noise or recoil.

The gray-eyed man had the muzzle of the Ingram pointed out the window. He held its stock with both hands, waiting for the professor's figure to enter the center of the notched gunsight. His right forefinger poised at the trigger. He could not slowly increase the trigger pressure, as he would normally do with most handguns. The trigger on the Ingram was sensitive to the slightest touch.

The professor moved into the center of the gunsight. The gunman took a deep breath and pressed the trigger all the way back to the guard. Siebold's arms flew apart, and his body lifted off the ground; then he fell heavily, face down, into the dirt. The fifteen 9-millimeter slugs shredded his chest cavity, blowing bits of bone and gristle out of his back, spraying the bloody residue up onto the benches fronting the dirt path.

The gunman exhaled and opened his right hand. The Ingram dropped into the water and sank instantly below the surface of the lake. The gunman then turned back to the interior of the cabin. The actions of the passengers were normal. They had not heard or seen anything unusual. The gunman rose, walked through the cabin, and went up on deck. He noticed a father and son fishing near the Atlantic landing, and farther up the dirt path, two joggers ran side by side. No one on the shoreline noticed the fallen figure of Professor Wolf Siebold.

The sound of the public boat's engines decreased, and it glided into the Atlantic landing.

The gunman left the boat, crossed the street and entered the lobby of the Atlantic Hotel. He went down a flight of carpeted stairs and walked slowly up to a public phone booth. He dropped the proper amount of pfennigs into the slot and dialed a number in the Wannsee suburb of Berlin.

It was 8:24 A.M. Sunday morning, and Friedrich Diestel reclined on his terrace lounge that overlooked Lake Havel. He permitted himself a small smile when the phone rang. He knew Professor Siebold was dead before he lifted the receiver. He took no special pleasure in Siebold's death. His satisfaction was confined to the precise execution of orders. Order made life possible, and order made death meaningful.

CHAPTER

51 ⊠

THE TAXI HAD BEEN CLIMBING THROUGH THE FOREST FOR THE LAST fifteen minutes. Lisa looked at the tall pines and thought that if the business with Esau went according to plan, Barney would be out of danger. They would have no reason to harm him. But if the old man did something unforeseen, something unprogrammed. . . .

She squeezed Barney's hand, trying to dispel her thoughts. Barney put his arm around her and drew her close. A great shaft of sunlight suddenly broke through the clouds, turning the dark green forest into a brilliant emerald, and the fresh smell of pine permeated the taxi.

The single-lane macadam road came up to a crest, then sloped down for several hundred feet before climbing steeply again. The driver shifted into low gear as the road arched up at almost a ninety-degree grade. They reached the top of the hill and swung off onto a dirt track whose entrance was marked with a sign that read: "Kessenger Haus—Private Road."

Dr. Esau's study was a huge high-ceilinged ornate room. Its decor and furnishings were out of the Belle Epoque. There were large, dark, brooding Flemish canvases on the walls. The domed ceiling was painted with rose-colored dancing cherubs. A magnificent crystal chandelier hung from the ceiling. There was a stale odor in the study that smelled of disuse and old money that had nothing left to purchase.

The huge oak doors were opened by Esau's nurse, Karl Plieger, a stocky man with a jovial face. He wheeled the old man into the study, placing the wheelchair opposite Barney and Lisa.

Barney stared at the apparition facing him. There were tufts of gray hair clinging to the sides of a small skull that appeared so fragile a smile would crack its skin. Dr. Esau's black eyes were bright but had receded into almost hollow sockets. His straight nose was thin and long. His mouth was slack, and through the open robe the shriveled skin at Esau's throat reminded Barney of a turkey's neck.

Plieger adjusted the blanket around Esau's scrawny shoulders, and the old man waved him away. Plieger went to a large gold-leafed antique desk and sat down.

Esau stared at them silently. Barney found it hard to believe that this relic, this skeleton of a man, had once wielded incredible power, that this cancer-ridden ghost had possessed the genius that provided the energy requirements for the Reich.

The slack mouth gathered itself, and his lips moved slowly. "The French are building an atomic reactor in northern Iraq."

Barney was speechless. It was one of those non sequiturs that defied answer.

"Did you know that?" Esau rasped.

Barney shook his head. "No. I didn't."

"The French will do anything for a profit. During the occupation their scientists worked hand and glove with me. The resistance was a myth. All through the war the Parisian nightclubs were open. The racetracks ran; the restaurants were full. The French are a people whose principal character trait is 'accommodation.' And now they sell the Iraqis an atomic reactor." He coughed twice and wiped some spittle from his lips. "The world will end within two centuries; of that there can be no question. But to me it has no relevance. Because I am ending." He paused, and the tips of his bony fingers drummed against the arms of the wheelchair. His bright sunken eyes glanced at Lisa. "I am told you are the stepchild of Paul Obermann."

"Yes," she said. "Paul Obermann raised me."

Barney thought she lied well.

"You are how old?" Esau inquired.

"Thirty-three," she said.

While his body was desiccated, his brain was not. Esau calculated instantly. "You were born in 1945?"

"Yes."

"A fateful year. It marked the decline of the West."

Barney cleared his throat and asked, "You were taken prisoner by the Russians in 1945?"

The small turkey head bobbed. "Yes. They came down Prinz Albrechtstrasse into the Kaiser Wilhelm Institute. Mongolians in white uniforms with machine guns. They kept flushing my toilet. Can you imagine the German nation losing a war to people who had never seen a toilet?"

There was a slight pink tone in his yellow cheeks. And Barney asked, "Where were you taken?"

"First Zossen. Then Kiev. Then Moscow. They wanted the Genesis Formula. The one that contained the Mangan catalyst." A glint of triumph entered the sunken eyes. "I designed a pilot hydrogenation plant at the Academy of Science with their foremost engineers. The process failed. It was a purposeful failure. After five years and millions of rubles, they placed me in Lubyanka Prison."

"You never revealed the final formula?"

"Never. They knew we made oil from coal through hydrogenation. They knew it costly and required slave labor. But they did not know we had perfected the ultimate catalyst."

Esau's lips drew back in a self-satisfied grin, and Barney permitted the old man a moment of victorious reminiscence before he asked, "What happened to the formula?"

"Reimeck probably informed you of the clandestine meeting in the old Adlon Hotel. Did he not?"

"Yes." Barney nodded.

"The convoy containing the formula was captured by the Americans. They in turn sent it to the British in Hamburg."

Barney craved a cigarette but did not dare smoke in the presence of Esau, who seemed to have trouble drawing enough oxygen to speak. "I know about that convoy," Barney said. "What I'm asking you, Doctor, is what happened to the formula after the war."

The doctor glanced at Lisa, then back over his shoulder to Plieger, who sat at the antique desk fondling a gold letter opener.

Esau gathered the blanket tighter around his thin shoulders. "From what I've learned about you"—the old man coughed violently twice, then wheezed—"you are not a stupid man. You're a man who has achieved degrees of learning, a man with years of service in sensitive areas. The answer to your question is obvious, is it not?" He sucked the stale air. "After the oil embargo of '73 all the oil reserves of the seven major American companies increased in value by four hundred percent. OPEC is their creation. They have joined with large banking interests and armament manufacturers to prevent the manufacture of synthetic fuel. Of course, there is a conspiracy." His voice trembled and rose. "They will continue to withhold synthetic fuel until their profit position is assured." He leaned forward in the chair, and drops of spittle fell from his lips onto his robe. "They purchased my freedom from the Soviets. They have furnished me with sufficient funds to live in the grand manner."

Barney glanced at Lisa, but she merely stared transfixed at the apparition of the old man. She was beginning to feel uneasy.

Barney asked, "You keep referring to 'they.' Who are 'they'?"

"The cartel," Esau rasped. "They have maintained my life because I possess the formula." He leaned back. "They permitted me to stay alive because I agreed to withhold its publication. And should I die under abnormal circumstances, that formula would be delivered to certain Swiss industrial interests."

"By whom?" Barney asked.

"By my old and trusted colleague Professor Wolf Siebold." Esau then turned and snapped his fingers at Plieger. "Cognac!"

Plieger got up from the desk, went to a portable table, poured a brandy into a crystal glass, and brought it to Esau. The old man held the glass in trembling hands and gulped it down in one long swallow.

A trace of color came into Esau's cheeks. "You are no doubt wondering why I agreed to see you."

Barney nodded. Lisa waited for the old man's response with a sense of foreboding.

The old man licked his lips. "I agreed to see you for one reason. The ultimate reason for any man to perform any act. The reason is the assurance of my own immortality." He leaned back in the wheelchair, his cheeks flushed by cognac.

Barney shifted in his chair. He wondered whether to press him or wait for the old man to continue.

Esau's black eyes were bright and wide. "It's quite simple, really. I have only a very limited time left. Therefore, I am no longer concerned with my personal safety. Or the safety of anyone else. I do not care about past crimes. Slave labor. I do not care that thousands died to prove my theories. I am a scientist. A very great one. I want my formula for synthetic fuel published and produced." His raspy voice rose. "It wasn't Siebold who perfected the Mangan catalyst. It was I! It was my discovery! And that catalyst not only produced motor fuel from coal at an economic price but also produced methanol. Yes. Methanol, the magic substance that will fuel the energy requirements of future mankind."

"Why do you call methanol magic?" Barney asked.

"Because it can be made from wood, trees, pulp, grain. It only requires that a car have no carburetor, rather a fuel injector. It produces no pollutants. It burns cleanly, producing no carbon buildup on the engine. It requires only the planting and replanting of trees and wheat." He paused. "And along with regular fuel, my formula permits"

—he gasped and wheezed for breath—"permits synthesized petrochemical products completely uncontaminated by sulfur. Of course, immediate production would be made from coal. But then wood and grain will take over. When the natural supply of oil is exhausted, even the cartel will have to turn to my process. But I cannot wait for that day. I have no time!"

He rubbed his chest and said, "The civilized world must be made to know that it owes its existence to the genius of Abraham Esau. And you, Mr. Caine, are in a position to insure that knowledge." He gasped and coughed and snapped his fingers at Plieger and screamed, *"Den Akt!"* The spasmodic coughing continued.

Plieger carried a manila envelope over to the doctor and handed it to him. He then poured another cognac and brought it to the old man, who drank it off in one gulp. The coughing subsided, and Esau looked at Barney.

His voice was barely audible. "This envelope contains the final formula."

The adrenaline ran, and a cube of ice formed in the center of Barney's chest. He was overwhelmed by an insane desire to grab the envelope and run, as if some unseen force would make it vanish before he got possession of it. But he made no move for the envelope.

Lisa stared at the old man as if he were a cobra about to strike. Her worst fears had been realized.

The old man leaned forward, and spittle drooled out his slack lips. "I want your solemn oath that this formula will be placed in the proper hands to insure its public use. And that it is known forever as the 'Esau Catalytic Synthol Process.'" His voice rose, and his hands trembled, and the skull was waxen against the flush of his cheeks. "Promise me!" he shouted, then caught his breath, and his voice subsided. "You have all the proper motives." He shot a look at Lisa. "Both of you. Your stepfather was killed for this. Thousands died to perfect it!" He stared at Barney. "Can you promise to have this formula published?"

Barney could not move or speak. It was as if he were hypnotized by the piercing eyes that burned out of the skeletal head.

"Can you make that promise?" Esau repeated.

Barney nodded, and his voice sounded as if it belonged to someone else. "Yes. I'll see to it. You can sleep on it."

"I will do more than sleep on your word. I will die on it." Esau then leaned forward. "There is a saying that a man finds immortality only if he produces a son, or builds a house, or plants a tree. I have done none of those things. But this envelope assures my immortality because its

contents will prevent the world from drifting into permanent darkness."
He leaned his trembling arm across to Barney, who took the envelope. "I have been waiting for someone like you for twenty-eight years. For a situation like this. For a professional, a man well schooled in police methods. A man outside the influence of the cartel. A man with pure motives."

"How can you be certain of my motives?" Barney asked.

"I know all about the killing of the Neeleys."

Esau went into another fitful spasm of coughing. His head fell back, bobbing on his wrinkled neck; spittle oozed out of his open mouth. Plieger grabbed the old man's wrists and began to massage them vigorously. After a moment Esau's head came forward, and the coughing ceased. He leaned so far forward in his chair that Plieger had to restrain him.

Esau's black eyes blazed at Barney. "You must not fail. It is your sacred task!" The tone of his voice was no longer a plea. It was an order. And in that moment Barney could imagine the imposing strength that had once resided in the ravaged body. He could see Dr. Esau standing with the leaders of the Reich. Hitler and Göring and the top scientist at Farben. He could see a healthy Esau resisting the threats of the KGB and deceiving the Soviets. He was a madman blessed with a scientific skill for which countless thousands had paid with their lives.

"Do not fail me!" he commanded. Then Plieger turned the chair and wheeled Esau out of the ornate room.

They were back on the winding macadam highway when Barney opened the envelope. He removed eight pages of expensive linen stock. The pages contained complex three-dimensional engineering diagrams, surrounded by chemical formations. There was an accompanying text in German. Barney shook his head and wished he had majored in chemistry. The language and diagram in his hand were meaningless to him.

Lisa glanced at the documents. "Can I see them?"

Barney handed them to her. Her forehead furrowed as she examined each page in its turn. She felt empty and helpless. The pages she scanned were in effect Barney's death warrant.

"Does any of it translate?" he asked.

She shook her head. "One would have to be a chemical engineer. But in the diagrams I can define the words 'coal,' 'gas,' 'hydrogen methane,' 'ethylene,' 'propylene,' 'butane,' and 'synthol.'" She went to another page. "Here is something with the catalyst. You see here." Barney leaned over. "It says *Katalysator,* and the words 'manganese,' 'molybdenum,' 'platinum,' and 'iridium,' along with the chemical symbols for each of those metals. But it might as well be in Greek." She handed the pages back to Barney and looked pensively at him as he tucked the pages back into the envelope and asked, "Do you think Esau had another copy?"

Barney nodded. "But I'd go to my own grave believing these are the originals."

"How can you be certain?"

Barney sighed. "Immortality is one hell of a motive."

They were coming down the sloping road, into the green pines.

"But Siebold also has a copy," Lisa remarked.

"Yes. But I would doubt that Siebold would go up against the cartel under any circumstances, not if he wants to keep playing that flute."

"But Esau thought he would," she insisted. "He gave Siebold the formula years ago to guarantee his own safety."

"I think Siebold used that copy to keep himself alive," Barney replied.

"It's ironic to think so many died for eight pages of scientific equations," she said thoughtfully.

Barney did not respond, but he thought about the truth of her words. He thought about those who had perished. The slaves. The inmate workers at I. G. Farben–Auschwitz. And all the others, at the fifteen hydrogenation plants. Those huge factories and refineries that had mysteriously escaped Allied bombing. His thoughts then skipped forty years to Tom Neeley and Kay, and he could clearly see their torn, shattered bodies. And Obermann bleeding to death at the base of the prehistoric stone monster and Kaladi and Clements blown to pieces in a shower of blood, bone, and Confederate money. All of them destroyed, chasing after the eight pages he held in his hand. Barney felt an icy current of sudden truth course through his body as his own position hit him with full clarity.

He was in a taxi, going through a Bavarian forest with a lovely but deadly German girl. A girl he was totally obsessed with. And sitting in his lap was an envelope whose contents made him one of the most powerful men on earth. He had the final Nazi formula, containing the Mangan catalyst. The catalyst which made the production of synthetic fuel instantly feasible!

His heart began to race and pound, and he rubbed the center of his chest with his right hand.

Lisa looked at him. "What's the matter?"

"Nothing."

"Your face is white."

"I'm fine."

But she knew better. Lisa was a student of fear. She knew Barney was frightened. But there was nothing she could do. It was now up to Hoess. The little man in the dark coat. The man who had tailed Barney in Berlin. The little man Barney had seen in the street in Hamburg. The man on the Mozart Express. The man who'd been assigned to cover her moves by Diestel. She would have to report to Hoess.

The post office in Baden-Baden was in a small circular square in the center of town, not far from the casino. The West German flag flew over the low single-story building. The lobby of the post office was wide and well lit. There were mail clerks' windows to one side and writing desks set against the opposite wall. Barney felt a wave of relief as he saw the green Siemens copying machine just to the right of the entrance. Lisa explained the operating instructions to Barney, which were standard and simple. Barney placed each page of the formula face down on the photographic plate, then closed the lid over the page. He set a knob on the face of the machine to "3" for number of copies and pressed a red button. The machine clicked and whirred, and the copy slid out into one tray and the original into another tray. Lisa watched him make three complete copies, knowing that as each copy slid into the tray, Barney was drawing closer to his own violent end.

He collated the copies into three separate sets, and went up to the clerk and asked for a manila envelope. Barney carefully inscribed Louis Yosuta's Los Angeles address on the face of the envelope and used Hans Lehmans's Berlin office as the return. He asked Lisa, "Tell the clerk I want this sent air special, and ask him when he thinks it will arrive in Los Angeles."

She translated the clerk's words for Barney. "It will leave here in one hour and be taken to the small postal airfield at the edge of town. A mail plane will take it to Frankfurt with all the other overseas mail. It will leave Frankfurt for London and then be placed on a direct flight, over the Pole, to Los Angeles. He thinks it will be delivered sometime tomorrow evening."

Barney nodded and paid the clerk, who applied the necessary stamps and the red seal indicating "Special" and dropped it in a huge mail sack. Barney tucked the remaining two copies into his inside jacket pocket.

On the ride back to the hotel he thought how curious it was that there was no one else to send it to. He could not chance the envelope's lying around the lobby of his own apartment building in Los Angeles. He did not trust Nolan. And could not endanger Alice and his son, Timmy, by sending it to his ex-wife's home in Bel-Air. He considered for a moment sending it to Kathy Barnes, care of her airline at the L.A. International Airport, but that was risky, and besides, he had no right to place Kathy in danger. The Israeli drop was to be used only as a last resort; it could only be initiated from America. No. He had done the right thing. He would keep one copy in his possession and give the other copy to Hans Lehmans.

It was still remarkably difficult for him to consider that Lisa was on the other side, playing her own game. A game directed by Diestel. And in his haste and excitement to get the formula off to Louis, she had been at his side and had seen Louis's address. But hell, Barney sighed. Louis was in no danger as long as there were other copies. Besides, Louis was a professional. He could take care of himself. In any case he would phone Louis and alert him.

The gray-haired concierge with the white dueling scar and permanent smile gave Barney two hotel envelopes. Barney sealed them and said, "I want these placed in your vault."

The concierge took the envelopes. "Come with me, please."

Lisa waited at the desk as Barney followed the concierge to an anteroom. The walls were lined with small metal squares that had two key insertions placed in their center. The concierge went to a box at eye level, removed the two keys that protruded from the box, and drew it open. He placed the envelopes in the box and slid the box back into its place. He locked the metal container with both keys and handed one to Barney. "You present your key whenever you wish to remove them."

Barney thanked him and gave him a ten-mark tip.

Once they were in the room, Lisa asked, "Would you like to try the baths?"

"No. I've got some calls to make. You go ahead."

"You're sure?"

"Yes. I've got things to do."

She came to him. "Like what?" she asked softly.

"Oh, important things, like taking a bath and making reservations for tonight."

"What sort of reservations?"

He touched her cheek. "We're going on the town. Dinner. Then the casino. Then maybe a little disco dancing. The brochure says there's a marvelous discothèque called La Flotilla."

"Well then"—she smiled—"I'll have to try to look pretty."

He kissed her softly. "That's the world's greatest cinch."

Barney walked up to her, and placed his hands on her wide shoulders. He stared at her, trying to discern the killer in that beautiful oval face. But all that came back to him was the portrait of fragile beauty.

"You look exhausted," she said. "You're certain you want to go out?"

He nodded. "The taxpayers owe me a night. Besides, I'll take a nap. I'll be fine."

"I suppose my nightmare didn't help last night."

"What nightmare?" He smiled.

She kissed him quickly on the lips, then turned and left.

She walked down the long corridor, puzzling over the fact that Barney still held her above suspicion. She attributed it to the thoroughness of Diestel. They must have removed Obermann's file from the federal records at Wiesbaden. It was that and the fact that she had fooled other men in the past. Tough, intelligent men. Dedicated men.

The only man in recent years she had failed to entice was Frank Tedesco. She remembered the night at Tedesco's Haitian villa, high up in the mountains of Pétionville, above the stench and poverty of Port-au-Prince. They had been served a sumptuous dinner, augmented by a seemingly endless flow of Dom Pérignon. And after dinner a servant brought out a tray of rolled Colombian grass. They smoked and drank, and she had tried all her tricks, but Tedesco had only smiled and remarked about the importance of her mission. And after a while a stunning black girl with great flashing eyes and a dancer's body joined them on the terrace. Tedesco introduced them, then put his arm around the black girl's narrow waist and smiled at Lisa. "If you'd like to gamble, I have an open line of credit at the casino." The black girl said something in Creole, and they both laughed and left her there.

Men like Tedesco were special. They were immunized against temptation and compassion. But Barney was special, too, in a much different way. Barney was a professional in a brutal world, but he had never lost his compassion. He had been genuinely saddened by Obermann's murder. And he was driven by the emotional need to avenge the death of his friends, the Neeleys. He was a man of loyalty and feelings. And she cared for him. Despite herself, she cared about him. She had to. Barney had restored her as a woman. She would try her best to save him. It was for Lisa an act of atonement.

She entered the elevator and pressed the button for the second floor instead of the one marked "B" for baths.

She walked down the second-floor corridor, stopping at Room 219. She knocked softly, twice, and almost instantly a heavy voice answered, *"Ja?"*

She whispered. "Lisa Spangler."

There was a pause; then the small man opened the door. His disguise was gone. He wore no beard and sported no goatee, but had his thick-lensed glasses on. He smiled. *"Bitte. . . ."*

CHAPTER

52 ⊠

BARNEY WAS STRETCHED OUT ON THE BED. HE HAD PLACED A CALL TO Louis Yosuta; it would be four in the morning in L.A. The operator said there would be a slight delay. Barney thought about lunch but had no appetite. He still retained the grotesque vision of Dr. Esau's skeletal head and raspy voice pleading for immortality. He reached into his pocket and took out the small vault key with the number 34: all the events that had begun with that German truck convoy, the convoy of secrets that left Zossen in April 1945 had come down to this tiny grooved key.

The phone rang sharply, and Barney placed the key back in his pocket. He picked up the receiver and was surprised to hear Lehmans's voice. "I'm in the lobby. Can you come right down?"

They were in a taxi traveling on a country road. Barney had filled Lehmans in on everything since they last spoke. Lehmans listened attentively but did not offer much. When Barney concluded, he asked, "You haven't yet confronted the girl?"

"No. Not yet," Barney replied. "Let me play it my way. You gave me forty-eight hours."

Lehmans looked more fatigued than usual and did not offer any protest. Barney asked, "Where are we going?"

"To a small postal airfield."

"Jesus Christ!" Barney exclaimed.

"What is it?" Lehmans asked.

"I forgot to give you the copy of the formula. It's in the hotel vault."

"How many copies?"

"Two. One for you. One for me."

"You have sent the original to Los Angeles?"

"Yes. I told you."

"Well then, no matter. You can give me my copy in Berlin."

"We can go back," Barney offered.

Lehmans shook his head. "I have no time. I flew down here on my way to Zurich. The Swiss federal police have captured those two terrorists who broke out of Moabit Prison. I'm late now, but Baden was on the way. I took a chance that I would find you in the hotel."

"I was going to call you," Barney said.

"Yes. I know." Lehmans stared off in the direction of the towering Alpine ridge that bordered Germany, Switzerland, and France. After a moment he spoke to Barney. "Sometime before nine this morning Professor Wolf Siebold was found shot to death on the dirt path at the foot of Lake Alster."

Barney felt numb. His throat muscles contracted, and he could not respond.

Lehmans continued. "Siebold was hit by fifteen nine-millimeter bullets. The bullets bore groove marks indicating the use of a silencer." Lehmans looked straight ahead and continued. "Siebold's chest cavity exploded. He was literally cut in half. He was hit from the lakeside, probably from a passing boat."

"How do you know that?" Barney asked hoarsely.

"Because we found bits of bone and flesh sticking to the park benches which are set back from the water."

Barney sucked his breath in and let it out. "Any witnesses?"

"None. There was a man and his son fishing not thirty meters from where Siebold's body lay. But they saw nothing."

"Did they hear anything?" Barney asked.

Lehmans shook his head. "Only the sound of the public boat as it approached the Atlantic landing. We questioned the captain of the boat and the conductor. But to them, passengers are faceless, just bodies they move from one point to another. The deckhand only remembered two small children who were making fun of an elderly deaf woman."

Barney sighed. "Fifteen slugs. Christ Almighty. What kind of a machine gun can be silenced?"

"It was a machine pistol. Very unique. Very expensive. We found it sixty feet from shore. The water is only ten feet deep. We dragged the bottom in a thirty-yard radius from where the body lay."

"What make was it?"

"Our ballistics experts identified it as an Ingram Parabellum automatic. It can accommodate clips from fifteen to two hundred bullets. It fires a clip in less than two seconds with no recoil and can easily be fitted for a silencer. My experts further informed me that the weapon is manufactured in your country. South Carolina, I believe."

The BMW taxi reached a cutoff on the highway and swung onto a dirt road marked *"Flugfeld."* They came over a small grassy rise, and Barney could see a tall pole with an attached windsock. There was a barnlike wooden hangar, with a smaller whitewashed building alongside. A red and white twin-engine Cherokee plane was parked at the top of the strip, facing into the wind.

Lehmans told the driver to stop and wait. They got out of the taxi and started walking slowly through the tall weeds that bordered the dirt strip. "The professor's apartment was ransacked," Lehmans said. "A wall safe was blown open. We found a medal. A Knight's Cross awarded to Siebold by Göring. Nothing else. Except the housekeeper who was bound, blindfolded, and gagged in a closet. She could tell us nothing."

They walked in silence for a moment; then Barney said, "I know why Siebold was killed. And I know who killed him."

Lehmans stopped, looked at Barney, and asked, "More theory?"

"No, fact," Barney stated. "I can't prove it, but it's fact."

Lehmans resumed walking, and Barney continued, "Remember, Esau gave a copy of the formula to Siebold. If anything violent happened to Esau, Siebold was to make the formula public."

"Yes. You told me. It was Esau's life insurance policy. How does that tell you who the killer is?"

"It has be Diestel," Barney replied. "You said he controlled the surviving Genesis team. They reported to Diestel. Siebold was killed and the formula taken on Diestel's orders. Diestel is the finger man. He planted the girl with me and had Obermann killed, too."

Lehmans turned his coat collar up. "It's conjecture," he said, "but it's the right conjecture. That's why I wanted to pick them all up. We need corroboration." Lehmans's steely gray eyes fastened on Barney. "I've lost Siebold. My only corroboration is Fräulein Spangler."

Barney shrugged. "Even if one of them cracked, it wouldn't matter."

"Why not?" Lehmans asked quizzically.

"Because Diestel is only the local executioner. We've got to find out who gives Diestel his orders."

Lehmans shook his head. "You have to determine that. All I require is the killer of Obermann and Siebold. I'm not concerned with exposing some international cartel that's in league with OPEC. I have no interest in the intricacies of geopolitical power games. I am faced only with the solution of two German homicides."

They drew close to the plane, and Barney could now see the word "POLIZEI" emblazoned on its side. The pilot opened the cabin door, and Lehmans nodded at the man.

"Did Esau say who it was he feared?" Lehmans asked.

Barney nodded. "The same people who arranged his release from the Russians, and supported him all these years. The cartel."

"What cartel?"

"He implied they were oil interests," Barney said. "The Americans arranged his release from the Soviets in '56."

"Well," Lehmans sighed, "by now this mysterious cartel knows you have the formula. And I don't think they will permit Dr. Esau to die of cancer. He won't have his few weeks or months."

"Why not?" Barney asked. "Why kill him? He's already a dead man."

"It's fairly obvious they are eliminating the Genesis scientists. They'll kill him," Lehmans replied.

The pilot leaned out of the cockpit window and shouted something to Lehmans, who replied, *"Eine Minute!"* The pilot turned over the port engine, and the propeller began to spin with increasing velocity. The tall weeds bordering the dirt strip swayed in the wash.

"I want Diestel," Lehmans said.

"You'd better pick up Reimeck first," Barney cautioned. "He's the last Indian. The only one who can nail Diestel."

"What about Esau?" Lehmans asked.

"Forget it. He's certifiably insane. Nothing he could say would stand up. You've got to get Reimeck."

The starboard motor turned over, and Lehmans had to shout, "And the girl?"

Barney shouted back, "We have an agreement. I still have thirty-six hours. I want Tedesco!"

The pilot throttled the engines down, and Lehmans lowered his voice. "You want me to send a man down here?"

"No. I'm okay."

"They know you have the formula."

"True. But they also know I've sent it off to L.A. Killing me isn't going to help them."

"How do they know it's gone to L.A.?"

"The girl was with me when I mailed it."

"That was smart," Lehmans said sarcastically.

Barney shrugged. "I didn't plan on it, but in a sense it was the perfect thing to do. If they know the formula's gone to L.A., it may keep me alive."

"For a while, perhaps." Lehmans sighed.

The pilot held his thumb up to Lehmans who nodded and motioned he'd be a minute. He turned to Barney. "You realize that every Genesis scientist you've spoken to has been eliminated."

"Yes. And I think I know why. And when I'm certain, I'll know what to do."

Lehmans shook Barney's hand. "I'll be back in Berlin tomorrow afternoon."

"I'll have a message waiting for you," Barney replied.

Lehmans nodded and climbed up into the cabin and closed the door. Barney stood in the backwash as the propellers revved up to full power. The pilot released the hydraulic brakes, checked his fuel mixture, pressure gauge, and RPM synchronization. He placed the flaps down at twenty degrees, opened the throttle, and the Cherokee moved down the strip, gathering speed and throwing a cloud of red dust behind its tail. As it neared the end of the strip, it reluctantly became airborne, and banked left, heading southwest toward Switzerland.

CHAPTER

53 ⊠

MANFRED REIMECK CAME OUT OF HIS FIFTH-FLOOR OFFICE AND WALKED down three flights to the second-floor aeronautic exhibit. It was late in the day, but the museum was still busy with visitors. Reimeck made his way through the crowds to the balcony railing and stared down at the great hall below. The visitors crowded around the 1895 sailing vessel, and at the north end of the hall children swarmed over the gleaming vintage locomotive engines.

Reimeck enjoyed the Sunday visitors. They were always the most enthusiastic. He rubbed his boneless, squashed nose. His wife had been after him for years to have his disfigured nose reconstructed. But he could not bring himself to explain to her why he refused to undergo the cosmetic surgery.

Reimeck had never seen combat and was secretly ashamed of that fact. His smashed nose was at the heart of a self-imposed fantasy, and he wore the disfigurement like a badge of honor. He had been test-driving the new Porsche Tiger tank in May 1943. The tank had been fitted with an advanced version of the 88-millimeter cannon. Reimeck had been standing in the interior of the tank to the rear of the driver and the gunner. The order to fire was given, and the gunner squeezed the six-inch trigger mechanism. There was a sharp crack and recoil. The shell casing flew out of the breech and slammed into the center of Reimeck's face, turning his nose into a shapeless red pulp. The medical team at the Stuttgart test facility did what they could for him. Six months later he was awarded an Iron Cross, Second Class. And while Reimeck's injury did not measure up to the hideous wounds of his comrades, it did give him a certain stature at the annual reunions of the Waffen SS.

Reimeck glanced up at the guide wires fixed to the old combat aircraft that swayed above his head. They were a mix of World War I

Fokkers and biplanes and World War II Messerschmitts, Stukas, and Junkers 111s. But his favorite aircraft, the one that had taken on legendary proportions in his mind, was the ME-262 twin-engine jet fighter. The first pure jet aircraft in the history of aviation. He studied its graceful lines lovingly, but with a certain sadness.

Because of the design genius of Messerschmitt, the jet fighter had been ready for mass production as early as April 1941. There was nothing in the air its equal, and had it been manufactured in quantity, it would have altered the entire course of the war. The skies over the Reich would have been free of enemy bombers. Herr Messerschmitt had pleaded its case with Speer, stating he could have one thousand ME-262 jets in the air by late '42. Speer had taken the issue up with Hitler. But that psychotic paperhanger had refused all of Speer's pleas. And now, almost forty years later, it swayed above Reimeck's head: a curiosity, a museum piece. A forlorn relic that had propelled the world into the jet age. Reimeck stood silently admiring the jet. He was in no position to see his killers.

A powerful hand grabbed him under each armpit, lifting his body above the railing and propelling him out over the ledge. For a split second Reimeck thought he might float slowly down. But gravity grabbed him, pulling him down, his arms spread-eagled, his legs kicking the empty air. He heard someone scream seconds before he crashed into the wooden deck of the great sailing ship.

In the ensuing panic, the two former Waffen SS men strolled calmly through the panicked crowd. They walked down the stairs to the ground-floor lobby and out into the cobblestone courtyard.

CHAPTER

54 ☒

THE TURN-OF-THE-CENTURY LAMPS WERE ON, AND THE SIDEWALK CAFÉS displayed multicolored lights above their awnings. Barney and Lisa sat at a choice window table at the Stahlbad Restaurant.

Barney's call to Louis had gone through fifteen minutes after he returned from the small postal airfield. He advised Louis of the imminent arrival of the envelope containing the original copy of the formula. Louis asked no questions. He assured Barney he would place the envelope in the safe at Tactical Headquarters the moment it arrived. He informed Barney that Nolan had been trying to locate him, that he wanted him home. Barney replied that he planned to return in forty-eight hours. That he had one final task to perform. He had to nail Frank Tedesco.

Lisa interrupted his thoughts and asked, "Is there more champagne?" Barney lifted the bottle of Laurent-Perrier 1956 out of the silver ice bucket and refilled her glass. She sipped the champagne and said, "The concierge was right. The fish was delicious."

"Couldn't be better," Barney agreed.

She took out one of her German cigarettes, and he lit it for her. Her hair shimmered in the candlelight, and the lighting made her oval face seem smaller and dramatized her high cheekbones. Her light blue eyes were darker and more intense. She wore a black St. Laurent dress, a string of snowy pearls circled her throat, and two small diamonds sparkled at her earlobes.

The waiter inquired about dessert; they ordered chocolate mousse and espresso. Lisa smiled. "Do all American detectives travel in this style?"

Barney shook his head. "Only those who have charge cards." He did not tell her about Siebold's killing or Lehmans's unexpected visit. He drank the champagne but felt no glow. The impending confrontation with her was only hours away. They finished their desserts and strolled through the narrow, gaily lit streets, heading toward the soft neon of the casino.

The casino had once been the summer palace of German royalty. It reeked of old money, and its decor and architecture were pure Renaissance. The roulette wheels were spinning, and all eyes were fastened on the small white ball as it bounced from number to number.

They watched the action at the roulette tables for a while, then drifted into another room, which was taken up exclusively by a table of chemin de fer.

An immaculately dressed Arab held the bank. There was a bucket of champagne at his side and a long cigarette holder in his lips. There was a sign suspended over the table that read: "Pas de limite." The plaques were three inches long and two inches wide. Each plaque was worth ten thousand marks, or five thousand dollars. Barney guessed there was almost two hundred thousand dollars' worth of plaques in the game. The cards spun out of the shoe, and in three draws the Arab broke the other players, and the stickman pushed a pile of gold plaques across the table to the Arab.

An exotic-looking Eurasian girl sat beside the Arab. She stacked the plaques into neat piles. The Arab sipped the champagne and whispered briefly to the Eurasian girl. She picked up a few smaller plaques and tossed them to the stickman, who smiled, *"Merci."*

The Arab glanced up at Lisa, motioning her to join the game. But she shook her head, and Barney and Lisa went back to the roulette tables.

They played the wheel for an hour. Barney staying with red and even, increasing and decreasing his bets trying to play the percentages. Lisa played number 32, placing a ten-mark chip on every spin. At the end of the hour, number 32 had come up twice, and discounting her investments, she had won almost three hundred marks.

They cashed their chips and went out of the sixteenth-century casino, down a long flight of carpeted stairs, to the lobby, where they entered a door marked in red neon, "La Flotilla."

The crash of Rod Stewart's "Maggie May" greeted them, along with the mixed aromas of perfume, sweat, and the sweet smell of grass. The room was small with shiny black patent leather walls and a black patent leather ceiling. Fantastic images, coming from an unseen projector, played off the gleaming walls and ceiling.

For the first time, Barney and Lisa saw young people in Baden-

Baden. They were the youth of the resort's industry: waiters, waitresses, clerks, bellhops, and muscular masseurs who toiled in the baths. And sprinkled amongst the gyrating youth were a few older, elegantly dressed couples who seemed out of place in the midst of the jeaned youths.

They were seated at a table at the rear of the room. They ordered scotch and Perrier water and stared off at the dancers. "Maggie May" ended, and the Bee Gees came on with "Staying Alive." And Barney was struck again with the curious American tug, that same loneliness he had experienced that first night in Berlin. He glanced at Lisa. The projected phantoms and bizarre kaleidoscope images slid across her face.

They drank their scotch in a hurry, and Barney said, "Come on. Let's do it."

They worked their way through the outer ring of dancers and moved to the center of the dance floor. Lisa's body barely moved; all her action came from the rhythmic swaying of her hips. Barney knew one basic step and stayed with it. They were packed so close together that whatever they did went unnoticed. Barney was beginning to feel the champagne and the scotch, and the driving dynamics of the soft disco rock took him along. The sweet aroma of Lisa's perfume came at him in a rush.

A tall blond girl dancing with a young boy sidled up alongside Lisa. Barney could see that the girl's eyes were abnormally bright and her pupils were dilated. She was on speed or coke or a blend of both. The Bee Gees ended, and the lights suddenly dimmed, everything went blue, and Parisian street scenes appeared on the black walls. Aznavour sang "Que C'est Triste Venise," and the dancers melted into one another. Barney's arms went around Lisa. They moved in place, feeling each other's body warmth, and as the number concluded, Lisa whispered, "There ought to be a law against Aznavour."

A wildly percussive acid-rock tune came on, and they changed tempos. A phantasmagoria of images flashed over the walls and slid across the ceiling.

The images came and went with machine-gun rapidity: *Dracula, Superman, Chaplin, Hitler, Zorro, Delon, Belmondo, Hemingway, El Cordobes, Franco. James Dean and Stalin. The Beatles. Soviet troops fighting through the rubble of Berlin. Mick Jagger, the atomic mushroom at Alamagordo, Tuesday Weld and an endless cemetery of crosses. The Pope, Marilyn Monroe, Muhammad Ali, Garbo, Himmler, Louis Armstrong. An American patrol in a jungle.* The barrages of images increased in tempo flashing in an unrelated bizarre rush. *Kennedy smiled in the open car in the Dallas sunshine. Presley did bumps and grinds. Jack Ruby pointed a gun, and Oswald winced in pain. Christ walked on water. Nixon had his raised fingers giving the V. Skeletal heads smiled up at young British soldiers. Eichmann, Peggy Lee, Calley. Linda Lovelace, Ho Chi Minh, and Orphan Annie.* The flashing images carried an end-of-the-world dimension, making the pulsing room an insane sanctuary, an isolated mad refuge from all exterior reality.

The number concluded, and as they started back to their table, the tall blond girl touched Lisa's arm and stared at her out of feverish eyes and spoke quickly in hushed tones. Lisa smiled at the tall girl but shook her head.

They walked through the grounds of the hotel. The trees were wet, and the smell of fresh pine was exhilarating after the closeness of the discothèque.

"What did that girl want?" Barney asked.

Lisa sighed. "She wanted to make love to me, while you and her boyfriend watched."

"Nice," Barney said.

They strolled across the wooden bridge and heard the rushing sound of the stream below. They were nearing the entrance of the hotel when she said, "The smell of pines reminds me of all the sweet things in my life that never happened."

They undressed slowly, almost methodically. The darkness of the bedroom relieved by a streaky spill of moonlight coming through the open terrace windows.

Barney sat on the edge of the bed, sipping some cognac as he watched her step out of her panties. She stood erect, her wide shoulders back, her curving breasts thrust out. She stared at him for a moment, then walked over to the bed, took the glass out of his hand, and pressed him back down onto the bed.

She knelt over him, planting soft kisses over his face, neck, and down his chest. He felt the moist warmth of her mouth everywhere. And they made love soundlessly. Concentrating. Moving slowly. Her hands squeezing both sides of his waist. He felt the first delicious pangs of orgasm, and she whispered, "Not yet . . . please. . . ."

They neither spoke nor moved for a long time. She asked him for a cigarette, and he went over to the bureau, lit one, and handed it to her.

She raised herself up in bed and leaned against the headboard. He sat down on the other side of the bed, watching her features as they alternately lit up and went dark, by the red glow of her cigarette. She finished the cigarette, looked at him for a brief moment, then got up and went into the bathroom.

Barney listened to the shower running and knew he was out of time.

The bathroom door opened. She came out wearing a white terry-cloth robe and stood just outside the bathroom, her figure backlit by the stream of light coming out of the open bathroom door. She reached into her handbag and removed a small vial of perfume and sprayed her neck and shoulders. Her actions were exactly like those of Laura Gregson after she had balled him that night in his apartment. The night that now seemed an eternity ago.

Barney heard himself speak, but it was as if the words belonged to someone else. "Why don't you reach back into that bag and take out that twenty-two automatic and pump seven shots into me? The same way you did to Tom Neeley."

There was a long moment of silence, and she whispered, "I don't understand."

Barney sat up and leaned back against the headboard. "Sure you do. You're no more related to Paul Obermann than I am."

He waited for a response, but there was none. She just stared at him, unmoving, betraying nothing.

Barney went on, "Paul Obermann was taken to England in late '45. He was there for six years. There was no way in the world he could have raised you."

She walked slowly over to the bureau and lit a cigarette, then turned to him. "It's true. But he sent checks for my care every month."

Barney smiled sarcastically. "You're good. Christ, you're terrific. But your friends left you out in the cold. They should have removed Paul Obermann's file from the federal police records. I'm sure the Fraternal Order has a few fingers in that pie. But they dumped you. Obermann had no sister. He was not related to your mother. You never met him until a couple of weeks before I came to Berlin."

Barney got up and slipped his robe on. He looked out the terrace windows for a moment, then turned back to her. "You must have died trying to keep from laughing. All that sweet melancholy, that poetic ceremony on the lake, spreading Obermann's ashes, and that silent walk through the woods. And that coy stuff at the table, letting me sell you on going to Zehlendorf with me. And helping me. When you were just following orders." Barney shook his head. "I bet you never had an easier mark. Neeley must have been a tougher case than I was."

She showed no emotion. She just met his eyes with her own. Barney suddenly slapped her face hard with his open palm, back and forth, and shouted, "Well, talk! Goddammit! I'm listening!"

She rubbed the side of her cheek, and tears began to well up in her eyes. "You've been lied to by Lehmans," she said. "None of it is true."

"Oh, really!" Barney exclaimed. "Well, what about that phony French passport they found in your Berlin apartment?"

For the first time there was genuine fear in her eyes. "What passport?" she murmured.

"The forged French passport that has an entry date in Miami the week before Neeley was killed. You left Tedesco in Haiti, came in to Miami, had the voodoo doll filled with coke in Miami. Then flew to Los Angeles and delivered it to Neeley."

"You can think what you like," she said.

"You're goddamn right I can. That phony passport also has entry dates for Tripoli, Damascus, and Beirut. You worked with those two terrorists in L.A. One of whom I nailed on the beach at Kay Neeley's. The name of the man I killed was Primo Santiago. Does that ring any bells?"

Tears coursed down her cheeks, and she shook her head. "I don't know anything."

"But I do," Barney snapped. "You're a terrorist lady, aren't you?"

"What does it matter?" She sighed, brushing the tears away.

"It matters because two friends of mine were killed."

For the first time there was a trace of protest in her voice. "Your friends were themselves criminals."

"Kay Neeley was no criminal," Barney replied angrily. "And Tom was old. Frightened. He didn't rate what he got. He somehow tripped onto Genesis after thirty-three years. Neeley's fatal mistake was telling Clements, who took the information to some higher authority. Clements was put in touch with Tedesco. It was Tedesco who hired you. They needed someone who could gain Neeley's confidence. They set Neeley up in the cocaine business with you as the courier. You and your comrades made Neeley's death look like a cocaine hit. But you came up empty. Because Neeley didn't talk. He couldn't talk. He had no idea where the formula was. Only a thin lead back to Obermann from the good old days in Hamburg."

Barney lit one of her German cigarettes, then went to the foot of the bed, sat down, and faced her.

"Are you finished?" she asked angrily.

"Almost. I'm guessing now. But I think you went to Clements to get permission for your two PLO comrades to interview Kay Neeley. Only by then I had begun to put a few pieces together. Too late to save Kay." Barney paused. "Someone in L.A. passed the word that I was on my way to Berlin with Obermann's name in my pocket. You care to take it from there?"

Lisa rose and walked to the window. She stared out at the moonlit grounds. "I want you to understand something about me." She turned to him. "Do you think you can?" she asked softly.

Barney sighed. "Later. I'll try my best. But right now I'd appreciate it if you would fill in the missing spaces."

"All right," she answered. "It's true we knew you were coming. Diestel introduced me to Obermann before you arrived. My photograph was placed in his apartment. Diestel instructed Obermann to follow his orders. Diestel sent me to see you at the Kempinski with Obermann's knowledge. He ordered Obermann to meet you at the zoo." She paused. "I had no idea that Paul was to be killed."

"Neither did I," Barney said caustically. "You fooled me. Your performance at the lake was first-class. Just like in Hamburg."

She glared at him. "Whatever we did in bed had nothing to do with the rest of it. You can choose not to believe that if you wish." Her voice sagged. "It doesn't matter."

Barney rose and paced. "It doesn't matter," he mimicked her. "It doesn't matter." He faced her and shouted, "What the hell does matter?"

"The formula matters," she said coldly. "It must not be used."

"No matter who gets killed?" Barney replied.

She chewed on her lower lip for a second, then sighed. "Try and listen to me now." She took a deep breath and let it out. "My father's name was Fritz Suhrens. He was the commander of the Ravensbrück concentration camp. Three hundred thousand women were gassed and burned at that place. I was born there in my father's villa, at that killing center. Toward the end my mother hid me in a room full of teeth. Jars of gold teeth." She leaned against the bureau. "My mother escaped with me two days before the Soviet troops came. My father was hanged, but we survived. My mother was quite beautiful. We were taken care of by the Fraternal Order. When I grew up, I found out what my father had been. I read every document I could find. I loathed him. And despised everything my parents' generation stood for. And later I hated the new Germany for building their power structure without regard for the past. The new Germany is run by the same monsters. I despised the West for permitting the rise of the so-called new Germany, and I despised the Soviets for the murder of freedom in East Germany and Czechoslovakia and Hungary. And the Americans for Vietnam. I felt I had to do something. Something that would save humanity. I had to take a stand. I had to atone for what my father was. I met the people in Baader-Meinhof. And I found a way to act. And a goal to achieve."

"What goal?" Barney asked gently.

"The universal brotherhood of mankind." She walked over to him, and her lips trembled. "I was sent to Damascus. I was trained by Habash. I spent months of indoctrination. Of confinement. Living in mud hovels in human excrement. They made me submit to every sexual indignity. With men. With women. With animals. And I didn't care, because for me it was a purge. A payment to those women who died at Ravensbrück. I became in my mind one of those inmate women. They made me watch hours of film, of violence, of torn and maimed flesh. They taught me to use firearms and schooled me in terror tactics. After eight months I was sworn into the cause, in a torchlight ceremony at Sidon, in Lebanon."

She crushed her cigarette and said, "My mind was free of all past conceptions, of all conscience. I was transformed. And for the first time in my life, I had something to believe in. I knew that terror and violence were the only means."

"The means to what?" he asked.

She stared into his eyes. "Chaos."

"Then what?" he asked.

"With chaos comes a void. That void will be filled by our movement." She paused. "We are funded by the Saudis. The synthetic fuel formula is a dire threat to them. And to other interests that I have no feeling for but are nevertheless allied. So I accepted the assignment."

"Why were Tom and Kay Neeley tortured?"

"We had to know whether Neeley had met with the Swiss."

"What Swiss?"

"The industrialist," she said. "The same man who contacted Obermann. The Swiss worried them."

"Who's them?" Barney asked.

She shrugged. "I don't know. We only followed orders."

"Whose orders?"

"Tedesco's," she answered.

"Shit." Barney sighed.

"Is thicker than blood," she said automatically.

"What?" he asked.

"Carlos said that. It's his favorite quotation. 'Shit is thicker than blood.' Make shit out of them."

"That's a terrific philosophy for the 'brotherhood of man,' " Barney said, then angrily asked, "You agree with that?"

Lisa did not respond. She merely stared at him. Vacantly. Without emotion.

Barney walked over to Lisa and grabbed her arms pulling her to her feet. "Tell me, what it was like to fuck Neeley, then watch him die?"

She broke free of his arms and slapped him viciously across the face. She started another swing, but he grabbed her wrists, and she shook her head and sobbed. "I hate everything you stand for. But I don't hate you. You believe in what you do." She paused, trying to regain control. "You see, we're both professionals."

He released her hands. "And since we're professionals," Barney said, "let's do some business."

"Would you give me a brandy, please?" she asked.

He looked at her, and despite everything, he could have taken her in his arms and made love to her all over again. He turned away and got her the brandy.

She drank half of it in one swallow, then looked at him and asked, "What kind of business do you wish to do?"

"That depends."

"On what?"

"An answer to one simple question: Who gives Diestel his orders?"

She stared at him, her eyes flashing, calculating for a long time. Then she said, "Tedesco."

The name hung in the air like a magical code that would open the mysteries of time.

"Okay," Barney said. "I want Tedesco. And you can give him to me."

"Why should I?" she asked defiantly.

"Because you have no choice. Lehmans is going to pick you up as an accessory to the murders of Obermann and Siebold."

Her eyes widened in surprise.

"Oh, I forgot to tell you," Barney said. "They blew the good professor to pieces this morning. He never got to play that flute. Now, you take me to Tedesco, and I'll buy you some time with Lehmans."

She walked past Barney, up to the window. She tipped the miniature brandy bottle up to her lips and drained it. "I do have doubts. Terrible doubts. I stopped caring months ago whether I lived or died. I can't hurt anyone. Not anymore." She turned from the window. "But I still believe there has to be a new way. The old way is the road to oblivion for all of us." She paused. "I'm sorry I had to deceive you. I'm sorry you found out about me. I'm sorry it ended like this."

She turned and went out onto the small terrace. Barney followed her. They stood side by side on the small balcony, feeling the cool Bavarian night wind and listening to the moan of the pines. Their faces were molded in chiaroscuro tones cast by the moonlight. She shivered slightly. Her lips trembled, and she whispered, "Tedesco is in Berlin."

CHAPTER

55 ⊠

THE KURFÜRSTENDAMM THROBBED WITH ITS NOCTURNAL ACTION. THE pimps, peddlers, and pushers worked the sidewalk cafés, and the orange and blue neon of the Berlin sex clubs flashed: Mireille's, Ilona's, The Adam and Eve, the Triangle.

Barney and Lisa stared silently at the passing glitter, each lost in thought; unaware of the gray Mercedes that had been following them since Tegel Airport.

The Mercedes parked diagonally across and fifty feet north of the hotel entrance. Lehmans sat in the rear seat of the Mercedes, puffing nervously on a cigarette. A heavyset man sat in the front seat, alongside the driver. The three men watched as Barney and Lisa got out of the taxi and entered the lobby of the hotel.

Barney gave the concierge the envelopes containing the copies of the formula. Once again he was given a small numbered key and told to present the key when he wished to remove the envelopes.

They were given a room at the far end of the third-floor corridor. Barney ordered steak sandwiches and two bottles of Moselle. They had been like prisoners in their own care on the train from Baden-Baden to the Munich airport. A wall of introspective silence had risen between them. She needed his help with Lehmans, and he needed her help with Tedesco.

Barney had phoned Lehmans from the Munich airport and left a message that he would be at the Kempinski by nine.

Lisa picked at her food but drank three glasses of wine. Her cheeks were flushed as she rose from the table and went into the bathroom. Barney shoved his plate away and glanced at his watch. It was 8:50 P.M. He felt bone-tired and mentally drained. This day of travel by train and plane had been excruciating. The confrontation with Lisa had left him desolate and helpless. He hated what she stood for but in a curious way felt closer to her than he ever had. He wanted to protect her. Lisa was a casualty. A victim of her own desperate need to atone for her father's crimes and the crimes of an entire German generation. She had been irreparably damaged by the sins of the world she inherited. She was an easy mark for the fanatics, the mind fuckers.

Barney had seen similar victims. In Spain. The kids who had gone up against Franco's Guardia Civil. And he had seen them in his own country, in the late sixties. Those college kids victimized by the rhetoric of celebrity-seeking rabble-rousers. The kids went to hospitals, while their speech-making leaders showed up on Walter Cronkite and sold articles to national magazines.

The celebrity "revolutionaries" took credit for halting the Vietnam War but ducked the responsibility for Kent State. Barney despised the assholes that directed the National Guard and the imbeciles who had placed live ammunition in their M-1 rifles. But the rhetoric of the mind fuckers had made Kent State an inevitability. There are certain events once set in motion that cannot be stopped.

And now no one would be able to save this German girl. She was in too deep to get out; and she had told the truth when she said she didn't care anymore. But Barney cared. Maybe, just maybe, there was a way through Tedesco to keep her alive. Frank Tedesco, the Brooklyn street hustler, the amorphous link between Genesis and the thing that Dr. Esau had called the cartel.

Lisa came out of the bathroom and went over to the bed and sat down on the edge and reached for the phone.

"What are you doing?" Barney asked.

"You want Tedesco, don't you?" she replied, and lifted the receiver. "I'll have to speak in German."

Barney nodded and watched her dial.

Her face tensed as she spoke into the phone. "Fräulein Spangler." She waited a few seconds and continued. *"Ja, natürlich das ist möglich."* She paused. *"Ich werde die Hotel Halle um halb zehn verlassen."* There was another pause, and she stole a quick glance at Barney, then spoke into the phone. *"Ich verstehe. Ich werde ein Paar schritte von ihm entsernt gehen. Ja, auf wiedersehen."* She placed the receiver back onto its cradle and looked at Barney. "We must leave the lobby at exactly nine-thirty."

"Then what?"

"There will be a car waiting at the entrance. The car will take us to Tedesco."

Barney didn't like the idea of getting into a strange car with a girl who was probably doomed and relying solely on possession of the formula for his own safety. The cartel was not above killing a cop, especially a cop who was operating in alien country without authority. But he had come too far to back away now. Frank Tedesco was the end of the line. It could still be a setup, he thought. Tedesco might be sitting on his terrace in Pétionville. Yet she had followed Barney's instructions.

"Is Tedesco going to be in the car?" he asked.

"I don't know." She shrugged. "I would suppose he would send a driver."

"You understand if anything happens to me," he said, "the formula is still secure. If I'm hit, they're out of business."

"Yes. They know that."

She rose and walked over to the serving table, sat down, poured another glass of wine, and parted her straight pale hair, brushing it away from the sides of her face. "Not that it matters anymore"—she sighed—"but I want you to know that I had no idea Neeley was going to be killed. I delivered the voodoo doll." Lisa sipped the wine and avoided Barney's eyes. "I made love to him, showered, and opened the front door. Neeley was still in bed. The men came in, and I left. When Neeley failed to give them any information, I asked Clements's permission for them to see Kay Neeley."

"But you knew that once they saw Kay, they'd have to kill her."

Lisa shook her head. "They didn't have to kill her."

"Well, that's swell," Barney replied. "Then you have nothing on your conscience."

She stared at him for an instant, then went over to the window. She watched the blue neon Mercedes sign revolve slowly in the Berlin night. "I don't take matters of life and death lightly." She turned, and their eyes met. "I don't take love lightly either," she whispered.

Barney rose wearily and walked over to her. "For Christsake." He sighed. "Why carry on the charade?"

"I don't care what you believe," she said quietly. "It's what I believe. It's what I feel. Before I met you, I was emotionally dead. I came back to life with you. I need you. Whether that's love, I have no idea. But you know damn well what I mean."

She was an accomplished liar and expert at role playing. But there was no deceit in her sad blue eyes. And there was no reason for her to lie about that. Not anymore. Barney cupped her face in his hands.

"What the hell is going to happen to you?"

She shrugged. "Does it really matter to you?"

And by that bizarre human logic, that special emotional man-woman logic that defies the most sophisticated computers, Barney owed her the words. "Yes. It matters. Because I'm in love with you."

He put his arms around her, folding her into him. And they clung together in a final hopeless embrace, caught in an intricate, deadly web that spun out of a clandestine meeting in the old Adlon Hotel, whose remnants were still standing not two kilometers away.

CHAPTER

56 ⊠

THE DIGITAL CLOCK OVER THE DESK READ 9:28 P.M. AS THEY WALKED through the lobby. Lisa wore a beige trench coat over her jeans and walked slightly ahead of Barney.

Across the street, in the back seat of the big Mercedes, Lehmans saw her come out. He spoke to his driver, who turned the engine over. Barney was going through the revolving door when he saw a man spring out of a dark sedan parked directly in front of the entrance. The man grabbed Lisa and shoved her violently into the open rear of the sedan. Barney bolted toward the sedan just as the door slammed. The car's motion wrenched his hand from the door. There was a screeching sound of tires being propelled across the asphalt, and a cloud of acrid smoke covered Barney as the sedan roared off.

Across the street Lehmans screamed at his driver, and the Mercedes roared up to the entrance. The rear door swung open, and Lehmans shouted, "Get in!"

Barney jumped inside, slamming the door. The driver gunned the engine, chasing the Mercedes after the disappearing tail lights of the black sedan. They careened down Fasanenstrasse. Lehmans shouted something in German at his driver. The high whoop of the siren came on, along with a rotating blue light on the roof of the Mercedes. They reached the end of Fasanenstrasse, turned right, and raced along a cobblestoned street in a run-down section not far from the Berlin Wall. They swerved around a Volkswagen and narrowly missed an oncoming bus. They shot under the elevated S-Bahn and jumped the curb. Barney and Lehmans were thrown against each other as they spun around and turned into Budapesterstrasse.

The tail lights of the sedan appeared up ahead. Lehmans's driver pressed the accelerator to the floor and Barney saw the needle of the speedometer move into the extreme end of the red zone. The tail lights of the sedan moved toward the south entrance of the Tiergarten Park. Barney could see the illuminated watchtowers of the East Berlin guards in the distance. They careened in and around civilian traffic that desperately tried to get out of their way. Lehmans shouted, "Radio!" at the big man in the front seat. The man picked up a hand mike and began broadcasting a stream of instructions in German.

They shot through the arch at the park entrance to the "Hall of Heroes" and went up onto the lawn, cutting diagonally across toward the parallel roadway, trying to cut off the sedan. They bumped hard as they leaped from the lawn back onto the roadway. The sedan was only a hundred feet ahead. They heard an ominous ping as a bullet ripped through the Mercedes's right fender. Lehmans and the big man in front ducked reflexively, as the whine of another bullet whizzed past the right side.

They raced along the park drive, passing the crumbling ruins of the old Spanish Embassy, past the lake where Obermann's ashes resided. The sedan suddenly swerved off the road and swung into the lakeside restaurant, smashing tables, and roared out of the north gate. The maneuver placed the sedan far ahead of the following Mercedes.

The big man in front placed the radio mike back on its hook, took out a P-38 Luger, and lowered his window.

"For Christ's sake," Barney shouted. "Don't kill the girl!"

A half a mile ahead they saw the sedan enter the Stresse des 17 Juni. The Mercedes driver crossed over to a street called Invaliden that bisected the 17 Juni. The maneuver picked up a quarter of a mile on the sedan.

They were now hurtling down a street that bordered the wall. The wailing siren of the Mercedes alerted the East German guards, and powerful, blinding spotlights began to stab at the western side of the wall. There was another ping sound, and the upper right portion of the windshield turned into lacework. The big man fired his Luger twice at the tail lights of the sedan.

They suddenly rose up in the air, and their heads slammed against the roof of the car as they hit a speed bump in the road. Lehmans cursed in German. His driver apologized and swung the wheel hard to the left. They were roaring straight toward the lights of Checkpoint Charlie.

They saw the sedan screech to a halt at the checkpoint. The rear door flew open, and Lisa was shoved out. She ran up toward the checkpoint. The sedan shot away, heading back toward the Invaliden. Lehmans tapped the driver and said, *"Halten Sie!"* The driver slowed down as they approached the checkpoint. A voice crackled on the radio, and the big man picked up the mike and answered. The driver killed the siren and the flashing blue light. The Mercedes stopped at the foot of Friedrichstrasse. Lehmans and Barney got out of the car and walked along the worn cobblestones toward the sentry booths.

They were bathed in hot white lights coming from the semicircle of East German watchtowers, which were set back two hundred feet from the American sentry booths. The distance between the watchtowers and the sentry booths was studded by giant cement teeth, barbed wire, and oval cement slabs.

And looming up behind the watchtowers, on the east side of the wall like a ghostly presence of the Nazi past, was the magnificent arch of the Brandenburg Gate.

There was a gleaming limousine parked a few feet past the sentry box. Lisa was standing just outside its open right door. A uniformed chauffeur and a black American staff sergeant stood on either side of her. A tall, rangy captain walked toward Barney and Lehmans.

The checkpoint was as light as day. Barney could see the dark uniformed figures of the East German gunners moving in their watchtowers, the deadly snouts of their 50-caliber machine guns pointed in their direction. Their breaths vaporized in the cold night air as they approached the captain.

The captain saluted and asked Lehmans for his ID card. He looked at the card, handed it back, and asked Barney, "Who are you?" Barney showed him his identification, and the captain examined it carefully, paying special attention to the gold badge.

Lehmans said, "We want that girl. She is a primary suspect in three homicides."

Barney glanced at Lehmans in surprise. "They got Reimeck. Yesterday," Lehmans explained.

The captain said, "I don't know what the hell this is all about, and I don't want to know. Your credentials are in order. But you can't touch that girl."

"Why not?" Barney asked.

"That limousine has CD plates. That's Corps Diplomatique. They can go anywhere with total immunity."

Barney remembered asking Lisa about the CD plate he had seen before they left for Hamburg. "What country does that limo belong to?" he asked.

"Haiti," the captain replied.

"Look, Captain," Barney said. "The girl's name is Lisa Spangler. She is also a material witness to two American homicides."

The captain glanced back at Lisa. "I'm sorry, there's nothing I can do," he said.

"Can I talk to her?" Barney asked.

The captain sighed and glanced up at the East German watchtowers. "Those guys in those towers don't fuck around. You can walk with me. Slow and steady. Do not—I repeat—do not make any overt moves. That CD limo is on the way to their side. We have no legal basis for holding it. Now, I'm taking a chance with you. Understood?"

They followed the captain, walking methodically toward the black limousine. Barney felt naked in the hot glare of the arc lights. He tried to define Lisa's face, but in the blaze of light her features were a blur.

They walked twenty-five feet up to the rear fender of the limousine. He could see her clearly now. The black sergeant stood alongside her. The chauffeur had gone back behind the wheel. The captain looked at Barney. "This is as far as we go. You want to talk? Go ahead."

Barney's hands flexed, and the muscles in his face tensed. He stared at Lisa with a touch of grudging admiration. She had set it up this way. Her only refuge was East Berlin, but for how long? They knew she had failed. They knew Barney had the formula. But she was buying time. He began to feel a trickle of adrenaline starting its chilly path through his chest. He was separated from her by less than twenty feet.

Lehmans saw the adrenaline doing strange things to Barney's eyes. He grabbed Barney's wrist. "Don't! Don't even think it!"

The captain growled at Barney. "We haven't got all night, mister. You got something to say to the lady, go ahead and say it."

"I have nothing to say." Barney sighed.

At that moment the left rear door of the limousine opened, and a tall, handsome man, wearing a dark cashmere coat, got out and walked slowly up to them. The man smiled at Barney. "I'm Frank Tedesco. I understand you want to see me."

Barney stared at Tedesco's black eyes. They reminded him of the eyes of Leo Mirell's chauffeur. They were pimp's eyes, hustler's eyes. But the tall, good-looking man was no ordinary hustler. He was an underworld celebrity and an overworld functionary. Tedesco had survived and prospered in a murderous world where the first mistake was the last.

Lisa had kept her part of the bargain. Barney was face to face with Frank Tedesco. The man represented everything that Barney had fought against all his life, and he had him cold. But couldn't touch him. "Well,

Mr. Caine, I'm waiting," Tedesco said. "I thought you had something to say."

"Yeah." Barney sighed. "I've got something to say."

And in that fractional second of time, Barney forgot the circumstances. He brought the punch up from the cobblestones, throwing the power of his shoulder behind his right hand. His fist crashed into Tedesco's face, landing high up on his right cheek, sending a sharp flash of pain from Barney's wrist radiating up to his shoulder.

Tedesco fell. The black sergeant and the tall captain moved quickly, grabbing Barney and slamming him against the rear of the limousine. Lehmans bent over Tedesco, trying to help him up, but Tedesco angrily brushed Lehmans's arm away.

Tedesco sat up on the wet cobblestones and shook his head, trying to clear the shock of the blow. He looked blankly into the glare of the floodlights. There was a trickle of blood running from the split skin in his cheek. Tedesco glanced over at Barney, still pinned against the car. "It's all right," Tedesco said to the captain. "Let him go."

They released Barney, and the captain warned him, "You make one move, mister, and it's your ass! You got that?"

Barney rubbed his right wrist. "Yeah. I got it."

Tedesco slowly got to his feet. He took out a handkerchief and daubed at the trickle of blood on his cheek. He took a cigarette out of a silver case, lit one, and blew the smoke at Barney. "That wasn't smart," he said. "You're directing your frustrations at the wrong man. I don't rate any hatred, Mr. Caine. I'm not a happy man. I'm a man forced to live in exile." He drew hard on the cigarette, and his voice picked up some charm. "You can't imagine how I long for America. There is no action in the world like America." He glanced at Lisa for a second, then back to Barney. "All those beautiful women on Fifth Avenue. All those beautiful banks. The Sunday football games. The races at Saratoga in the summer. And those marvelous East Side restaurants. Christ, I'd give anything to be able to go back."

"You can," Barney said. "I can guarantee it."

"How?" Tedesco asked.

"Go to jail. It's easy, Frank. You just walk in and sit down."

Tedesco smiled and daubed at the blood that had begun to congeal. "It's a little late in the game for me to do ten years in some federal prison. Besides, I don't deserve it. I'm just a man in the middle. A man who receives and makes phone calls."

"For whom?" Barney asked.

"Whoever pays." Tedesco shrugged. "I'm a broker. People come to me with problems, and I solve their problems for the right price."

"And that price is sometimes murder," Barney stated.

Tedesco shook his head. "I've always been opposed to murder. I believe there has never been any problem that couldn't be bought."

"You gave Diestel the okay to have the Genesis scientists hit," Barney said. "Do you call that murder?"

Tedesco looked at the bloodspots on his handkerchief. "I never heard of Genesis."

"How about names?" Barney snapped. "Names like Neeley, Obermann, Siebold, and Reimeck?"

"I'm sorry, Caine. I can't help you." Tedesco looked at Lehmans. "I can help you, though, Inspector. You've been exposed to some trouble, and that disturbs my sense of fair play, so you can forget the German aspect of this case. As I told Mr. Caine, I receive phone calls. And I got one about an hour ago. It seems Diestel went wading in Lake Havel, right in front of his villa." Tedesco dropped his cigarette and stepped on it. "There's a sandbank a few feet from shore with a severe drop." He smiled. "One of those tragic accidents."

Lehmans and Barney exchanged a quick glance. Tedesco continued. "You know what they say, it's the good swimmer who always drowns." Tedesco smiled at Lehmans. "From your point of view the case is closed. You can chalk these fatalities up to a falling out amongst the old Fraternal Order." Tedesco then glared at Barney. "Instead of being angry, Mr. Caine, you ought to think of rewarding me. You suffer a narrow view of your own position."

"Yeah. I have that habit," Barney muttered.

"You know who killed the Neeleys," Tedesco said. "That's what you came to Germany for. Besides, you got a hell of a lot more than you bargained for. That poor cancer-ridden old man gave you the formula. Hell, you'll probably get a commendation."

Tedesco noticed Barney staring at Lisa. "And by the way," he added, "should you ever want to take a holiday, let me know. I've got lots of room. A wonderful place up on a mountain. There's always a breeze off the Caribbean. And who knows?" He glanced at Lisa. "I might even arrange to have your German lady present. Think about it, Lieutenant."

"Who gives you the orders, Frank?" Barney asked.

Tedesco turned and walked to the limousine. He opened the rear door and looked back at Barney. "You're a bright boy, Caine. You ought to be able to figure that one out."

"I have," Barney replied.

Tedesco glared at Barney for a moment, then entered the huge sedan and slammed the door.

Lisa glanced at Barney. Their eyes met for a final second; then she quickly got into the back seat of the limousine.

The big car moved ahead slowly, threading its way through the twisting path of cement teeth and steel barricades. Barney and Lehmans watched as the limousine's tail lights disappeared into East Berlin.

CHAPTER

57 ☒

LEHMANS DROVE BARNEY OUT TO TAGEL AIRFIELD AT NINE IN THE morning. Barney was booked on the 10:30 Pan Am flight from Berlin to London; with a connecting flight from London to Los Angeles, arriving in L.A. at 3:50 P.M. Pacific coast time.

Diestel's body had been washed up on the beach at Lake Havel at 5:30 A.M. that morning. Lehmans had scheduled a press conference for later that afternoon. He would officially state that the deaths of Obermann, Siebold, Reimeck, and Diestel were connected to their past activities during World War II. And the case had been turned over to the federal authorities in Wiesbaden.

Lehmans got Barney through the preliminary security check, and they went up to the VIP Pan Am lounge. Barney had half an hour before the flight commenced boarding. The attendant in the lounge was a plain-looking, efficient girl, who spoke English fluently. She fixed the men two Bloody Marys and returned to her reception desk.

Barney stared out the window for a moment, while Lehmans lit his perennial cigarette. "You think she can be traded off?" Barney asked.

"For what?"

"The formula."

Lehmans stared at Barney and said, "You mean to say that after all you've been through, you would trade that formula for the girl?"

Barney nodded. "Yeah, I think so. Why the hell should I crusade for this fucking oil thing?"

Lehmans sighed. "The girl's fate is sealed. They'll add her up like a column of figures. If the pluses outweigh the minuses, they'll keep her alive." Lehmans coughed twice. "I know how they operate. When Fräulein Spangler has served her purpose"—Lehmans shrugged—"then . . ." Lehmans touched Barney's arm. "For God's sake, man, make that formula public. Get it out in the open. The goddamn Arabs, the banks, the interlocking cartel of oil companies are choking the life out of the Western democracies. And if they fall, you have another Germany of the thirties. Make it public, Barney."

Barney smiled. "And you were the guy who wasn't concerned about geopolitical conspiracies."

"That was said in the heat of the night," Lehmans replied. He drained his glass, crushed the cigarette. His gray eyes met Barney's, and he offered his hand.

Barney grasped it and said, "What the hell can I say, Hans?"

"There's nothing to say," Lehmans replied. "You would have done no less for me."

"I almost forgot," Barney said, and took out one of the sealed envelopes and handed it to Lehmans. "If anything happens to me, get this to someone you trust in the West German government."

"And if you succeed?"

"Keep it as a souvenir." Barney smiled.

Lehmans nodded, then turned and started out. His big shoulders were slightly stooped, and his walk was stiff. It was the walk of a man beyond his years.

Barney went up to the receptionist and gave her Louis Yosuta's number and said he would pay for time and charges.

"Is this an official police matter?" she asked.

Barney nodded.

"Then it won't be necessary," she said. "We have a charge code for official calls." The receptionist dialed the overseas operator.

Barney walked over to the portable bar and added some ice and vodka to his Bloody Mary. He sat down on a sofa and picked up a *Newsweek* magazine. There was a cover story on international terrorism. The thrust of the article was that the United States was the next logical terrorist target. Several minutes passed before the receptionist called to him.

"I'm sorry, Mr. Caine, but your number in Los Angeles is temporarily out of service."

Barney didn't like the words "out of service." It was 3:40 A.M. in Los Angeles. An odd time for a phone problem. Line disruptions usually occurred at the height of usage during the business day, when the load was greatest. But then people did jar receivers loose from their cradles. Besides, Louis had received the formula sometime yesterday, probably toward the evening. By now it would be safely tucked away in the vault at Tactical Headquarters. And in any case, the copy was in Barney's jacket pocket.

He sipped the Bloody Mary and continued reading the *Newsweek* article. After a moment, the receptionist called to him again. "There is a phone call for you. You can take it there." She indicated a phone at the far end of the sofa.

It was Lisa. Her voice was breathless. "I only have minutes. Louis Yosuta is in grave peril."

Barney felt a throbbing in his temples and instantly understood why Louis's line was out of service.

Lisa spoke rapidly. "The man who followed you in Berlin was the same man you saw in the street that night in Hamburg. He followed us to Baden. I told him you sent the formula to Louis Yosuta and gave him the address."

Barney contained his anger. She had followed her orders, and she didn't have to make this call. "Why would they go after Louis?" Barney asked. "I still have a copy, and Lehmans has a copy."

"You have nothing. And Lehmans has nothing," she said. "Look at the envelope. Quickly!"

Barney placed the receiver on the table and took out the envelope. He tore it open and removed eight pages of chemical numerals and symbols that were labeled "Hydrocarbons." They had been Xeroxed in the Berlin public library. He cursed himself for not having checked its contents since leaving Baden-Baden. He lifted the receiver, and his voice thickened in anger and frustration. "How did they manage the switch?"

"The small man: Hoess. He knew someone at the hotel. That's why I was instructed to take you to that hotel."

"It was the concierge, right?" Barney asked. "The gray-haired guy with the scar and the permanent smile."

"I don't know," she said. "All that matters now is your partner's life."

She was right, and he asked, "Why are you telling me this?"

There was a slight pause. "Because I owe you that much." He heard the sound of door chimes behind her voice, and she whispered, "Goodbye, Barney." The line clicked and went dead.

Barney walked up to the receptionist. "Take this down, please." The girl picked up a pen and looked at him. Barney said, "I want you to place an official police emergency call to Los Angeles: two-one-three-four-eight-five-three thousand." The girl jotted the number, and he continued. "I want the watch commander at Detective Division. Metro

Headquarters." Beads of perspiration began to appear on Barney's forehead. He wiped them away as the girl spoke into the phone.

The connection went through in less than two minutes. The receptionist nodded at Barney and once again indicated the phone at the sofa. He picked up the receiver. "Hello?"

A tired voice on the other end of the line said, "Watch Commander, Belgrave."

Barney spoke fast. "This is Lieutenant Barney Caine." He spelled "Caine." "I'm on a classified case out of Tactical. I'm calling from Tegel Airport, in West Berlin. I have reason to believe my partner on this case, back in L.A., Sergeant Louis Yosuta, is in imminent danger."

The tired voice woke up. "Who's your superior, Caine?"

"John Nolan, Tactical Chief."

"Hold on!"

The receptionist came up to Barney and said, "You don't have much time. The flight to London is now boarding."

"Can you advise the gate this is an emergency?"

"I'll do what I can." She went back to her desk.

Barney knew that Belgrave was following precedure. He was feeding the information Barney had given him into the giant computer at Parker Center. The process took less than thirty seconds but seemed an eternity.

Belgrave's voice came on. "Okay, Caine. We confirm your case. Go ahead."

"Send a Metro car to Three-six-five South Alameda. That's Sergeant Yosuta's home." Barney paused. "Tell them to proceed with extreme caution."

"Got it," Belgrave snapped. "Anything else?"

"Yeah," Barney said. "But send that first."

There was another brief delay. Then Belgrave said, "A black-and-white is on the way."

"Okay," Barney replied. "Now arrange a Metro car to meet my plane. It's Pan Am Number Three-three, out of London, arriving L.A. at three-thirty-five P.M. Alert those assholes at customs. I can't get hung up there."

"Got you," Belgrave said.

"One other item," Barney said. "Have someone check Sergeant Yosuta's time log at Tactical for the last twenty-four hours."

"Done," Belgrave snapped.

"That's it," Barney said.

"Have a safe flight, Lieutenant. We'll be waiting."

Barney hung up, went over to the desk, picked up his canvas bag, and slung it over his shoulder. The receptionist accompanied him through the final security check of hand luggage. She wished him well. He thanked her and raced down the long tiled tunnel. He passed gate after gate. Barney thought: It never failed, when you were in a jam for time, your gate was always at the end of the terminal. He boarded the 747 just as the stewardess was about to close the door.

The flight to London was just over two hours, and Barney made the connecting polar flight without difficulty.

The rear cabin of the giant 747 was half empty, and after takeoff, Barney moved into a vacant row of five seats. He took two pillows and a blanket down from the overhead rack, tilted all five seats back, and stretched out.

He closed his eyes and saw the face of the concierge. The man's features came back to Barney with perfect clarity: the fine gray hair, the whitish scar, and the pasted-on smile that masked his abiding hatred of those foreign tourists he was obliged to serve. The concierge had to have been Diestel's contact. There was no other way they could have made the switch. But that became clear only in retrospect. He should have checked the goddamn envelope when he withdrew it from the safety box. But how could he have assumed Diestel had a strong connection with the hotel personnel? Well, why not? The Kameradschaft was as strong as ever. And the cartel's influence stretched over seven thousand miles and four decades. No, it had been a mistake. His mistake. And he had made another mistake earlier. He should have told Lehmans about the little man who had posed as a pimp that first night in Berlin. That had been an error of omission. And those mental lapses may have cost Louis Yosuta his life. But if Louis had placed the formula envelope in the Tactical vault, there was still a chance to save him. For the moment Barney had done all he could for Louis. And for that he could thank Lisa.

In the end, in the twisted logic that ruled her mind, she had tried to balance the scales. And in his heart Barney forgave her everything. He wished she were with him now. He remembered the wistful look in her eyes that last night in Baden. When she sadly said, "The smell of pines reminds me of all the sweet things in my life that never happened."

CHAPTER

58 ⊠

THE HUGE 747 CAME IN LOW OVER HOLLYWOOD PARK RACETRACK. ITS engines thundered over the stucco cottages of Inglewood as it approached the number 4-B east-west runway. The enormous wheels absorbed the shock of its three hundred tons kissing the runway. The four Pratt-Whitney engines screamed in protest as they were thrust in reverse and the brakes applied. The twelve-hour six-thousand-mile flight was arriving fifteen minutes ahead of schedule.

Barney identified himself to the chief steward and was the first passenger to exit. He came down a ramp onto the macadam and blinked in the smoggy sunlight. A uniformed Pan American official called his name, and Barney waved to the man. They walked through a tunnel toward passport control, and the man informed Barney that his onboard luggage would be forwarded to his home.

The guard at passport control checked Barney's name against the list of subversives and wanted criminals in his ledger. He stamped Barney's passport and said, "Welcome home, Mr. Caine."

There was a slim dark-complected man standing alongside a tough-looking female customs agent. The man greeted Barney. "George Santoro. Metro—Detective Squad. Welcome back, Lieutenant."

Barney shook the man's hand.

The customs woman asked, "Anything in that shoulder bag, Lieutenant?"

"Toiletries. Shirts and dirty underwear."

She said, "Open it, please." She zipped it open, and she rummaged around for a moment, then zipped it closed. He handed her his customs card. She looked at it. "You purchased nothing in Germany?"

"No. No purchases. No diamonds. No cocaine. No grass. No hash. No furs. No apples or flowers or fruits."

"Thank you," she hissed.

"You're welcome. Sweetheart."

They pounded down the moving electric walkway, adding their own velocity to that of the treadmill. Santoro spoke English with a Spanish cadence. "We got to Sergeant Yosuta's house at four-fourteen A.M. The place was a fucking mess. Even the walls were shredded. Yosuta's wife was unconscious. She was beaten up bad. The little boy was tied up in his bed. Mrs. Yosuta's in Good Samaritan. She may require cosmetic surgery. But she's not critical."

"What about Louis?" Barney asked.

"Three men in ski masks came into the house. They tied up the kid, grabbed Louis, held a gun to his head. They asked him about an envelope. When he refused to answer, they hit his wife. Over and over. But Louis never spoke."

They were nearing the end of the treadmill, coming toward the terminal's entrance. Santoro said, "They took Sergeant Yosuta with them."

The black-and-white Metro car was at the curb. They got in, and the driver, a beefy red-faced man, growled, "Where to?"

"Tactical," Barney said.

Santoro took a sheet of paper out of his pocket and showed it to Barney. "Here's Sergeant Yosuta's time log for the last twenty-four hours."

Barney felt a dull throbbing pain over each eye. He studied Louis's time log, and his heart pounded. He spotted something that sent a surge of hope and relief through his tired body.

There was the normal entry at 9:15 A.M. and the normal out at 6:15 P.M. But farther down the sheet there was an entry at 8:45 P.M. and an out at 9:05 P.M. Barney knew that Louis's life depended on the twenty minutes between those two entries.

He handed the sheet back to Santoro. "You did a thorough job here, Santoro."

"Thanks, Lieutenant. I been on it since we got the call. We got an APB out on Yosuta. The commissioner's on it. Nolan's on it. Half the Metro dicks are on it."

Nolan's dowdy longtime secretary, Mary Corona, said that Nolan was with the commissioner and had been since Sergeant Yosuta was first reported missing.

Barney's fear, fatigue, and frustration were turning to rising anger. But his voice was calm. "Listen to me, Mary. Listen carefully. I want you to open the Control safe. I want you to open the safe right now."

She removed her bifocals and shook her head, spraying a snowfall of dandruff over the shoulders of her blouse. She said, "I'm not allowed to open that safe without proper authorization."

Barney grabbed a pen and paper off her desk. He scribbled a note, signed it, and handed it to her. She studied the note and said, "Well, I don't know that this is sufficient authorization."

Santoro stepped forward and smiled at the nervous woman. "I'm Detective George Santoro, Metro Squad. I've been on this case since three A.M. I can cosign that authorization."

Barney admired Santoro's persuasiveness and the pointed way he called the note an authorization.

Nolan's secretary stared at the handsome detective. She was beginning to waver, and Santoro added, "You have to open that safe. Sergeant Yosuta's life is in your hands."

She bit her lip and said, "All right."

Mary Corona bent over the gun-metal safe in the Operations Room. They watched in silence as she carefully turned the small knob on the safe's combination. They heard the clicking as the dial moved from number to number. She stopped after each turn, consulting a note that contained the code.

Barney snapped, "Come on. For Christ's sake!"

"I am. I'm—I'm trying to be careful," she stammered. She peered through her bifocals at the tiny numerals and slowly moved the dial to 14. Then she glanced at the code note and said, "Damn!"

"What's wrong?" Barney asked.

"That should have been fifteen," she said.

Barney sighed. "All right, Mary. It's my fault. I've made you nervous. Now start over and take your time."

She began again. Twisting the knob and consulting the code. Number after number. Left and right. The clicking of the wheel sounding like an ominous countdown before a missile launch.

She ended on 32. The number stirred Barney's memory. It was the same number that Lisa had played at the roulette table that last night in Baden-Baden.

Mary Corona was now showing beads of sweat on her upper lip. She grasped the safe's handle with her right hand, sighed heavily, and yanked it straight down. The handle responded easily, and she swung the safe open.

Barney shoved her aside, knelt down, and began to search through the jumble of documents, currency, evidence bags, ledgers, and canceled checks. He rifled the contents, desperately seeking the manila envelope. He threw the papers aside, emptying the contents of the second shelf onto the floor. He then lowered himself and peered into the bottom shelf of the safe. He moved a stack of ledgers, and as the pile of gray ledgers receded, he saw the manila envelope standing in a vertical position against the rear wall of the safe.

He grabbed the envelope, stood up, and tore the flap open. He removed the eight pages of the formula and checked them quickly but carefully. He turned to Mary Corona. "Run three copies of each page!"

She nodded, took the pages, and asked no questions. The middle-aged secretary had slipped out of her normal bureaucratic attitude. She was now an active participant in a life-and-death situation.

They followed her into the Communications Room. She placed each page face down, reproducing three copies. She repeated the process eight times. Barney collated the copies into sets of three.

He said, "Get me three manila envelopes and ten dollars' worth of stamps."

"Right away, Lieutenant," she replied.

Santoro peered at the pages in Barney's hand. "What the hell is that stuff?"

"Sergeant Yosuta's life insurance policy."

Mary Corona came back with the envelopes and stamps.

Barney went over to a steel desk and sat down. He took a piece of paper out of his wallet and carefully copied an address onto the face of a manila envelope. He then licked and pasted the ten dollars' worth of stamps across the top of the envelope. He handed the envelope to Santoro. "Hold onto that." Barney then placed a complete set of formula pages inside the remaining two envelopes. He folded one of the envelopes into his inside jacket pocket and handed the remaining envelope to Nolan's secretary. "Put that back in the safe, then phone Tidal Oil, ask for Adam Steiffel's secretary. Tell her that Barney Caine is on his way over to see her boss, on official police business." Barney paused. "Tell her to inform Mr. Steiffel that I have a personal greeting for him from Dr. Esau."

Her face turned into a puzzled frown. "Who?"

"E-S-A-U."

The big digital clock on the Bank of America building showed 4:52 P.M. Barney couldn't believe he was in a car moving along Wilshire Boulevard. The time gap of nine hours and the jet lag gave him a curious high, a transient euphoria that tortured reality.

They parked in a red zone on Wilshire in front of the towering concave glass building with its large chrome letters. "TIDAL OIL."

Barney and Santoro got out of the car, and Barney indicated a mailbox at the corner. "Drop that stamped envelope in that mailbox, and stand right there until I come down." He paused and added, "Let me have your service revolver."

Santoro looked at Barney for a moment, then nodded.

Barney tucked the .38 Smith and Wesson into his belt. He waited until Santoro reached the mailbox and dropped the manila envelope inside. He then entered the soaring five-story atrium lobby with its rushing waterfall and live palm trees.

Steiffel's pleasant-looking secretary smiled. "Go right in, Mr. Caine." She pressed the hidden button underneath the lid of her desk, tripping the automatic lock on Steiffel's office door.

Steiffel's office was in the familiar state of semidarkness. Adam Steiffel sat in the tomblike silence, behind his circular desk. The blue light coming from the tinted windows cast his face in granite. His accusatory eyes stared at Barney. He had a cigar clenched between his teeth. He said nothing for a long moment. He then leaned back in the high leather chair and brushed his snow-white mane. His lips moved, and the grim, hollow voice floated across the darkened room. "What can I do for you, son?"

Barney took the envelope out, removed the eight Xeroxed pages, crossed to the desk, and dropped the pages.

Steiffel looked at Barney for a moment, then picked up the pages. He examined each page carefully, then placed them in a neat pile. He flicked an ash off his cigar. "I repeat, what can I do for you?"

Barney's voice was icy but calm. "Release Louis Yosuta, and we do business."

The old man shook his head. "I never heard of the gentleman."

"I know that," Barney said, "but make the call anyway."

Steiffel leaned back and puffed thoughtfully on the cigar. "What assurance do I have that all the formula copies will be returned?"

"You have my word. Nothing more."

Steiffel smiled at Barney. "That's not much, son."

Barney's temples throbbed, and his face tensed. "Listen to me carefully, Mr. Steiffel. I don't give a fuck about your goddamn formula. You can go on milking the public till the cows come home." Barney gasped a lungful of air and exhaled. "Make that call. And make it now."

"Or what?" the old man asked. Steiffel swiveled around and stared out the huge tinted window. "I'm seventy-eight years old. I'm prepared for my mortality. At my age a bullet is even preferable to a failing liver or kidney or the gray monster of cancer." He turned to Barney. "Death holds no terror for me."

Barney felt the cold steel of the .38 against his belly and wondered whether to test the old man's bravado. But if he were forced to use the gun, he couldn't. It would be first-degree murder. The gun was just a prop. "All right." Barney sighed. "No Louis. No business."

Steiffel stared at him for a moment. "You mean what you say about the return of the formula?" he asked.

"I'm not responsible for the salvation of the American economy," Barney said. "I pay my own bills. I run no empires. I'm a cop."

Steiffel brushed his magnificent silver hair and pursed his lips. "Do you have any proof that connects me to a missing police officer named Louis Yosuta?"

"No."

The old man nodded, stared at Barney for an instant, then said, "Please remove your jacket and open your shirt."

"I have no bugs. No wires," Barney said.

"Do you want to do business?" the old man asked.

Barney rose and removed his jacket. He tossed it at Steiffel, who caught it deftly and searched its pockets and lining. He handed it back to Barney, who now had his shirt open, exposing the handle of the .38. The old man saw the gun handle but ignored it.

"Now turn your pockets inside out, and roll up your pant legs."

Barney followed Steiffel's instructions.

The old man inspected Barney carefully; then the birdlike eyes seemed to relax. "I think we can do business." Steiffel waited for Barney to button his shirt and put his jacket back on, then said, "Come with me."

Steiffel went to a panel in the wall, over which hung the slogan "When money talks, people listen." He pressed a button, and the panel slid open. "After you," Steiffel said agreeably.

The room was all copper: ceiling, walls, and floor, dull red copper. There was a scattering of teak furniture, but there were no windows. The old man pressed a button on the copper side of the door, and it slid closed, sealing them into the metallic chamber.

Barney felt as if he had entered the tomb of some ancient pharaoh.

"This room may surprise you," Steiffel explained, "but it is really quite old in concept. I first saw a copper room at a meeting with Howard Hughes back in 1940. In this city, at his offices. Mr. Hughes was ahead of us all." Steiffel paused. "The copper precludes penetration by any long-range electronic sound devices. It is absolutely immune to the most sophisticated eavesdropping mechanisms."

The old man went behind the teak desk and sat down. "I'm very impressed with you, Caine. You're quite a cowboy. The CIA lost a hell of a man when you resigned." Steiffel lifted the receiver and pushed a combination of buttons at the base of the phone. He spoke quickly into the phone. "The weather is clearing. You can release the forecast. And—"

He was about to conclude when Barney cut in. "Tell them to have Louis phone me here, from John Nolan's office."

Steiffel repeated Barney's message, only he referred to Louis as the "weatherman," and hung up. "Satisfied?" he asked.

"When I speak to Louis," Barney replied. "Right now, I'd appreciate some answers."

Steiffel relit his cigar, blew some smoke, and shrugged. "You can't go anywhere with my answers. You know that. You and I are alone in this copper chamber without corroboration. Even the phone call I made is uncorroborated. Your partner was abducted by unknown assailants and released by unknown assailants." Steiffel smiled. "His abduction is probably unrelated to the Neeley case. You get my point. Don't you, son?"

"Absolutely," Barney agreed. "So why not give me some answers?"

Steiffel stroked his hair, placed the cigar in an ashtray, and looked at Barney, considering the merits of his request. Both their faces took on magenta tones from the overhead light bouncing off the copper walls. "All right." Steiffel sighed. "I think you're entitled to some answers."

He rose, paced for a moment and reflectively said, "Over the years we have been concerned with the continued existence of the surviving German scientists who worked on the Genesis program. But our concern was benign. After all, we controlled the oil from the sands to the pumps. And the manufacture of synthetic fuel was an economic impossibility. Therefore, we were content to let sleeping dogs lie. But when the Swiss industrialist contacted Obermann, everything changed."

Barney interrupted. "How did you know about the Swiss contact?"

"Obermann dutifully reported that contact to Diestel. And we became actively concerned."

"Why?" Barney asked. "What's wrong with making America self-sufficient in synthetic fuel?"

The old man stared at Barney with a look of total wonder. "Do you honestly expect a three-hundred-billion-dollar industry to undermine its own stake in the lucrative scarcity of oil by mass-producing synthetic fuel?"

Steiffel walked back to his desk and sat down. "We've had that formula in our possession since the conclusion of the war. British Intelligence turned it over to our chemists in early '46. We even imported a few German scientists to build pilot hydrogenation plants, to be certain the process was economically unsound. We terminated those plants in '56. But"—he paused—"that was twenty-two years ago. Things change. The price of crude oil has risen dramatically since '73, making the production of synthetic fuel an economic possibility. The Genesis Formula makes it an economic reality. Therefore, we could not risk the formula falling into the wrong hands."

"Enter Tom Neeley," Barney said.

"Correct," Steiffel said. "Neeley fitted all our requirements. He had in his youth been connected to Genesis, and he knew Paul Obermann."

"How did you know that?" Barney asked.

"Tom made money drops for me," Steiffel replied, "and when a man works for me, his past life is an open book." Steiffel inhaled the cigar smoke. "We had Tom's military records. We understood the importance of his last assignment, the transporting of the Genesis file to Hamburg, and his meeting Obermann was well known to us."

"How did Neeley stumble onto Genesis after thirty-three years?" Barney asked.

The old man peered at Barney through the cigar smoke and smiled. "Stumbled?" Steiffel shook his head. "He didn't stumble. We had Obermann write Neeley a letter, explaining the importance of Genesis and inviting Neeley to Berlin to explore the possibilities of reactivating the Genesis team."

Barney sighed. "And Neeley went for it."

"Naturally," Steiffel said. "Human greed being what it is. It was then that our design to eliminate the Genesis scientists took shape."

Barney felt himself hypnotized by the mellifluous voice and his own fatigue and the claustrophobic chamber.

The old man continued, "The girl, Lisa Spangler, was set up as the cocaine courier to gain Neeley's confidence."

Barney said, "You planted the German clues in Neeley's apartment?"

"Of course. We required that someone efficient be placed on the Genesis trail."

"How did you know it would be me?"

"We didn't. But it was obvious that the killing of a former police chief, living above his means and rumored to be engaged in nefarious activity, would attract a topnotch detective." Steiffel turned, and the fierce eyes penetrated Barney. "It did not matter who that detective was, so long as he served as our surrogate instrument to eliminate all the remaining German scientists."

"Why was it necessary to eliminate them?" Barney pressed.

"The Swiss consortium had the means to make the formula viable, to go into mass production of synthetic fuel. We couldn't tolerate that. But we couldn't be overt. We needed a cover."

Barney nodded. "And what could be a better cover for killing German citizens than their involvement with an American cop pursuing an American crime?"

The old man smiled. "Yes. We used you right from the start."

The impact of Steiffel's words struck Barney with a deadening force. He fell silent for a moment, his mind racing back over past events. The old man sucked and chewed on the wet end of the cigar. He seemed to be enjoying Barney's dissolution.

"Ah, don't take it personally, boy," Steiffel said. "After all, you were out of your milieu. You were a pawn. A soldier being moved by a master."

Barney felt a ball of heat collecting in his throat. "I halfway suspected it after I met with Diestel. He was too open. He cloaked it behind his Nazi philosophy, but he overplayed his hand. I was sure after Siebold led me to Reimeck. I just didn't want to believe someone was maneuvering all those people." Barney sighed. "I should have known you were calling the shots once Clements was hit."

"I deeply regretted that. But"—the old man shrugged—"Arthur had become too dependent on cocaine. However, I must confess a certain satisfaction with the demise of Yussef Kaladi."

"Yeah." Barney nodded. "That was a hell of a touch."

"What?" the old man asked.

"The Confederate money."

Steiffel smiled. "Unfortunately, I can't claim authorship. That idea came from one of my associates."

"Tell me," Barney said, "if you needed me, why was I shot at?"

"The Malibu incident was an accident," Steiffel said. "We didn't expect you to be moving that fast. The shots fired at you in the Berlin zoo were meant to miss. They served only to maintain a certain legitimacy. We wanted you healthy, bird-dogging the trail."

Barney nodded and lit a cigarillo. He blew some smoke at the copper ceiling, paced for a moment, then turned to Steiffel. "How did Tedesco fit in?"

"We commissioned him to engage the PLO gunmen. Tedesco informed them of Genesis. And their interest in suppressing the production of synthetic fuel is obvious. The involvement of the Muslim terrorists provided us with a further cover."

"The girl had been planted earlier," Barney said.

"Yes. She was the cocaine courier. Neeley had absolute faith in her."

Barney inhaled the bitter smoke of the cigarillo and sighed. "Christ, without the cocaine nothing would have happened."

The old man rose and brushed his silver hair. "Oh, something would have happened. Not quite so perfect, so well disguised. But we would have taken some action. The trigger was not cocaine. It was the Swiss contact with Obermann."

"How did you know I'd be authorized to go to Germany?"

"That was academic," Steiffel said. "Immediately after your first visit to me, I spoke to a certain party in city government."

Barney stared at the tall, frail-looking old man, digesting the full weight of his words.

"Is there anything else, son?"

"What about Diestel?" Barney asked.

"He was our man in Berlin. He was a high corporate officer of a West German firm we do business with. He held the Fraternal Order in his hand. He was most useful."

"Your only mistake was Dr. Esau," Barney said.

"Not exactly a mistake." The old man rose. "One cannot control everything. No plan is perfect. Do you know physics?"

"No. I never studied physics."

"A pity. You ought to read Heisenberg. The Uncertainty Principle. Random particles meeting in an isolated chamber changing their character and actions by pure chance. Like the Swiss contacting Obermann. Like Neeley and Genesis. Like cocaine and the Spangler girl. Like cancer chasing Dr. Esau after immortality. Like you and I, now in this chamber. You really ought to read Heisenberg."

The phone rang sharply, its tonality amplified by the copper room. Steiffel indicated his chair to Barney, who came around the desk and picked up the receiver.

"Hello?"

"It's me, Barney. I'm okay."

Barney felt a rush of relief at the sound of Louis's voice. "Where are you?" Barney asked.

"In Nolan's office."

"Put him on."

There was a pause, followed by the instant growl of Nolan's voice. "Goddammit, Caine! Where the fuck are you? I told you to—"

Barney dropped the receiver onto its cradle and said, "Okay. Let's get out of here."

The old man pressed the red button on the copper side of the panel, and it slid open. They reentered the office, and the copper door closed.

Steiffel walked up to the big glass window, and Barney sat down in a chair facing the circular desk. "Don't feel too disheartened, son," Steiffel said, turning to Barney. "We will manufacture synthetic fuel. And in great quantity. We already own most of the coal in the country. We know what's coming. We have the formula. We have the Mangan catalyst, and we have the technology. But we must be certain of profit. By 1990 the country will be on its knees to OPEC. The government will then turn to us. And in their desperation they will insure our profit position in the manufacture of synthetic fuel."

"Nice," Barney said.

"Business," Steiffel replied, "just business." He crossed from the window and walked toward Barney. "We are a team of giants nursing the lullaby of the masses."

Steiffel sat down on the sofa opposite Barney and peered across at him in the dim light. "You mustn't think of us as evil, rapacious men, clinging to the keys of our numbered Swiss accounts. On the contrary, we are a small family of simple businessmen seeking only the tranquil pursuit of profit. And we take great care to bestow sufficient largess on the citizens."

"Is this where you play 'The Star-Spangled Banner'?" Barney asked.

Steiffel smiled. "I understand your anger and therefore excuse it. You're an old-fashioned man. In a way the epitome of the American myth of the rugged individual. And I respect that. I come from a long line of strong-willed men. But like it or not, the world has changed. You're a policeman. You cannot possibly understand the complexities of global economics."

"No. But I understand murder."

"Only in a narrow, professional sense." The old man paused. "To you a dead man is a victim. To his family a personal loss. But to his undertaker he is a commodity. A profit. Life and death are only an extension of the economic cycle."

"Which gives you the moral license to kill," Barney replied.

Steiffel sipped some water. "This case cannot be equated with murder. A handful of greedy people. A few scientists who themselves committed unspeakable crimes in the name of their science. That's not murder. Their collective demise was simply economic pragmatism."

Barney said, "You never saw Tom and Kay Neeley's bodies, did you?"

Steiffel shrugged. "I grieve for the Neeleys, as I grieve for my dear friend Arthur Clements."

"What happens when there's no more profit left to squeeze from the citizens? When the whole goddamn world is on its knees?" Barney asked angrily.

The old man looked up at the ceiling for a moment, then stared at Barney. "In that case, the cartel performs its historic duty. We unleash the dogs of war. There are those times when war is both economically and ecologically necessary for the ultimate survival of the species." He rose, walked to the window, and looked out over the city. "Can we now do some business?"

Barney went over to the window and stood beside Steiffel. "Yeah. We can do business."

"You're going to tell me where the other copy is?" Steiffel asked.

Barney nodded.

"And you assure me there are no others."

"Only one. In my possession. You can call it a life insurance policy."

The old man smiled. "So it will remain with you?"

Barney nodded. "Until my death. Which I hope is after 1990, when you plan to manufacture synthetic fuel."

Steiffel turned from the window and looked at Barney. "You wouldn't go against us, son?"

"Me? Go up against a simple group of businessmen?"

"Fine. Then keep your insurance policy," he said. "Now, where's the other copy?"

Barney pointed down to the street. "You see that guy standing at the mailbox on the corner?"

Steiffel's eyes narrowed. "Yes, what about him?"

"He's a cop. A Metro detective. A half an hour ago he dropped the formula into that mailbox."

Steiffel's fierce blue eyes clouded. "I don't follow you."

"You will. That envelope is on its way to the Technion Institute in Haifa."

Steiffel's pallid cheeks turned crimson.

"I know you're powerful," Barney said, "but are you powerful enough to stop the U.S. mail?"

Steiffel's eyes widened, his lips quivered, and his voice trembled. He breathed the word as if he'd heard it for the first time, "Israel—why Israel?"

Barney said, "The formula went to Israel because they have no connections with big oil. It was circumstance, pure chance. It was Heisenberg. Those random particles—they'll kill you every time."

The old man turned, and moved to his desk. "You're out of my hands. You have created a situation that has removed you from my care. You are a damn fool, Mr. Caine. A suicidal maniac. You disappoint me. I gave you credit for more intelligence!"

"You made a mistake," Barney said. "You may be in a little bit of trouble, Mr. Steiffel." He turned and started for the door.

"Caine!" the old man shouted.

Barney looked back at the old man. The color had gone out of his cheeks, and his lips were blue. His voice was tense but composed. "Sending the formula to Israel is specious and futile. They have no coal. No minerals. No funds. All they have are oranges."

"But they have science," Barney said. "And they have connections. And you know how it is." Barney paused. "When money talks, people listen."

Adam Steiffel peered across the gloom of his office at the closed door. He then rose wearily and walked slowly to the window. He stared down at the detective standing on the corner. The man was leaning on the red, white, and blue mailbox.

CHAPTER

59 ⊠

BARNEY MET LOUIS AT THE GOOD SAMARITAN HOSPITAL. THE FLOOR nurse informed them Lou's wife was sleeping at the moment and that she was doing fine. They thanked the nurse and went down to the coffee shop just off the lobby.

"So legally he's clean." Louis sighed.

Barney nodded. "There's not a thing I can go to the DA with. But Steiffel's days are numbered."

"You just said he's clean," Louis replied.

"Legally. Not with his associates. He lost control of the formula, and they don't allow mistakes."

Louis said, "At least Neeley's killers got theirs." He paused. "Except Tedesco."

"Tedesco will be around as long as someone's willing to pay him," Barney said, then sipped some coffee and asked, "What about you? Can you nail the guys who grabbed you?"

Louis shook his head. "They wore masks. They spoke in Arabic. They kept me blindfolded all the time. Somewhere close to a freeway. I kept hearing the rush of cars. They shoved me out of the car blindfolded at Ventura and Coldwater."

"What language did they use when they questioned you?"

"English. They kept asking me about the envelope. When I said nothing, they hit my wife . . . over and over."

Barney looked at the calm, oval black eyes and softly asked, "How could you watch her get hit and not talk?"

"It's difficult for anyone to understand who isn't Japanese," Louis said. "We have codes of behavior that have been handed down for centuries. From generation to generation. I didn't speak because I thought it might endanger your life. That was my obligation, and my wife understood."

Barney nodded imperceptibly. Louis paid the bill and said, "Come on, I'll take you home."

Louis drove the unmarked Metro car. They were traveling west on Wilshire Boulevard, heading directly into a fiery scarlet sunset. The glass office buildings and the faces of the people on the teeming streets were cast in a red glow.

It seemed to Barney as if the dying sun was bleeding to death over the city. He could feel his eyes closing involuntarily and had to blink to keep them open. He glanced at his watch, which was still set on Berlin time. It read 2:43 A.M.

Barney lowered his window, and the balmy desert air floated against his face. He leaned over and turned the radio on, and Donna Summer was into a chorus of "Last Dance."

They stopped at a light on La Brea. Louis lit a cigarette and asked, "You think they'll go after you?"

Barney shook his head. "No. They're not the underworld. They don't practice vengeance. The overworld only acts out of necessity."

Louis sucked at the cigarette and asked, "But who makes the distinction between vengeance and necessity?"

Barney sighed. "A small group of simple businessmen."

The light changed. They crossed La Brea and passed the park where giant replicas of prehistoric monsters loomed up out of black pools of tar.

They rode in silence for a while, listening to Donna Summer. Just before the song ended, Louis glanced at Barney and asked, "What about the German girl?"

And in that moment, in the blood-red light and balmy desert air of Wilshire Boulevard, Lisa came back to Barney in a rush. His heart and mind ached for her light blue eyes, and her long pale hair, and her soft mouth, and the way her English sounded when she said, "I need you."

But Lisa was a memory, turning to a myth. She was part of something distant. Something that happened in Germany, a long time ago.